My Little Pony: Legends of Magic

Become our fan on Facebook **facebook.com/idwpublishing**
Follow us on Twitter **@idwpublishing**
Subscribe to us on YouTube **youtube.com/idwpublishing**
See what's new on Tumblr **tumblr.idwpublishing.com**
Check us out on Instagram **instagram.com/idwpublishing**

ISBN: 978-1-68405-158-8   21 20 19 18   1 2 3 4

COVER ART BY
BRENDA HICKEY

COLLECTION EDITS BY
JUSTIN EISINGER
AND ALONZO SIMON

COLLECTION DESIGN BY
RON ESTEVEZ

PUBLISHER
GREG GOLDSTEIN

MY LITTLE PONY: LEGENDS OF MAGIC, VOLUME 2. MAY 2018. FIRST PRINTING. HASBRO and its logo, MY LITTLE PONY, and all related characters are trademarks of Hasbro and are used with permission. © 2018 Hasbro. All Rights Reserved. The IDW logo is registered in the U.S. Patent and Trademark Office. IDW Publishing, a division of Idea and Design Works, LLC. Editorial offices: 2765 Truxtun Road, San Diego, CA 92106. Any similarities to persons living or dead are purely coincidental. With the exception of artwork used for review purposes, none of the contents of this publication may be reprinted without the permission of Idea and Design Works, LLC. Printed in Canada.
IDW Publishing does not read or accept unsolicited submissions of ideas, stories, or artwork.

Originally published as MY LITTLE PONY: LEGENDS OF MAGIC issues #7–12.

Greg Goldstein, President & Publisher
Robbie Robbins, EVP & Sr. Art Director
Chris Ryall, Chief Creative Officer & Editor-in-Chief
Matthew Ruzicka, CPA, Chief Financial Officer
David Hedgecock, Associate Publisher
Laurie Windrow, Senior Vice President of Sales & Marketing
Lorelei Bunjes, VP of Digital Services
Eric Moss, Sr. Director, Licensing & Business Development

Ted Adams, Founder & CEO of IDW Media Holdings

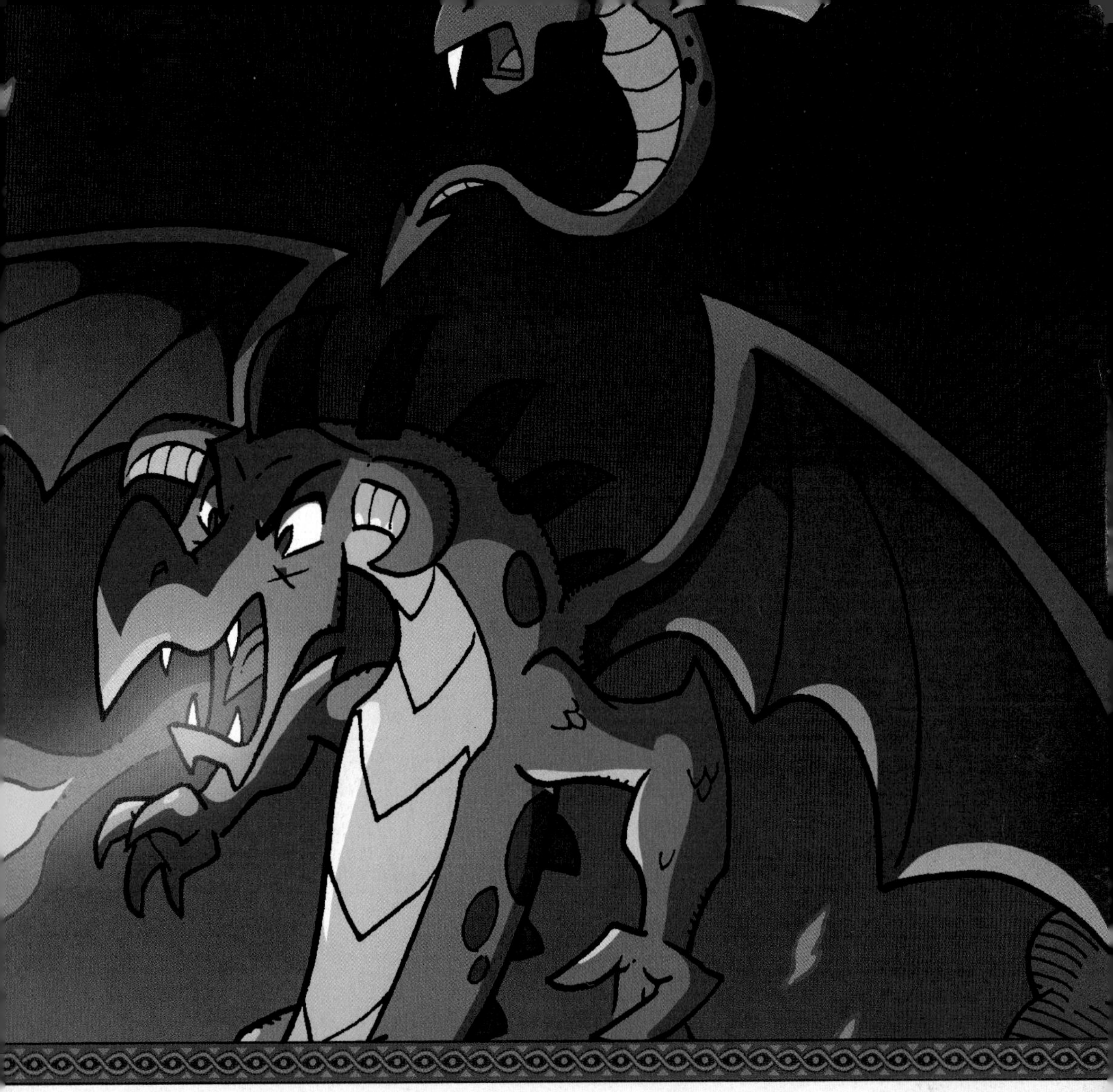

WRITTEN BY JEREMY WHITLEY

ART BY TONY FLEECS

COLORS BY HEATHER BRECKEL

LETTERS BY NEIL UYETAKE

SERIES EDITS BY BOBBY CURNOW

SPECIAL THANKS TO MEGHAN MCCARTHY, ELIZA HART, ED LANE, BETH ARTALE, AND MICHAEL KELLY.

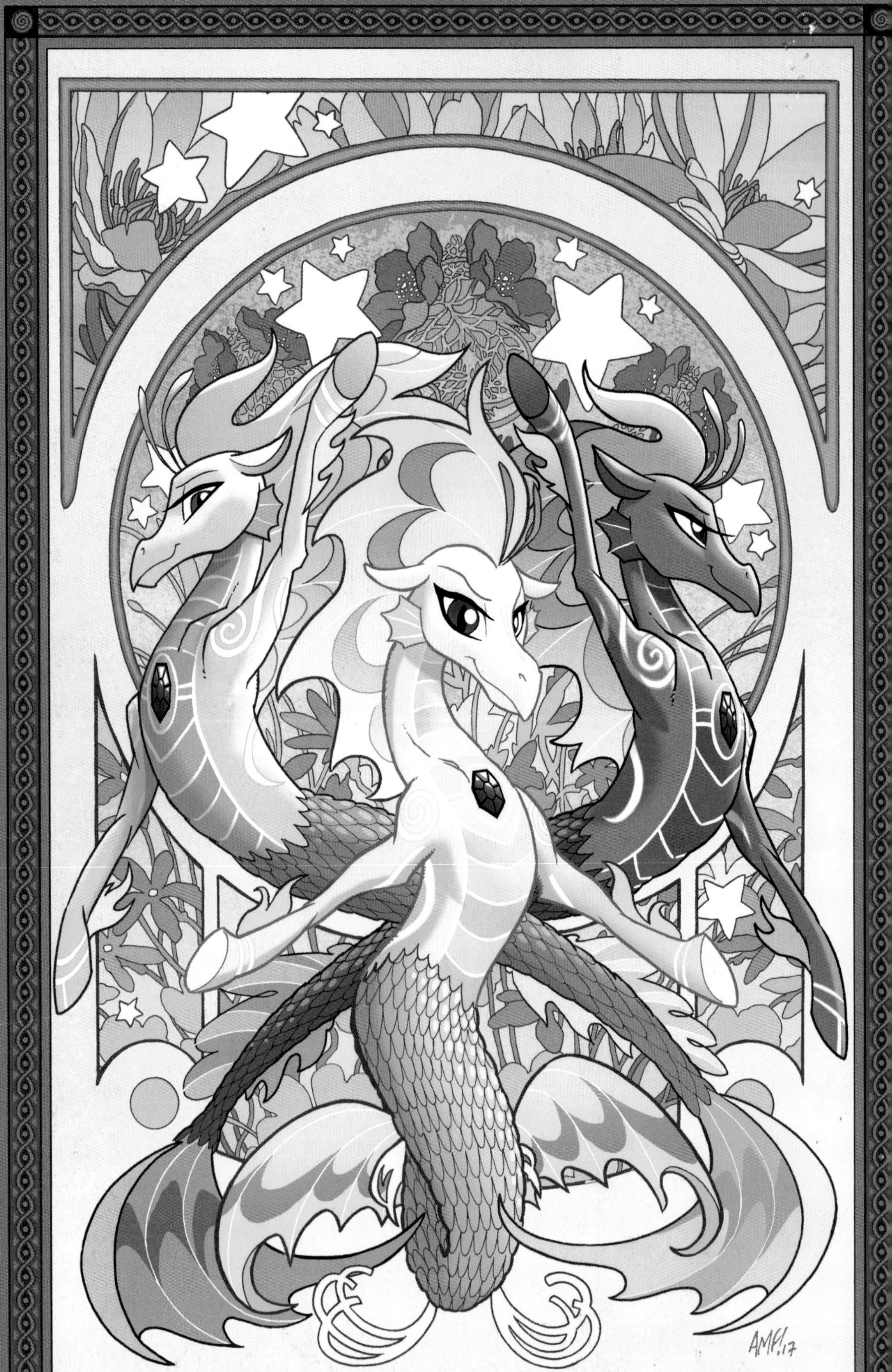

ART BY TONY FLEECS

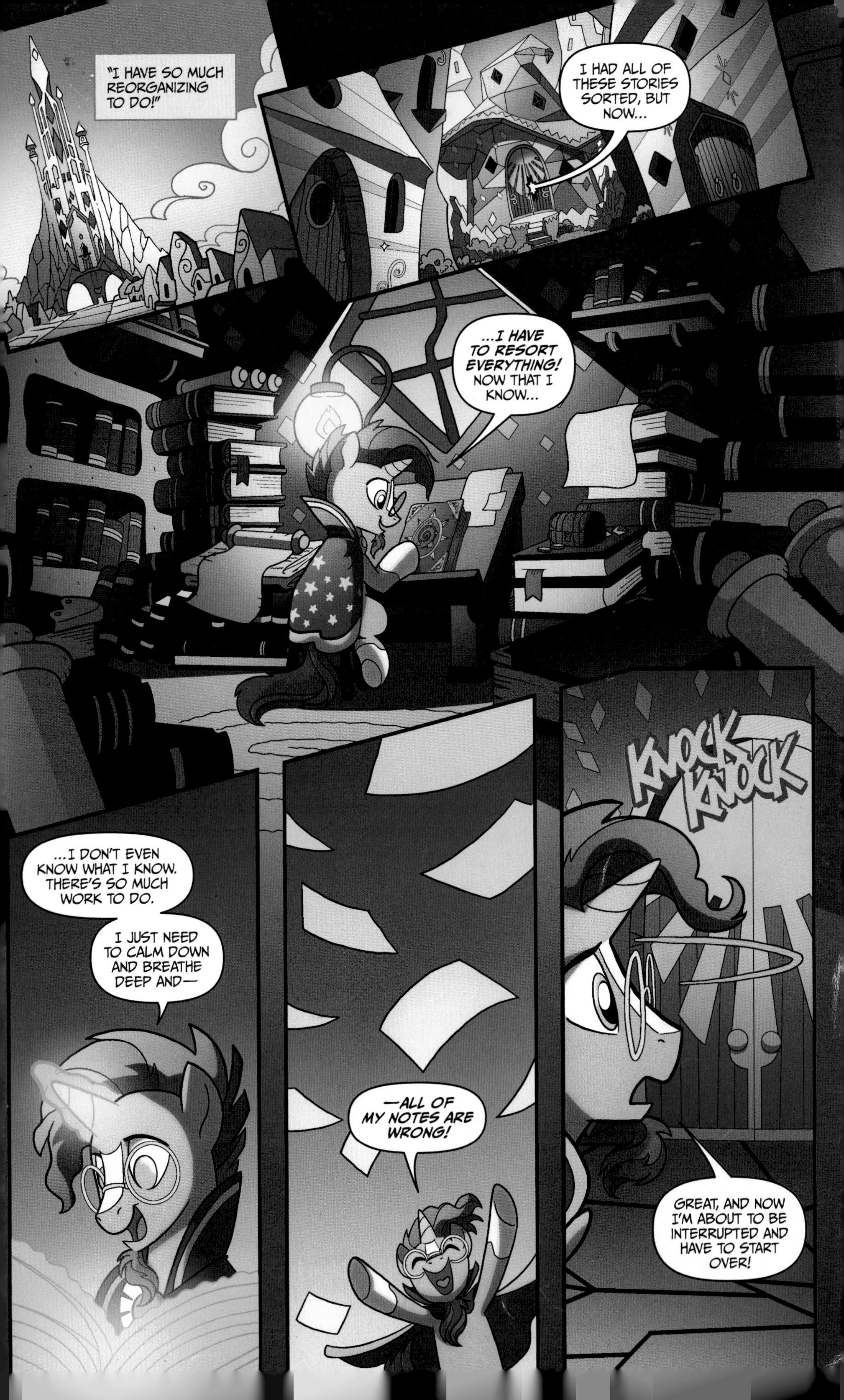
"I HAVE SO MUCH REORGANIZING TO DO!"
I HAD ALL OF THESE STORIES SORTED, BUT NOW...
...I HAVE TO RESORT EVERYTHING! NOW THAT I KNOW...
...I DON'T EVEN KNOW WHAT I KNOW. THERE'S SO MUCH WORK TO DO.
I JUST NEED TO CALM DOWN AND BREATHE DEEP AND—
—ALL OF MY NOTES ARE WRONG!
KNOCK KNOCK
GREAT, AND NOW I'M ABOUT TO BE INTERRUPTED AND HAVE TO START OVER!

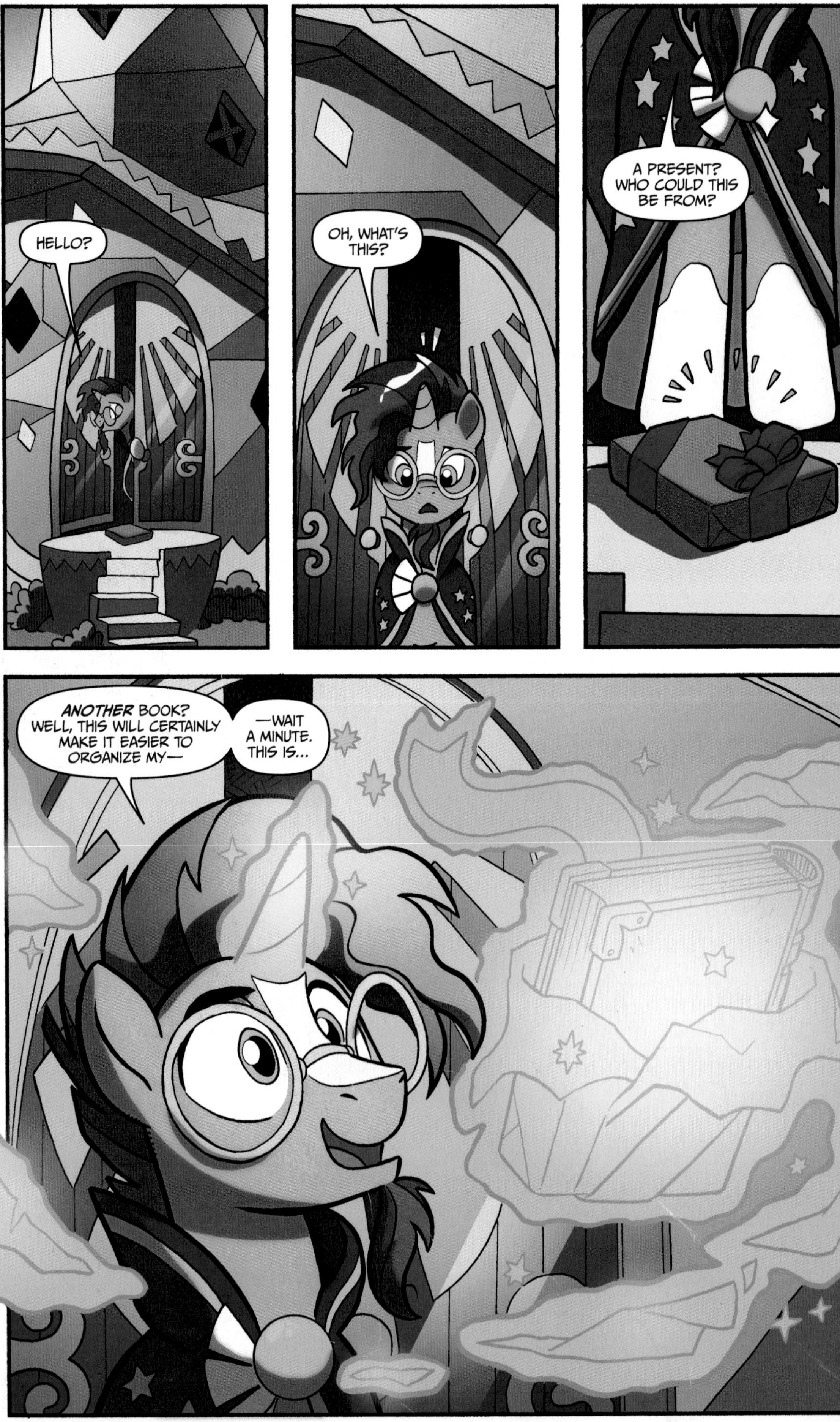
HELLO?
OH, WHAT'S THIS?
A PRESENT? WHO COULD THIS BE FROM?
ANOTHER BOOK? WELL, THIS WILL CERTAINLY MAKE IT EASIER TO ORGANIZE MY—
—WAIT A MINUTE. THIS IS...

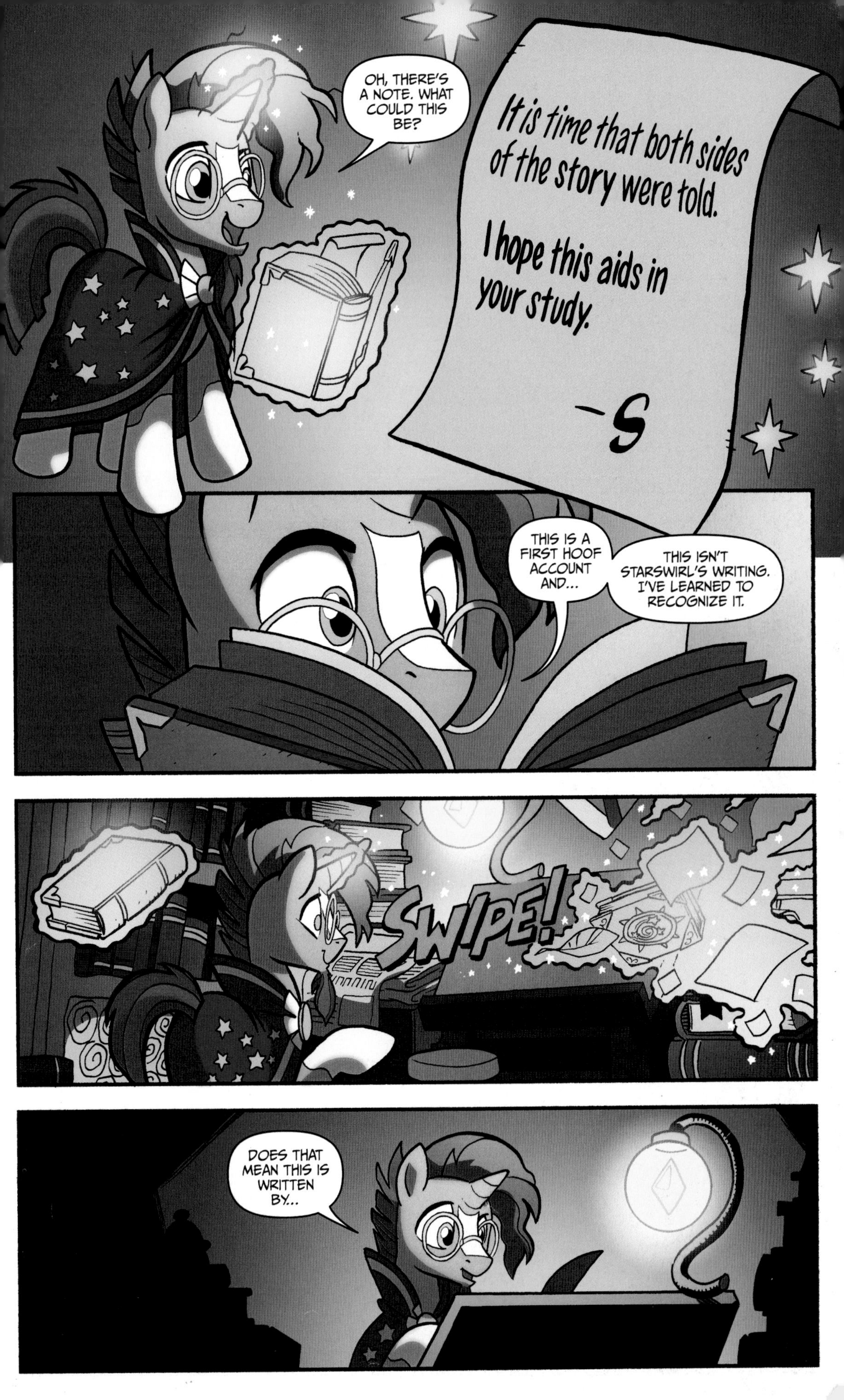
OH, THERE'S A NOTE. WHAT COULD THIS BE?
It is time that both sides of the story were told.
I hope this aids in your study.
-S
THIS IS A FIRST HOOF ACCOUNT AND...
THIS ISN'T STARSWIRL'S WRITING. I'VE LEARNED TO RECOGNIZE IT.
SWIPE!
DOES THAT MEAN THIS IS WRITTEN BY...

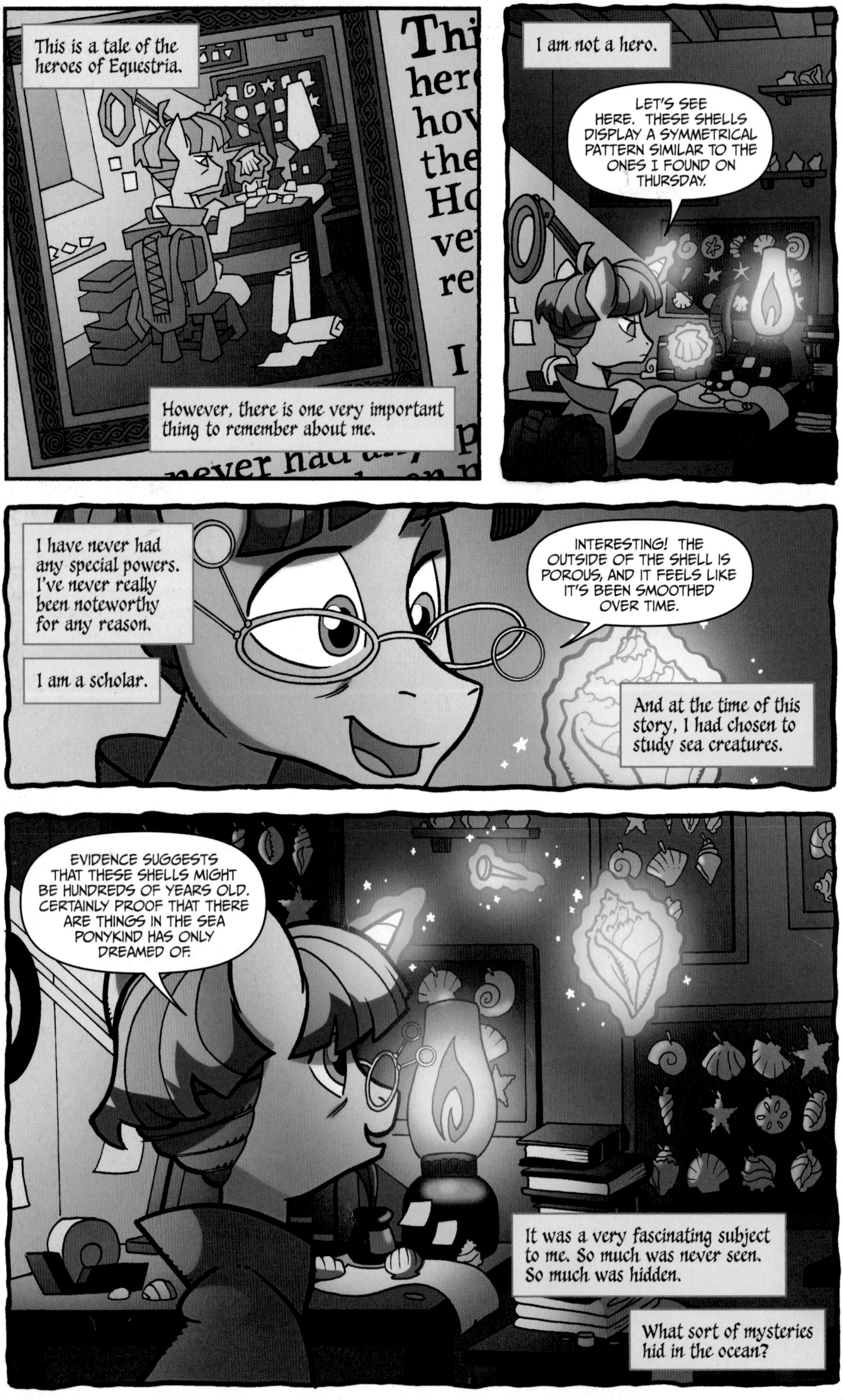
This is a tale of the heroes of Equestria.
However, there is one very important thing to remember about me.
I am not a hero.
LET'S SEE HERE. THESE SHELLS DISPLAY A SYMMETRICAL PATTERN SIMILAR TO THE ONES I FOUND ON THURSDAY.
I have never had any special powers. I've never really been noteworthy for any reason.
I am a scholar.
INTERESTING! THE OUTSIDE OF THE SHELL IS POROUS, AND IT FEELS LIKE IT'S BEEN SMOOTHED OVER TIME.
And at the time of this story, I had chosen to study sea creatures.
EVIDENCE SUGGESTS THAT THESE SHELLS MIGHT BE HUNDREDS OF YEARS OLD. CERTAINLY PROOF THAT THERE ARE THINGS IN THE SEA PONYKIND HAS ONLY DREAMED OF.
It was a very fascinating subject to me. So much was never seen. So much was hidden.
What sort of mysteries hid in the ocean?

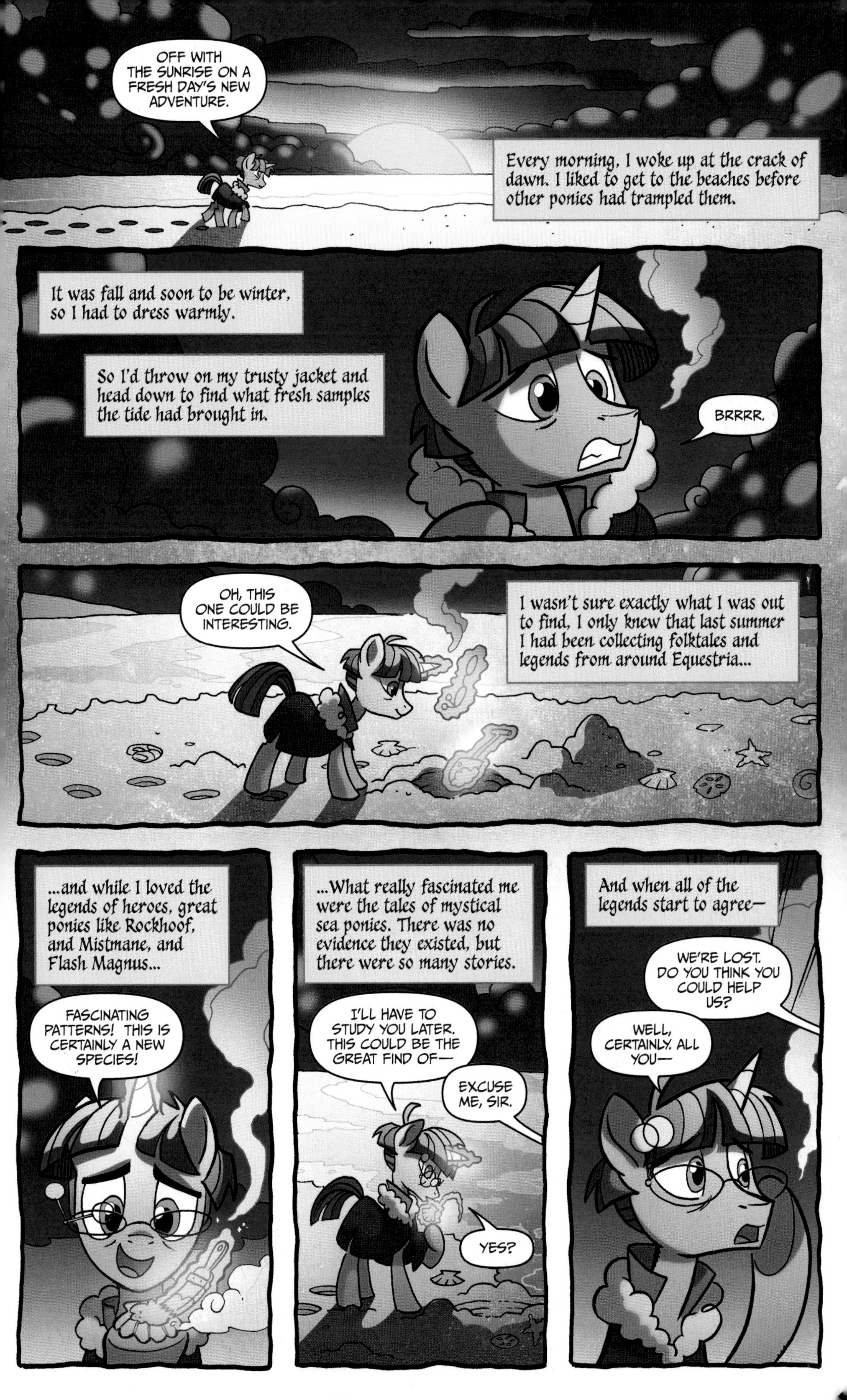
OFF WITH THE SUNRISE ON A FRESH DAY'S NEW ADVENTURE.
Every morning, I woke up at the crack of dawn. I liked to get to the beaches before other ponies had trampled them.
It was fall and soon to be winter, so I had to dress warmly.
So I'd throw on my trusty jacket and head down to find what fresh samples the tide had brought in.
BRRRR.
OH, THIS ONE COULD BE INTERESTING.
I wasn't sure exactly what I was out to find, I only knew that last summer I had been collecting folktales and legends from around Equestria...
...and while I loved the legends of heroes, great ponies like Rockhoof, and Mistmane, and Flash Magnus...
FASCINATING PATTERNS! THIS IS CERTAINLY A NEW SPECIES!
...What really fascinated me were the tales of mystical sea ponies. There was no evidence they existed, but there were so many stories.
I'LL HAVE TO STUDY YOU LATER. THIS COULD BE THE GREAT FIND OF—
EXCUSE ME, SIR.
YES?
And when all of the legends start to agree—
WE'RE LOST. DO YOU THINK YOU COULD HELP US?
WELL, CERTAINLY. ALL YOU—

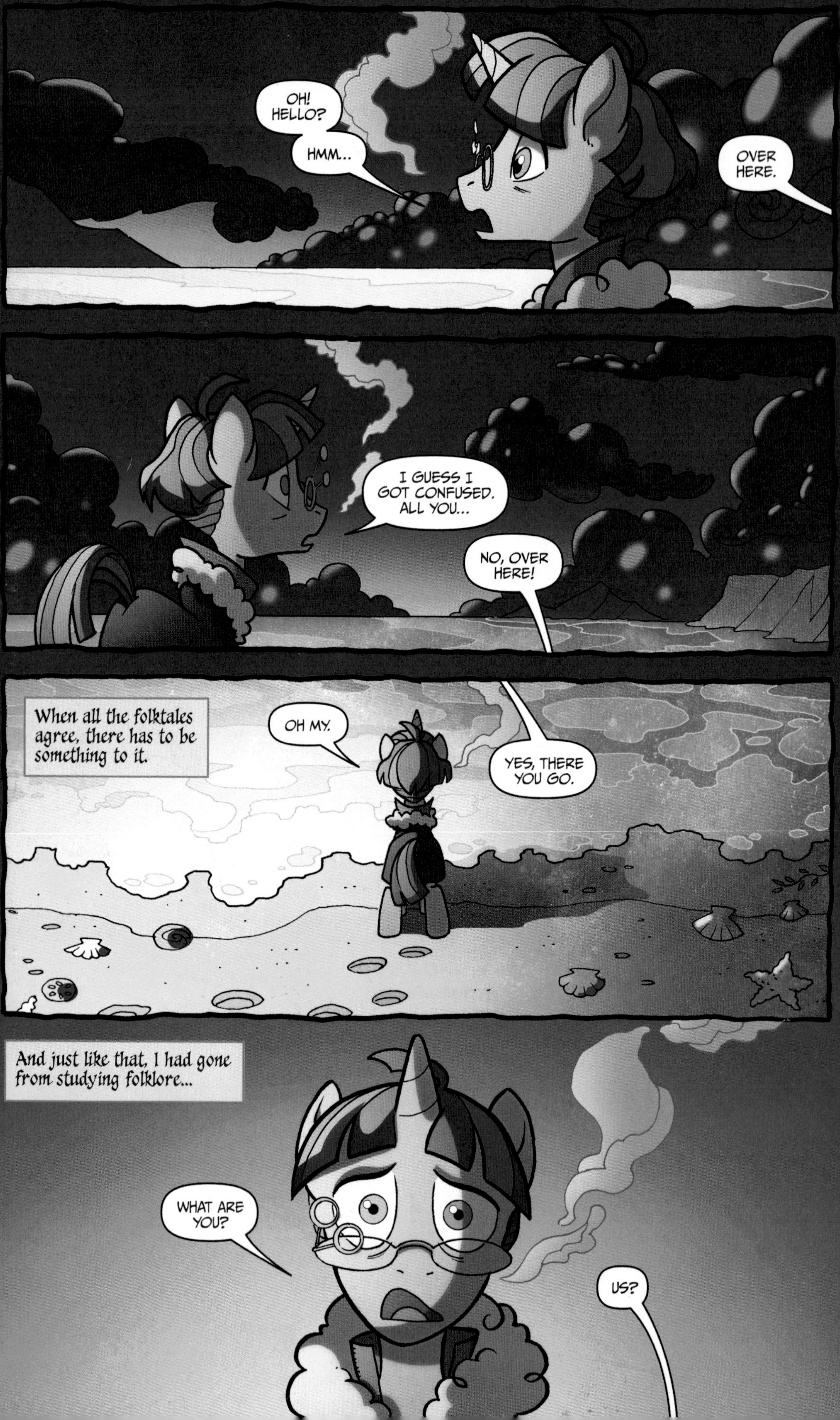
OH! HELLO?
HMM...
OVER HERE.
I GUESS I GOT CONFUSED. ALL YOU...
NO, OVER HERE!
When all the folktales agree, there has to be something to it.
OH MY.
YES, THERE YOU GO.
And just like that, I had gone from studying folklore...
WHAT ARE YOU?
US?

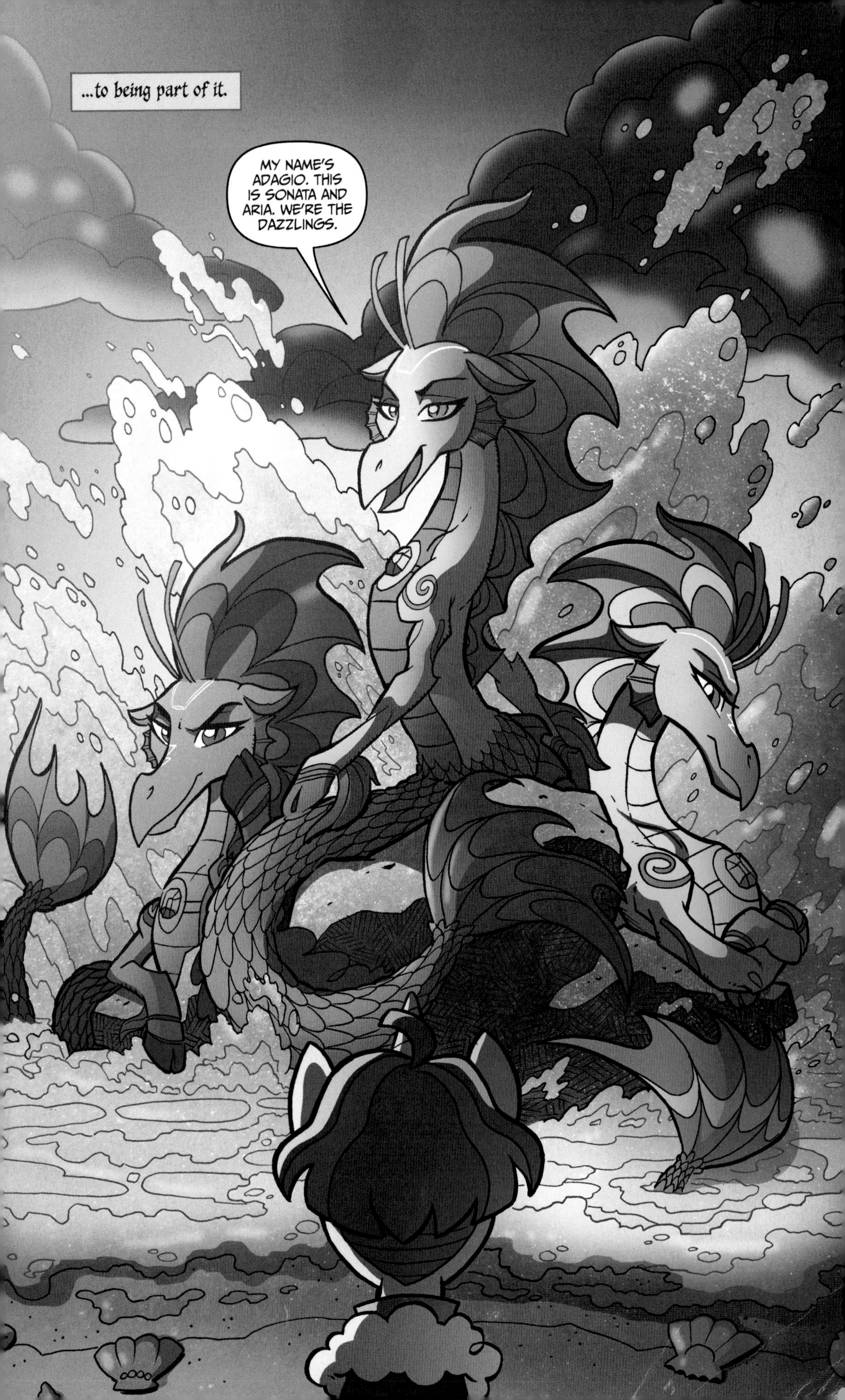
...to being part of it.
MY NAME'S ADAGIO. THIS IS SONATA AND ARIA. WE'RE THE DAZZLINGS.

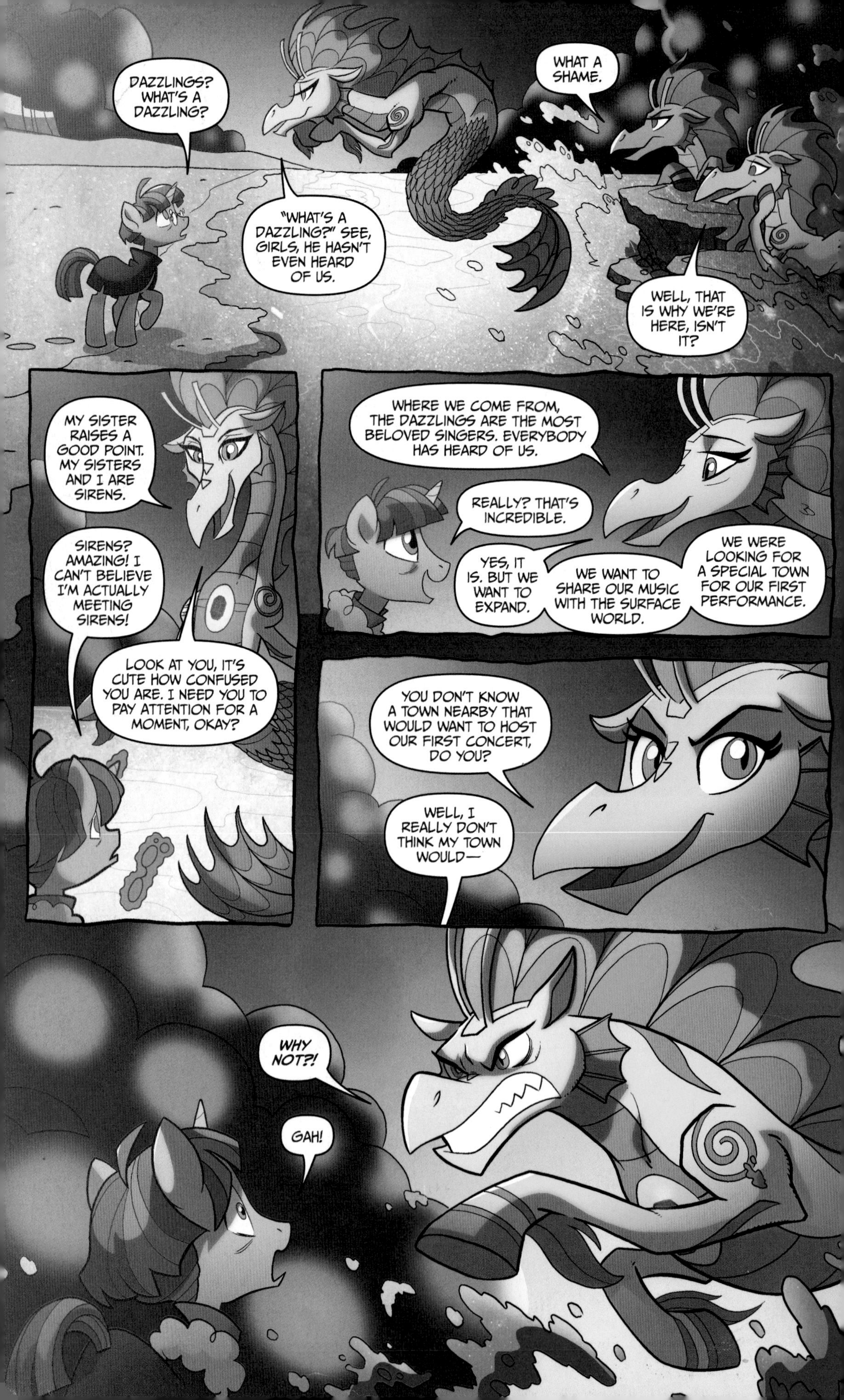
DAZZLINGS? WHAT'S A DAZZLING?
"WHAT'S A DAZZLING?" SEE, GIRLS, HE HASN'T EVEN HEARD OF US.
WHAT A SHAME.
WELL, THAT IS WHY WE'RE HERE, ISN'T IT?
MY SISTER RAISES A GOOD POINT. MY SISTERS AND I ARE SIRENS.
SIRENS? AMAZING! I CAN'T BELIEVE I'M ACTUALLY MEETING SIRENS!
LOOK AT YOU, IT'S CUTE HOW CONFUSED YOU ARE. I NEED YOU TO PAY ATTENTION FOR A MOMENT, OKAY?
WHERE WE COME FROM, THE DAZZLINGS ARE THE MOST BELOVED SINGERS. EVERYBODY HAS HEARD OF US.
REALLY? THAT'S INCREDIBLE.
YES, IT IS. BUT WE WANT TO EXPAND.
WE WANT TO SHARE OUR MUSIC WITH THE SURFACE WORLD.
WE WERE LOOKING FOR A SPECIAL TOWN FOR OUR FIRST PERFORMANCE.
YOU DON'T KNOW A TOWN NEARBY THAT WOULD WANT TO HOST OUR FIRST CONCERT, DO YOU?
WELL, I REALLY DON'T THINK MY TOWN WOULD—
WHY NOT?!
GAH!

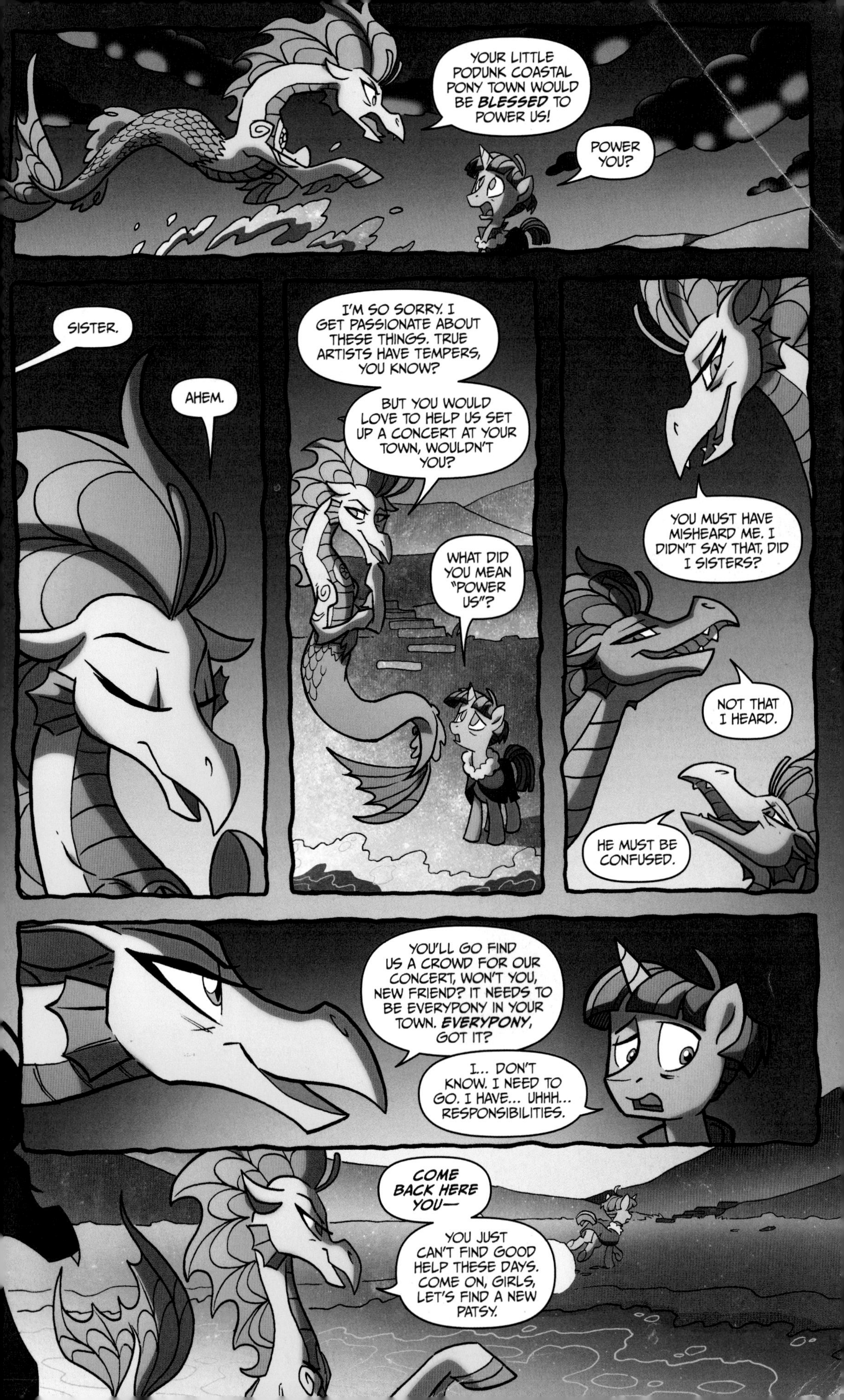

YOUR LITTLE PODUNK COASTAL PONY TOWN WOULD BE **BLESSED** TO POWER US!
POWER YOU?
SISTER.
AHEM.
I'M SO SORRY. I GET PASSIONATE ABOUT THESE THINGS. TRUE ARTISTS HAVE TEMPERS, YOU KNOW?
BUT YOU WOULD LOVE TO HELP US SET UP A CONCERT AT YOUR TOWN, WOULDN'T YOU?
WHAT DID YOU MEAN "POWER US"?
YOU MUST HAVE MISHEARD ME. I DIDN'T SAY THAT, DID I SISTERS?
NOT THAT I HEARD.
HE MUST BE CONFUSED.
YOU'LL GO FIND US A CROWD FOR OUR CONCERT, WON'T YOU, NEW FRIEND? IT NEEDS TO BE EVERYPONY IN YOUR TOWN. ***EVERYPONY***, GOT IT?
I... DON'T KNOW. I NEED TO GO. I HAVE... UHHH... RESPONSIBILITIES.
COME BACK HERE YOU—
YOU JUST CAN'T FIND GOOD HELP THESE DAYS. COME ON, GIRLS, LET'S FIND A NEW PATSY.

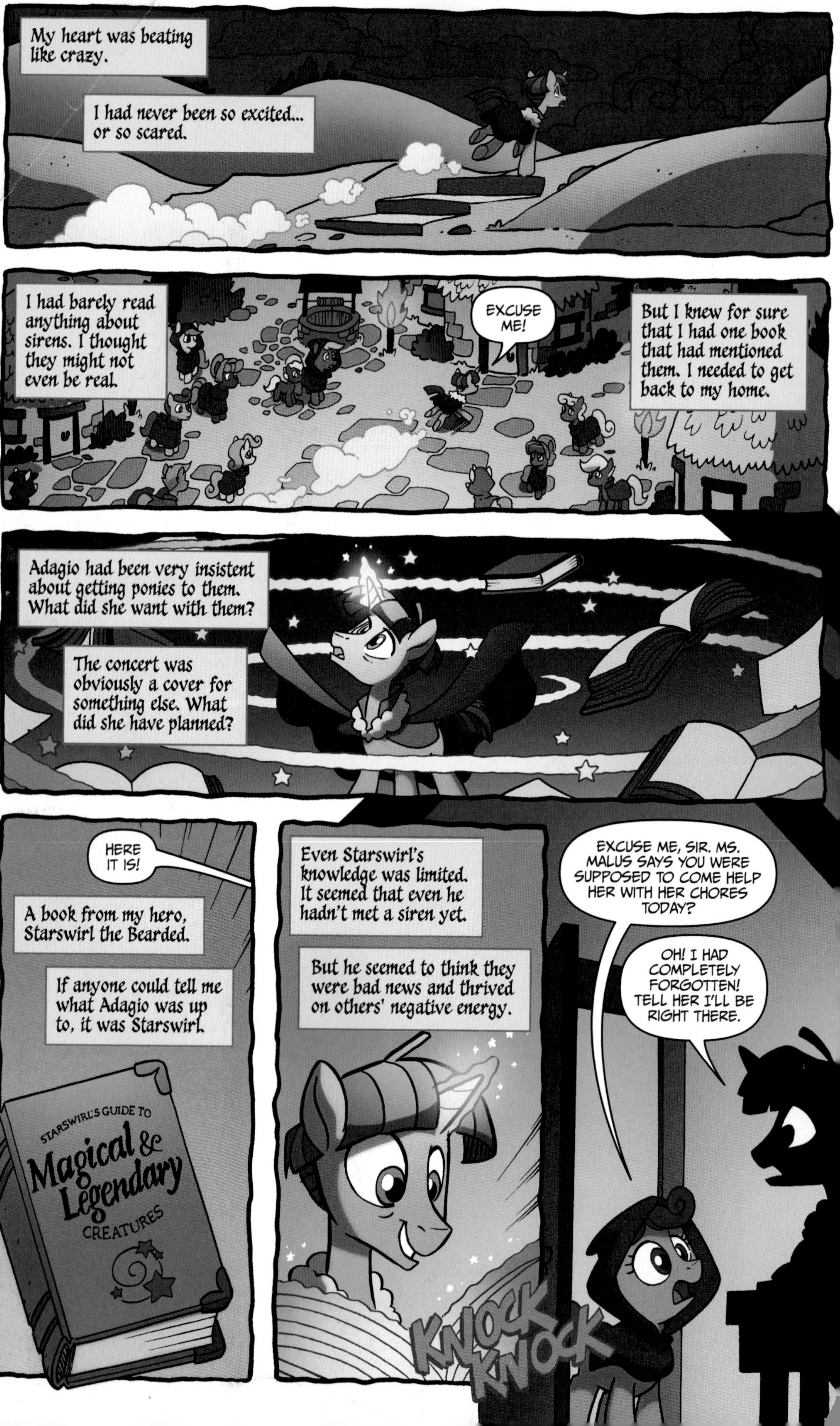
My heart was beating like crazy.
I had never been so excited... or so scared.
I had barely read anything about sirens. I thought they might not even be real.
EXCUSE ME!
But I knew for sure that I had one book that had mentioned them. I needed to get back to my home.
Adagio had been very insistent about getting ponies to them. What did she want with them?
The concert was obviously a cover for something else. What did she have planned?
HERE IT IS!
A book from my hero, Starswirl the Bearded.
If anyone could tell me what Adagio was up to, it was Starswirl.
STARSWIRL'S GUIDE TO Magical & Legendary CREATURES
Even Starswirl's knowledge was limited. It seemed that even he hadn't met a siren yet.
But he seemed to think they were bad news and thrived on others' negative energy.
KNOCK KNOCK
EXCUSE ME, SIR. MS. MALUS SAYS YOU WERE SUPPOSED TO COME HELP HER WITH HER CHORES TODAY?
OH! I HAD COMPLETELY FORGOTTEN! TELL HER I'LL BE RIGHT THERE.

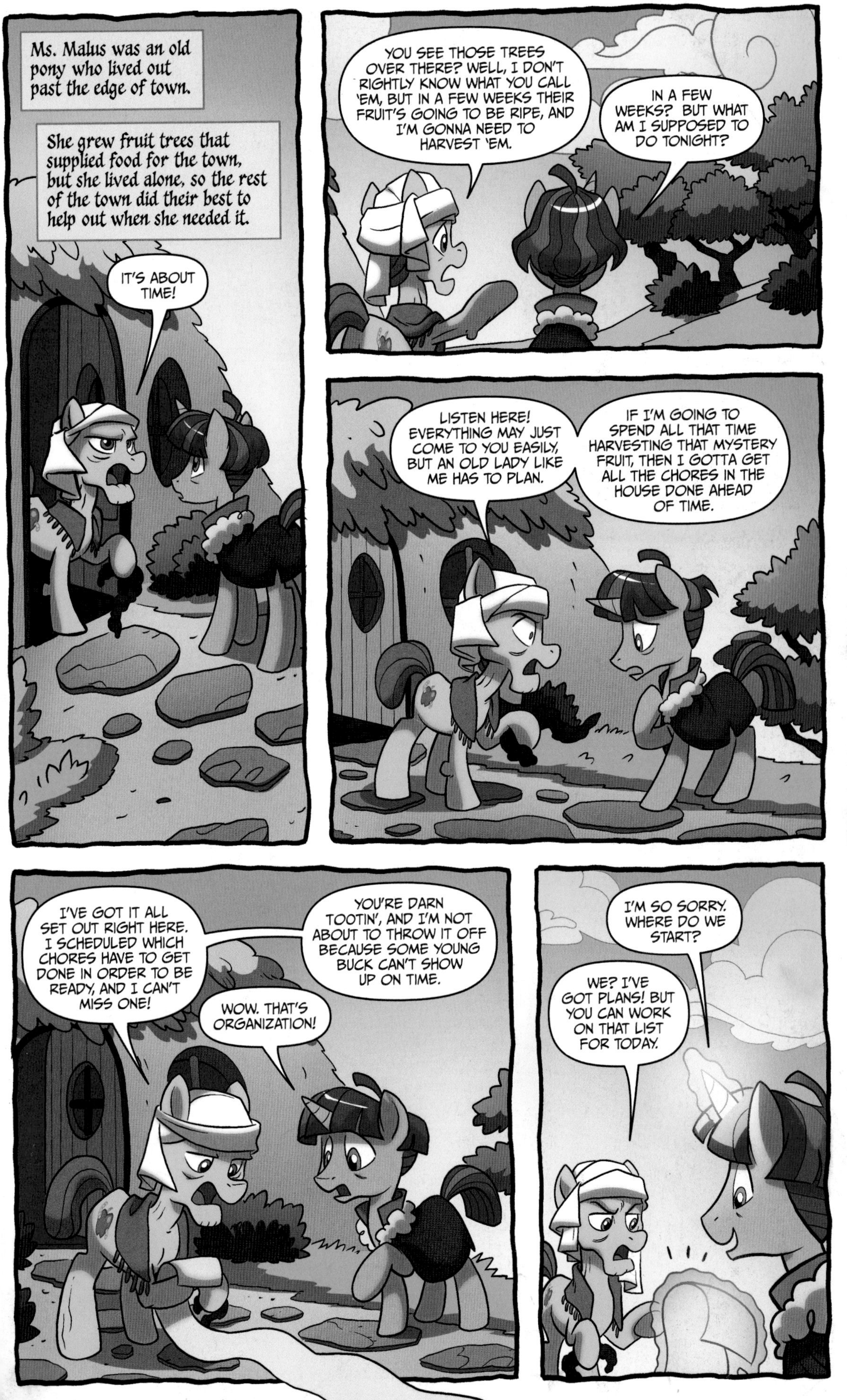

Ms. Malus was an old pony who lived out past the edge of town.
She grew fruit trees that supplied food for the town, but she lived alone, so the rest of the town did their best to help out when she needed it.
IT'S ABOUT TIME!
YOU SEE THOSE TREES OVER THERE? WELL, I DON'T RIGHTLY KNOW WHAT YOU CALL 'EM, BUT IN A FEW WEEKS THEIR FRUIT'S GOING TO BE RIPE, AND I'M GONNA NEED TO HARVEST 'EM.
IN A FEW WEEKS? BUT WHAT AM I SUPPOSED TO DO TONIGHT?
LISTEN HERE! EVERYTHING MAY JUST COME TO YOU EASILY, BUT AN OLD LADY LIKE ME HAS TO PLAN.
IF I'M GOING TO SPEND ALL THAT TIME HARVESTING THAT MYSTERY FRUIT, THEN I GOTTA GET ALL THE CHORES IN THE HOUSE DONE AHEAD OF TIME.
I'VE GOT IT ALL SET OUT RIGHT HERE. I SCHEDULED WHICH CHORES HAVE TO GET DONE IN ORDER TO BE READY, AND I CAN'T MISS ONE!
WOW. THAT'S ORGANIZATION!
YOU'RE DARN TOOTIN', AND I'M NOT ABOUT TO THROW IT OFF BECAUSE SOME YOUNG BUCK CAN'T SHOW UP ON TIME.
I'M SO SORRY. WHERE DO WE START?
WE? I'VE GOT PLANS! BUT YOU CAN WORK ON THAT LIST FOR TODAY.

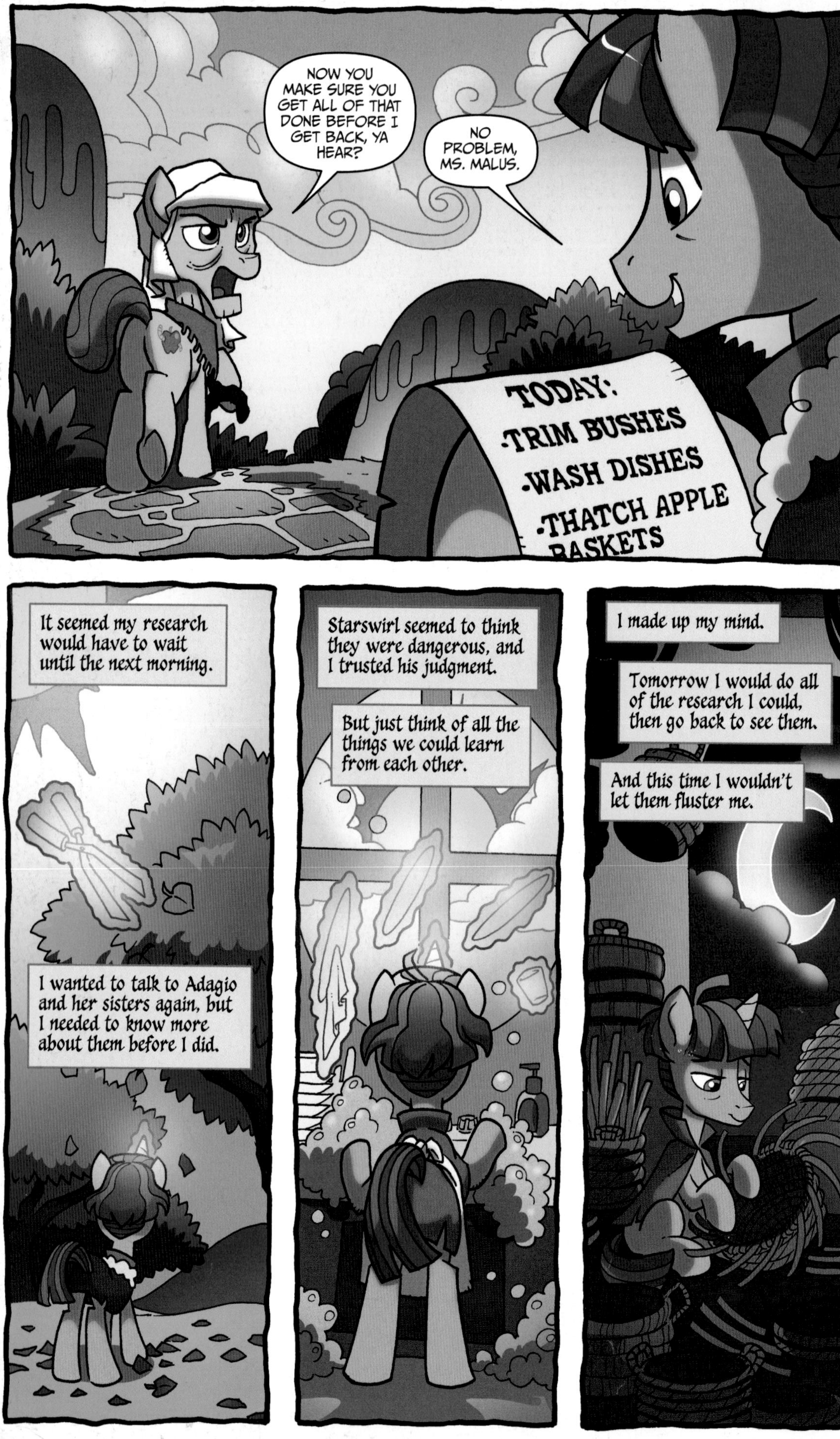
NOW YOU MAKE SURE YOU GET ALL OF THAT DONE BEFORE I GET BACK, YA HEAR?
NO PROBLEM, MS. MALUS.
TODAY:
-TRIM BUSHES
-WASH DISHES
-THATCH APPLE BASKETS
It seemed my research would have to wait until the next morning.
I wanted to talk to Adagio and her sisters again, but I needed to know more about them before I did.
Starswirl seemed to think they were dangerous, and I trusted his judgment.
But just think of all the things we could learn from each other.
I made up my mind.
Tomorrow I would do all of the research I could, then go back to see them.
And this time I wouldn't let them fluster me.

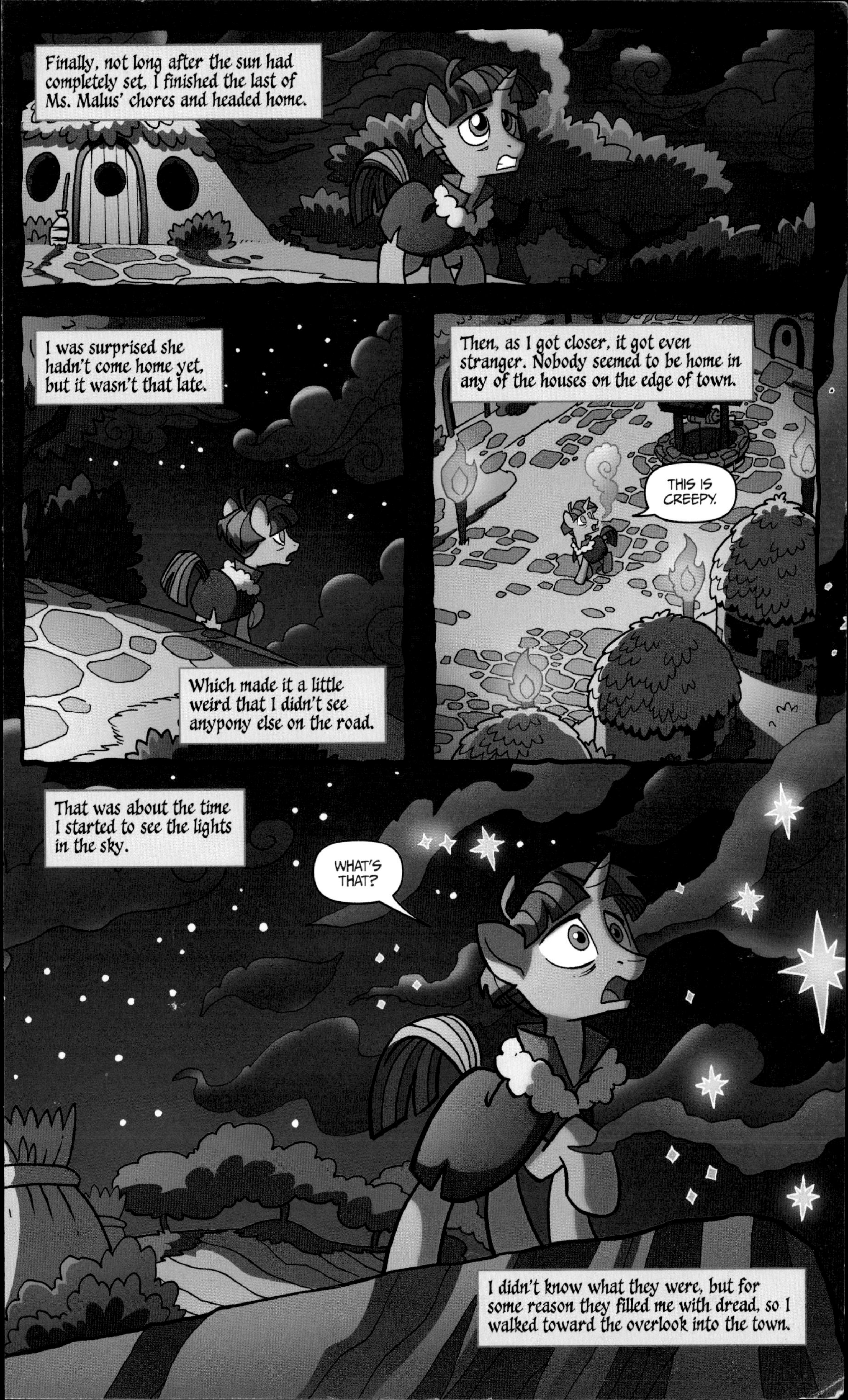

Finally, not long after the sun had completely set, I finished the last of Ms. Malus' chores and headed home.
I was surprised she hadn't come home yet, but it wasn't that late.
Which made it a little weird that I didn't see anypony else on the road.
Then, as I got closer, it got even stranger. Nobody seemed to be home in any of the houses on the edge of town.
THIS IS CREEPY.
That was about the time I started to see the lights in the sky.
WHAT'S THAT?
I didn't know what they were, but for some reason they filled me with dread, so I walked toward the overlook into the town.

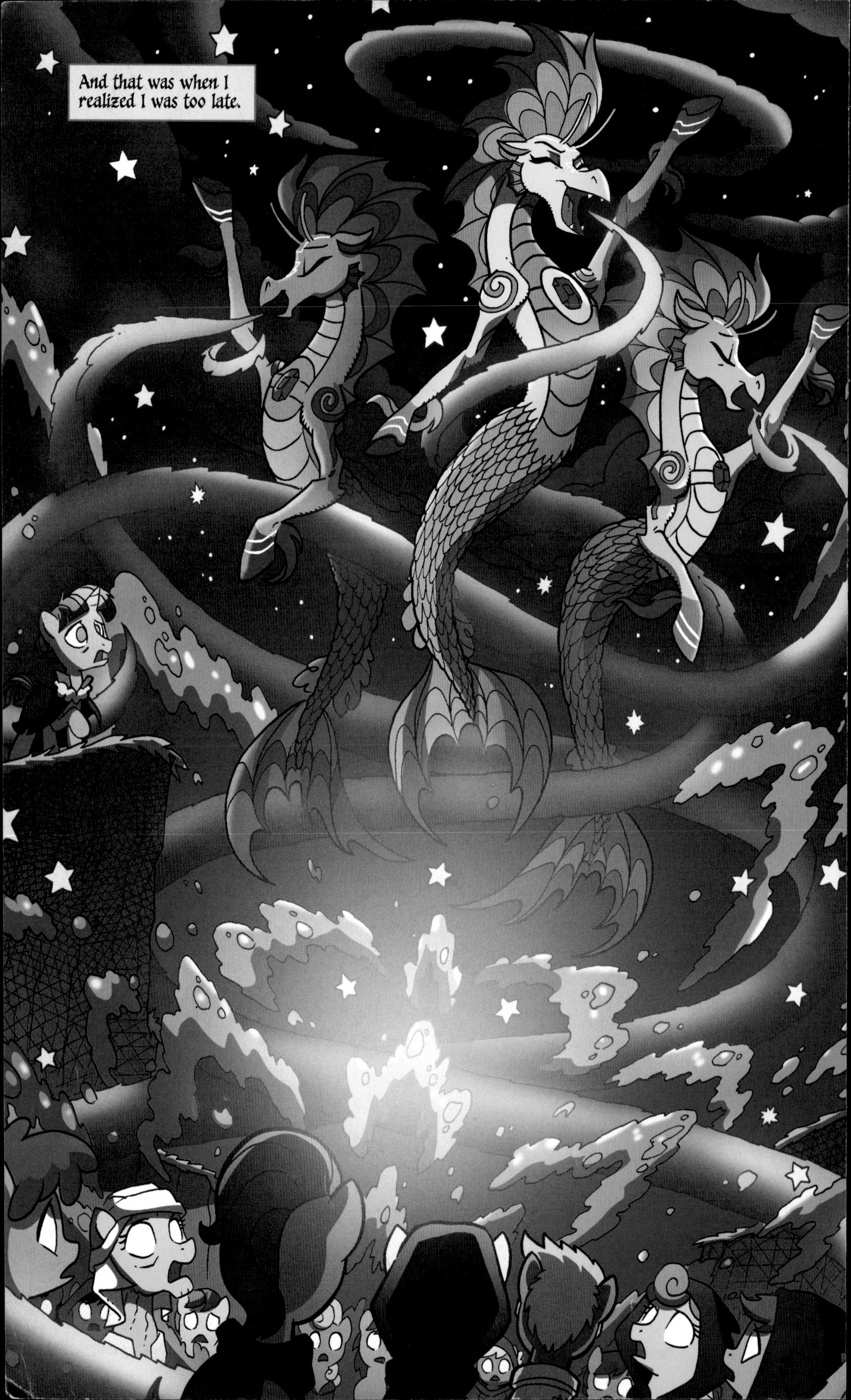
And that was when I realized I was too late.

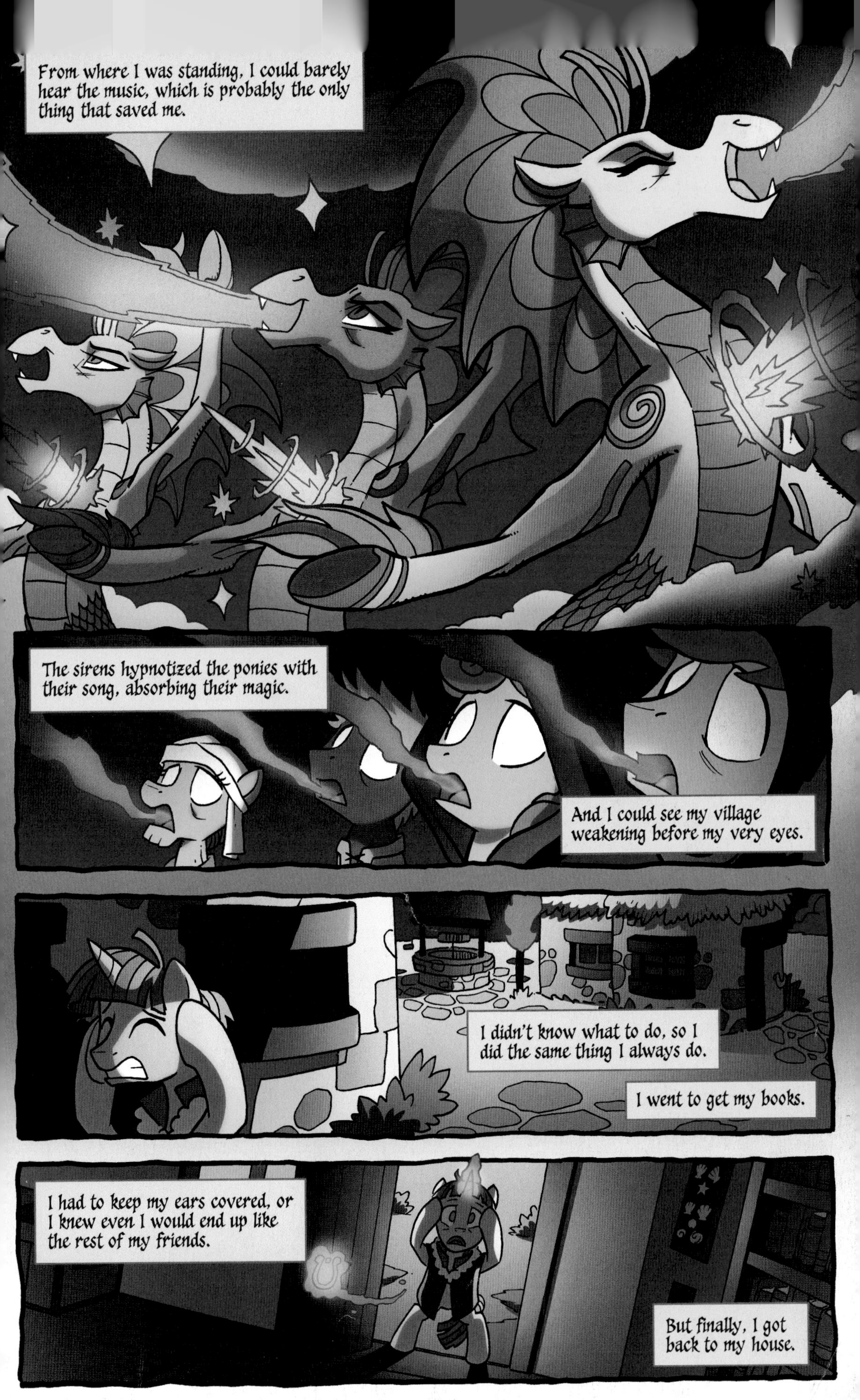
From where I was standing, I could barely hear the music, which is probably the only thing that saved me.
The sirens hypnotized the ponies with their song, absorbing their magic.
And I could see my village weakening before my very eyes.
I didn't know what to do, so I did the same thing I always do.
I went to get my books.
I had to keep my ears covered, or I knew even I would end up like the rest of my friends.
But finally, I got back to my house.

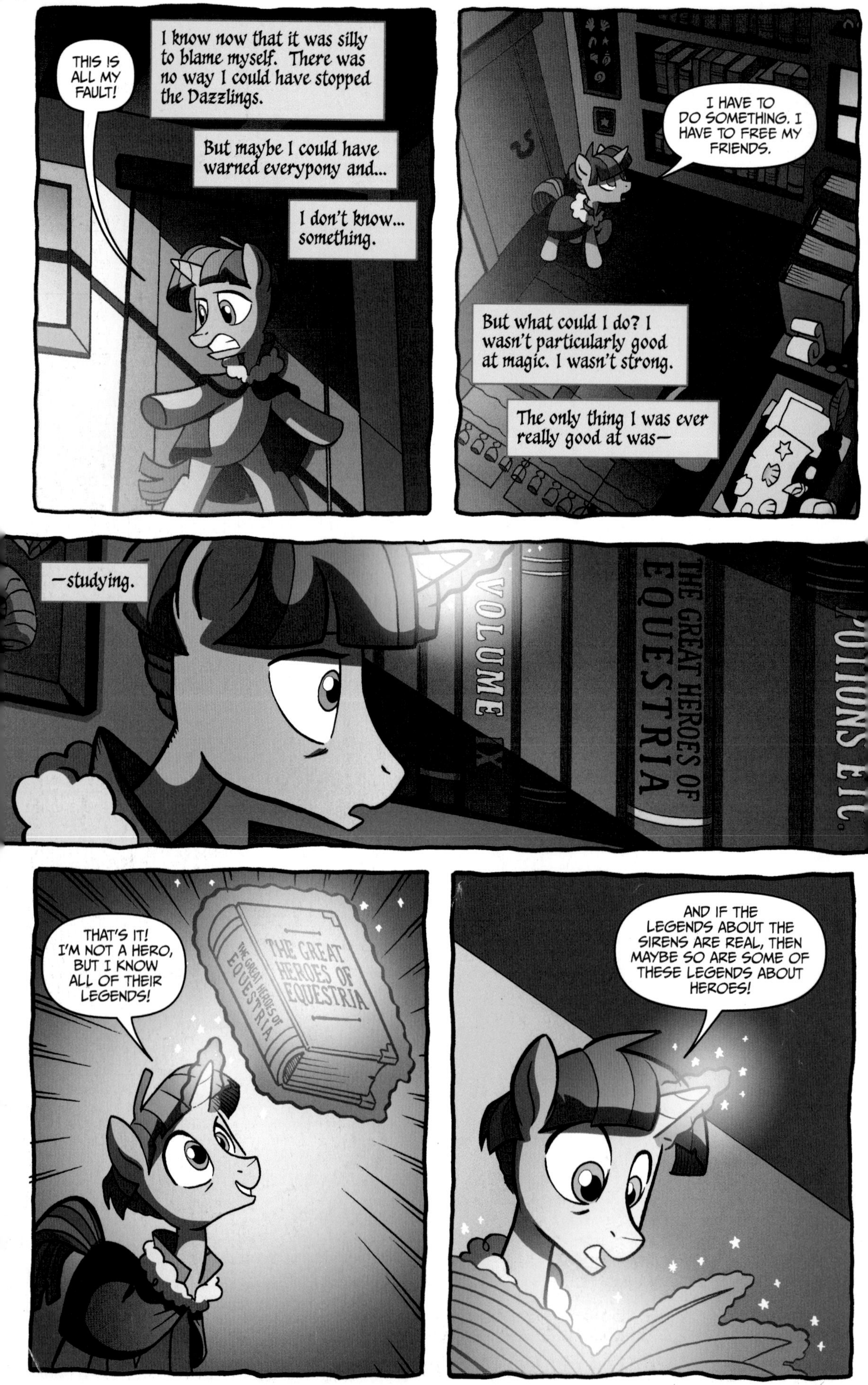
THIS IS ALL MY FAULT!
I know now that it was silly to blame myself. There was no way I could have stopped the Dazzlings.
But maybe I could have warned everypony and...
I don't know... something.
I HAVE TO DO SOMETHING. I HAVE TO FREE MY FRIENDS.
But what could I do? I wasn't particularly good at magic. I wasn't strong.
The only thing I was ever really good at was—
—studying.
VOLUME IX
THE GREAT HEROES OF EQUESTRIA
POTIONS ETC.
THAT'S IT! I'M NOT A HERO, BUT I KNOW ALL OF THEIR LEGENDS!
THE GREAT HEROES OF EQUESTRIA
AND IF THE LEGENDS ABOUT THE SIRENS ARE REAL, THEN MAYBE SO ARE SOME OF THESE LEGENDS ABOUT HEROES!

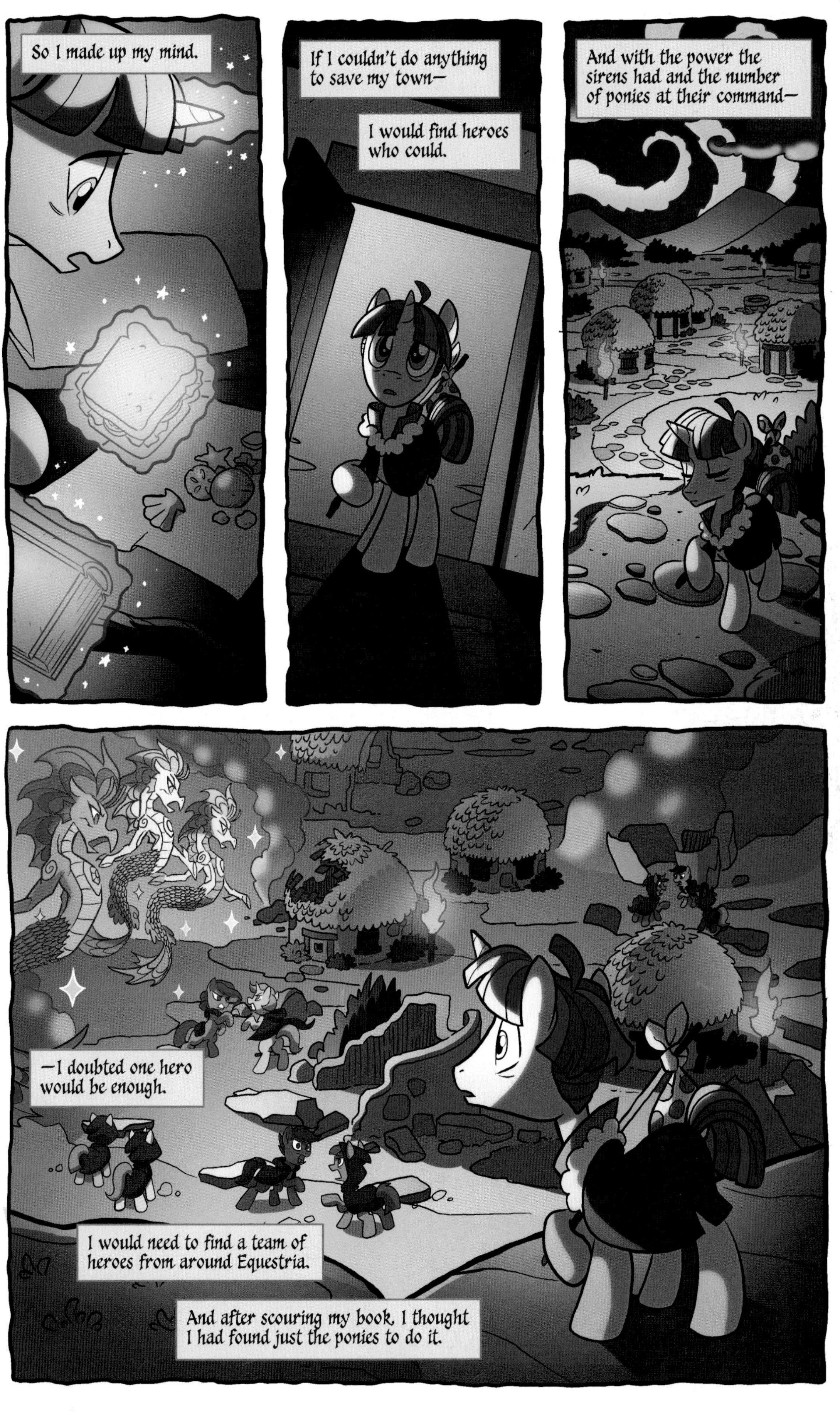
So I made up my mind.
If I couldn't do anything to save my town—
I would find heroes who could.
And with the power the sirens had and the number of ponies at their command—
—I doubted one hero would be enough.
I would need to find a team of heroes from around Equestria.
And after scouring my book, I thought I had found just the ponies to do it.

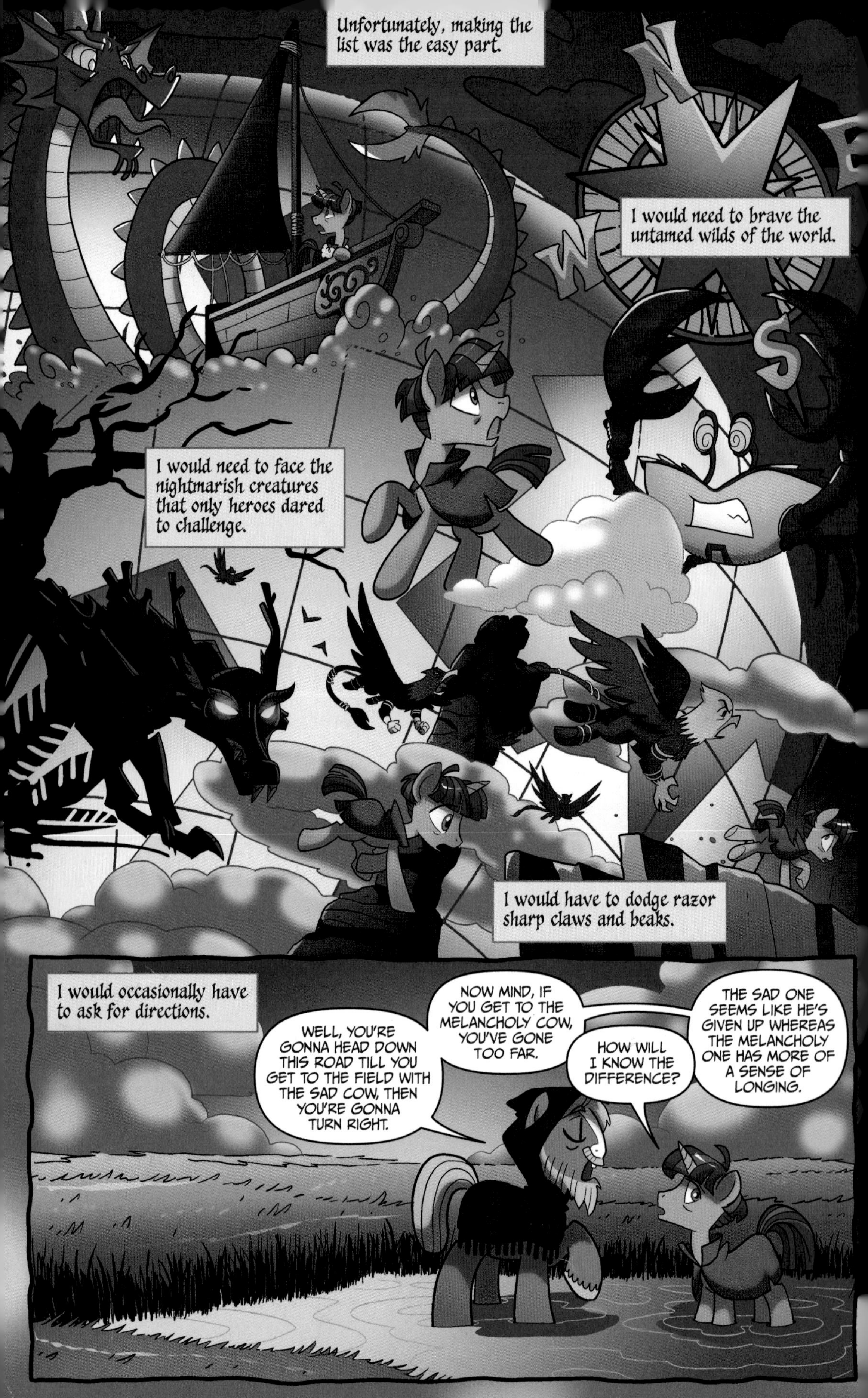
Unfortunately, making the list was the easy part.
N
E
W
S
I would need to brave the untamed wilds of the world.
I would need to face the nightmarish creatures that only heroes dared to challenge.
I would have to dodge razor sharp claws and beaks.
I would occasionally have to ask for directions.
WELL, YOU'RE GONNA HEAD DOWN THIS ROAD TILL YOU GET TO THE FIELD WITH THE SAD COW, THEN YOU'RE GONNA TURN RIGHT.
NOW MIND, IF YOU GET TO THE MELANCHOLY COW, YOU'VE GONE TOO FAR.
HOW WILL I KNOW THE DIFFERENCE?
THE SAD ONE SEEMS LIKE HE'S GIVEN UP WHEREAS THE MELANCHOLY ONE HAS MORE OF A SENSE OF LONGING.

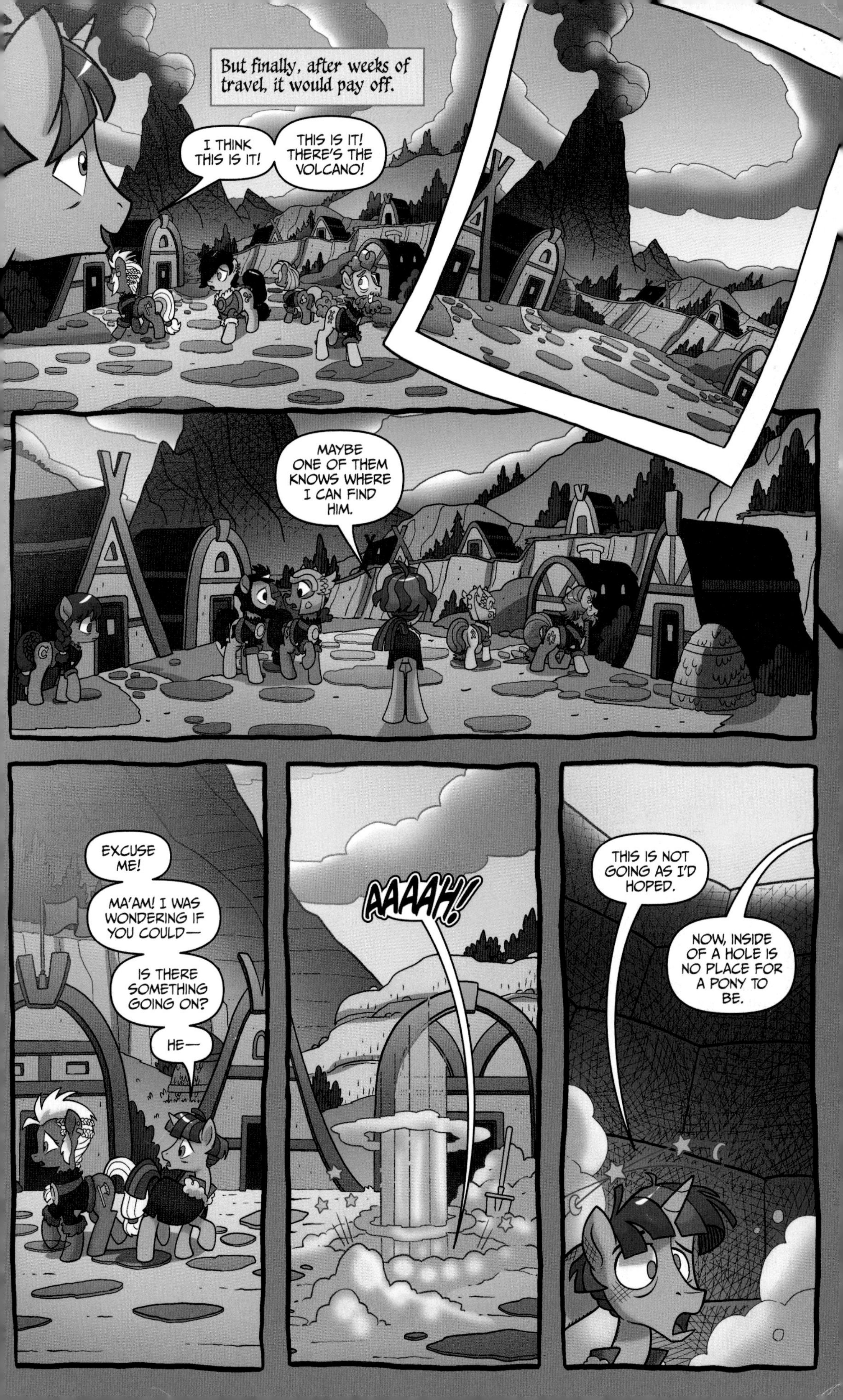
But finally, after weeks of travel, it would pay off.
I THINK THIS IS IT!
THIS IS IT! THERE'S THE VOLCANO!
MAYBE ONE OF THEM KNOWS WHERE I CAN FIND HIM.
EXCUSE ME!
MA'AM! I WAS WONDERING IF YOU COULD—
IS THERE SOMETHING GOING ON?
HE—
AAAAH!
THIS IS NOT GOING AS I'D HOPED.
NOW, INSIDE OF A HOLE IS NO PLACE FOR A PONY TO BE.

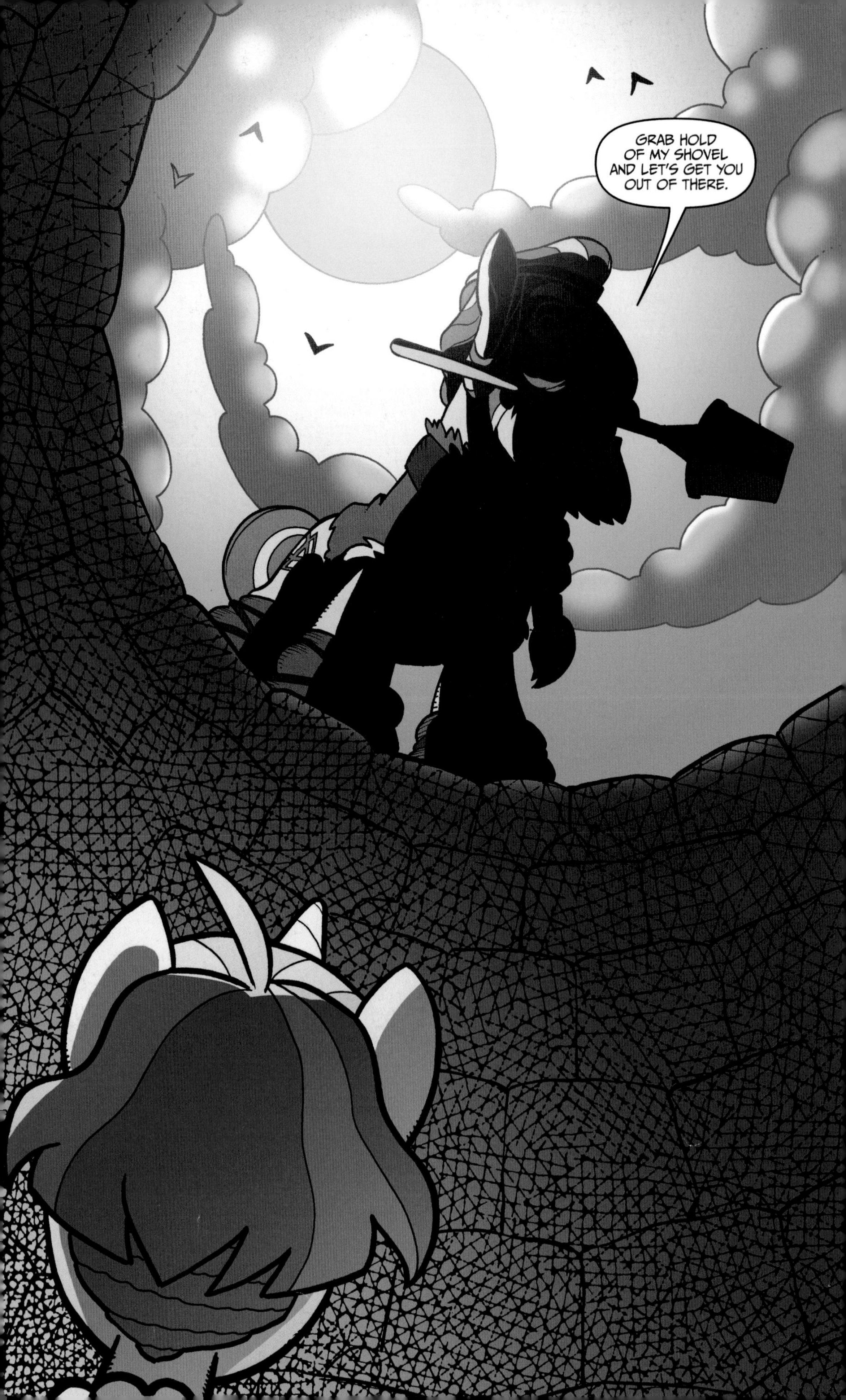
GRAB HOLD OF MY SHOVEL AND LET'S GET YOU OUT OF THERE.

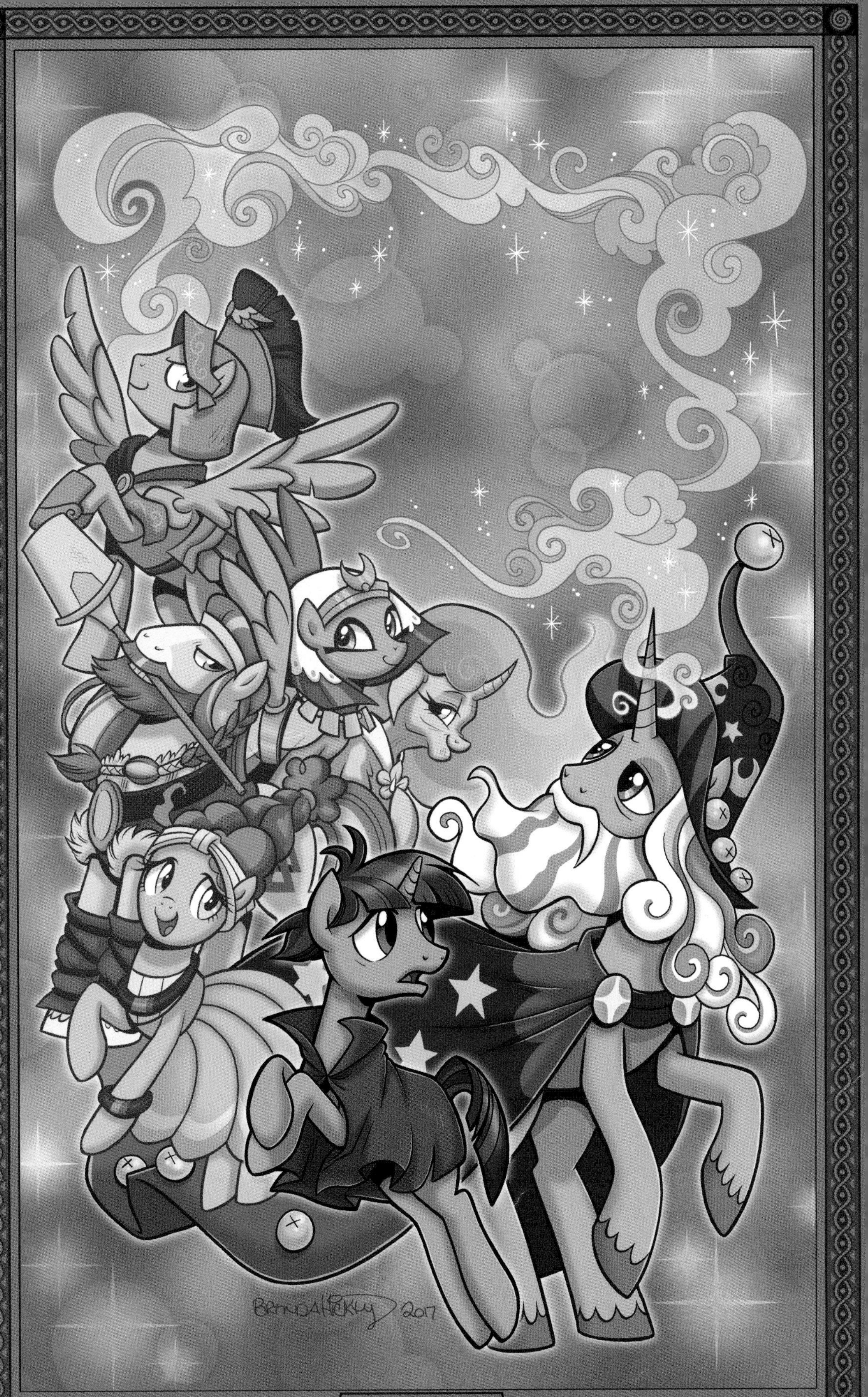
BRENDA HICKEY 2017

ART BY BRENDA HICKEY

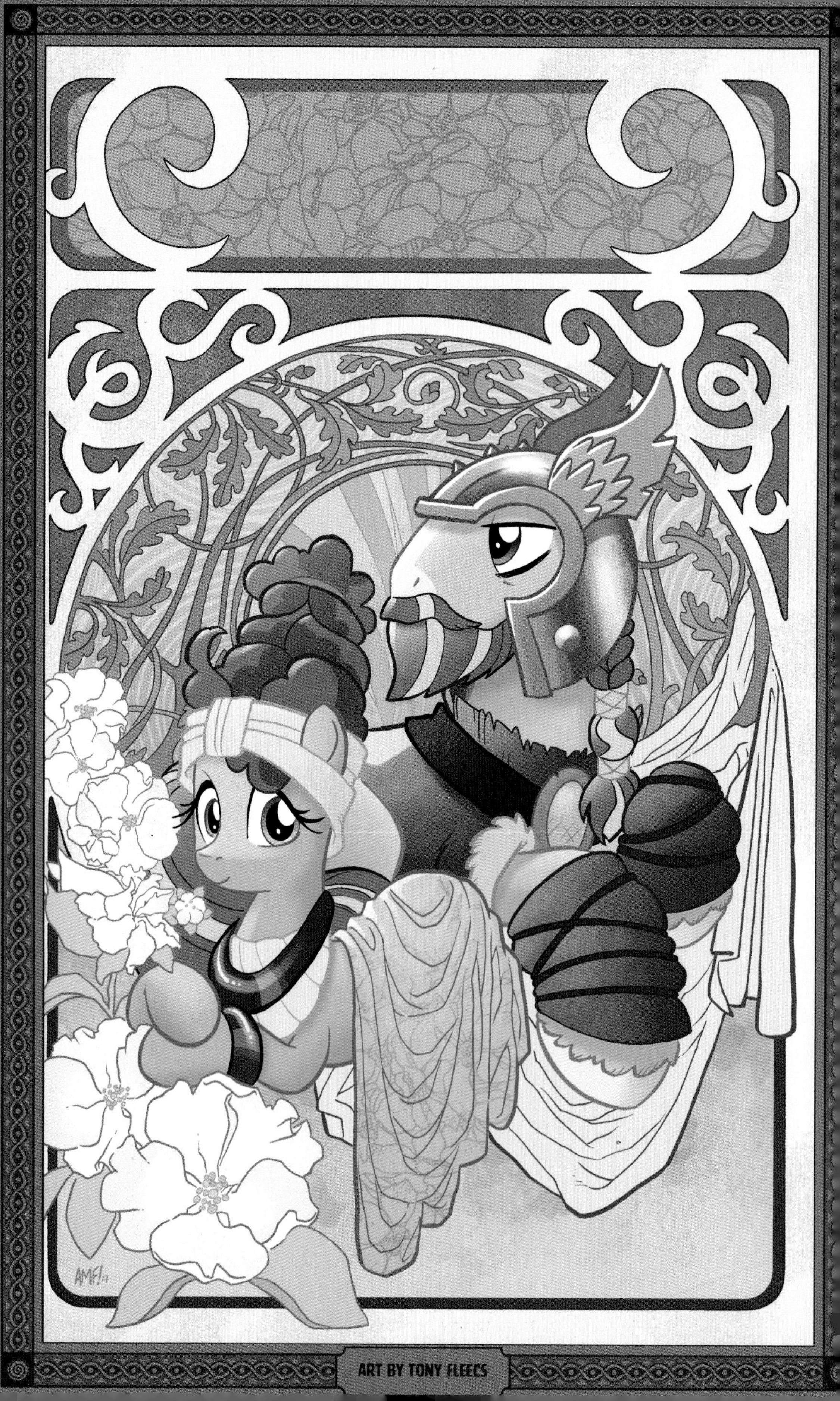
AMF!17

ART BY TONY FLEECS

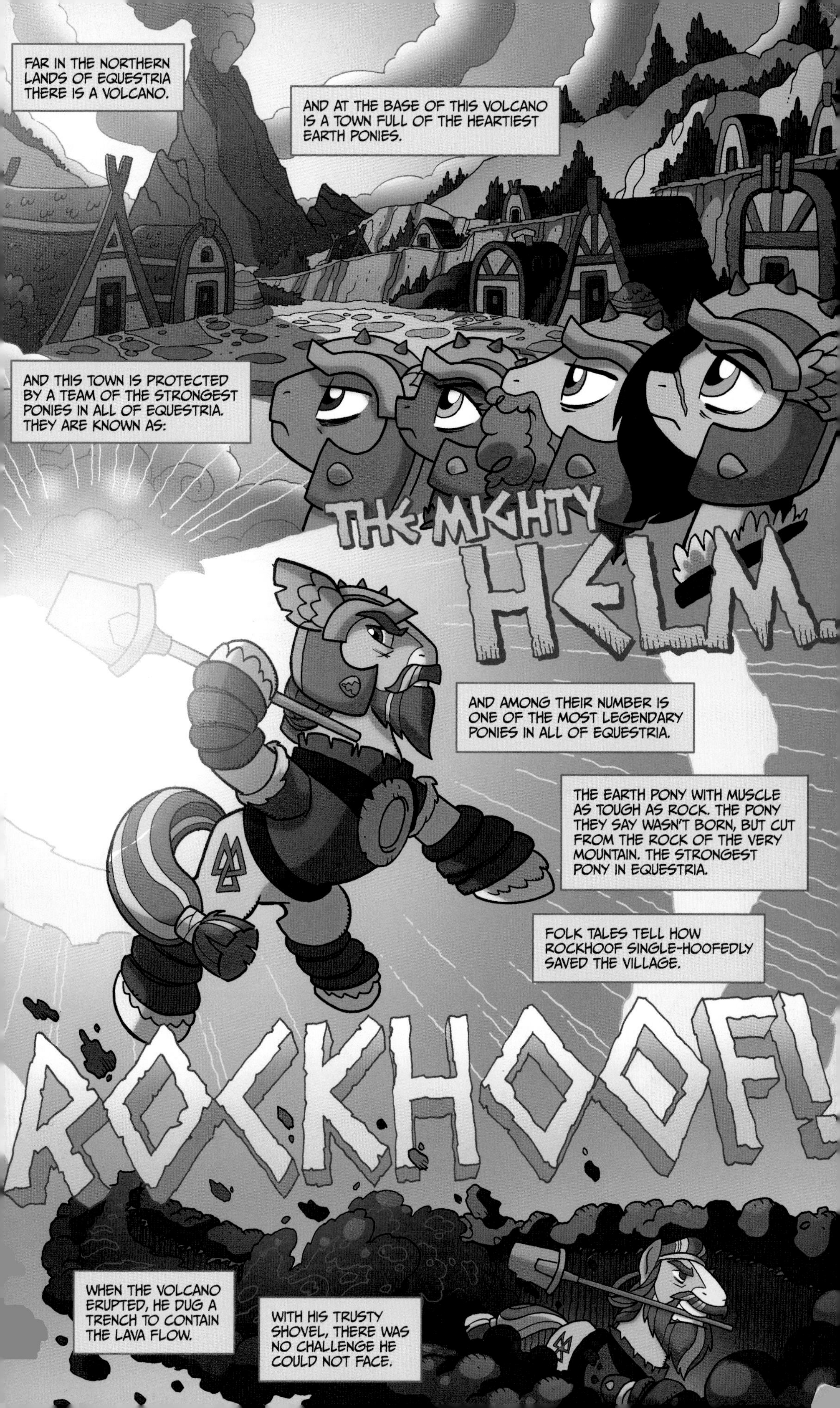
FAR IN THE NORTHERN LANDS OF EQUESTRIA THERE IS A VOLCANO.
AND AT THE BASE OF THIS VOLCANO IS A TOWN FULL OF THE HEARTIEST EARTH PONIES.
AND THIS TOWN IS PROTECTED BY A TEAM OF THE STRONGEST PONIES IN ALL OF EQUESTRIA. THEY ARE KNOWN AS:
THE MIGHTY HELM.
AND AMONG THEIR NUMBER IS ONE OF THE MOST LEGENDARY PONIES IN ALL OF EQUESTRIA.
THE EARTH PONY WITH MUSCLE AS TOUGH AS ROCK. THE PONY THEY SAY WASN'T BORN, BUT CUT FROM THE ROCK OF THE VERY MOUNTAIN. THE STRONGEST PONY IN EQUESTRIA.
FOLK TALES TELL HOW ROCKHOOF SINGLE-HOOFEDLY SAVED THE VILLAGE.
ROCKHOOF!
WHEN THE VOLCANO ERUPTED, HE DUG A TRENCH TO CONTAIN THE LAVA FLOW.
WITH HIS TRUSTY SHOVEL, THERE WAS NO CHALLENGE HE COULD NOT FACE.

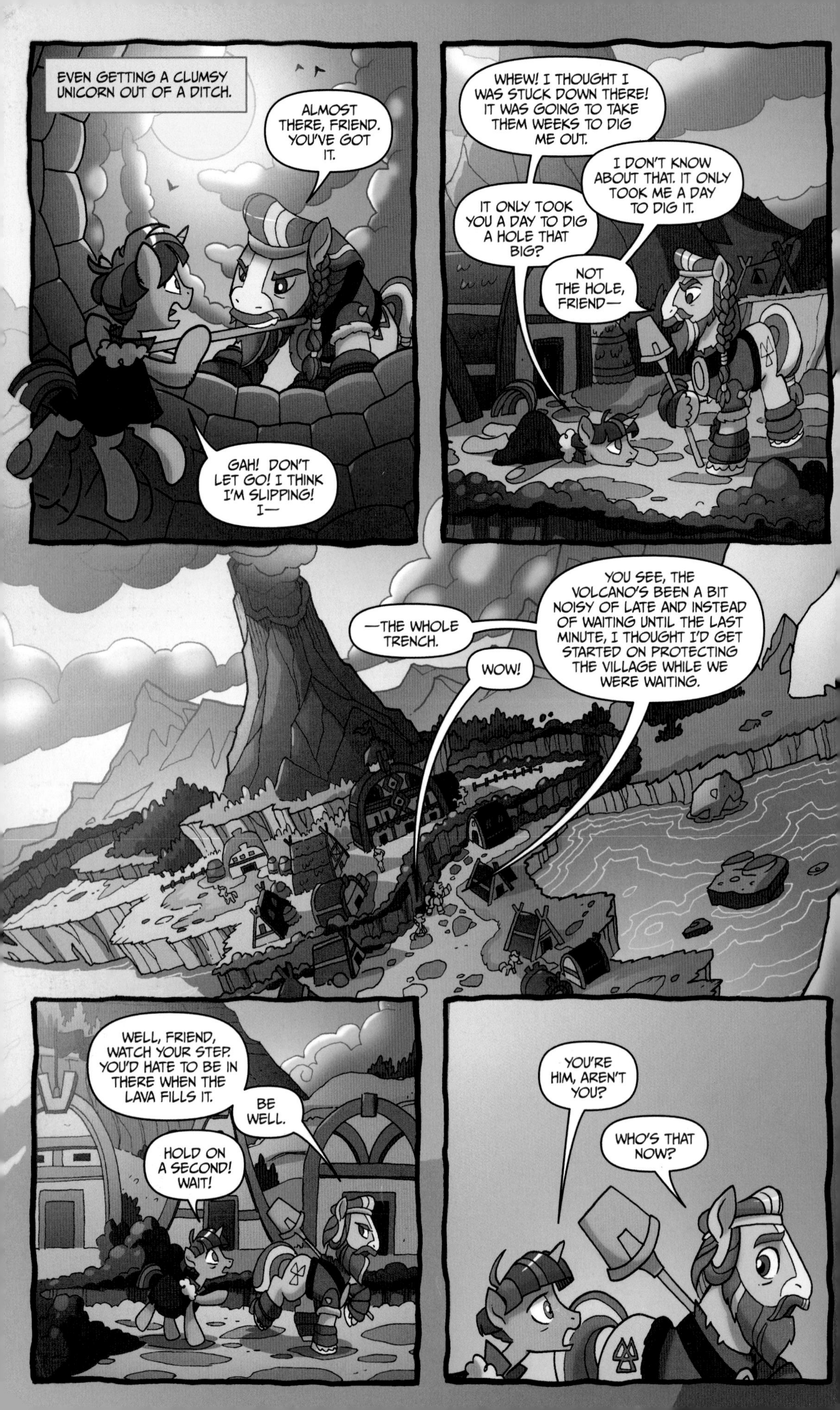

EVEN GETTING A CLUMSY UNICORN OUT OF A DITCH.
ALMOST THERE, FRIEND. YOU'VE GOT IT.
GAH! DON'T LET GO! I THINK I'M SLIPPING! I—
WHEW! I THOUGHT I WAS STUCK DOWN THERE! IT WAS GOING TO TAKE THEM WEEKS TO DIG ME OUT.
I DON'T KNOW ABOUT THAT. IT ONLY TOOK ME A DAY TO DIG IT.
IT ONLY TOOK YOU A DAY TO DIG A HOLE THAT BIG?
NOT THE HOLE, FRIEND—
—THE WHOLE TRENCH.
YOU SEE, THE VOLCANO'S BEEN A BIT NOISY OF LATE AND INSTEAD OF WAITING UNTIL THE LAST MINUTE, I THOUGHT I'D GET STARTED ON PROTECTING THE VILLAGE WHILE WE WERE WAITING.
WOW!
WELL, FRIEND, WATCH YOUR STEP. YOU'D HATE TO BE IN THERE WHEN THE LAVA FILLS IT.
BE WELL.
HOLD ON A SECOND! WAIT!
YOU'RE HIM, AREN'T YOU?
WHO'S THAT NOW?

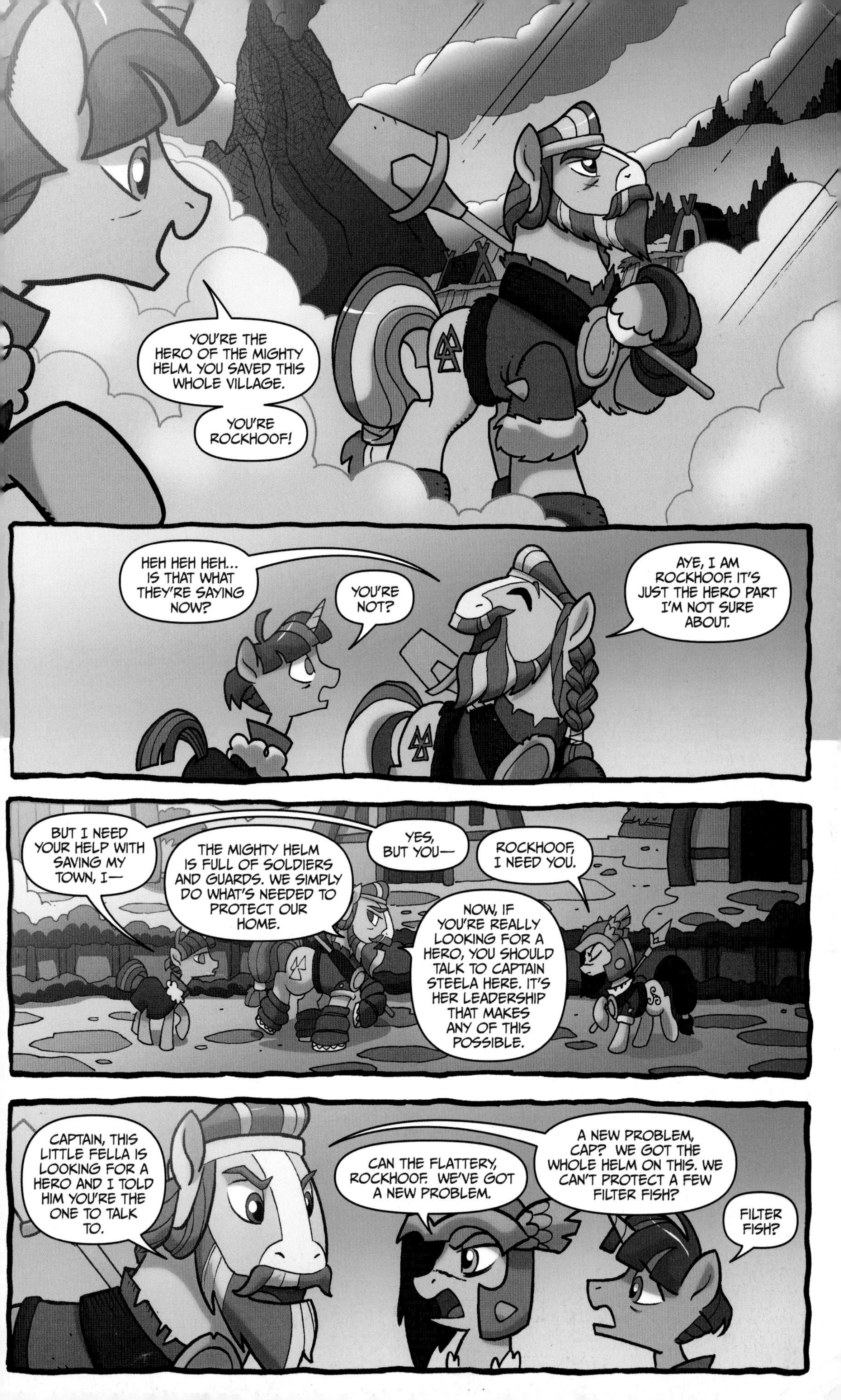
YOU'RE THE HERO OF THE MIGHTY HELM. YOU SAVED THIS WHOLE VILLAGE.
YOU'RE ROCKHOOF!
HEH HEH HEH... IS THAT WHAT THEY'RE SAYING NOW?
YOU'RE NOT?
AYE, I AM ROCKHOOF. IT'S JUST THE HERO PART I'M NOT SURE ABOUT.
BUT I NEED YOUR HELP WITH SAVING MY TOWN, I—
THE MIGHTY HELM IS FULL OF SOLDIERS AND GUARDS. WE SIMPLY DO WHAT'S NEEDED TO PROTECT OUR HOME.
YES, BUT YOU—
ROCKHOOF, I NEED YOU.
NOW, IF YOU'RE REALLY LOOKING FOR A HERO, YOU SHOULD TALK TO CAPTAIN STEELA HERE. IT'S HER LEADERSHIP THAT MAKES ANY OF THIS POSSIBLE.
CAPTAIN, THIS LITTLE FELLA IS LOOKING FOR A HERO AND I TOLD HIM YOU'RE THE ONE TO TALK TO.
CAN THE FLATTERY, ROCKHOOF. WE'VE GOT A NEW PROBLEM.
A NEW PROBLEM, CAP? WE GOT THE WHOLE HELM ON THIS. WE CAN'T PROTECT A FEW FILTER FISH?
FILTER FISH?

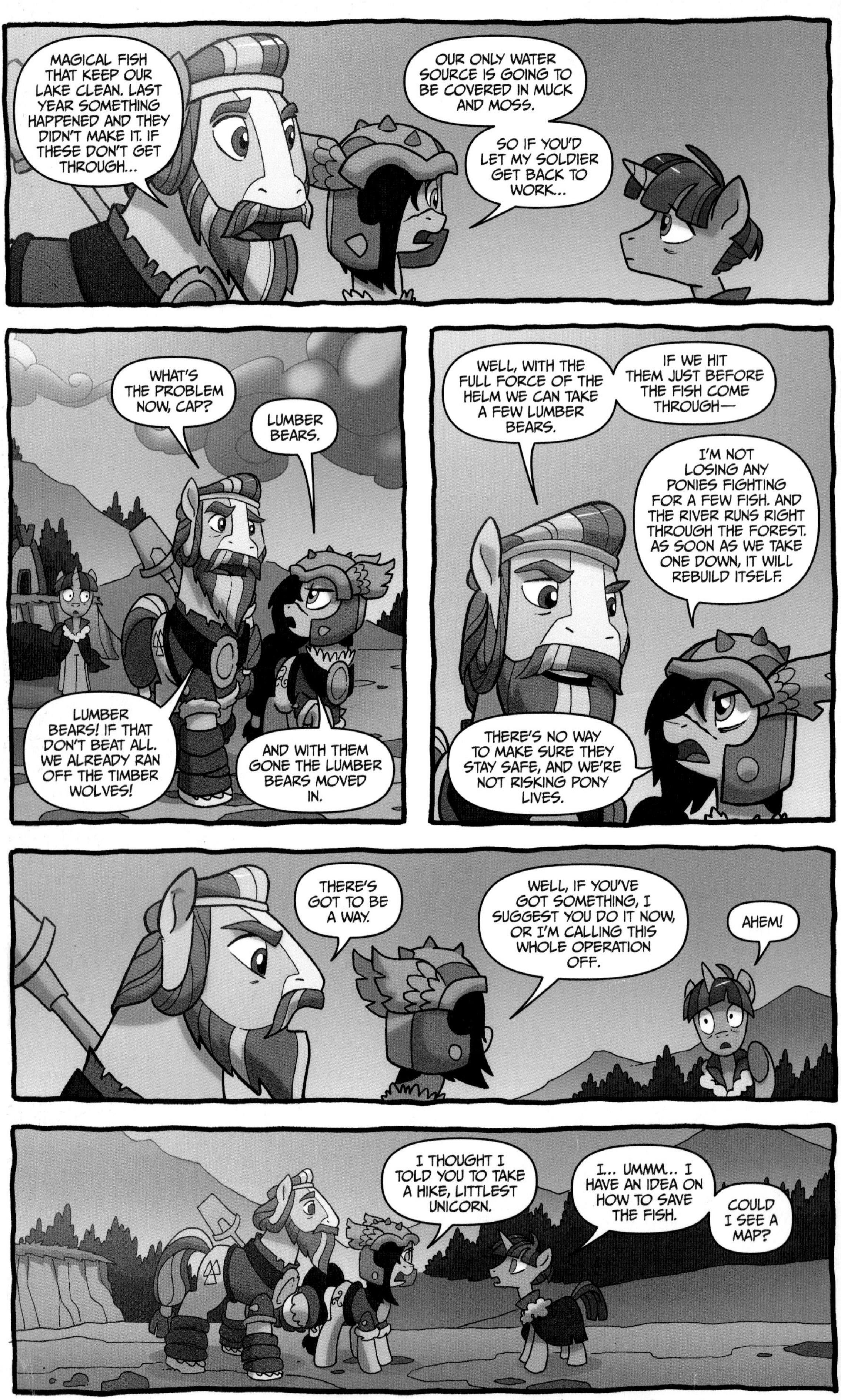
MAGICAL FISH THAT KEEP OUR LAKE CLEAN. LAST YEAR SOMETHING HAPPENED AND THEY DIDN'T MAKE IT. IF THESE DON'T GET THROUGH...
OUR ONLY WATER SOURCE IS GOING TO BE COVERED IN MUCK AND MOSS.
SO IF YOU'D LET MY SOLDIER GET BACK TO WORK...
WHAT'S THE PROBLEM NOW, CAP?
LUMBER BEARS.
LUMBER BEARS! IF THAT DON'T BEAT ALL. WE ALREADY RAN OFF THE TIMBER WOLVES!
AND WITH THEM GONE THE LUMBER BEARS MOVED IN.
WELL, WITH THE FULL FORCE OF THE HELM WE CAN TAKE A FEW LUMBER BEARS.
IF WE HIT THEM JUST BEFORE THE FISH COME THROUGH—
I'M NOT LOSING ANY PONIES FIGHTING FOR A FEW FISH. AND THE RIVER RUNS RIGHT THROUGH THE FOREST. AS SOON AS WE TAKE ONE DOWN, IT WILL REBUILD ITSELF.
THERE'S NO WAY TO MAKE SURE THEY STAY SAFE, AND WE'RE NOT RISKING PONY LIVES.
THERE'S GOT TO BE A WAY.
WELL, IF YOU'VE GOT SOMETHING, I SUGGEST YOU DO IT NOW, OR I'M CALLING THIS WHOLE OPERATION OFF.
AHEM!
I THOUGHT I TOLD YOU TO TAKE A HIKE, LITTLEST UNICORN.
I... UMMM... I HAVE AN IDEA ON HOW TO SAVE THE FISH.
COULD I SEE A MAP?

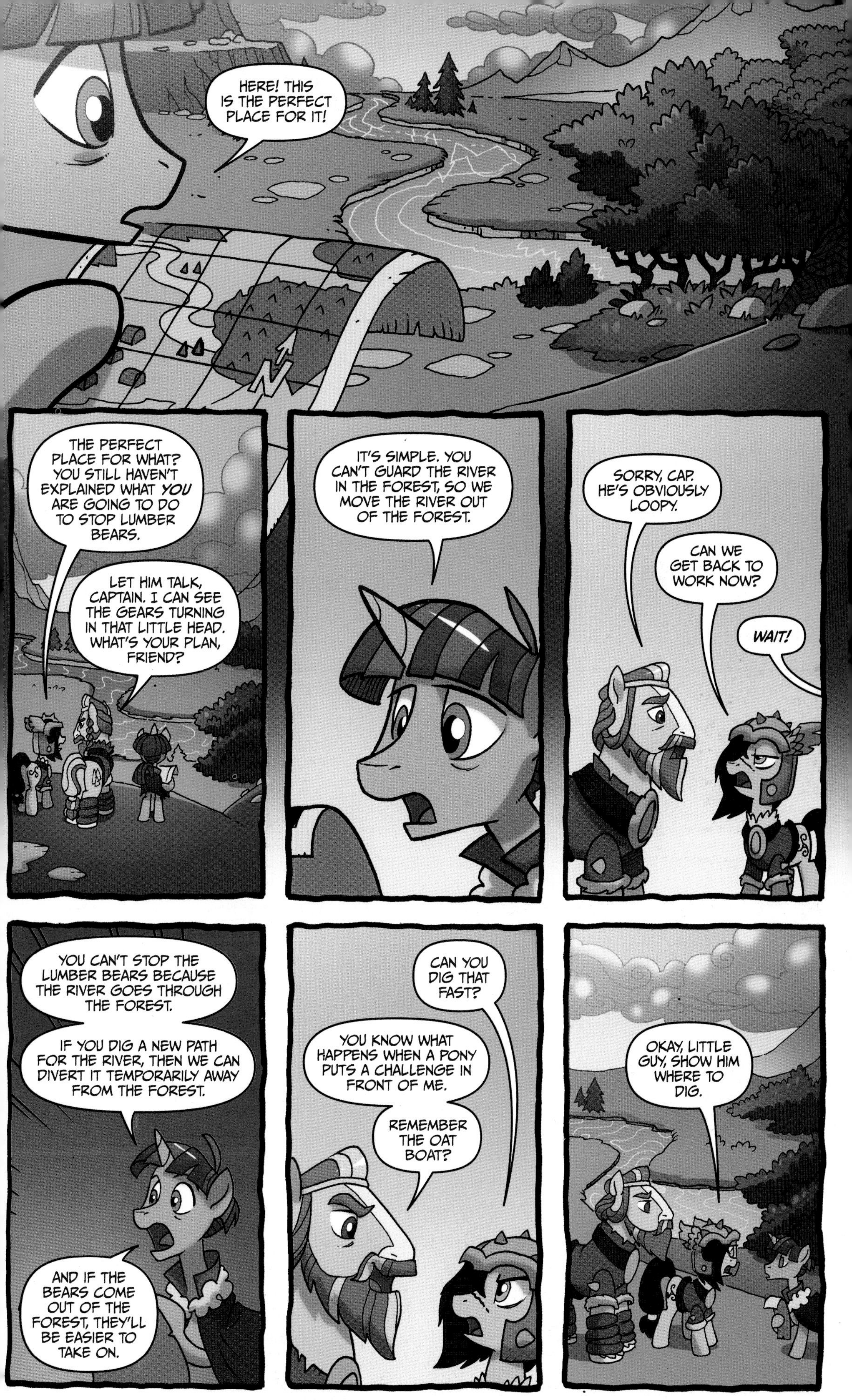
HERE! THIS IS THE PERFECT PLACE FOR IT!
N
THE PERFECT PLACE FOR WHAT? YOU STILL HAVEN'T EXPLAINED WHAT *YOU* ARE GOING TO DO TO STOP LUMBER BEARS.
LET HIM TALK, CAPTAIN. I CAN SEE THE GEARS TURNING IN THAT LITTLE HEAD. WHAT'S YOUR PLAN, FRIEND?
IT'S SIMPLE. YOU CAN'T GUARD THE RIVER IN THE FOREST, SO WE MOVE THE RIVER OUT OF THE FOREST.
SORRY, CAP. HE'S OBVIOUSLY LOOPY.
CAN WE GET BACK TO WORK NOW?
WAIT!
YOU CAN'T STOP THE LUMBER BEARS BECAUSE THE RIVER GOES THROUGH THE FOREST.
IF YOU DIG A NEW PATH FOR THE RIVER, THEN WE CAN DIVERT IT TEMPORARILY AWAY FROM THE FOREST.
AND IF THE BEARS COME OUT OF THE FOREST, THEY'LL BE EASIER TO TAKE ON.
CAN YOU DIG THAT FAST?
YOU KNOW WHAT HAPPENS WHEN A PONY PUTS A CHALLENGE IN FRONT OF ME.
REMEMBER THE OAT BOAT?
OKAY, LITTLE GUY, SHOW HIM WHERE TO DIG.

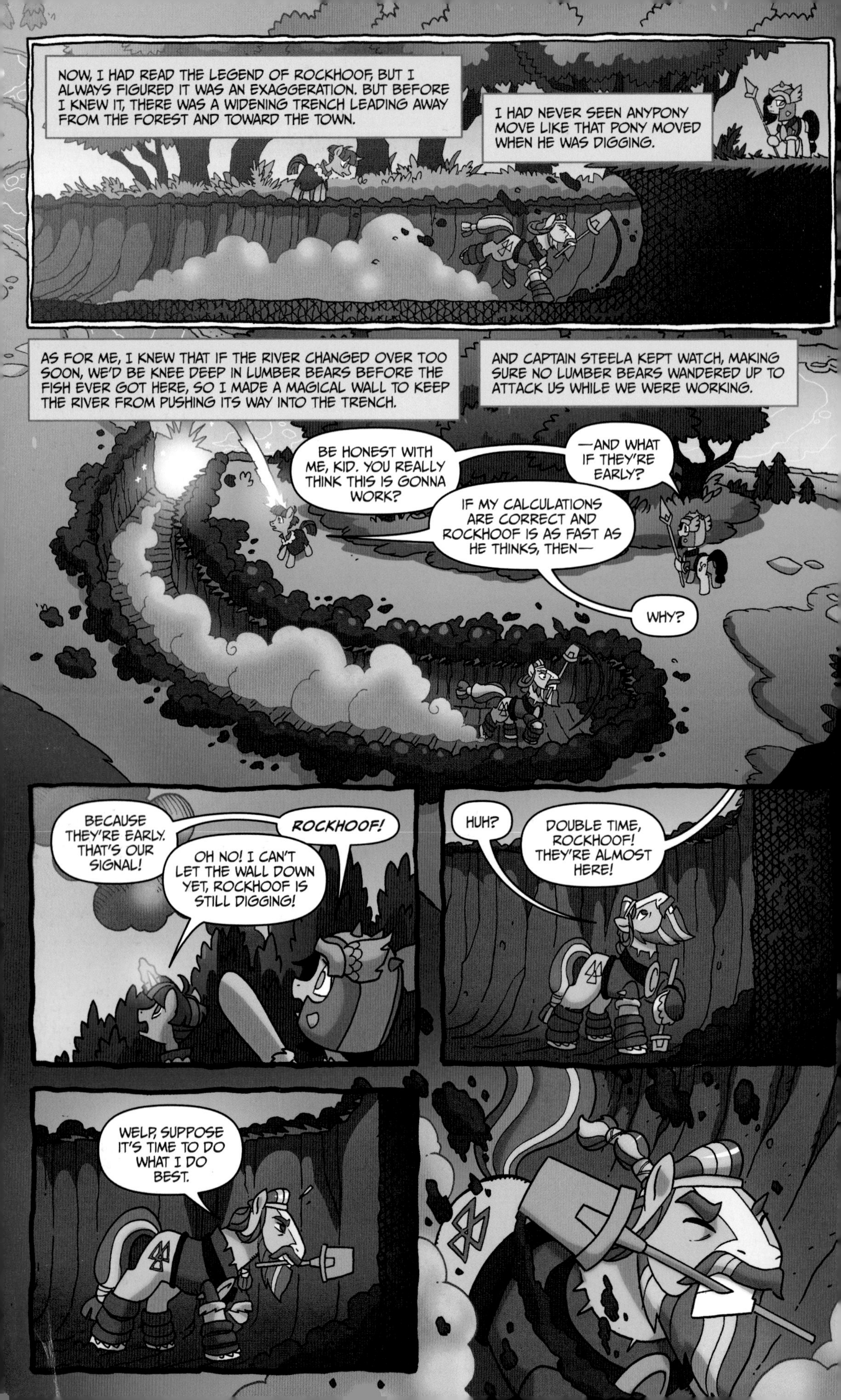
NOW, I HAD READ THE LEGEND OF ROCKHOOF, BUT I ALWAYS FIGURED IT WAS AN EXAGGERATION. BUT BEFORE I KNEW IT, THERE WAS A WIDENING TRENCH LEADING AWAY FROM THE FOREST AND TOWARD THE TOWN.
I HAD NEVER SEEN ANYPONY MOVE LIKE THAT PONY MOVED WHEN HE WAS DIGGING.
AS FOR ME, I KNEW THAT IF THE RIVER CHANGED OVER TOO SOON, WE'D BE KNEE DEEP IN LUMBER BEARS BEFORE THE FISH EVER GOT HERE, SO I MADE A MAGICAL WALL TO KEEP THE RIVER FROM PUSHING ITS WAY INTO THE TRENCH.
AND CAPTAIN STEELA KEPT WATCH, MAKING SURE NO LUMBER BEARS WANDERED UP TO ATTACK US WHILE WE WERE WORKING.
BE HONEST WITH ME, KID. YOU REALLY THINK THIS IS GONNA WORK?
IF MY CALCULATIONS ARE CORRECT AND ROCKHOOF IS AS FAST AS HE THINKS, THEN—
—AND WHAT IF THEY'RE EARLY?
WHY?
BECAUSE THEY'RE EARLY. THAT'S OUR SIGNAL!
ROCKHOOF!
OH NO! I CAN'T LET THE WALL DOWN YET, ROCKHOOF IS STILL DIGGING!
HUH?
DOUBLE TIME, ROCKHOOF! THEY'RE ALMOST HERE!
WELP, SUPPOSE IT'S TIME TO DO WHAT I DO BEST.

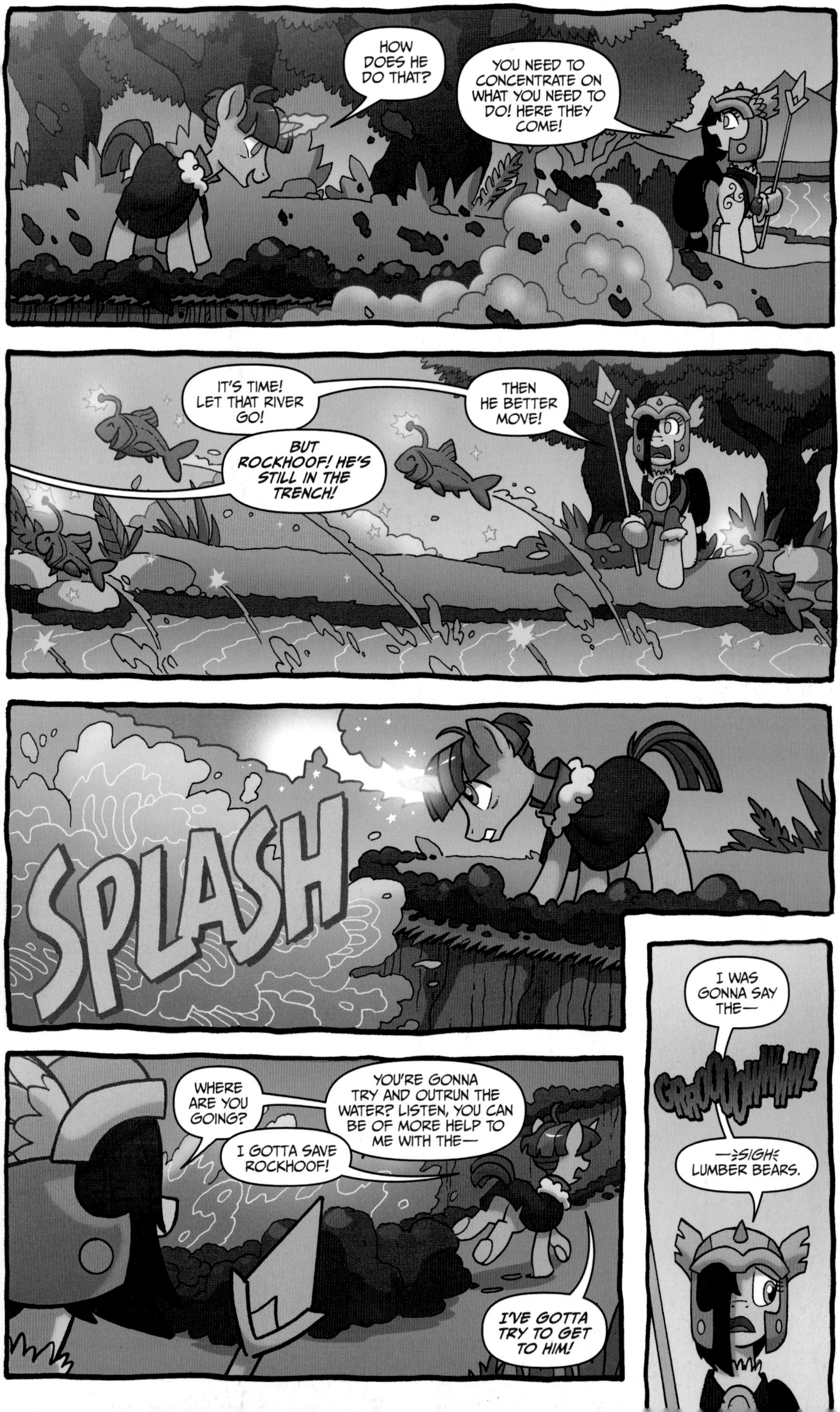

HOW DOES HE DO THAT?
YOU NEED TO CONCENTRATE ON WHAT YOU NEED TO DO! HERE THEY COME!
IT'S TIME! LET THAT RIVER GO!
THEN HE BETTER MOVE!
BUT ROCKHOOF! HE'S STILL IN THE TRENCH!
SPLASH
WHERE ARE YOU GOING?
I GOTTA SAVE ROCKHOOF!
YOU'RE GONNA TRY AND OUTRUN THE WATER? LISTEN, YOU CAN BE OF MORE HELP TO ME WITH THE—
I'VE GOTTA TRY TO GET TO HIM!
I WAS GONNA SAY THE—
GRROOOOWWWWL
—SIGH— LUMBER BEARS.

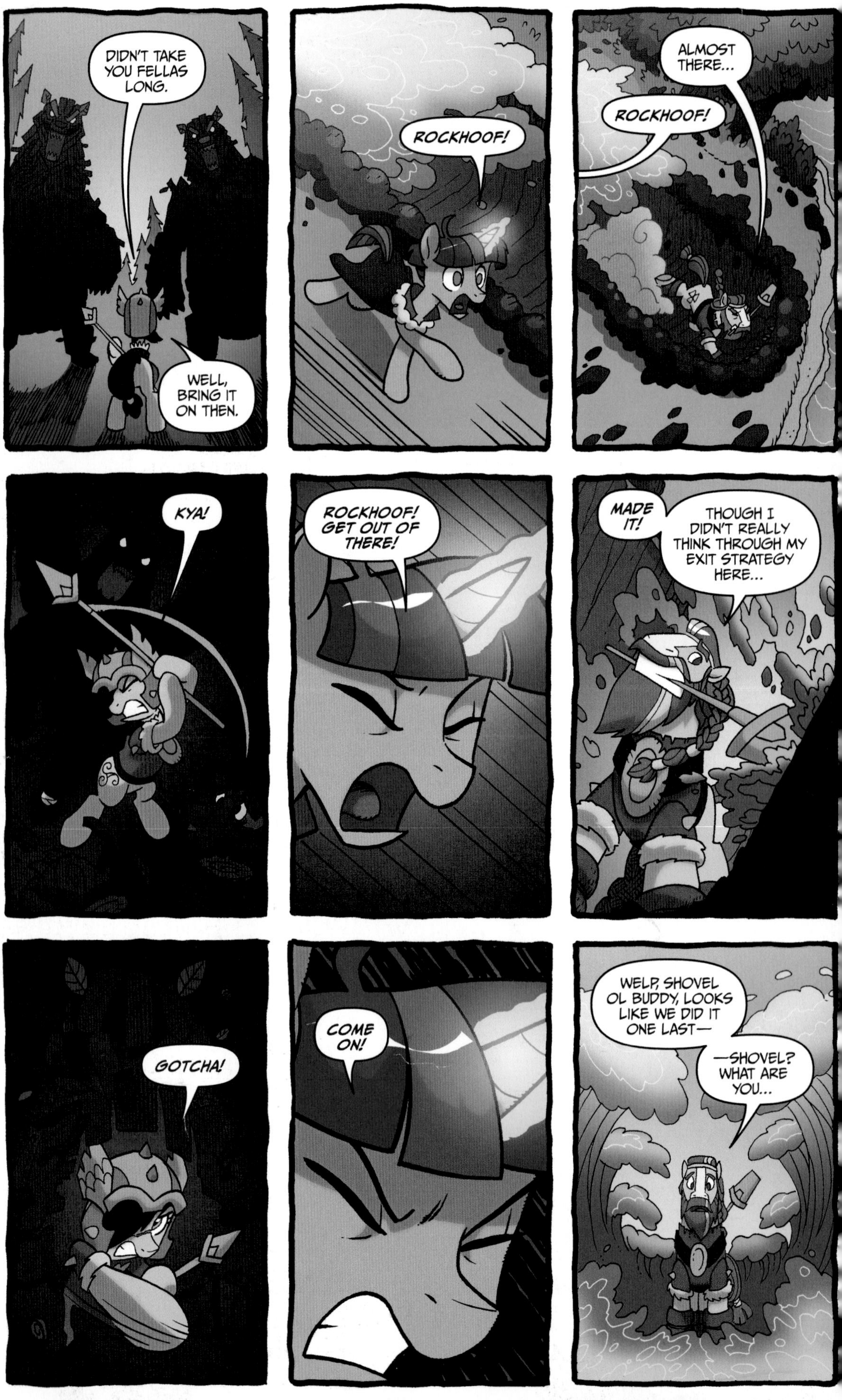
DIDN'T TAKE YOU FELLAS LONG.
WELL, BRING IT ON THEN.
ROCKHOOF!
ALMOST THERE...
ROCKHOOF!
KYA!
ROCKHOOF! GET OUT OF THERE!
MADE IT!
THOUGH I DIDN'T REALLY THINK THROUGH MY EXIT STRATEGY HERE...
GOTCHA!
COME ON!
WELP, SHOVEL OL BUDDY, LOOKS LIKE WE DID IT ONE LAST—
—SHOVEL? WHAT ARE YOU...

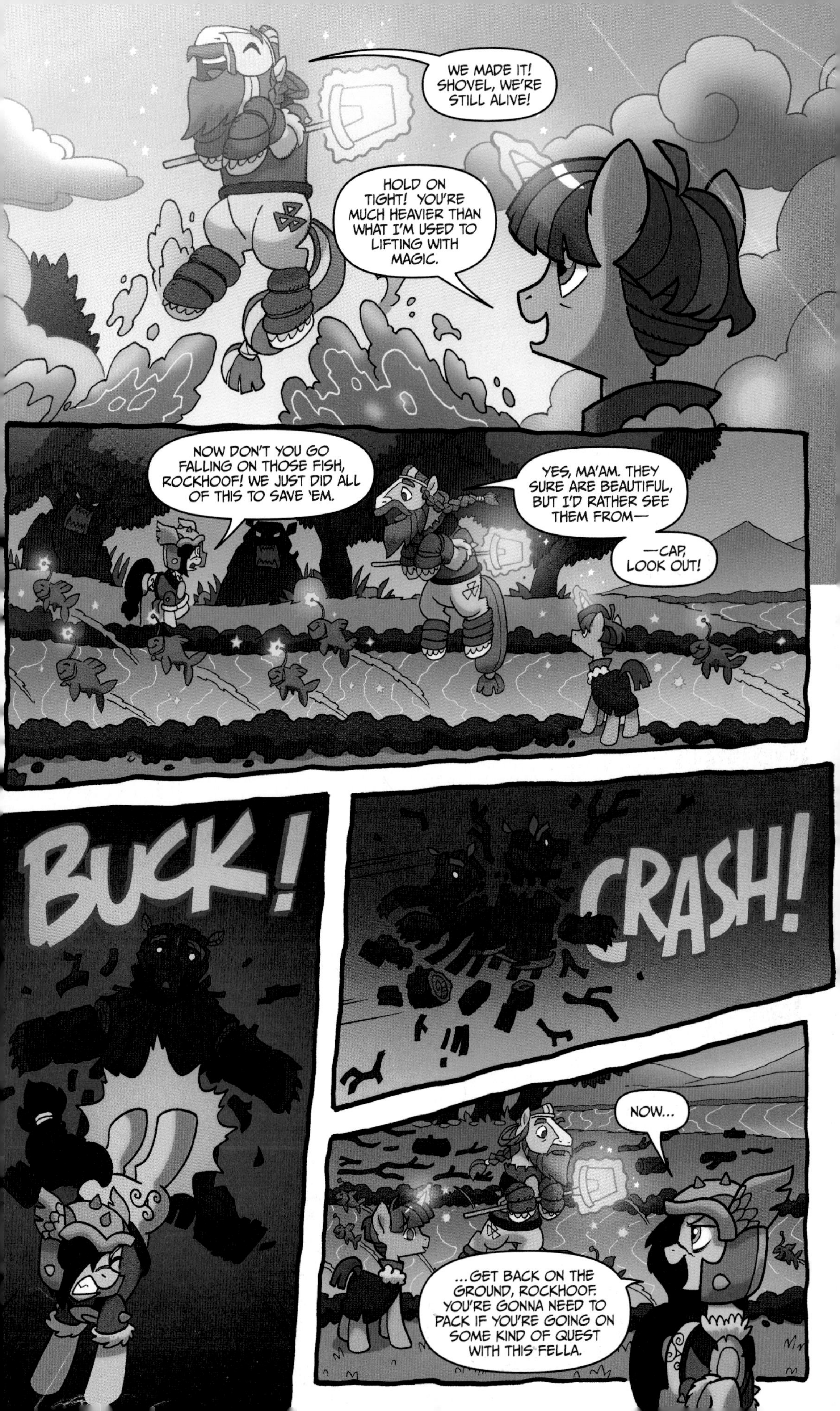

WE MADE IT! SHOVEL, WE'RE STILL ALIVE!
HOLD ON TIGHT! YOU'RE MUCH HEAVIER THAN WHAT I'M USED TO LIFTING WITH MAGIC.
NOW DON'T YOU GO FALLING ON THOSE FISH, ROCKHOOF! WE JUST DID ALL OF THIS TO SAVE 'EM.
YES, MA'AM. THEY SURE ARE BEAUTIFUL, BUT I'D RATHER SEE THEM FROM—
—CAP, LOOK OUT!
BUCK!
CRASH!
NOW...
...GET BACK ON THE GROUND, ROCKHOOF. YOU'RE GONNA NEED TO PACK IF YOU'RE GOING ON SOME KIND OF QUEST WITH THIS FELLA.

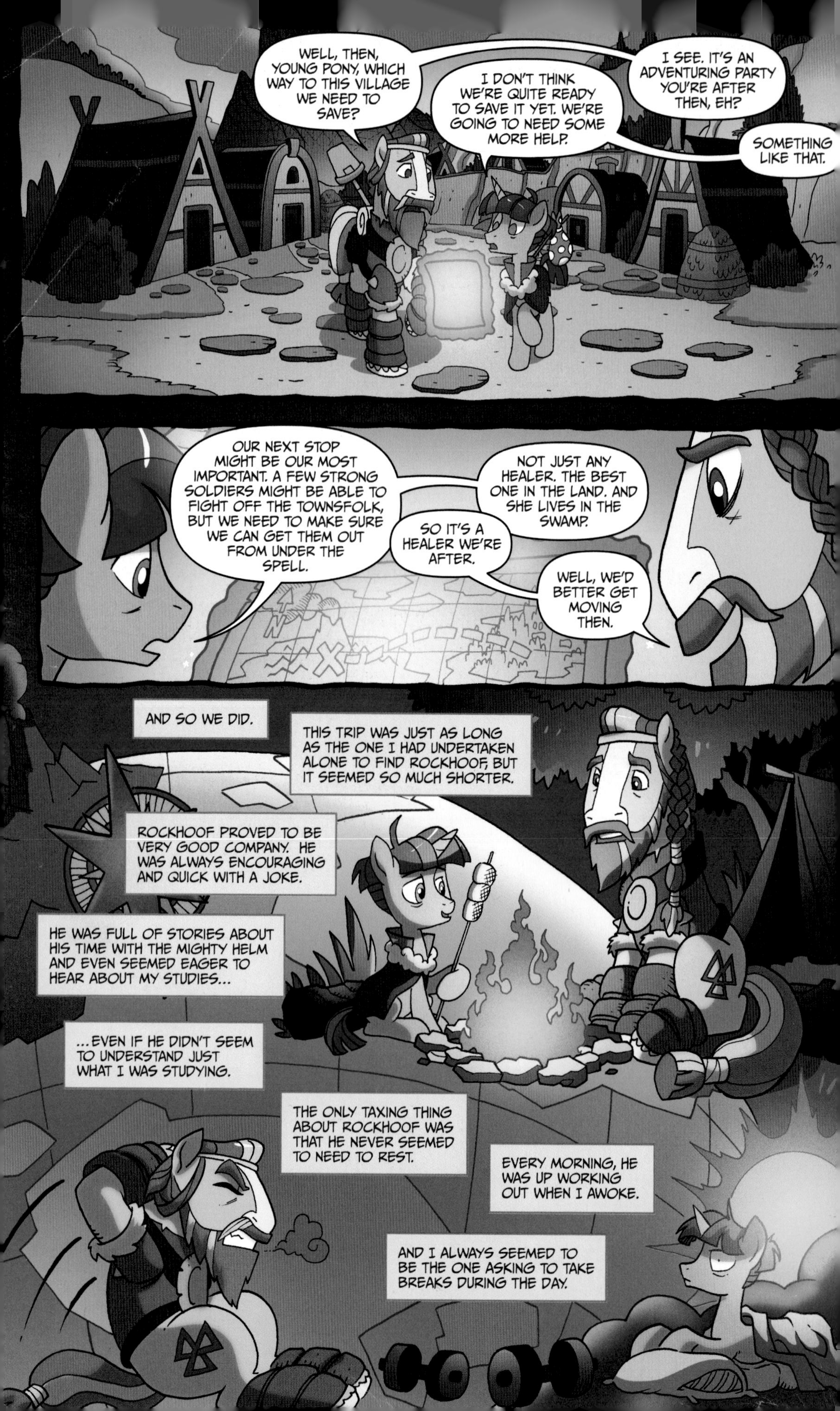
WELL, THEN, YOUNG PONY, WHICH WAY TO THIS VILLAGE WE NEED TO SAVE?
I DON'T THINK WE'RE QUITE READY TO SAVE IT YET. WE'RE GOING TO NEED SOME MORE HELP.
I SEE. IT'S AN ADVENTURING PARTY YOU'RE AFTER THEN, EH?
SOMETHING LIKE THAT.
OUR NEXT STOP MIGHT BE OUR MOST IMPORTANT. A FEW STRONG SOLDIERS MIGHT BE ABLE TO FIGHT OFF THE TOWNSFOLK, BUT WE NEED TO MAKE SURE WE CAN GET THEM OUT FROM UNDER THE SPELL.
SO IT'S A HEALER WE'RE AFTER.
NOT JUST ANY HEALER. THE BEST ONE IN THE LAND. AND SHE LIVES IN THE SWAMP.
WELL, WE'D BETTER GET MOVING THEN.
AND SO WE DID.
THIS TRIP WAS JUST AS LONG AS THE ONE I HAD UNDERTAKEN ALONE TO FIND ROCKHOOF, BUT IT SEEMED SO MUCH SHORTER.
ROCKHOOF PROVED TO BE VERY GOOD COMPANY. HE WAS ALWAYS ENCOURAGING AND QUICK WITH A JOKE.
HE WAS FULL OF STORIES ABOUT HIS TIME WITH THE MIGHTY HELM AND EVEN SEEMED EAGER TO HEAR ABOUT MY STUDIES...
...EVEN IF HE DIDN'T SEEM TO UNDERSTAND JUST WHAT I WAS STUDYING.
THE ONLY TAXING THING ABOUT ROCKHOOF WAS THAT HE NEVER SEEMED TO NEED TO REST.
EVERY MORNING, HE WAS UP WORKING OUT WHEN I AWOKE.
AND I ALWAYS SEEMED TO BE THE ONE ASKING TO TAKE BREAKS DURING THE DAY.

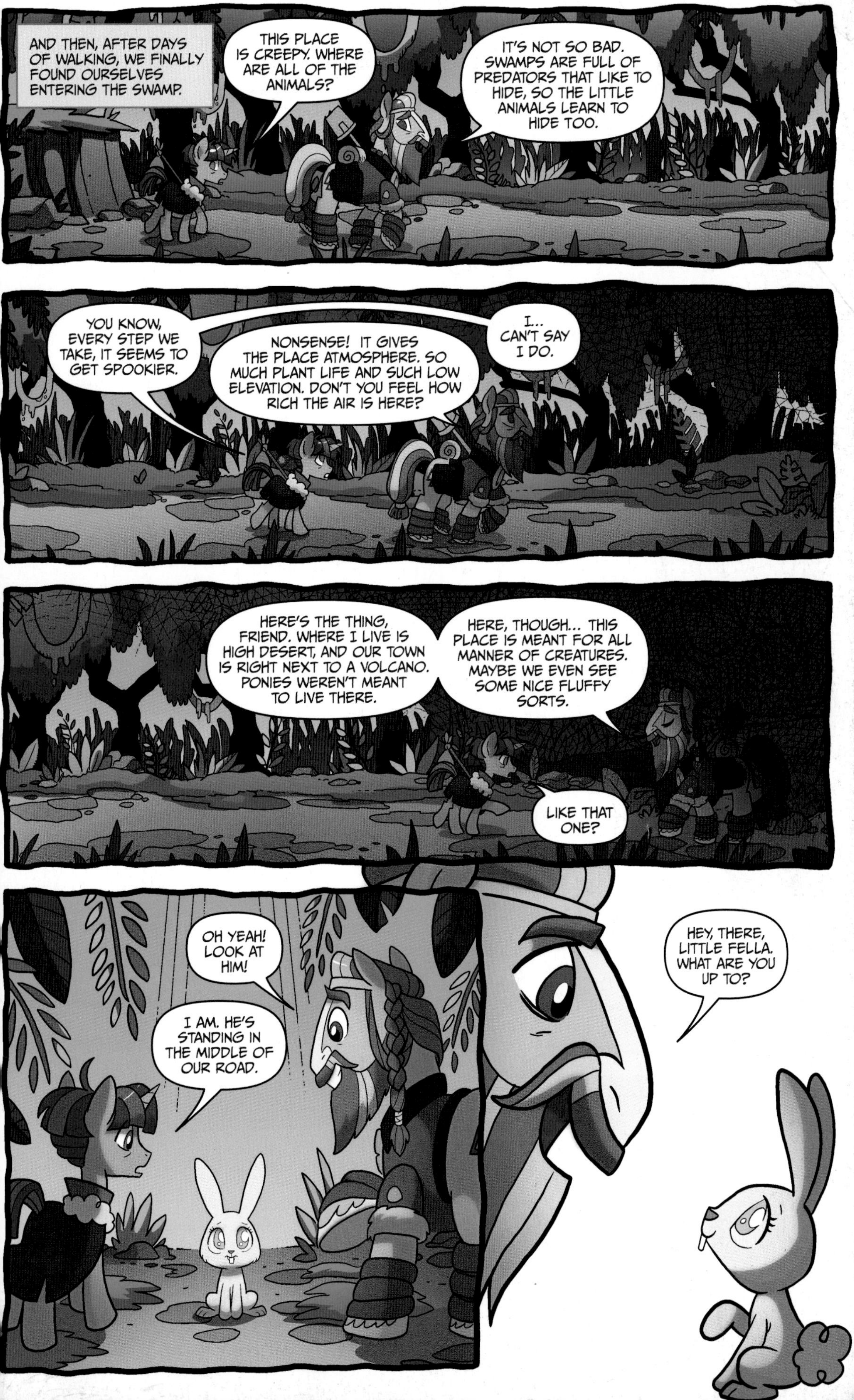
AND THEN, AFTER DAYS OF WALKING, WE FINALLY FOUND OURSELVES ENTERING THE SWAMP.
THIS PLACE IS CREEPY. WHERE ARE ALL OF THE ANIMALS?
IT'S NOT SO BAD. SWAMPS ARE FULL OF PREDATORS THAT LIKE TO HIDE, SO THE LITTLE ANIMALS LEARN TO HIDE TOO.
YOU KNOW, EVERY STEP WE TAKE, IT SEEMS TO GET SPOOKIER.
NONSENSE! IT GIVES THE PLACE ATMOSPHERE. SO MUCH PLANT LIFE AND SUCH LOW ELEVATION. DON'T YOU FEEL HOW RICH THE AIR IS HERE?
I... CAN'T SAY I DO.
HERE'S THE THING, FRIEND. WHERE I LIVE IS HIGH DESERT, AND OUR TOWN IS RIGHT NEXT TO A VOLCANO. PONIES WEREN'T MEANT TO LIVE THERE.
HERE, THOUGH... THIS PLACE IS MEANT FOR ALL MANNER OF CREATURES. MAYBE WE EVEN SEE SOME NICE FLUFFY SORTS.
LIKE THAT ONE?
OH YEAH! LOOK AT HIM!
I AM. HE'S STANDING IN THE MIDDLE OF OUR ROAD.
HEY, THERE, LITTLE FELLA. WHAT ARE YOU UP TO?

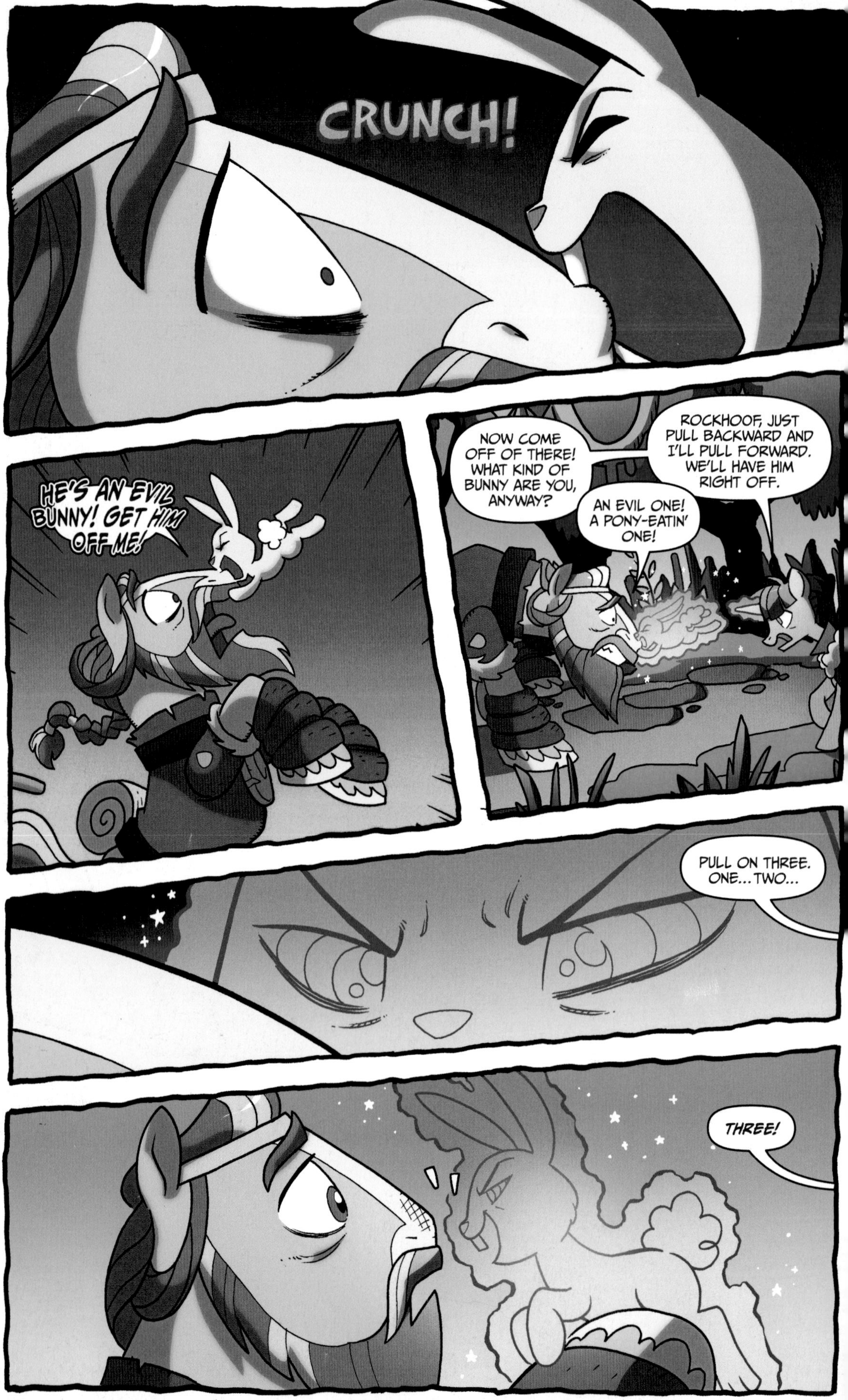
CRUNCH!
HE'S AN EVIL BUNNY! GET HIM OFF ME!
NOW COME OFF OF THERE! WHAT KIND OF BUNNY ARE YOU, ANYWAY?
ROCKHOOF, JUST PULL BACKWARD AND I'LL PULL FORWARD. WE'LL HAVE HIM RIGHT OFF.
AN EVIL ONE! A PONY-EATIN' ONE!
PULL ON THREE. ONE... TWO...
THREE!

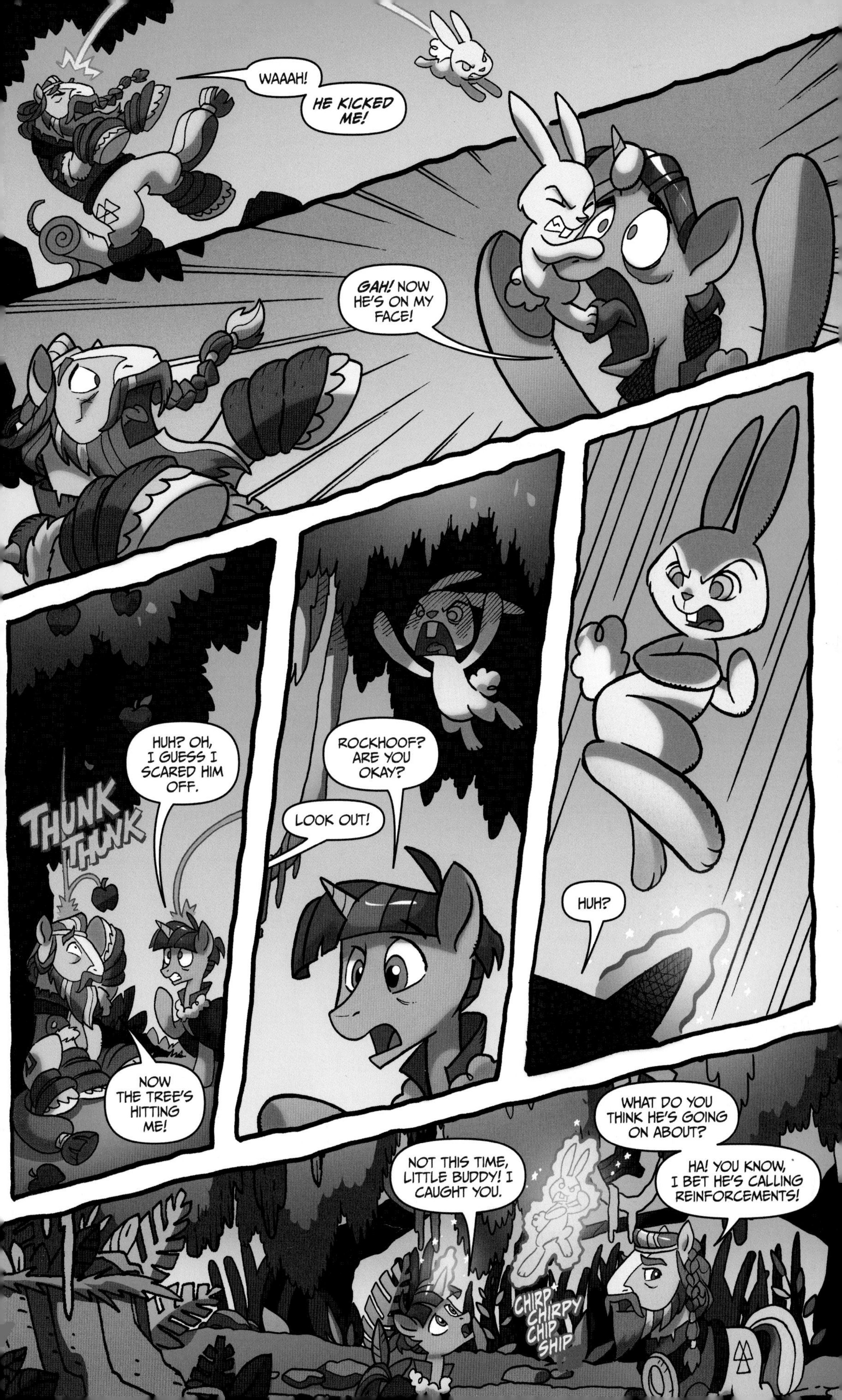
WAAAH!
HE KICKED ME!
GAH! NOW HE'S ON MY FACE!
HUH? OH, I GUESS I SCARED HIM OFF.
THUNK THUNK
NOW THE TREE'S HITTING ME!
ROCKHOOF? ARE YOU OKAY?
LOOK OUT!
HUH?
NOT THIS TIME, LITTLE BUDDY! I CAUGHT YOU.
WHAT DO YOU THINK HE'S GOING ON ABOUT?
HA! YOU KNOW, I BET HE'S CALLING REINFORCEMENTS!
CHIRP CHIRPY CHIP SHIP

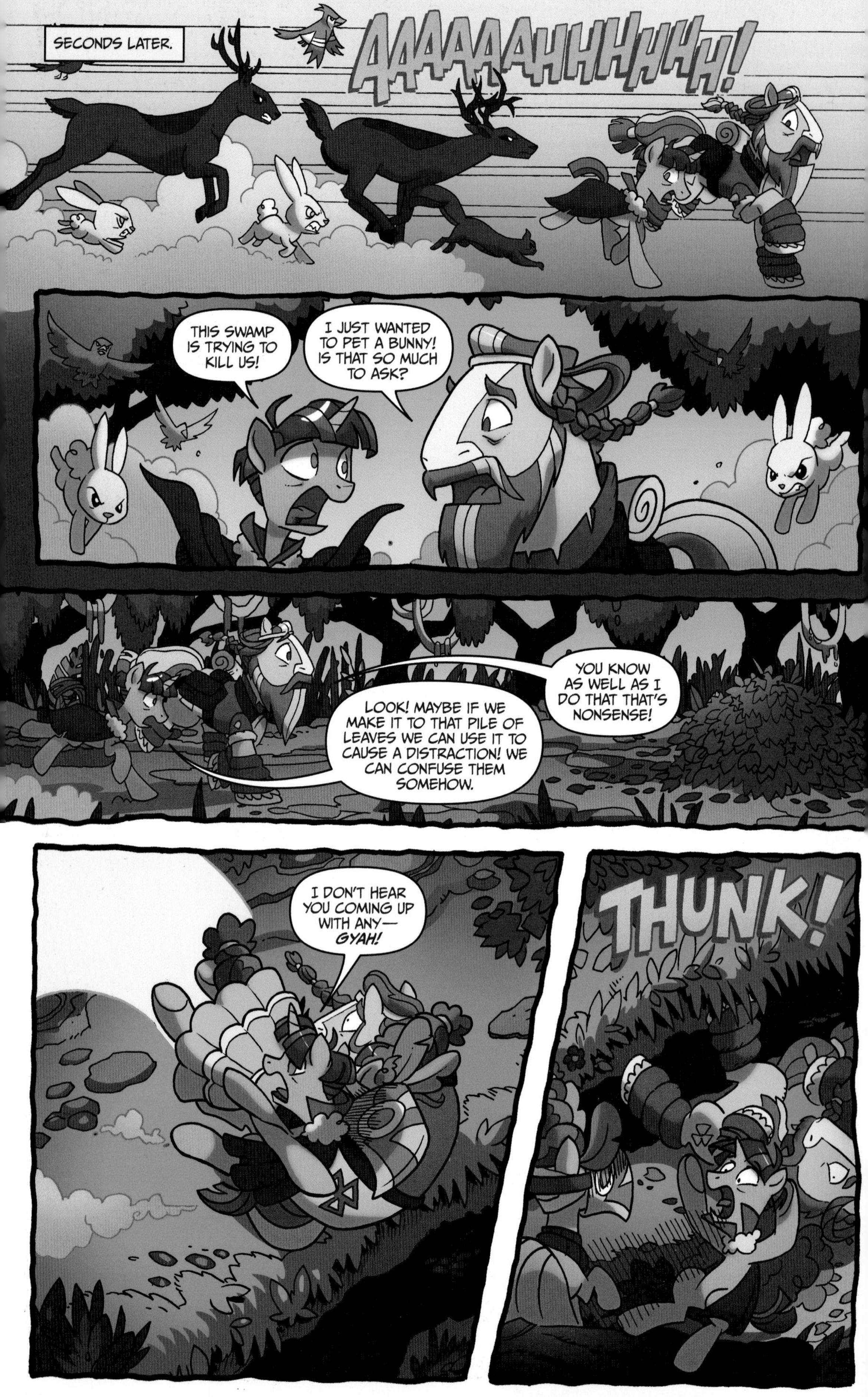
SECONDS LATER.
AAAAAAHHHHHH!
THIS SWAMP IS TRYING TO KILL US!
I JUST WANTED TO PET A BUNNY! IS THAT SO MUCH TO ASK?
LOOK! MAYBE IF WE MAKE IT TO THAT PILE OF LEAVES WE CAN USE IT TO CAUSE A DISTRACTION! WE CAN CONFUSE THEM SOMEHOW.
YOU KNOW AS WELL AS I DO THAT THAT'S NONSENSE!
I DON'T HEAR YOU COMING UP WITH ANY— GYAH!
THUNK!

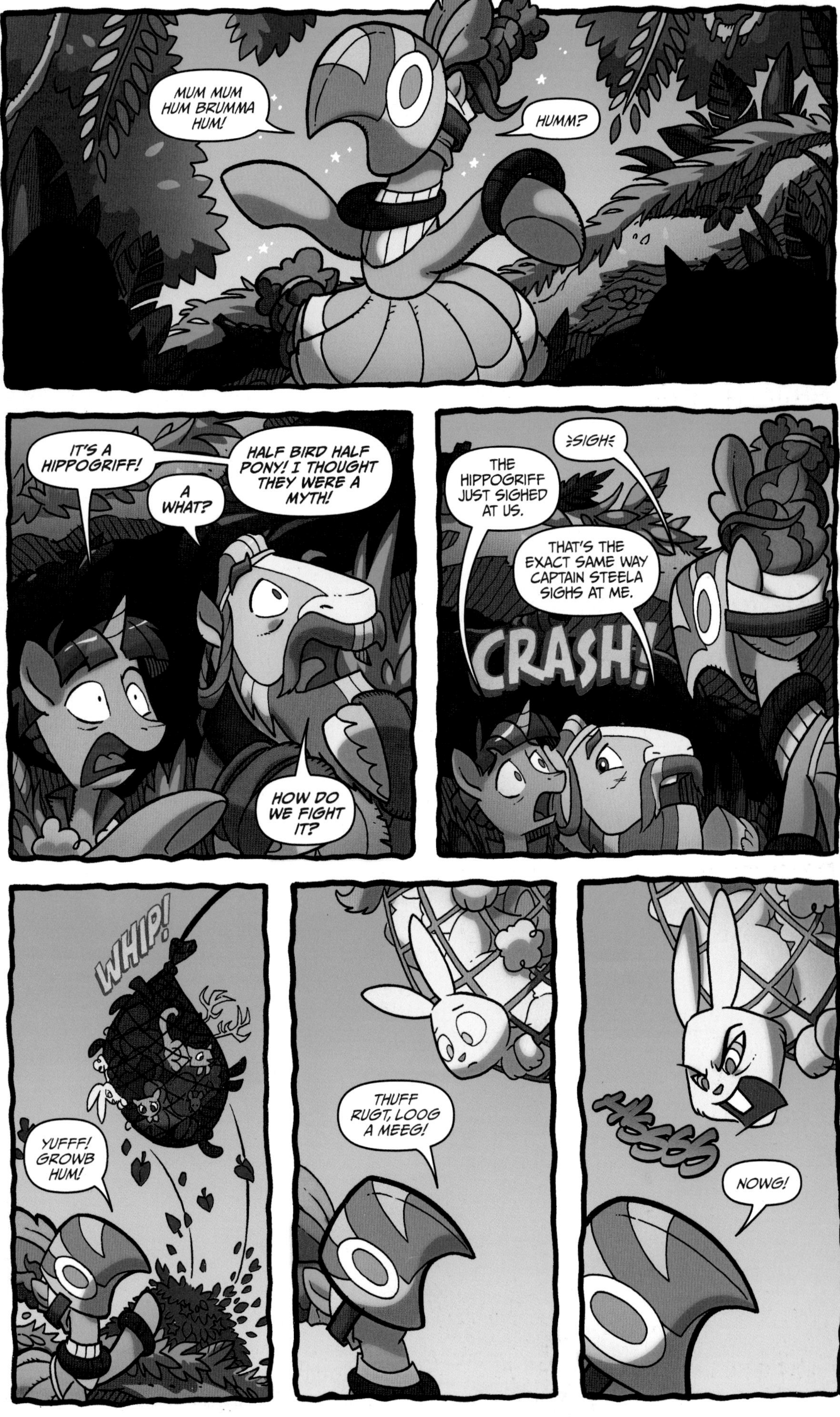
MUM MUM HUM BRUMMA HUM!
HUMM?
IT'S A HIPPOGRIFF!
A WHAT?
HALF BIRD HALF PONY! I THOUGHT THEY WERE A MYTH!
HOW DO WE FIGHT IT?
SIGH
THE HIPPOGRIFF JUST SIGHED AT US.
THAT'S THE EXACT SAME WAY CAPTAIN STEELA SIGHS AT ME.
CRASH!
WHIP!
YUFFF! GROWB HUM!
THUFF RUGT, LOOG A MEEG!
HSSSS
NOWG!

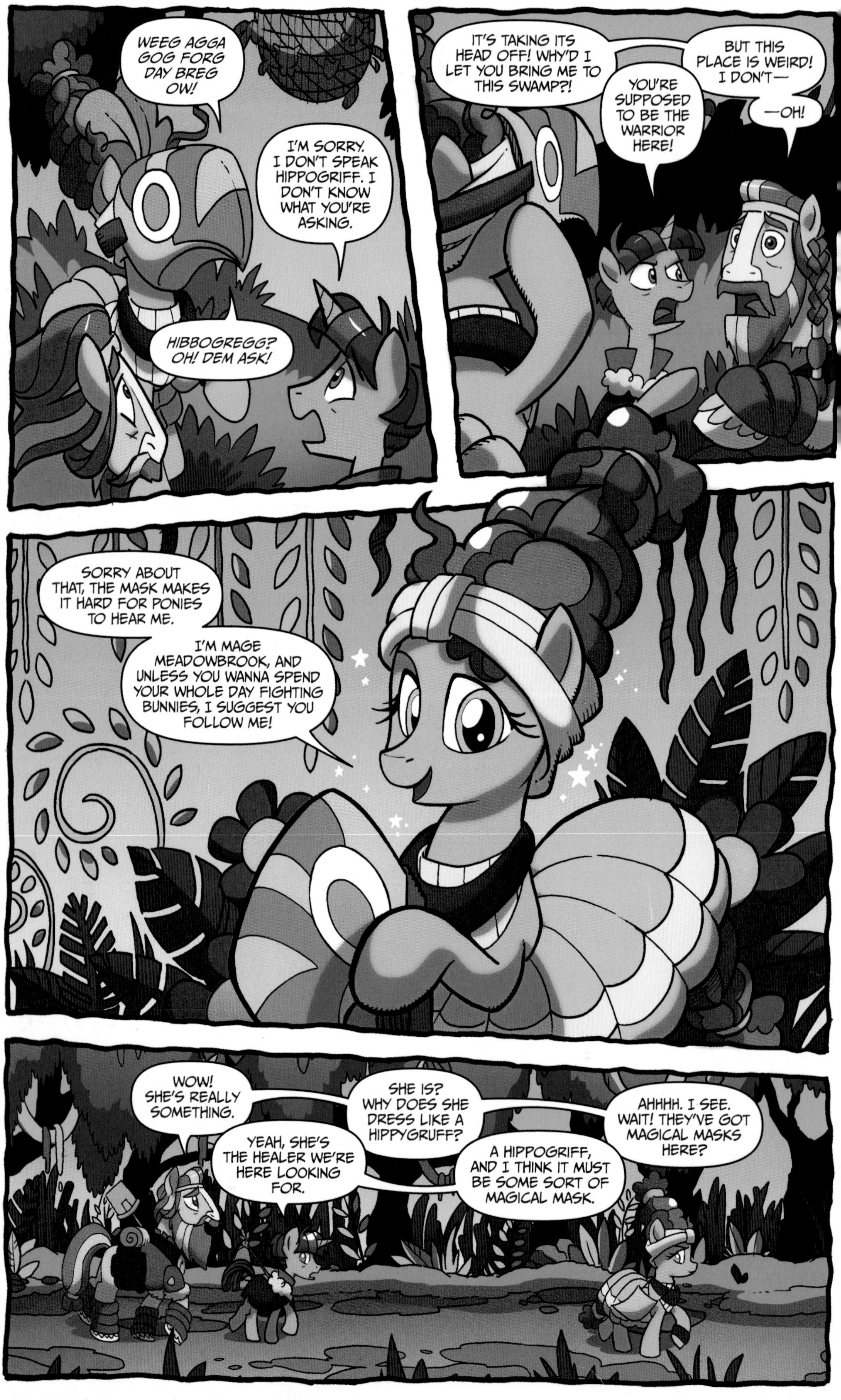
WEEG AGGA GOG FORG DAY BREG OW!
I'M SORRY. I DON'T SPEAK HIPPOGRIFF. I DON'T KNOW WHAT YOU'RE ASKING.
HIBBOGREGG? OH! DEM ASK!
IT'S TAKING ITS HEAD OFF! WHY'D I LET YOU BRING ME TO THIS SWAMP?!
YOU'RE SUPPOSED TO BE THE WARRIOR HERE!
BUT THIS PLACE IS WEIRD! I DON'T—
—OH!
SORRY ABOUT THAT, THE MASK MAKES IT HARD FOR PONIES TO HEAR ME.
I'M MAGE MEADOWBROOK, AND UNLESS YOU WANNA SPEND YOUR WHOLE DAY FIGHTING BUNNIES, I SUGGEST YOU FOLLOW ME!
WOW! SHE'S REALLY SOMETHING.
YEAH, SHE'S THE HEALER WE'RE HERE LOOKING FOR.
SHE IS? WHY DOES SHE DRESS LIKE A HIPPYGRUFF?
A HIPPOGRIFF, AND I THINK IT MUST BE SOME SORT OF MAGICAL MASK.
AHHHH. I SEE. WAIT! THEY'VE GOT MAGICAL MASKS HERE?

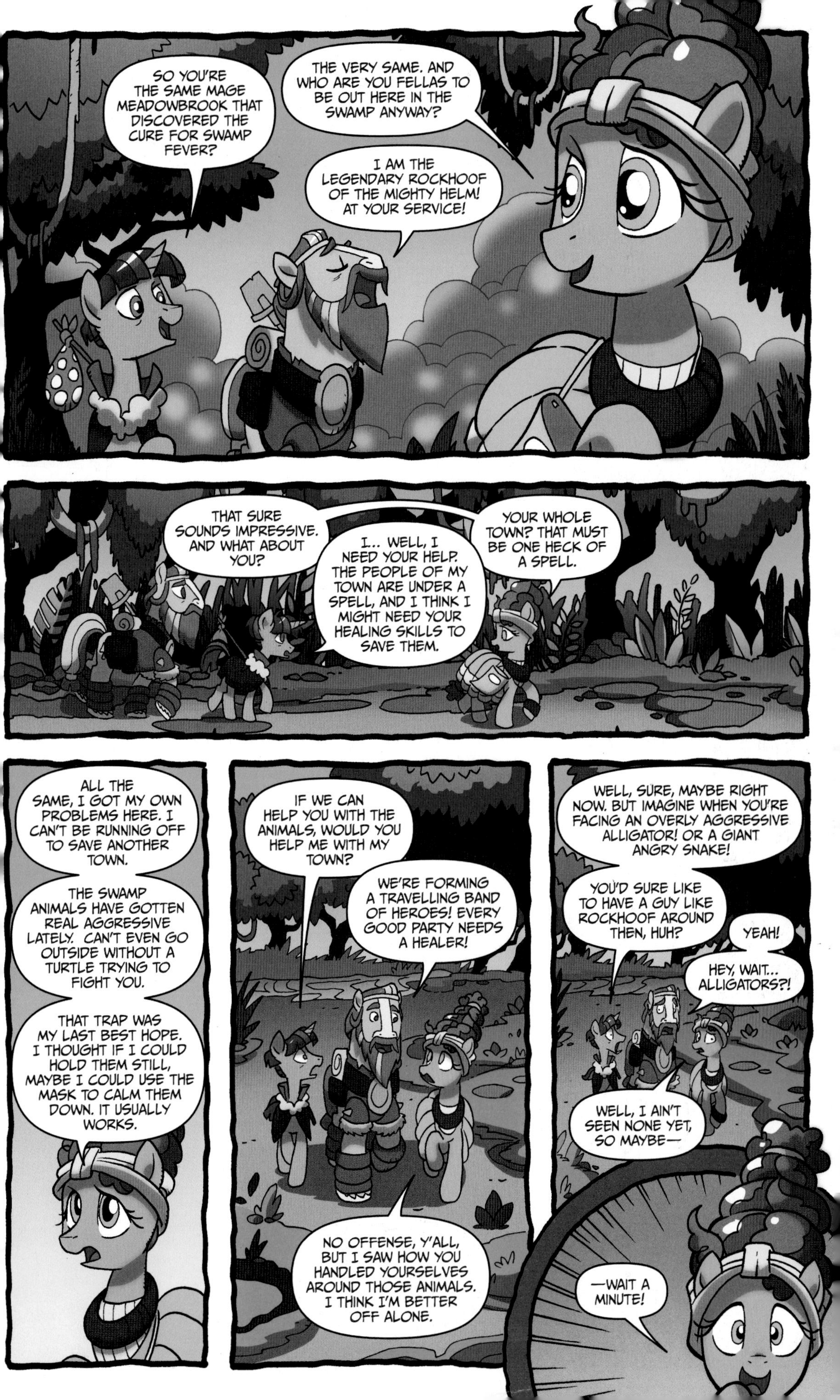

SO YOU'RE THE SAME MAGE MEADOWBROOK THAT DISCOVERED THE CURE FOR SWAMP FEVER?
THE VERY SAME. AND WHO ARE YOU FELLAS TO BE OUT HERE IN THE SWAMP ANYWAY?
I AM THE LEGENDARY ROCKHOOF OF THE MIGHTY HELM! AT YOUR SERVICE!
THAT SURE SOUNDS IMPRESSIVE. AND WHAT ABOUT YOU?
I... WELL, I NEED YOUR HELP. THE PEOPLE OF MY TOWN ARE UNDER A SPELL, AND I THINK I MIGHT NEED YOUR HEALING SKILLS TO SAVE THEM.
YOUR WHOLE TOWN? THAT MUST BE ONE HECK OF A SPELL.
ALL THE SAME, I GOT MY OWN PROBLEMS HERE. I CAN'T BE RUNNING OFF TO SAVE ANOTHER TOWN.
THE SWAMP ANIMALS HAVE GOTTEN REAL AGGRESSIVE LATELY. CAN'T EVEN GO OUTSIDE WITHOUT A TURTLE TRYING TO FIGHT YOU.
THAT TRAP WAS MY LAST BEST HOPE. I THOUGHT IF I COULD HOLD THEM STILL, MAYBE I COULD USE THE MASK TO CALM THEM DOWN. IT USUALLY WORKS.
IF WE CAN HELP YOU WITH THE ANIMALS, WOULD YOU HELP ME WITH MY TOWN?
WE'RE FORMING A TRAVELLING BAND OF HEROES! EVERY GOOD PARTY NEEDS A HEALER!
NO OFFENSE, Y'ALL, BUT I SAW HOW YOU HANDLED YOURSELVES AROUND THOSE ANIMALS. I THINK I'M BETTER OFF ALONE.
WELL, SURE, MAYBE RIGHT NOW. BUT IMAGINE WHEN YOU'RE FACING AN OVERLY AGGRESSIVE ALLIGATOR! OR A GIANT ANGRY SNAKE!
YOU'D SURE LIKE TO HAVE A GUY LIKE ROCKHOOF AROUND THEN, HUH?
YEAH!
HEY, WAIT... ALLIGATORS?!
WELL, I AIN'T SEEN NONE YET, SO MAYBE—
—WAIT A MINUTE!

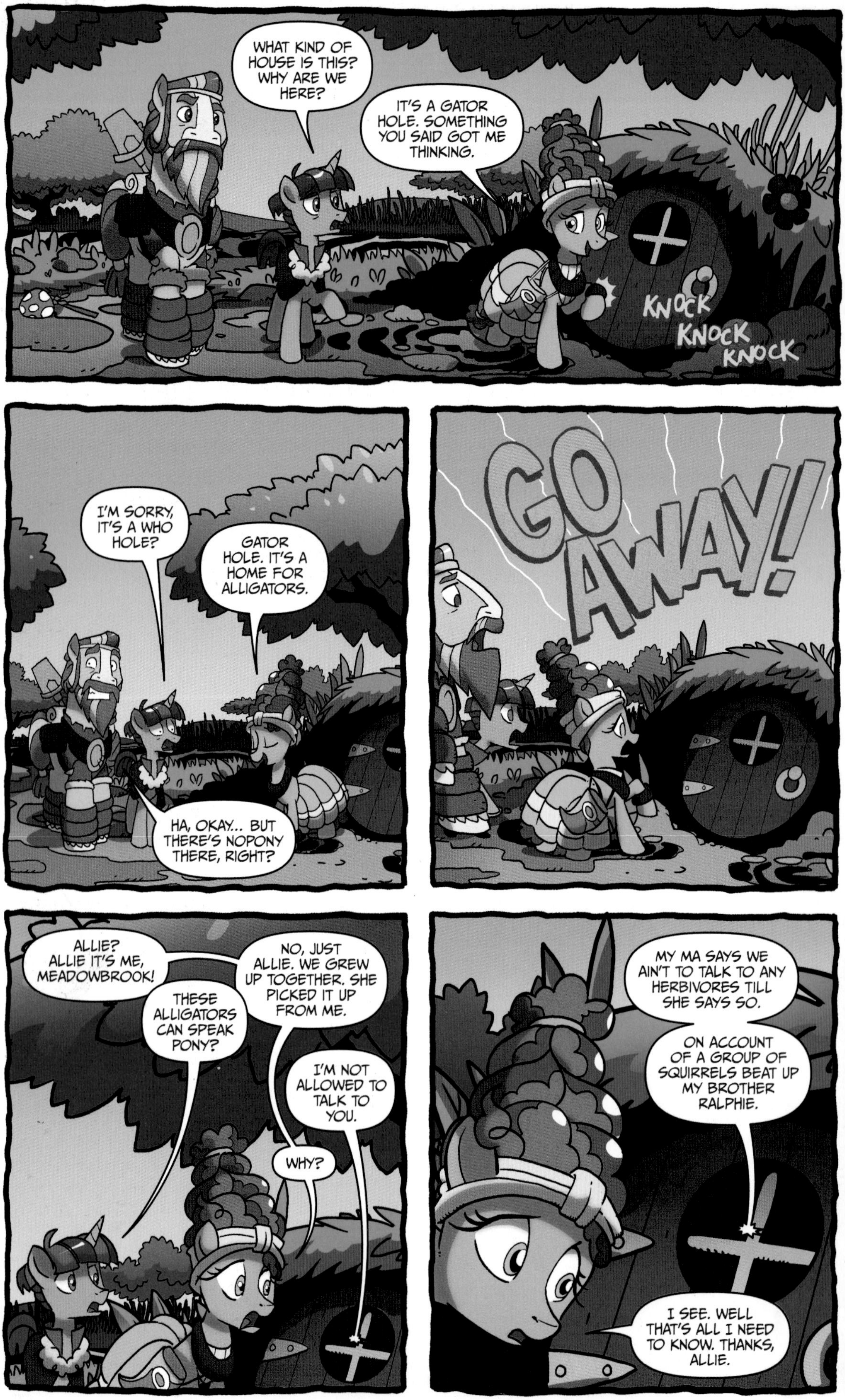
WHAT KIND OF HOUSE IS THIS? WHY ARE WE HERE?
IT'S A GATOR HOLE. SOMETHING YOU SAID GOT ME THINKING.
KNOCK KNOCK KNOCK
I'M SORRY, IT'S A WHO HOLE?
GATOR HOLE. IT'S A HOME FOR ALLIGATORS.
HA, OKAY... BUT THERE'S NOPONY THERE, RIGHT?
GO AWAY!
ALLIE? ALLIE IT'S ME, MEADOWBROOK!
THESE ALLIGATORS CAN SPEAK PONY?
NO, JUST ALLIE. WE GREW UP TOGETHER. SHE PICKED IT UP FROM ME.
I'M NOT ALLOWED TO TALK TO YOU.
WHY?
MY MA SAYS WE AIN'T TO TALK TO ANY HERBIVORES TILL SHE SAYS SO.
ON ACCOUNT OF A GROUP OF SQUIRRELS BEAT UP MY BROTHER RALPHIE.
I SEE. WELL THAT'S ALL I NEED TO KNOW. THANKS, ALLIE.

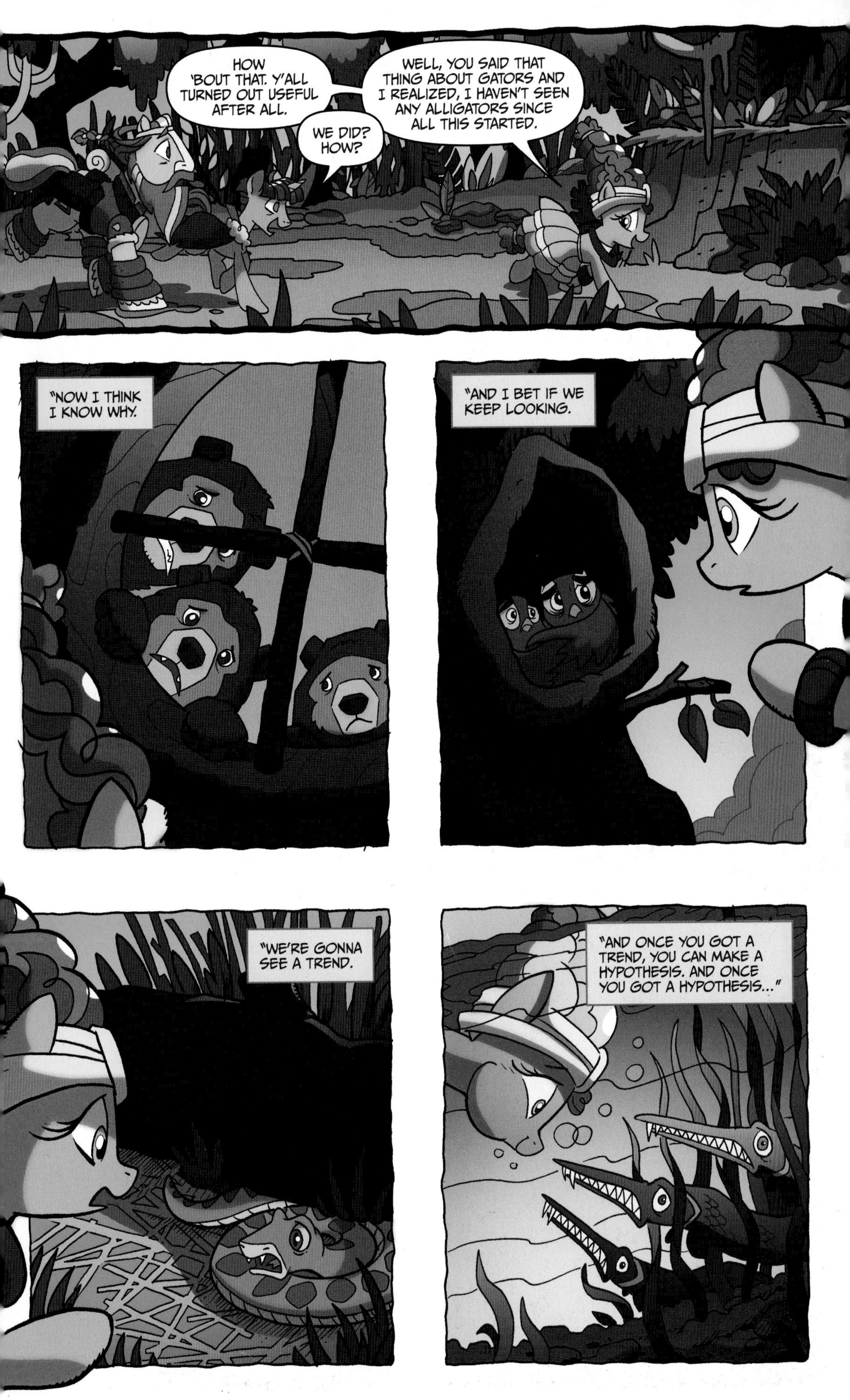
HOW 'BOUT THAT. Y'ALL TURNED OUT USEFUL AFTER ALL.
WE DID? HOW?
WELL, YOU SAID THAT THING ABOUT GATORS AND I REALIZED, I HAVEN'T SEEN ANY ALLIGATORS SINCE ALL THIS STARTED.
"NOW I THINK I KNOW WHY.
"AND I BET IF WE KEEP LOOKING.
"WE'RE GONNA SEE A TREND.
"AND ONCE YOU GOT A TREND, YOU CAN MAKE A HYPOTHESIS. AND ONCE YOU GOT A HYPOTHESIS..."

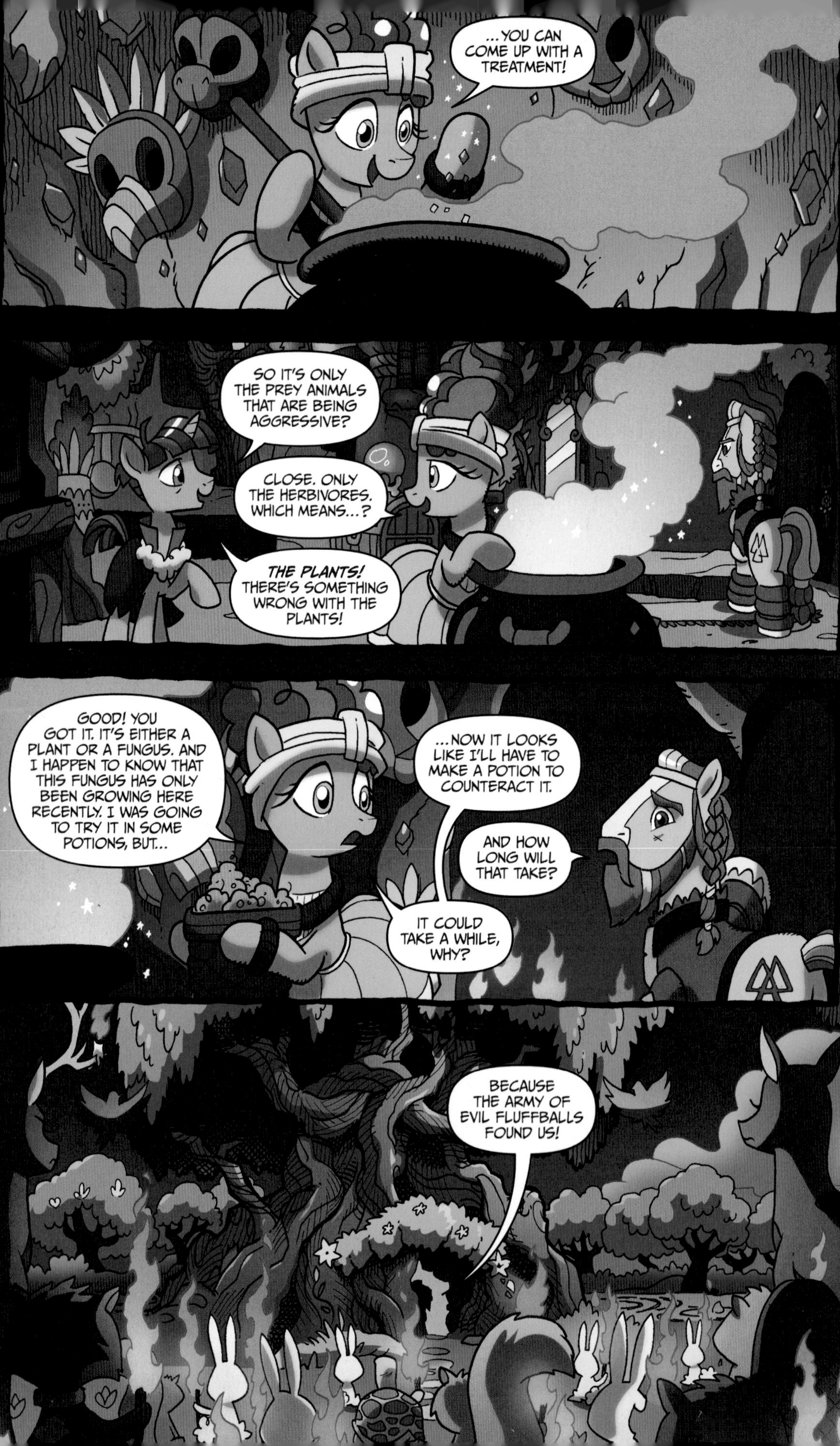
...YOU CAN COME UP WITH A TREATMENT!
SO IT'S ONLY THE PREY ANIMALS THAT ARE BEING AGGRESSIVE?
CLOSE. ONLY THE HERBIVORES. WHICH MEANS...?
THE PLANTS! THERE'S SOMETHING WRONG WITH THE PLANTS!
GOOD! YOU GOT IT. IT'S EITHER A PLANT OR A FUNGUS. AND I HAPPEN TO KNOW THAT THIS FUNGUS HAS ONLY BEEN GROWING HERE RECENTLY. I WAS GOING TO TRY IT IN SOME POTIONS, BUT...
...NOW IT LOOKS LIKE I'LL HAVE TO MAKE A POTION TO COUNTERACT IT.
AND HOW LONG WILL THAT TAKE?
IT COULD TAKE A WHILE, WHY?
BECAUSE THE ARMY OF EVIL FLUFFBALLS FOUND US!

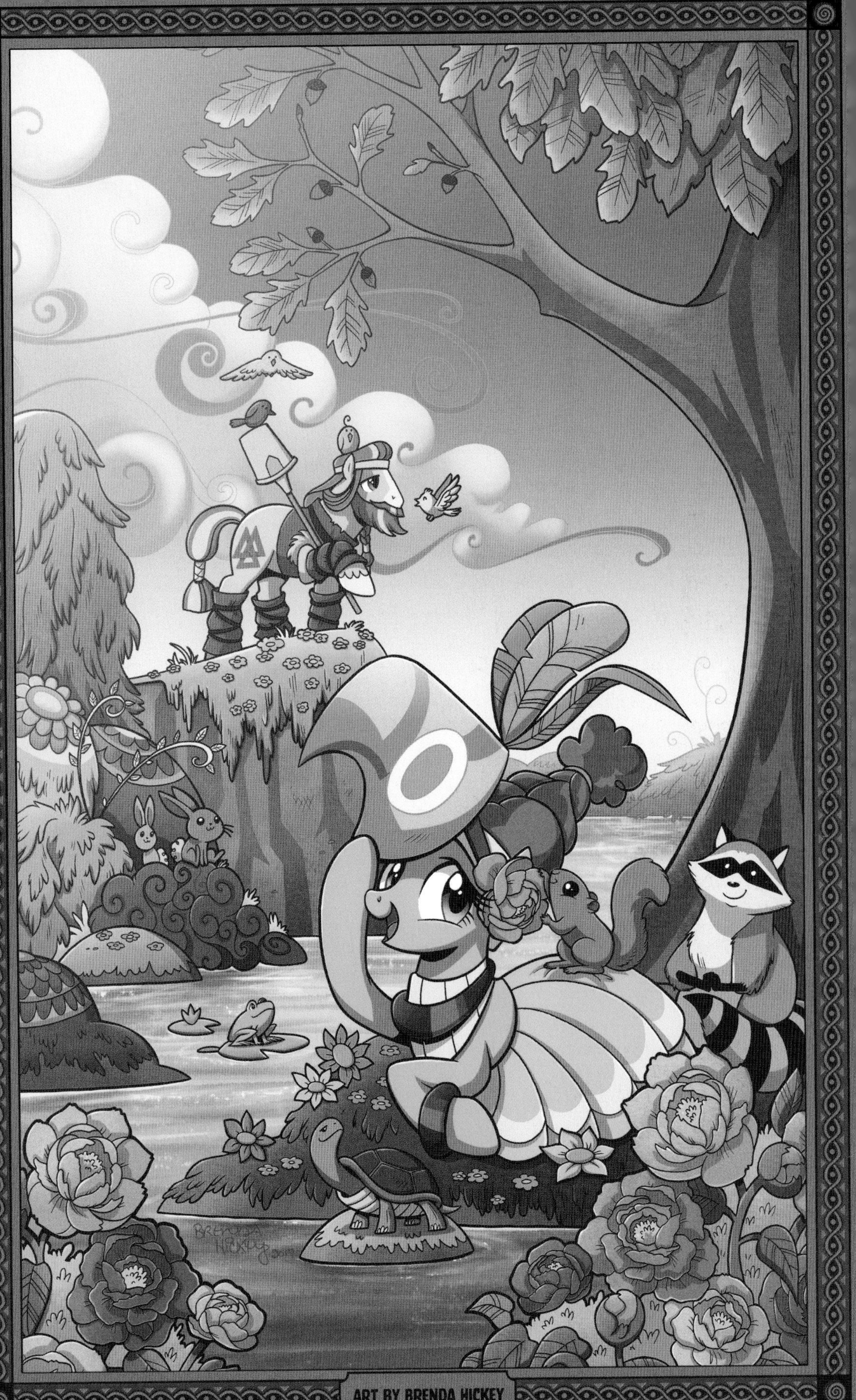

ART BY BRENDA HICKEY

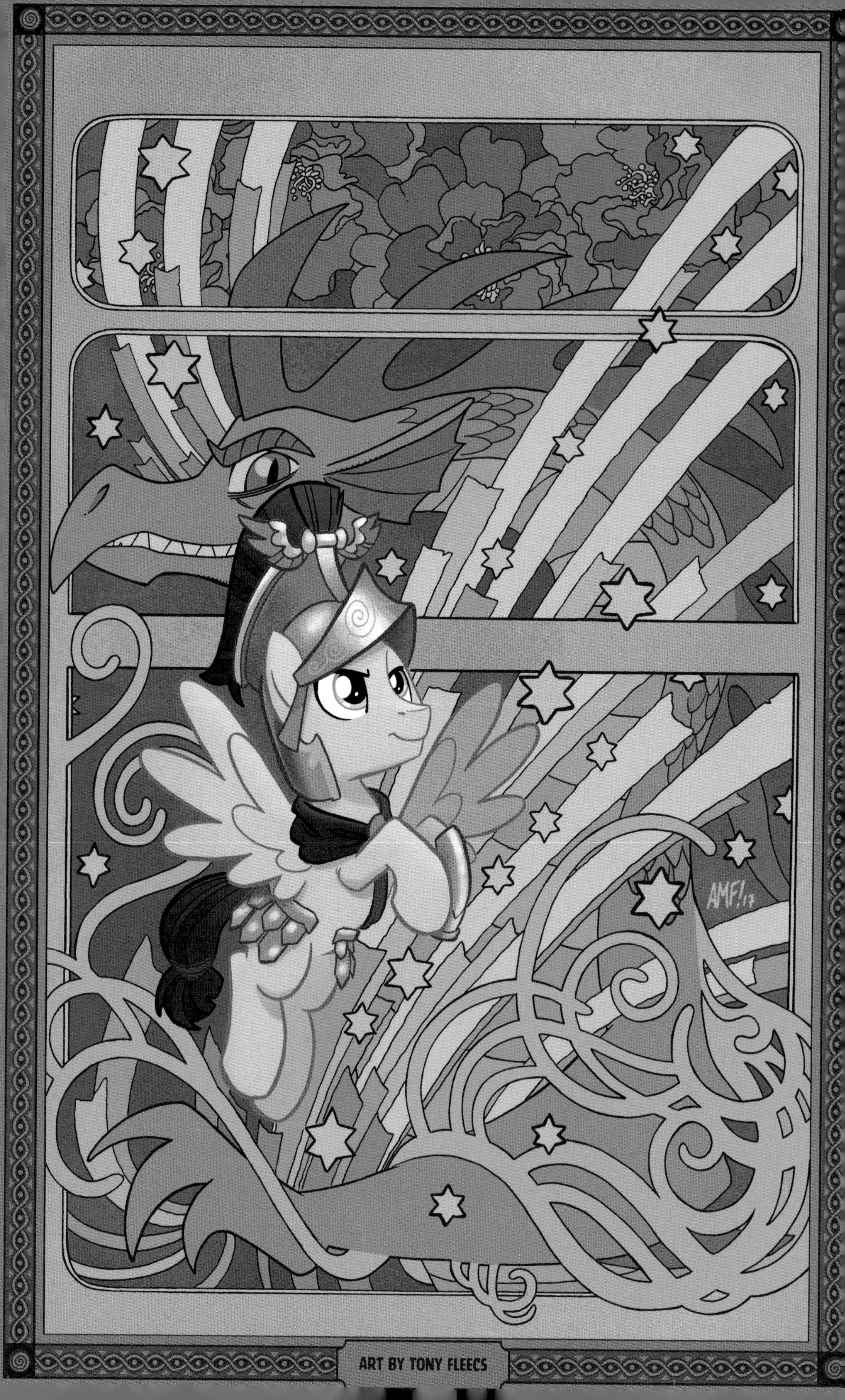
AMF!'17

ART BY TONY FLEECS

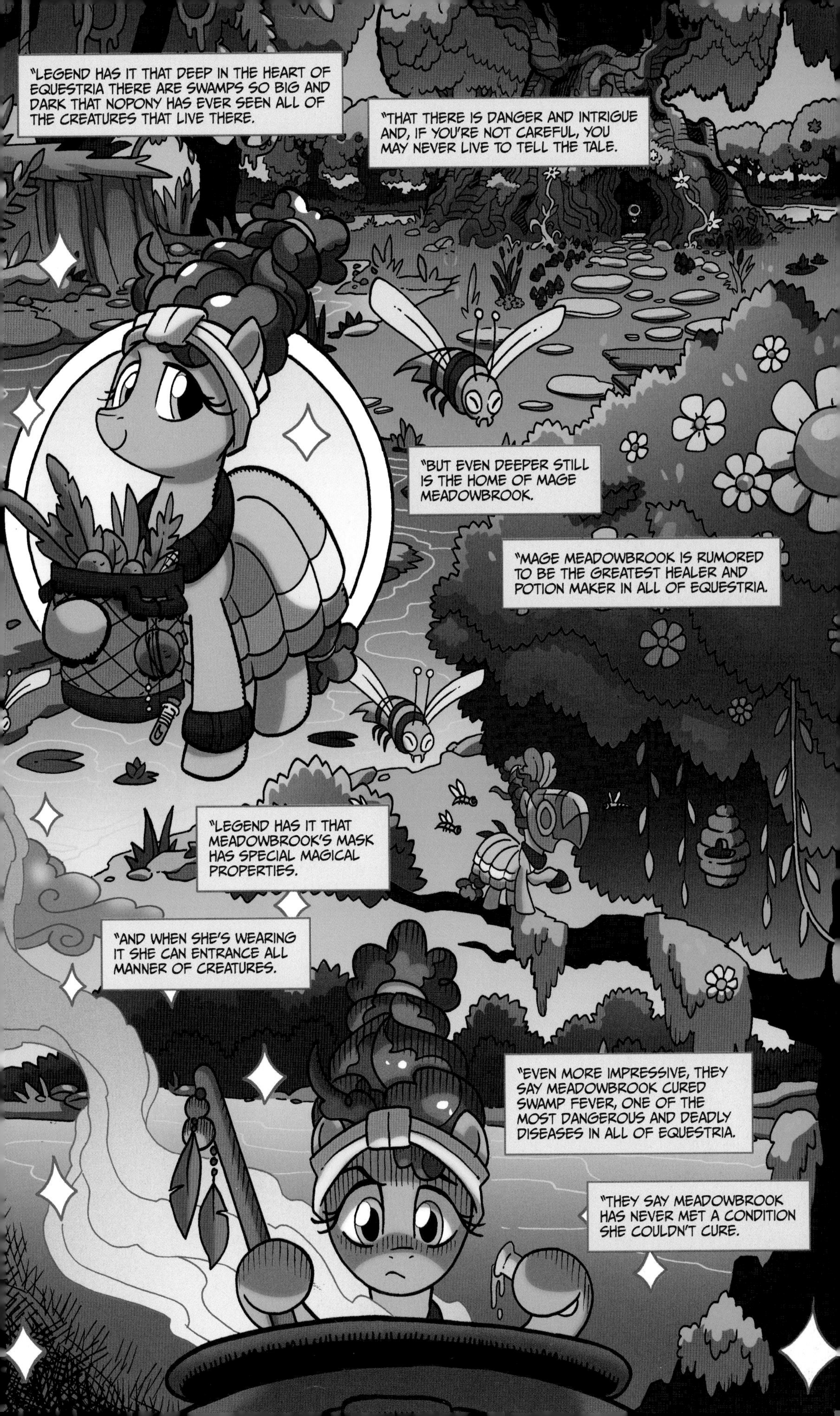
"LEGEND HAS IT THAT DEEP IN THE HEART OF EQUESTRIA THERE ARE SWAMPS SO BIG AND DARK THAT NOPONY HAS EVER SEEN ALL OF THE CREATURES THAT LIVE THERE.
"THAT THERE IS DANGER AND INTRIGUE AND, IF YOU'RE NOT CAREFUL, YOU MAY NEVER LIVE TO TELL THE TALE.
"BUT EVEN DEEPER STILL IS THE HOME OF MAGE MEADOWBROOK.
"MAGE MEADOWBROOK IS RUMORED TO BE THE GREATEST HEALER AND POTION MAKER IN ALL OF EQUESTRIA.
"LEGEND HAS IT THAT MEADOWBROOK'S MASK HAS SPECIAL MAGICAL PROPERTIES.
"AND WHEN SHE'S WEARING IT SHE CAN ENTRANCE ALL MANNER OF CREATURES.
"EVEN MORE IMPRESSIVE, THEY SAY MEADOWBROOK CURED SWAMP FEVER, ONE OF THE MOST DANGEROUS AND DEADLY DISEASES IN ALL OF EQUESTRIA.
"THEY SAY MEADOWBROOK HAS NEVER MET A CONDITION SHE COULDN'T CURE.

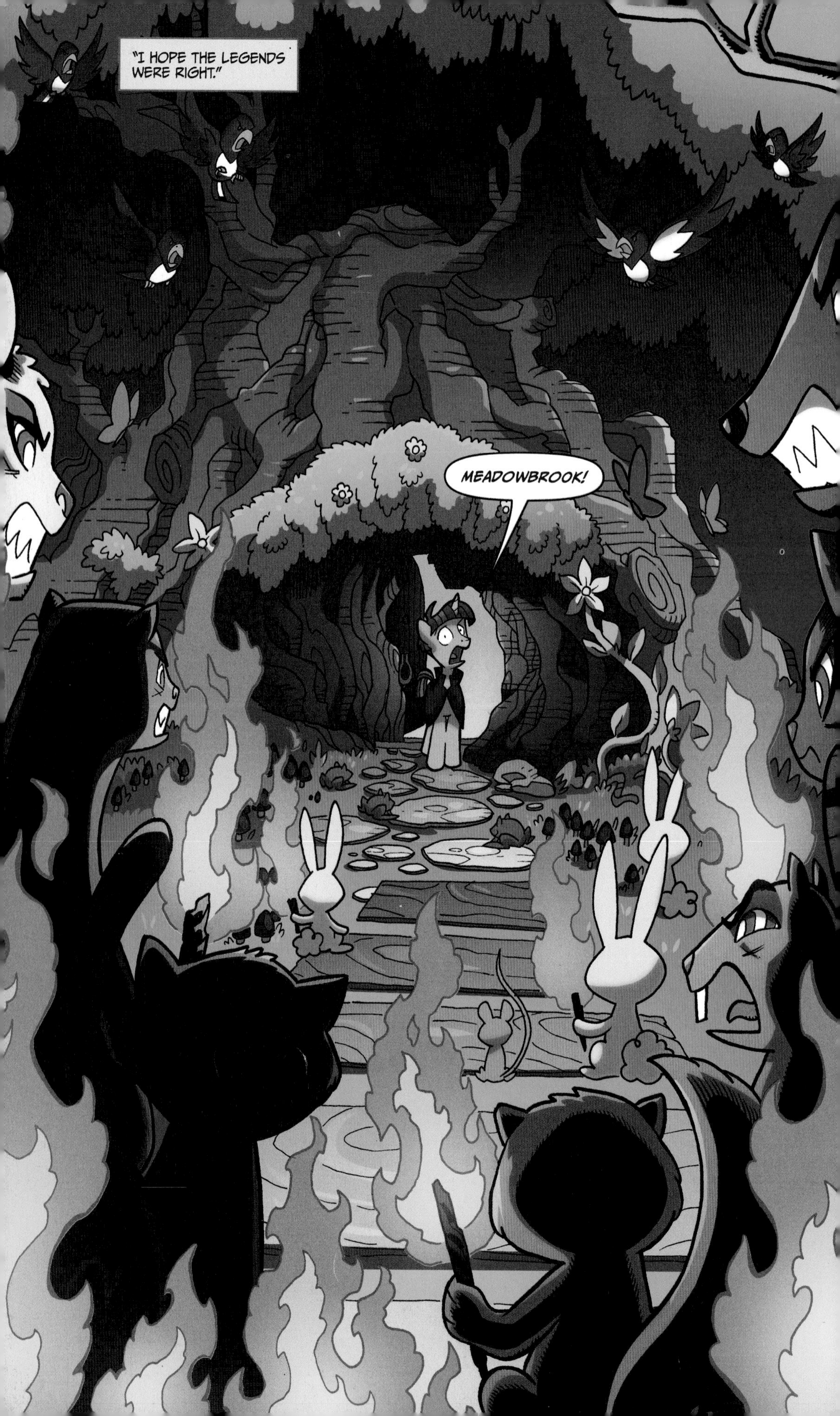
"I HOPE THE LEGENDS WERE RIGHT."
MEADOWBROOK!

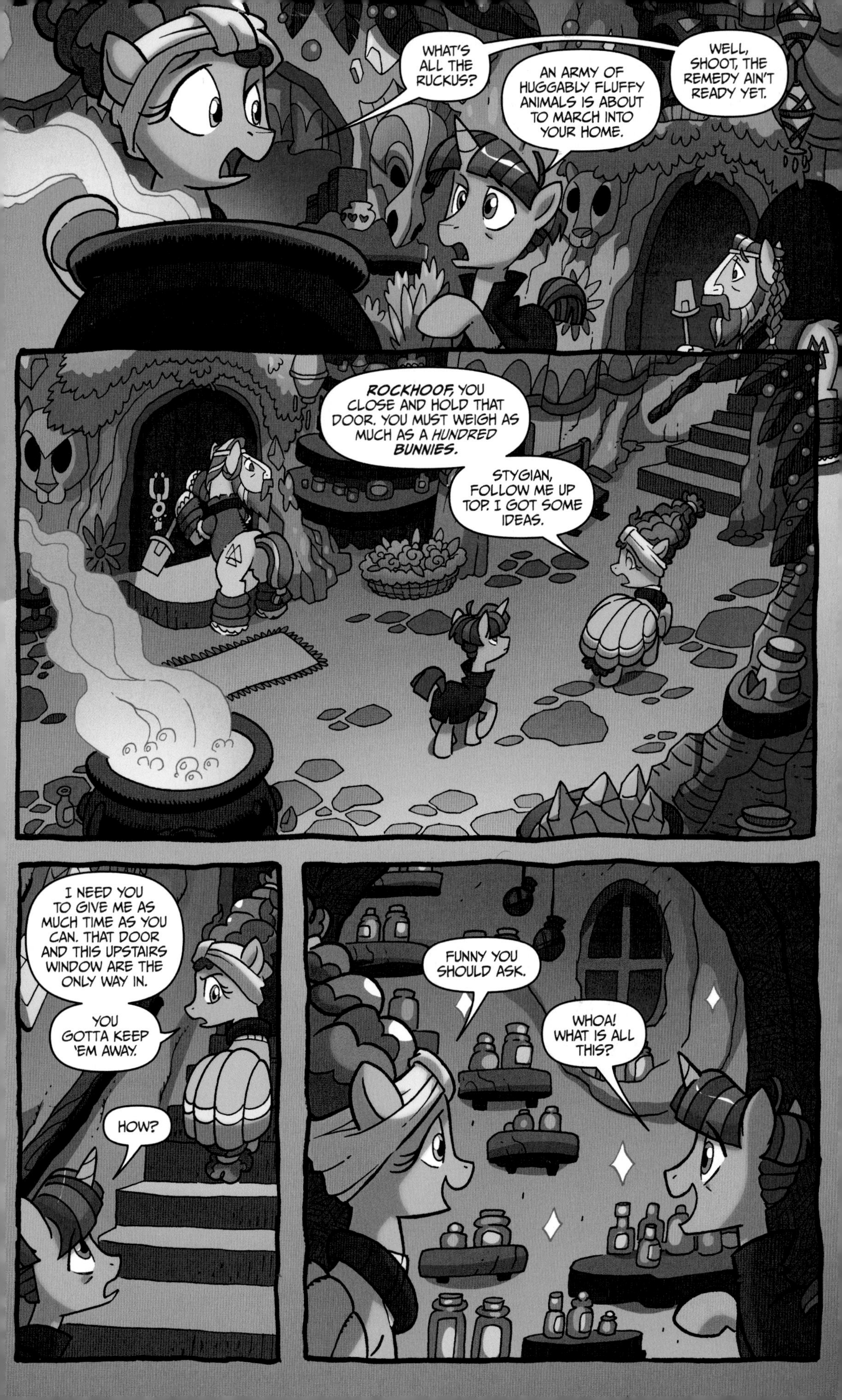
WHAT'S ALL THE RUCKUS?
AN ARMY OF HUGGABLY FLUFFY ANIMALS IS ABOUT TO MARCH INTO YOUR HOME.
WELL, SHOOT, THE REMEDY AIN'T READY YET.
ROCKHOOF, YOU CLOSE AND HOLD THAT DOOR. YOU MUST WEIGH AS MUCH AS A *HUNDRED* *BUNNIES.*
STYGIAN, FOLLOW ME UP TOP. I GOT SOME IDEAS.
I NEED YOU TO GIVE ME AS MUCH TIME AS YOU CAN. THAT DOOR AND THIS UPSTAIRS WINDOW ARE THE ONLY WAY IN.
YOU GOTTA KEEP 'EM AWAY.
HOW?
FUNNY YOU SHOULD ASK.
WHOA! WHAT IS ALL THIS?

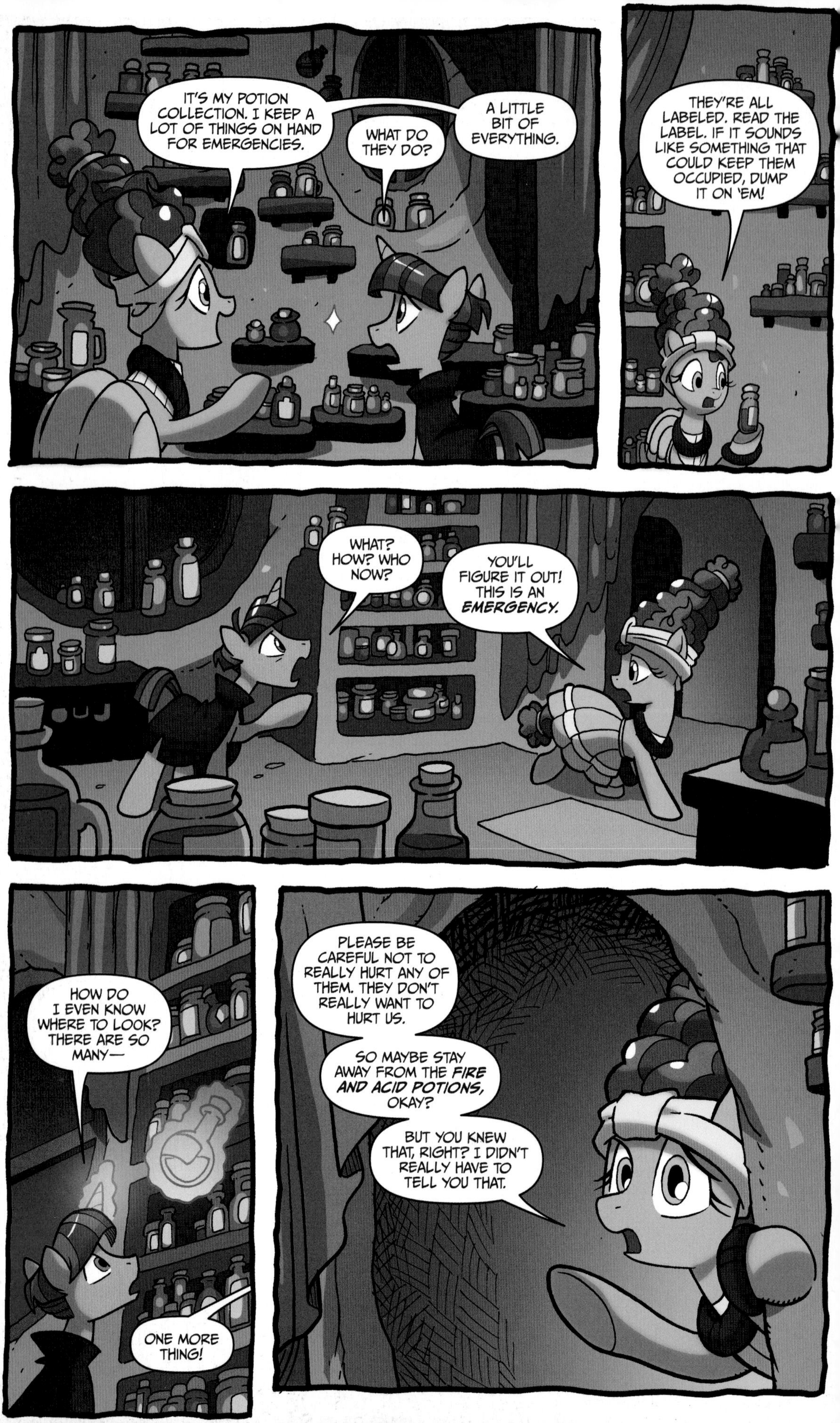
IT'S MY POTION COLLECTION. I KEEP A LOT OF THINGS ON HAND FOR EMERGENCIES.
WHAT DO THEY DO?
A LITTLE BIT OF EVERYTHING.
THEY'RE ALL LABELED. READ THE LABEL. IF IT SOUNDS LIKE SOMETHING THAT COULD KEEP THEM OCCUPIED, DUMP IT ON 'EM!
WHAT? HOW? WHO NOW?
YOU'LL FIGURE IT OUT! THIS IS AN EMERGENCY.
HOW DO I EVEN KNOW WHERE TO LOOK? THERE ARE SO MANY—
ONE MORE THING!
PLEASE BE CAREFUL NOT TO REALLY HURT ANY OF THEM. THEY DON'T REALLY WANT TO HURT US.
SO MAYBE STAY AWAY FROM THE FIRE AND ACID POTIONS, OKAY?
BUT YOU KNEW THAT, RIGHT? I DIDN'T REALLY HAVE TO TELL YOU THAT.

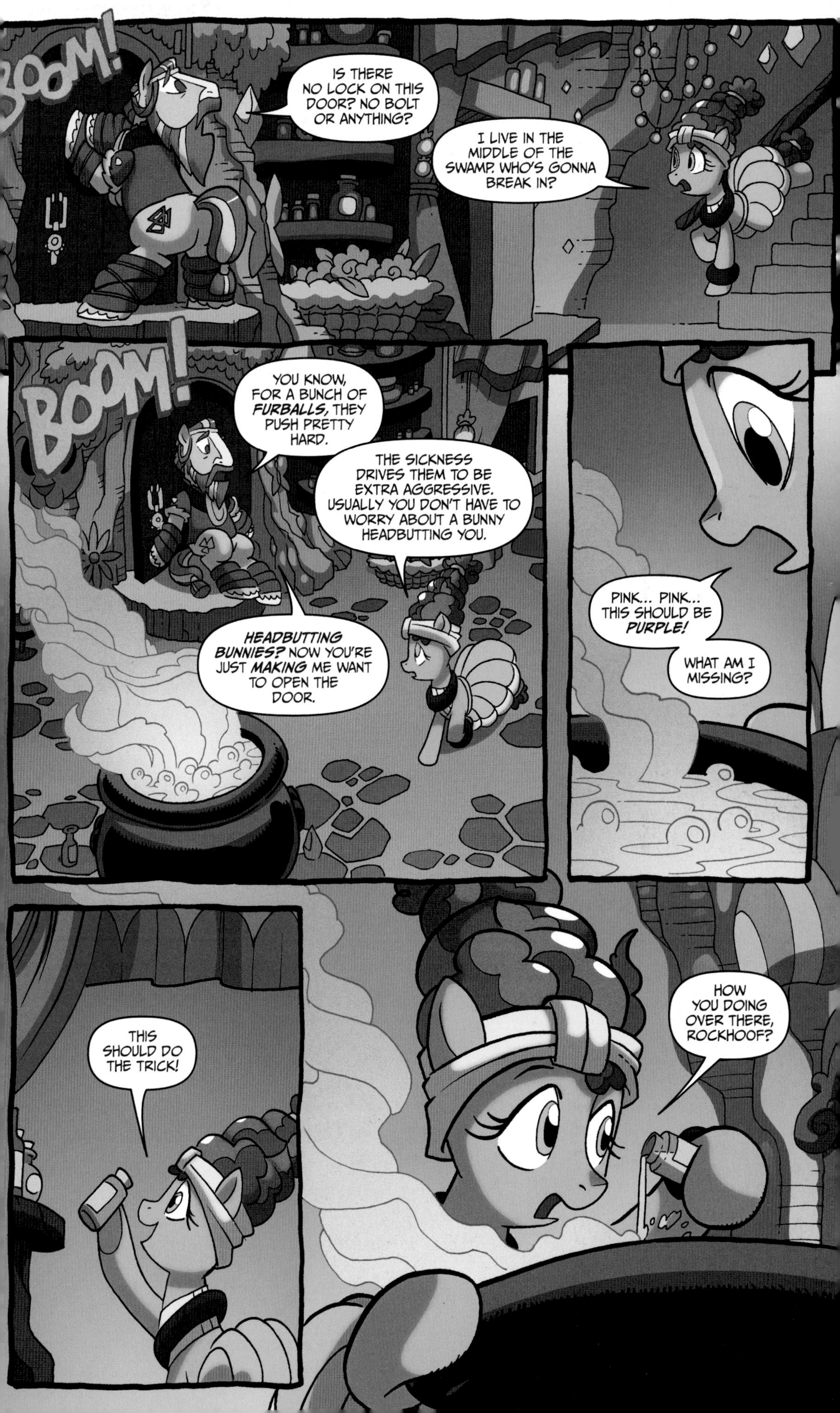
BOOM!
IS THERE NO LOCK ON THIS DOOR? NO BOLT OR ANYTHING?
I LIVE IN THE MIDDLE OF THE SWAMP. WHO'S GONNA BREAK IN?
BOOM!
YOU KNOW, FOR A BUNCH OF *FURBALLS,* THEY PUSH PRETTY HARD.
THE SICKNESS DRIVES THEM TO BE EXTRA AGGRESSIVE. USUALLY YOU DON'T HAVE TO WORRY ABOUT A BUNNY HEADBUTTING YOU.
HEADBUTTING BUNNIES? NOW YOU'RE JUST *MAKING* ME WANT TO OPEN THE DOOR.
PINK... PINK... THIS SHOULD BE *PURPLE!*
WHAT AM I MISSING?
THIS SHOULD DO THE TRICK!
HOW YOU DOING OVER THERE, ROCKHOOF?

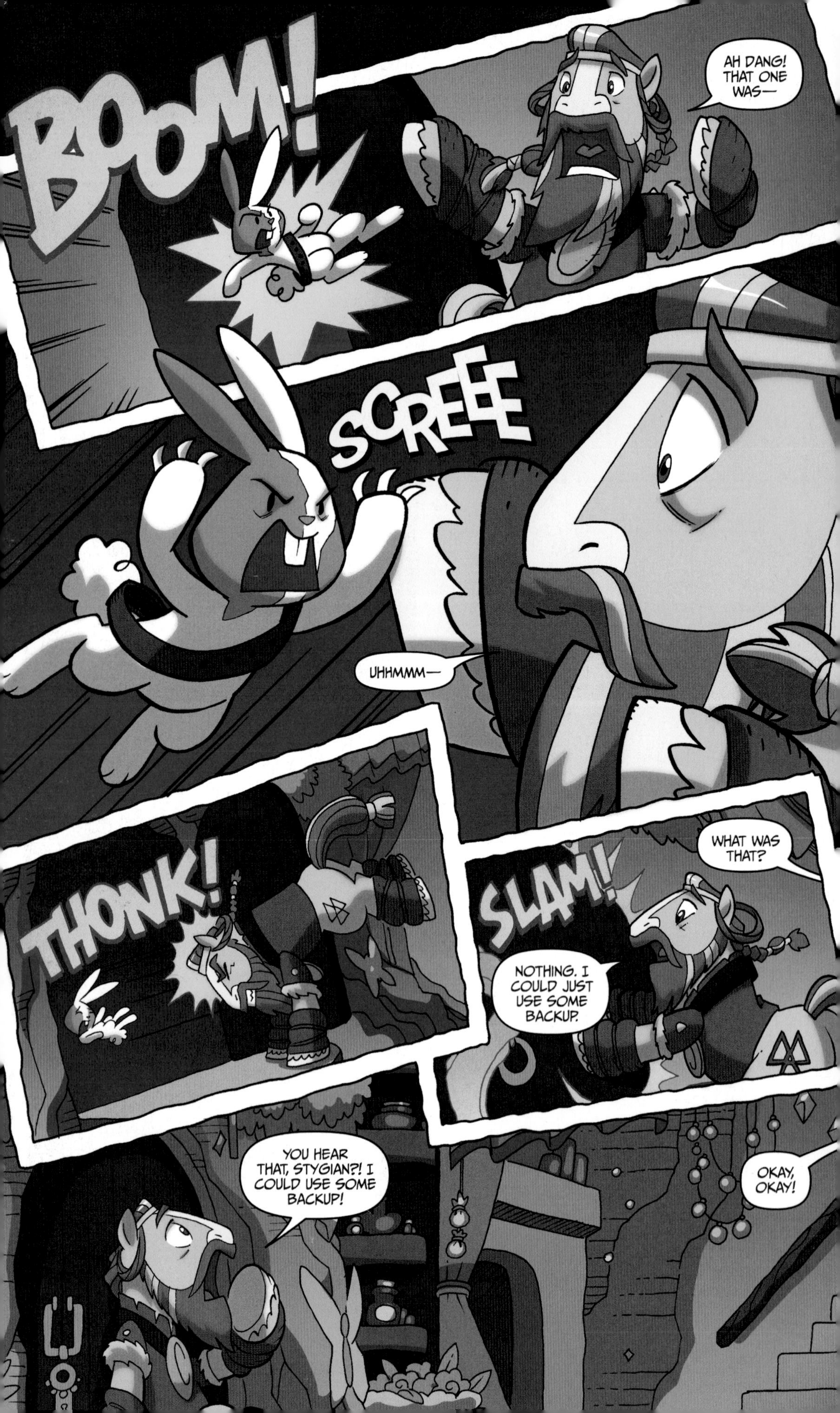
BOOM!
AH DANG! THAT ONE WAS—
SCREEE
UHHMMM—
THONK!
SLAM!
WHAT WAS THAT?
NOTHING. I COULD JUST USE SOME BACKUP.
YOU HEAR THAT, STYGIAN?! I COULD USE SOME BACKUP!
OKAY, OKAY!

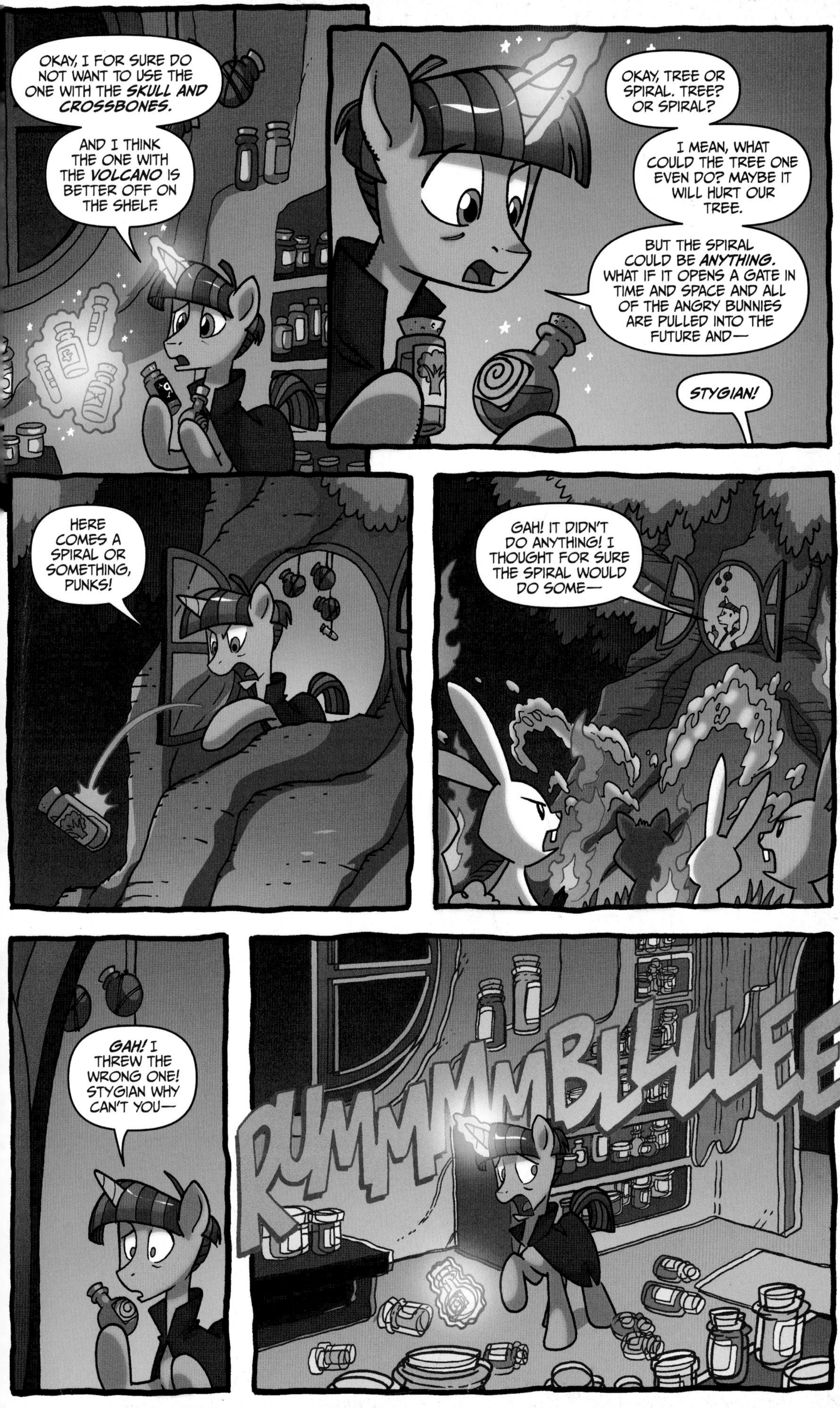

OKAY, I FOR SURE DO NOT WANT TO USE THE ONE WITH THE *SKULL AND CROSSBONES.*
AND I THINK THE ONE WITH THE *VOLCANO* IS BETTER OFF ON THE SHELF.
OKAY, TREE OR SPIRAL. TREE? OR SPIRAL?
I MEAN, WHAT COULD THE TREE ONE EVEN DO? MAYBE IT WILL HURT OUR TREE.
BUT THE SPIRAL COULD BE *ANYTHING.* WHAT IF IT OPENS A GATE IN TIME AND SPACE AND ALL OF THE ANGRY BUNNIES ARE PULLED INTO THE FUTURE AND—
STYGIAN!
HERE COMES A SPIRAL OR SOMETHING, PUNKS!
GAH! IT DIDN'T DO ANYTHING! I THOUGHT FOR SURE THE SPIRAL WOULD DO SOME—
GAH! I THREW THE WRONG ONE! STYGIAN WHY CAN'T YOU—
RUMMMMBLLLEE

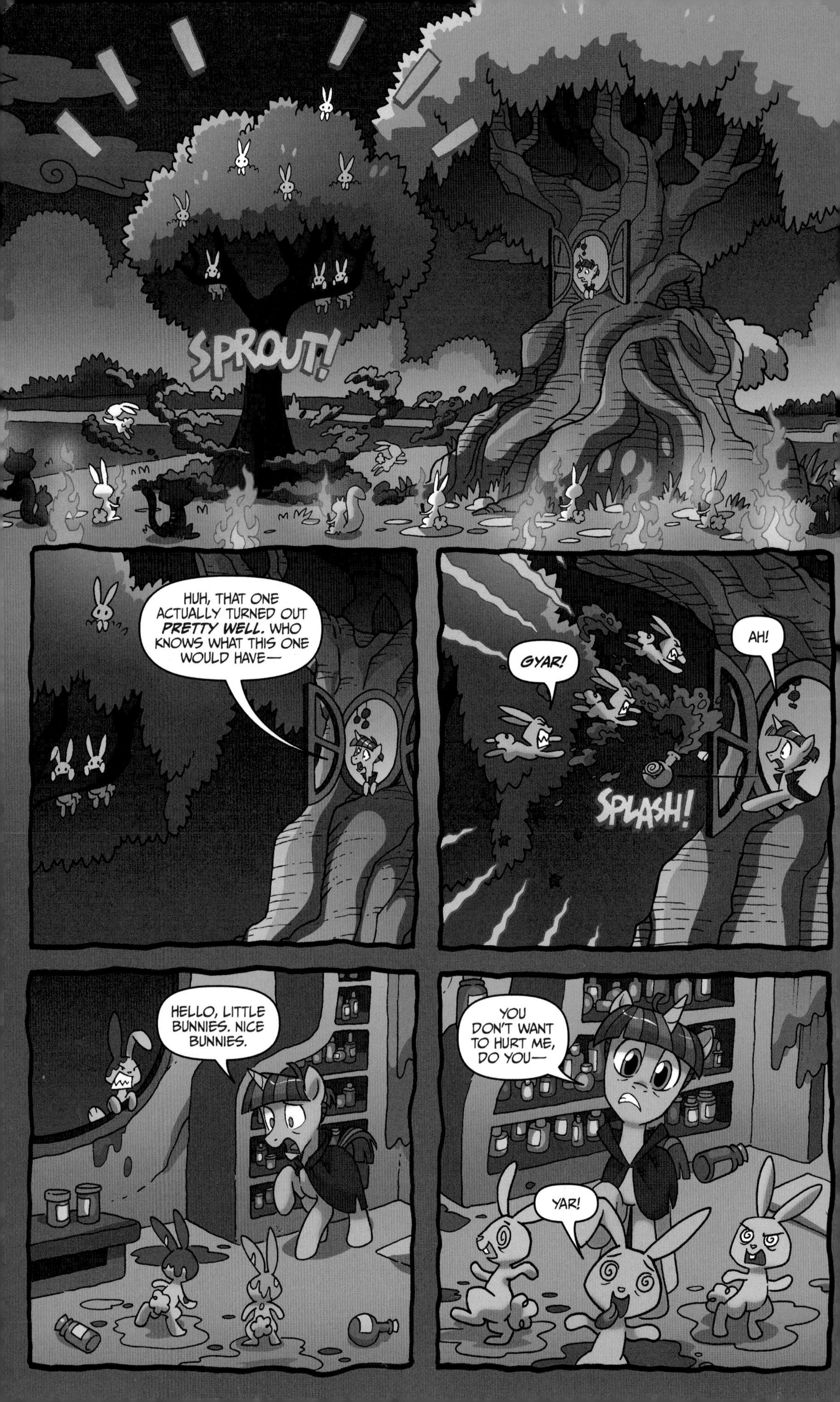
SPROUT!
HUH, THAT ONE ACTUALLY TURNED OUT PRETTY WELL. WHO KNOWS WHAT THIS ONE WOULD HAVE—
GYAR!
AH!
SPLASH!
HELLO, LITTLE BUNNIES. NICE BUNNIES.
YOU DON'T WANT TO HURT ME, DO YOU—
YAR!

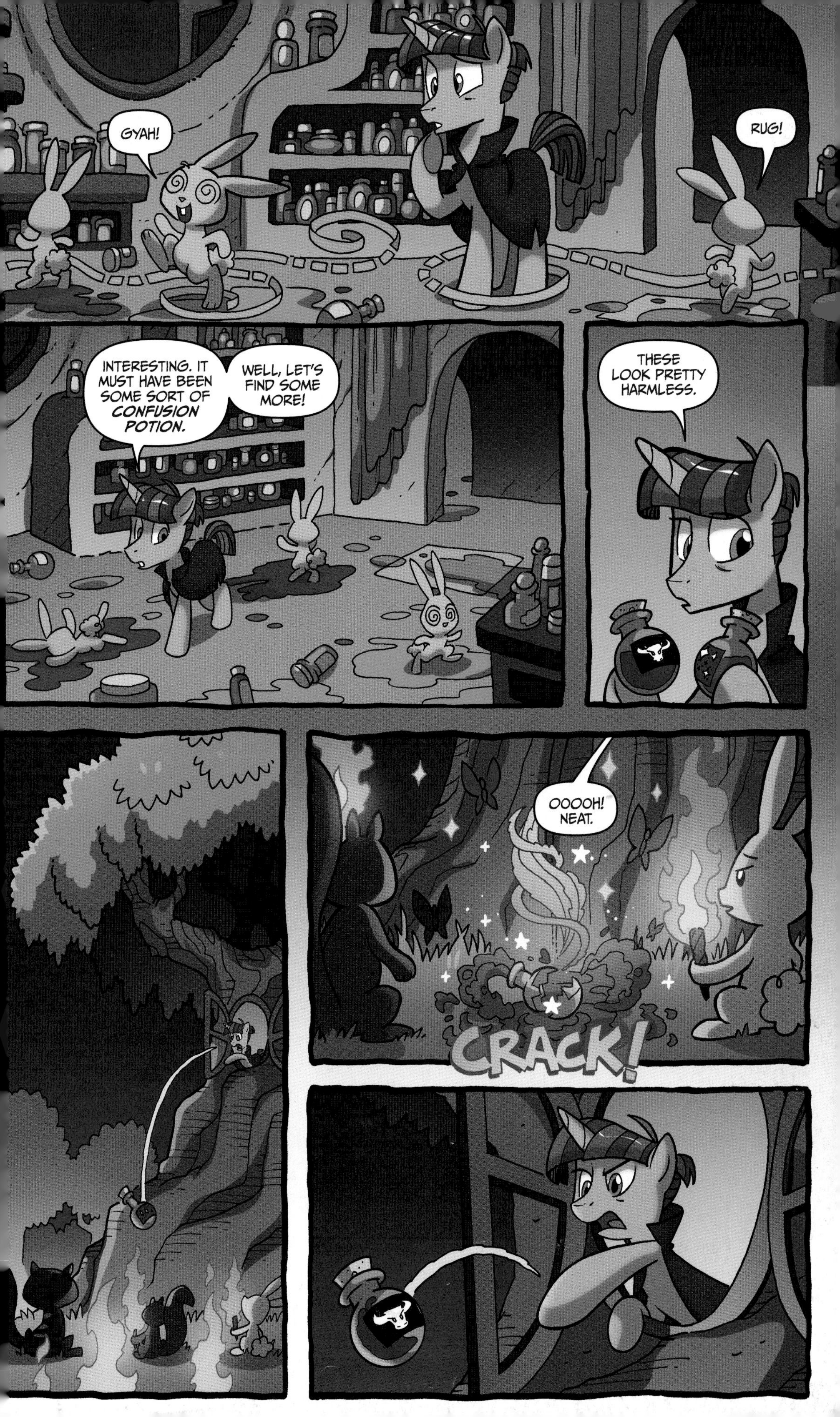
GYAH!
RUG!
INTERESTING. IT MUST HAVE BEEN SOME SORT OF *CONFUSION POTION.*
WELL, LET'S FIND SOME MORE!
THESE LOOK PRETTY HARMLESS.
OOOOH! NEAT.
CRACK!

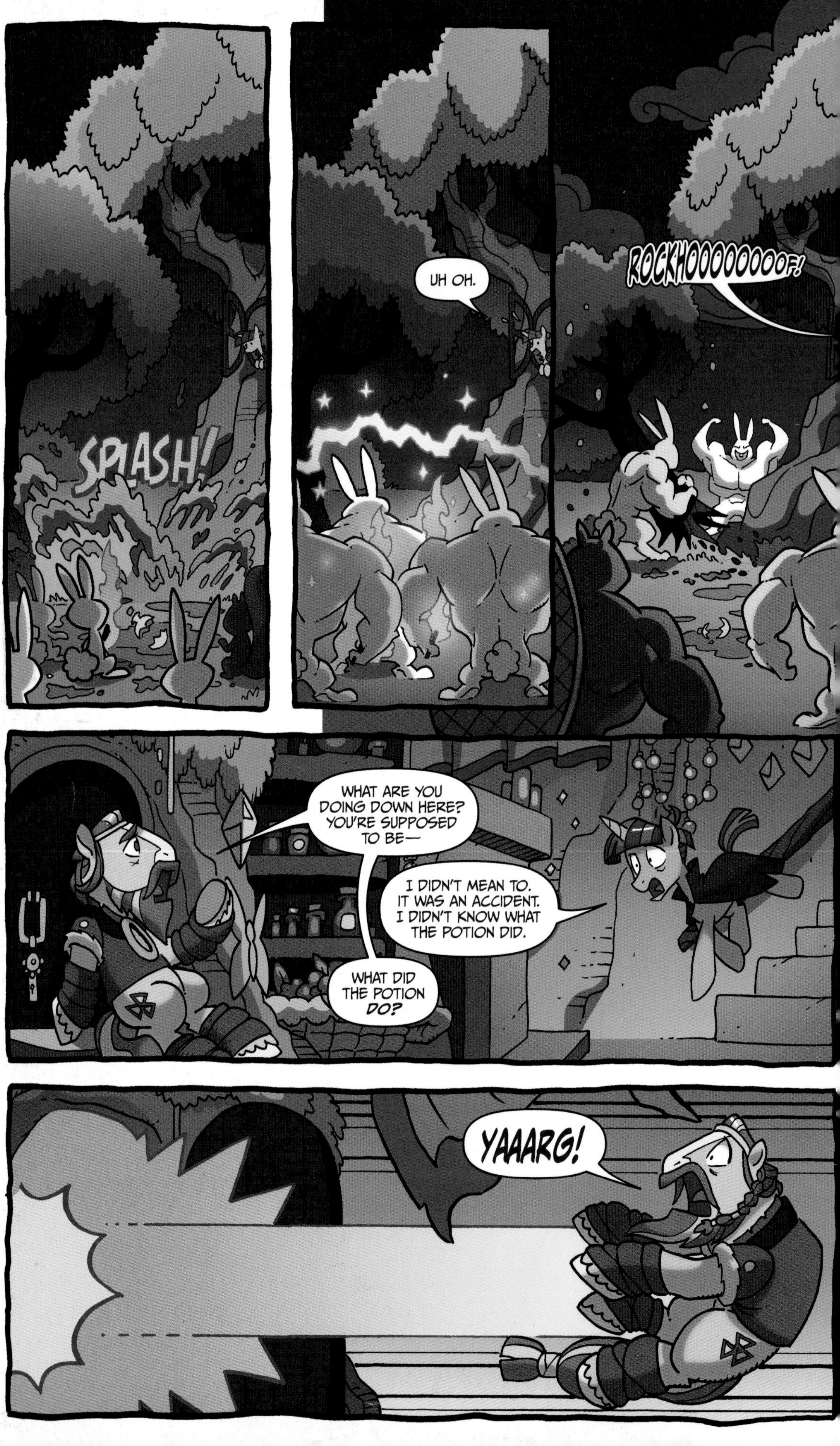
SPLASH!
UH OH.
ROCKHOOOOOOOOOF!
WHAT ARE YOU DOING DOWN HERE? YOU'RE SUPPOSED TO BE—
I DIDN'T MEAN TO. IT WAS AN ACCIDENT. I DIDN'T KNOW WHAT THE POTION DID.
WHAT DID THE POTION *DO?*
YAAARG!

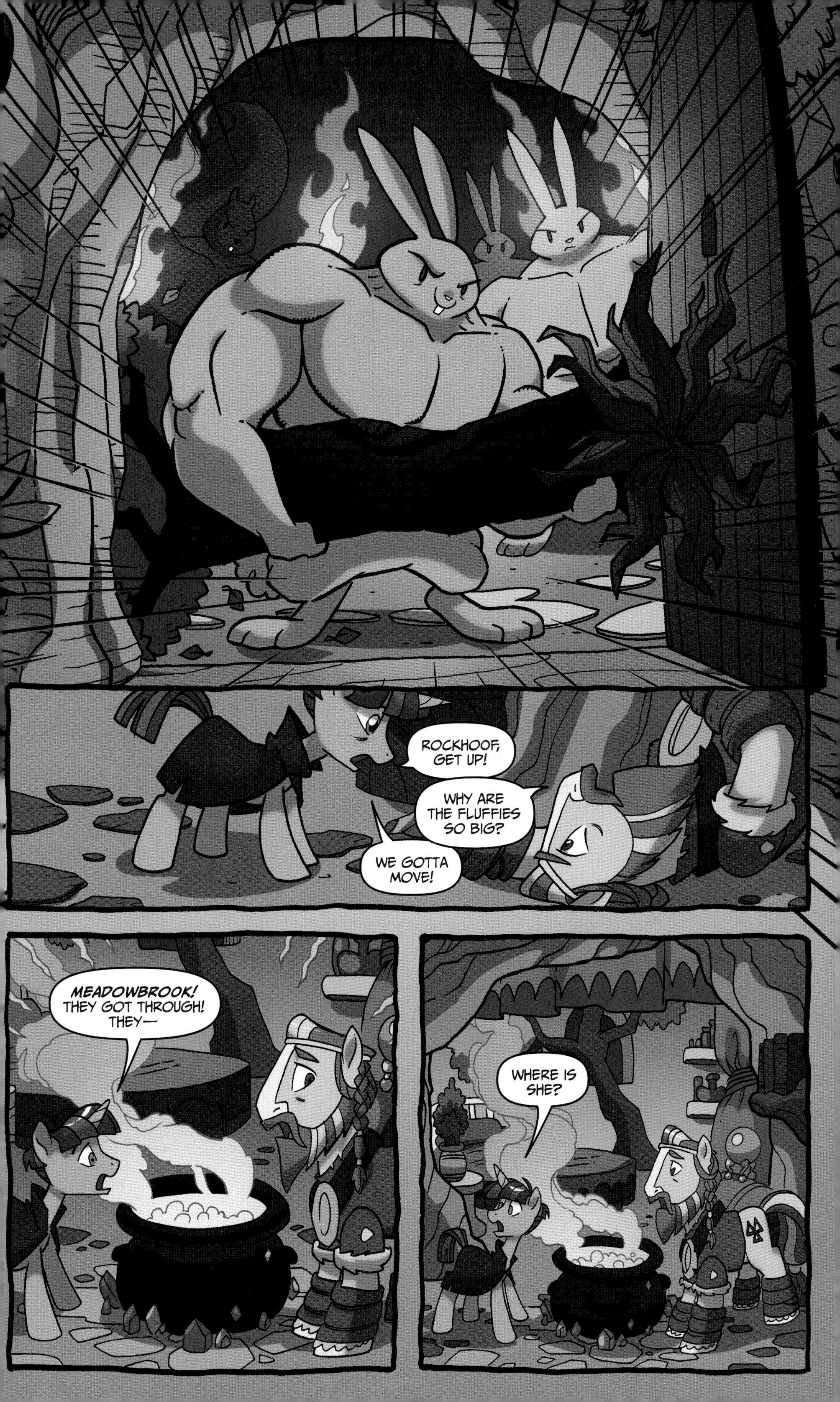
ROCKHOOF, GET UP!
WHY ARE THE FLUFFIES SO BIG?
WE GOTTA MOVE!
MEADOWBROOK! THEY GOT THROUGH! THEY—
WHERE IS SHE?

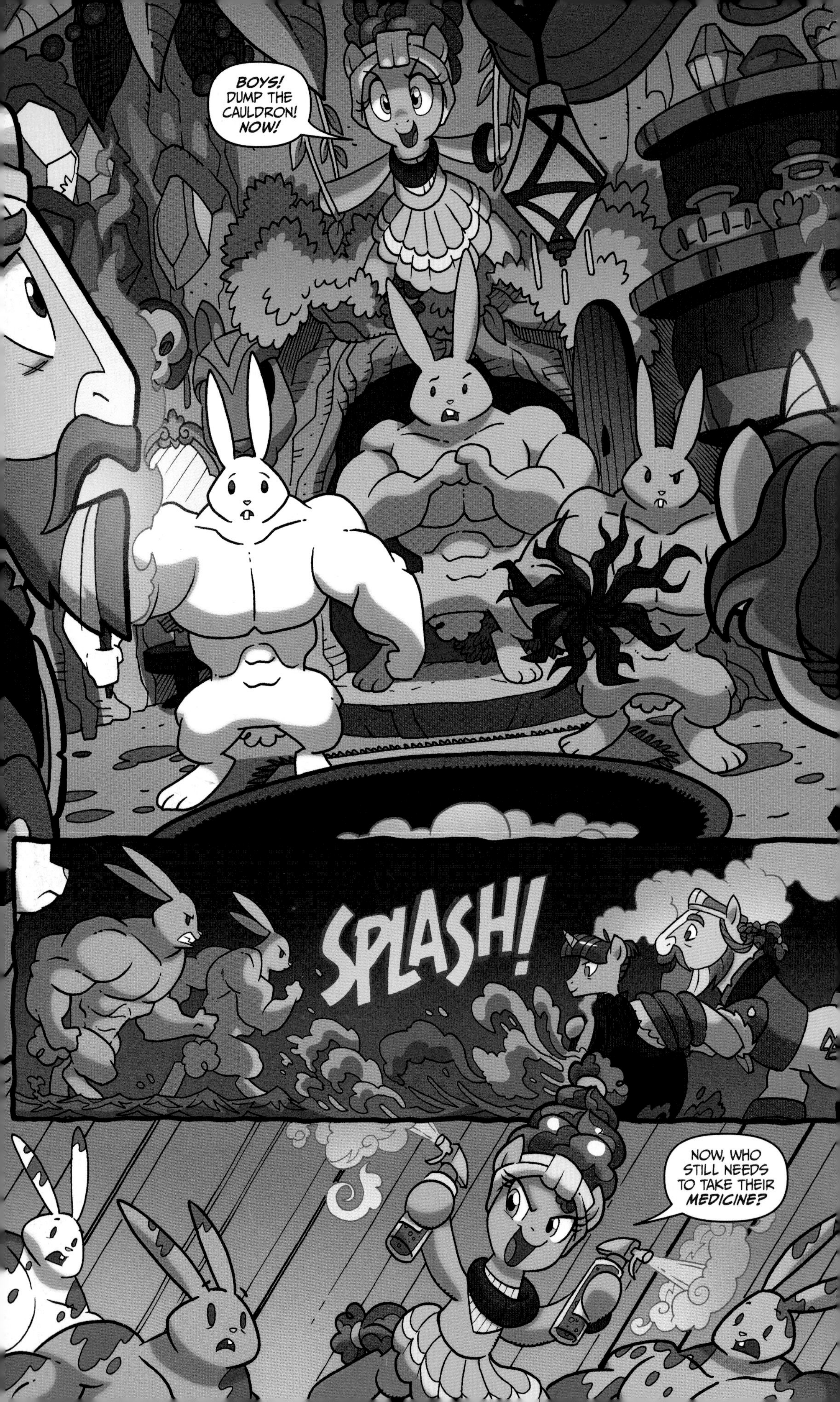
BOYS! DUMP THE CAULDRON! NOW!
SPLASH!
NOW, WHO STILL NEEDS TO TAKE THEIR MEDICINE?

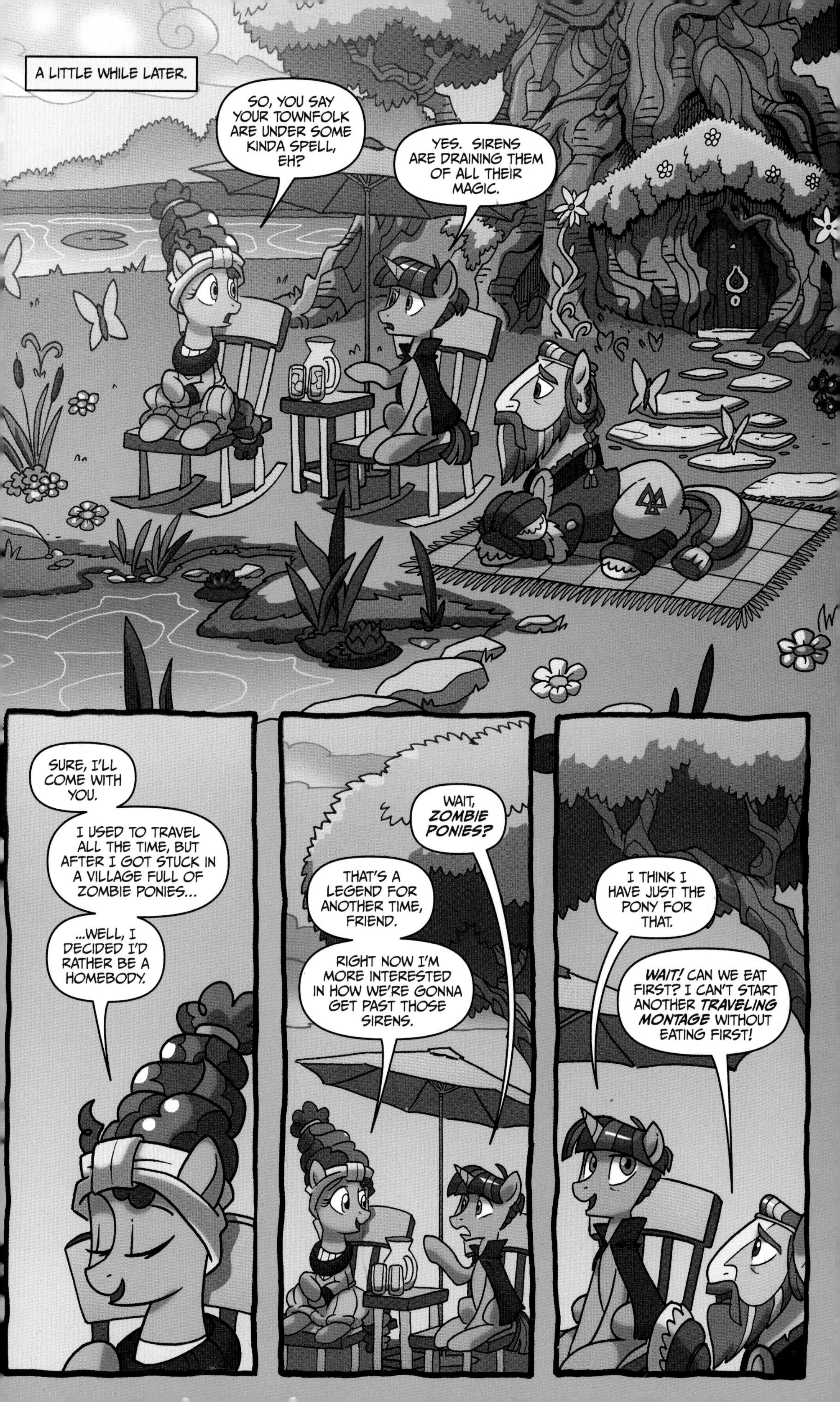

A LITTLE WHILE LATER.
SO, YOU SAY YOUR TOWNFOLK ARE UNDER SOME KINDA SPELL, EH?
YES. SIRENS ARE DRAINING THEM OF ALL THEIR MAGIC.
SURE, I'LL COME WITH YOU.
I USED TO TRAVEL ALL THE TIME, BUT AFTER I GOT STUCK IN A VILLAGE FULL OF ZOMBIE PONIES...
...WELL, I DECIDED I'D RATHER BE A HOMEBODY.
WAIT, *ZOMBIE PONIES?*
THAT'S A LEGEND FOR ANOTHER TIME, FRIEND.
RIGHT NOW I'M MORE INTERESTED IN HOW WE'RE GONNA GET PAST THOSE SIRENS.
I THINK I HAVE JUST THE PONY FOR THAT.
WAIT! CAN WE EAT FIRST? I CAN'T START ANOTHER *TRAVELING MONTAGE* WITHOUT EATING FIRST!

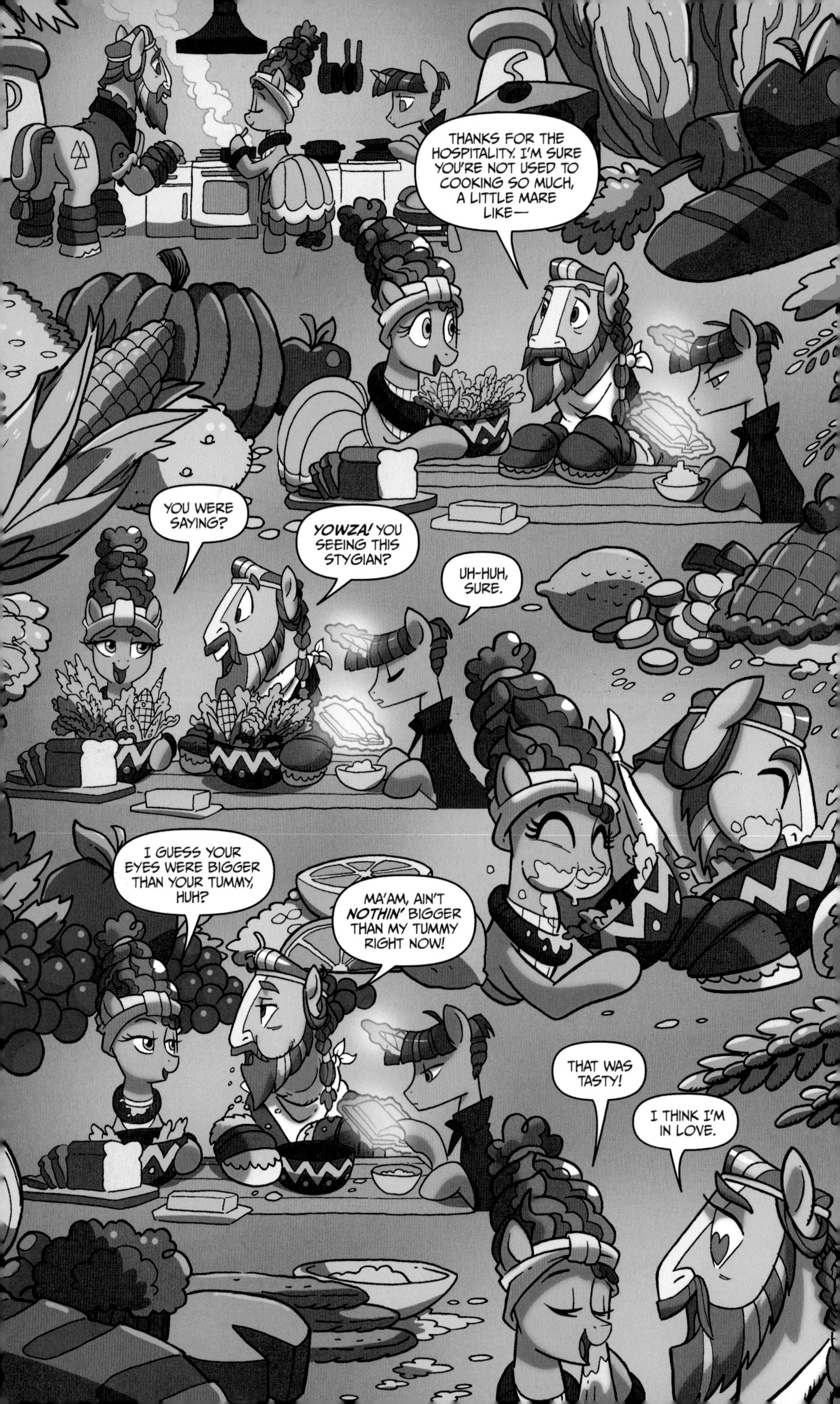
THANKS FOR THE HOSPITALITY. I'M SURE YOU'RE NOT USED TO COOKING SO MUCH, A LITTLE MARE LIKE—
YOU WERE SAYING?
YOWZA! YOU SEEING THIS STYGIAN?
UH-HUH, SURE.
I GUESS YOUR EYES WERE BIGGER THAN YOUR TUMMY, HUH?
MA'AM, AIN'T *NOTHIN'* BIGGER THAN MY TUMMY RIGHT NOW!
THAT WAS TASTY!
I THINK I'M IN LOVE.

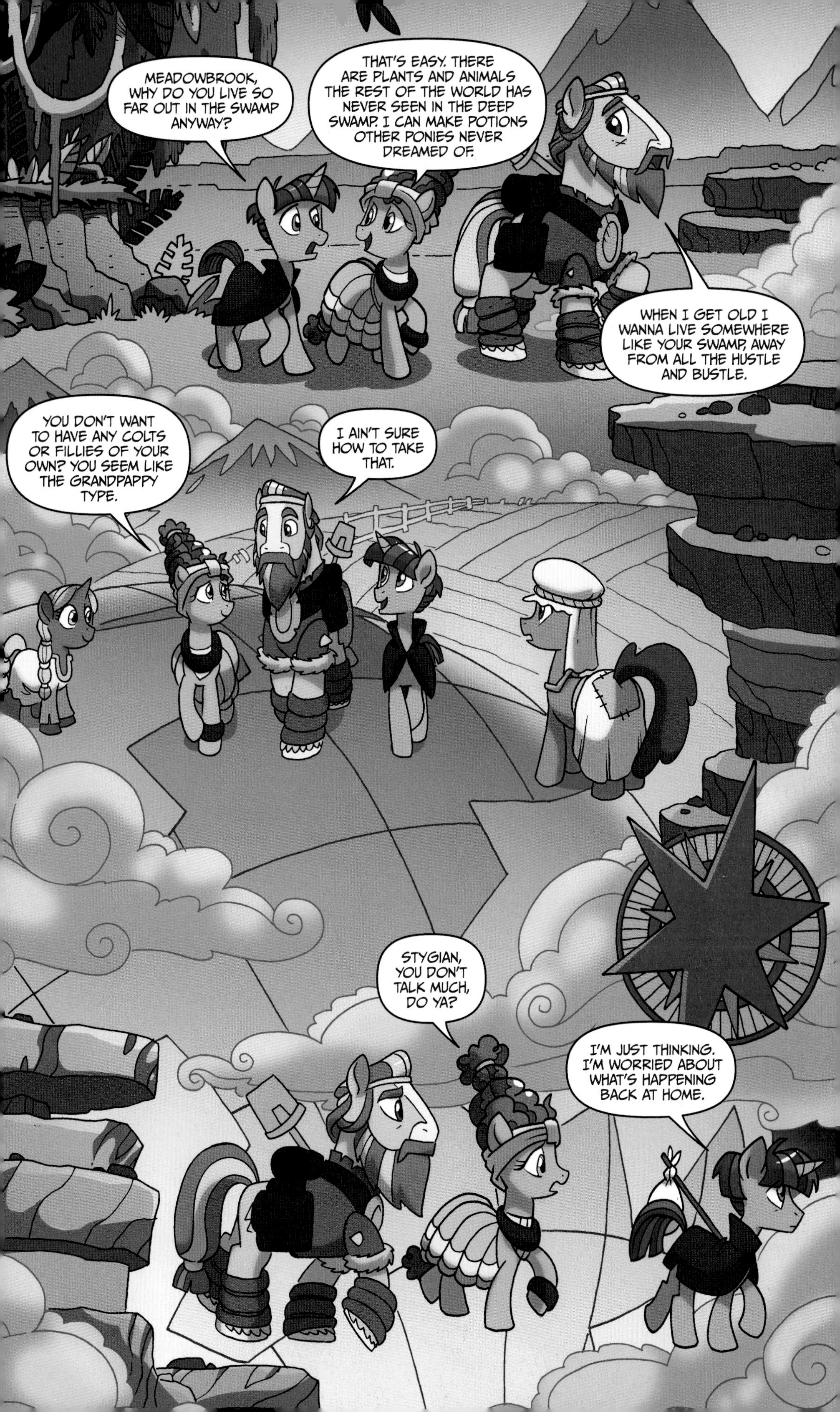
MEADOWBROOK, WHY DO YOU LIVE SO FAR OUT IN THE SWAMP ANYWAY?
THAT'S EASY. THERE ARE PLANTS AND ANIMALS THE REST OF THE WORLD HAS NEVER SEEN IN THE DEEP SWAMP. I CAN MAKE POTIONS OTHER PONIES NEVER DREAMED OF.
WHEN I GET OLD I WANNA LIVE SOMEWHERE LIKE YOUR SWAMP, AWAY FROM ALL THE HUSTLE AND BUSTLE.
YOU DON'T WANT TO HAVE ANY COLTS OR FILLIES OF YOUR OWN? YOU SEEM LIKE THE GRANDPAPPY TYPE.
I AIN'T SURE HOW TO TAKE THAT.
STYGIAN, YOU DON'T TALK MUCH, DO YA?
I'M JUST THINKING. I'M WORRIED ABOUT WHAT'S HAPPENING BACK AT HOME.

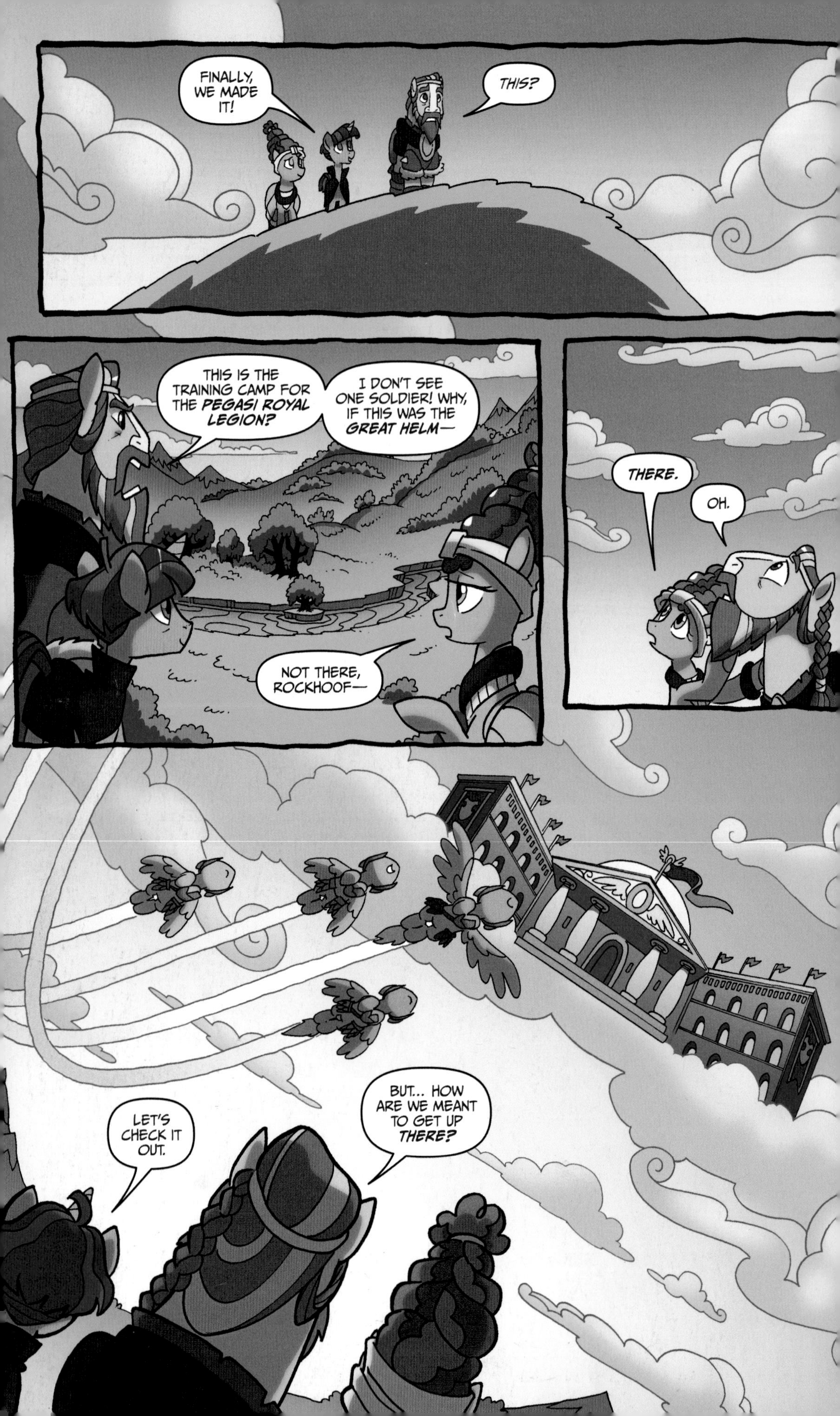
FINALLY, WE MADE IT!
THIS?
THIS IS THE TRAINING CAMP FOR THE PEGASI ROYAL LEGION?
I DON'T SEE ONE SOLDIER! WHY, IF THIS WAS THE GREAT HELM—
NOT THERE, ROCKHOOF—
THERE.
OH.
LET'S CHECK IT OUT.
BUT... HOW ARE WE MEANT TO GET UP THERE?

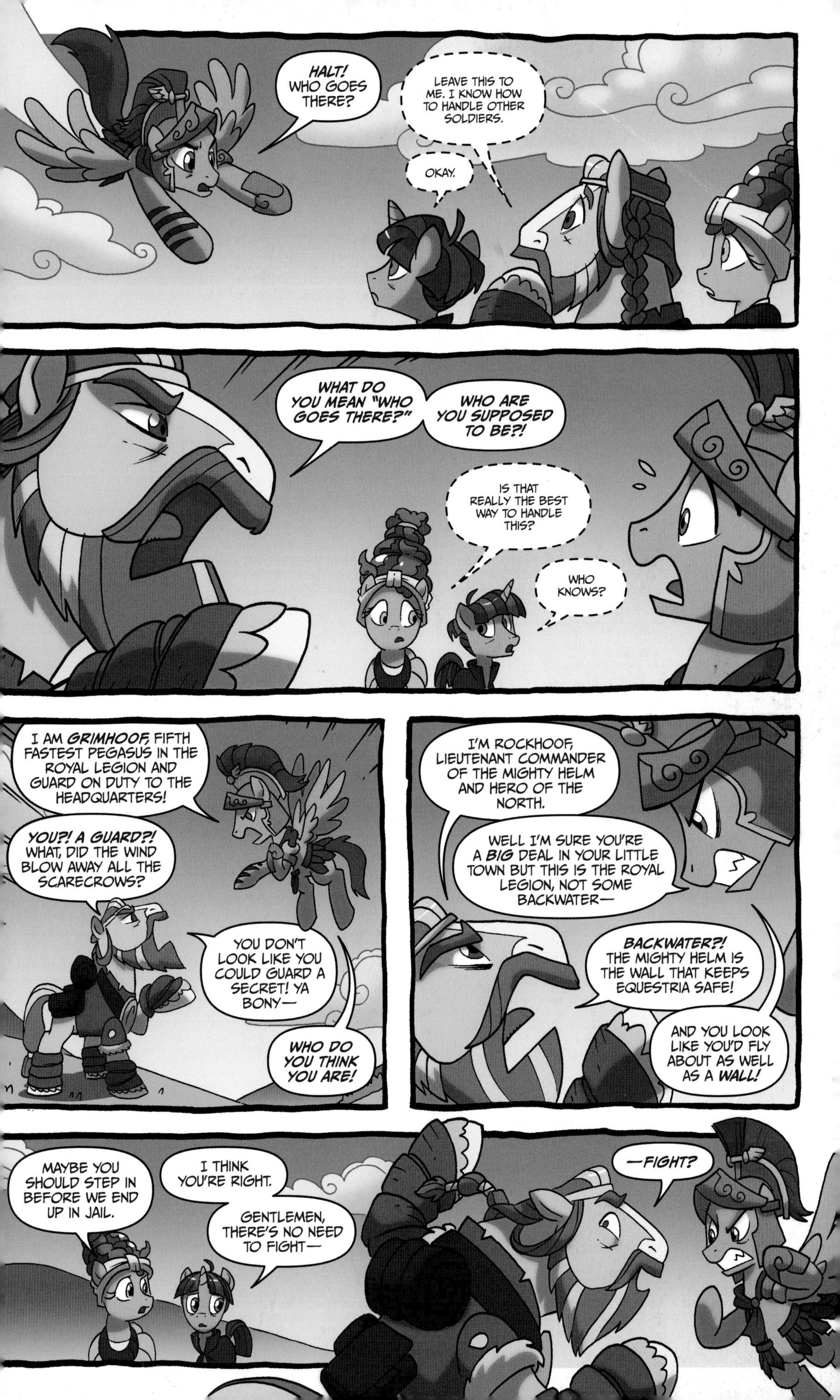
HALT! WHO GOES THERE?
LEAVE THIS TO ME. I KNOW HOW TO HANDLE OTHER SOLDIERS.
OKAY.
WHAT DO YOU MEAN "WHO GOES THERE?"
WHO ARE YOU SUPPOSED TO BE?!
IS THAT REALLY THE BEST WAY TO HANDLE THIS?
WHO KNOWS?
I AM GRIMHOOF, FIFTH FASTEST PEGASUS IN THE ROYAL LEGION AND GUARD ON DUTY TO THE HEADQUARTERS!
YOU?! A GUARD?! WHAT, DID THE WIND BLOW AWAY ALL THE SCARECROWS?
YOU DON'T LOOK LIKE YOU COULD GUARD A SECRET! YA BONY—
WHO DO YOU THINK YOU ARE!
I'M ROCKHOOF, LIEUTENANT COMMANDER OF THE MIGHTY HELM AND HERO OF THE NORTH.
WELL I'M SURE YOU'RE A BIG DEAL IN YOUR LITTLE TOWN BUT THIS IS THE ROYAL LEGION, NOT SOME BACKWATER—
BACKWATER?! THE MIGHTY HELM IS THE WALL THAT KEEPS EQUESTRIA SAFE!
AND YOU LOOK LIKE YOU'D FLY ABOUT AS WELL AS A WALL!
MAYBE YOU SHOULD STEP IN BEFORE WE END UP IN JAIL.
I THINK YOU'RE RIGHT.
GENTLEMEN, THERE'S NO NEED TO FIGHT—
—FIGHT?

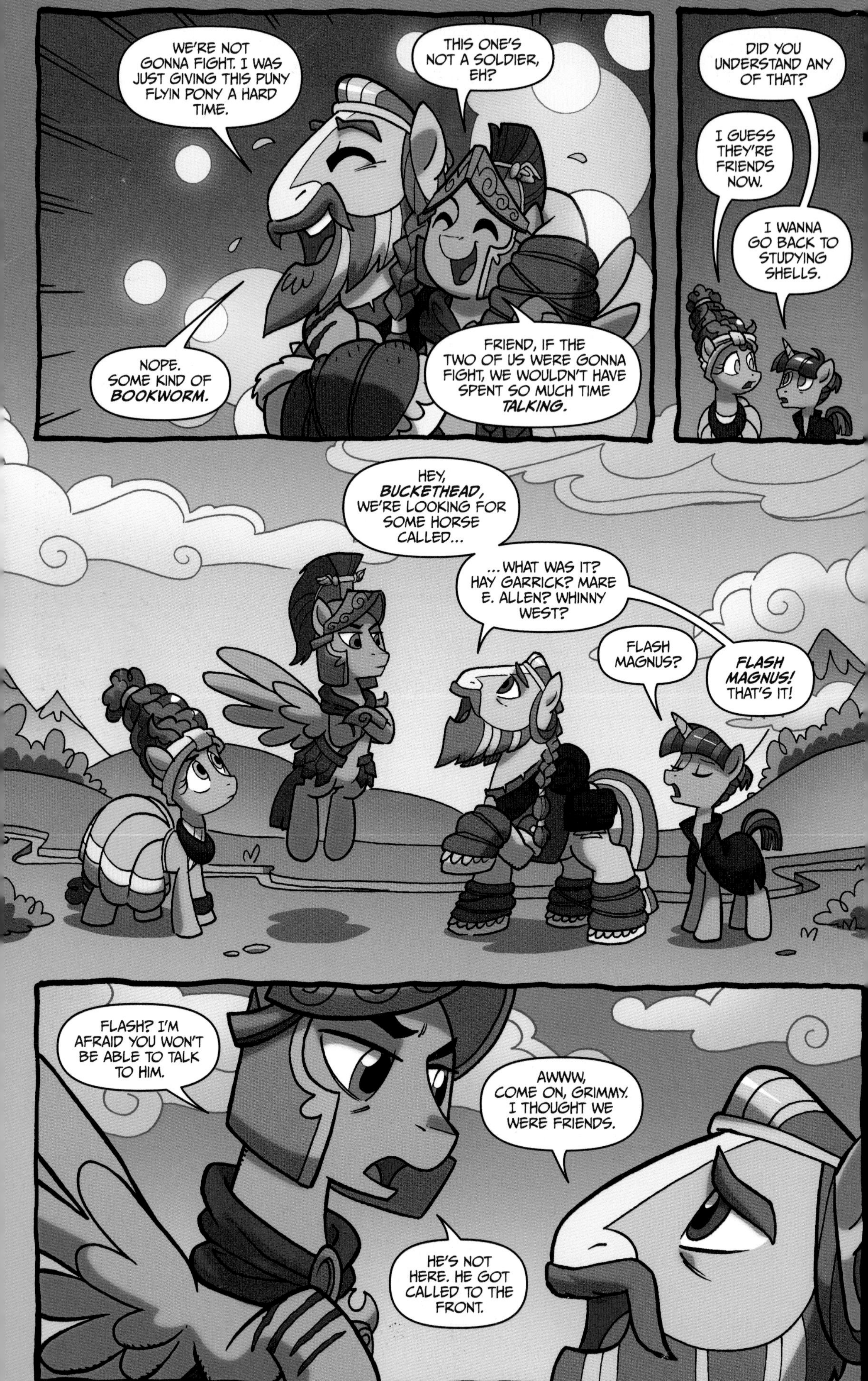
WE'RE NOT GONNA FIGHT. I WAS JUST GIVING THIS PUNY FLYIN PONY A HARD TIME.
THIS ONE'S NOT A SOLDIER, EH?
NOPE. SOME KIND OF *BOOKWORM.*
FRIEND, IF THE TWO OF US WERE GONNA FIGHT, WE WOULDN'T HAVE SPENT SO MUCH TIME *TALKING.*
DID YOU UNDERSTAND ANY OF THAT?
I GUESS THEY'RE FRIENDS NOW.
I WANNA GO BACK TO STUDYING SHELLS.
HEY, *BUCKETHEAD,* WE'RE LOOKING FOR SOME HORSE CALLED...
...WHAT WAS IT? HAY GARRICK? MARE E. ALLEN? WHINNY WEST?
FLASH MAGNUS?
FLASH MAGNUS! THAT'S IT!
FLASH? I'M AFRAID YOU WON'T BE ABLE TO TALK TO HIM.
AWWW, COME ON, GRIMMY. I THOUGHT WE WERE FRIENDS.
HE'S NOT HERE. HE GOT CALLED TO THE FRONT.

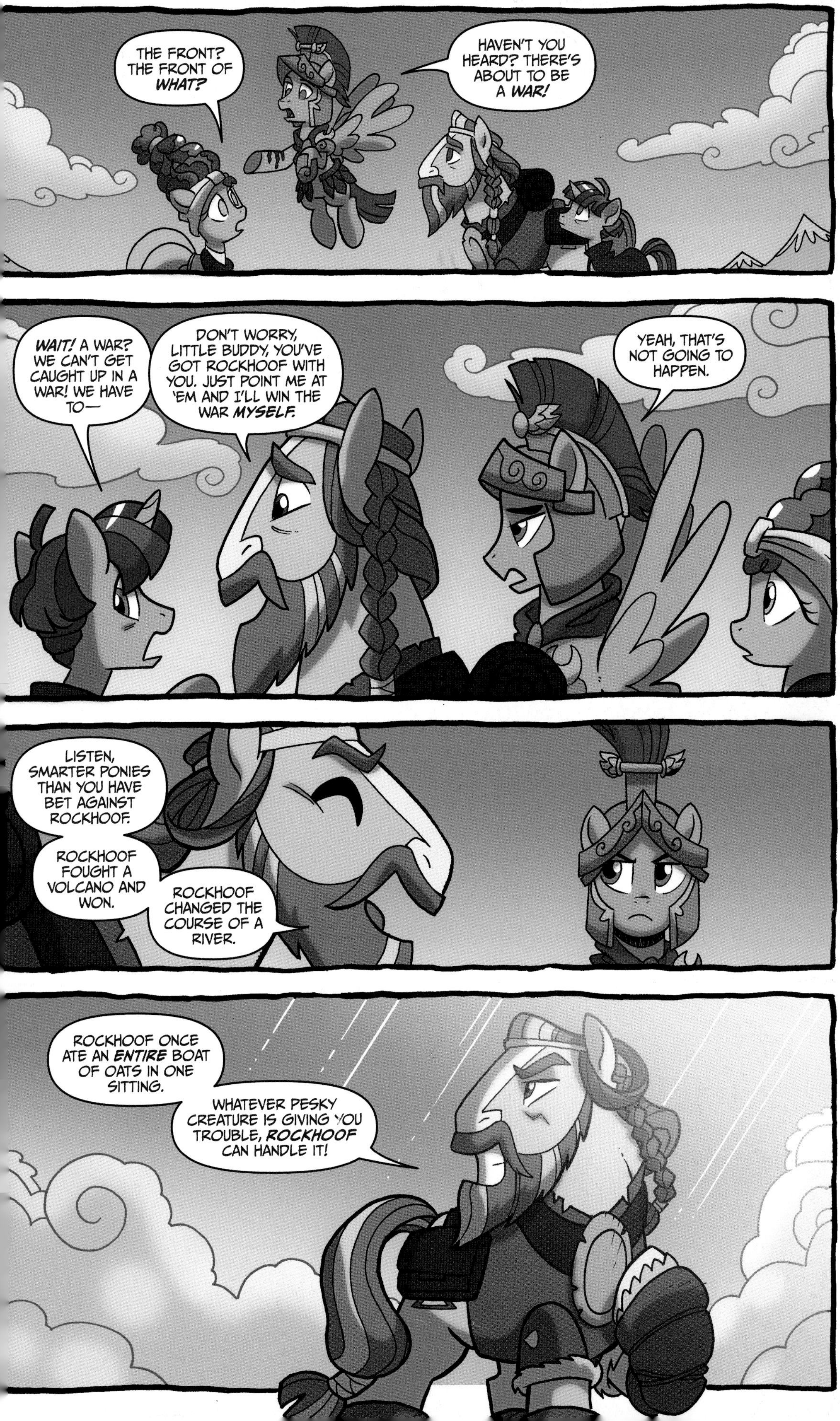
THE FRONT? THE FRONT OF *WHAT?*
HAVEN'T YOU HEARD? THERE'S ABOUT TO BE A *WAR!*
WAIT! A WAR? WE CAN'T GET CAUGHT UP IN A WAR! WE HAVE TO—
DON'T WORRY, LITTLE BUDDY, YOU'VE GOT ROCKHOOF WITH YOU. JUST POINT ME AT 'EM AND I'LL WIN THE WAR *MYSELF.*
YEAH, THAT'S NOT GOING TO HAPPEN.
LISTEN, SMARTER PONIES THAN YOU HAVE BET AGAINST ROCKHOOF.
ROCKHOOF FOUGHT A VOLCANO AND WON.
ROCKHOOF CHANGED THE COURSE OF A RIVER.
ROCKHOOF ONCE ATE AN *ENTIRE* BOAT OF OATS IN ONE SITTING.
WHATEVER PESKY CREATURE IS GIVING YOU TROUBLE, *ROCKHOOF* CAN HANDLE IT!

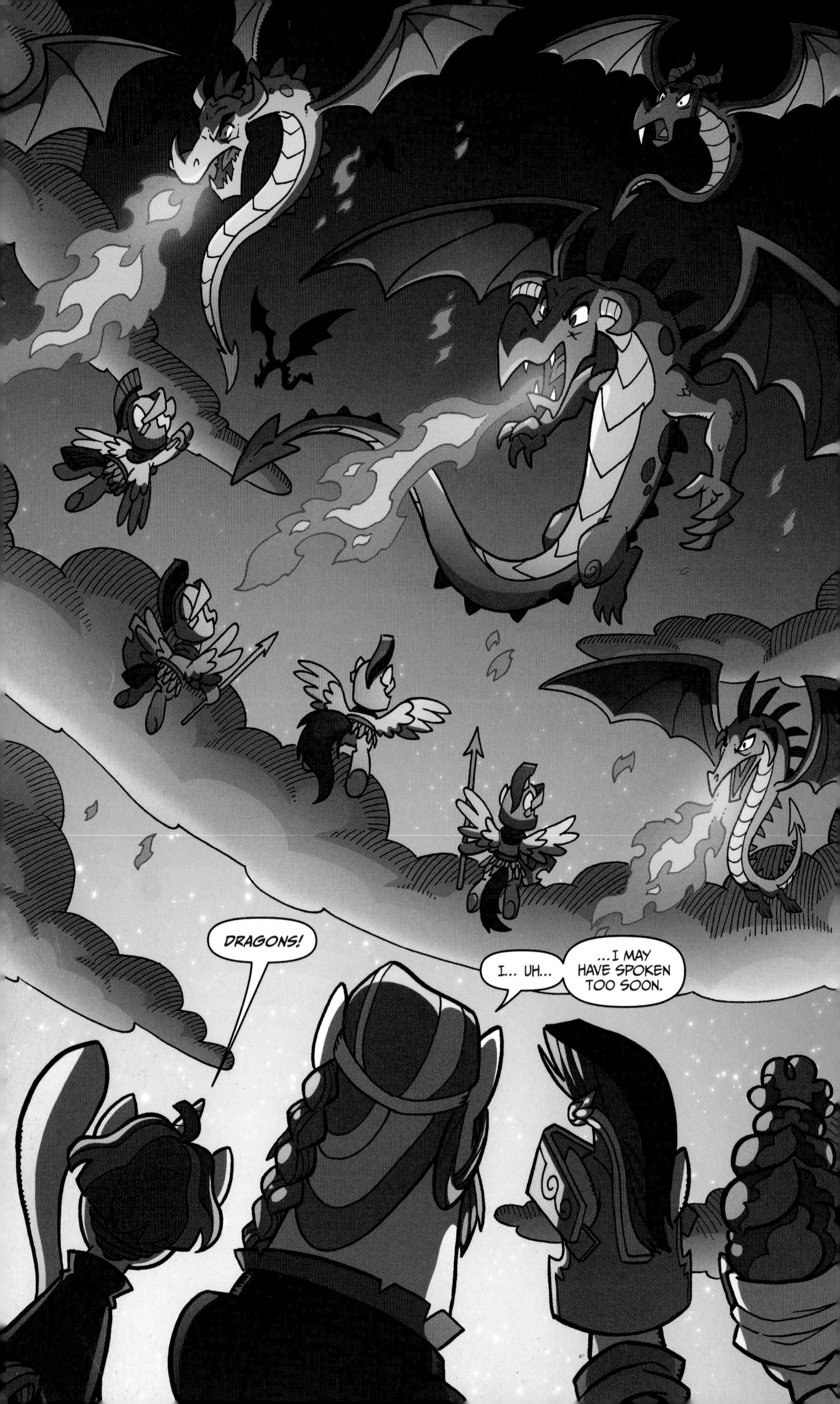
DRAGONS!
I... UH...
...I MAY HAVE SPOKEN TOO SOON.

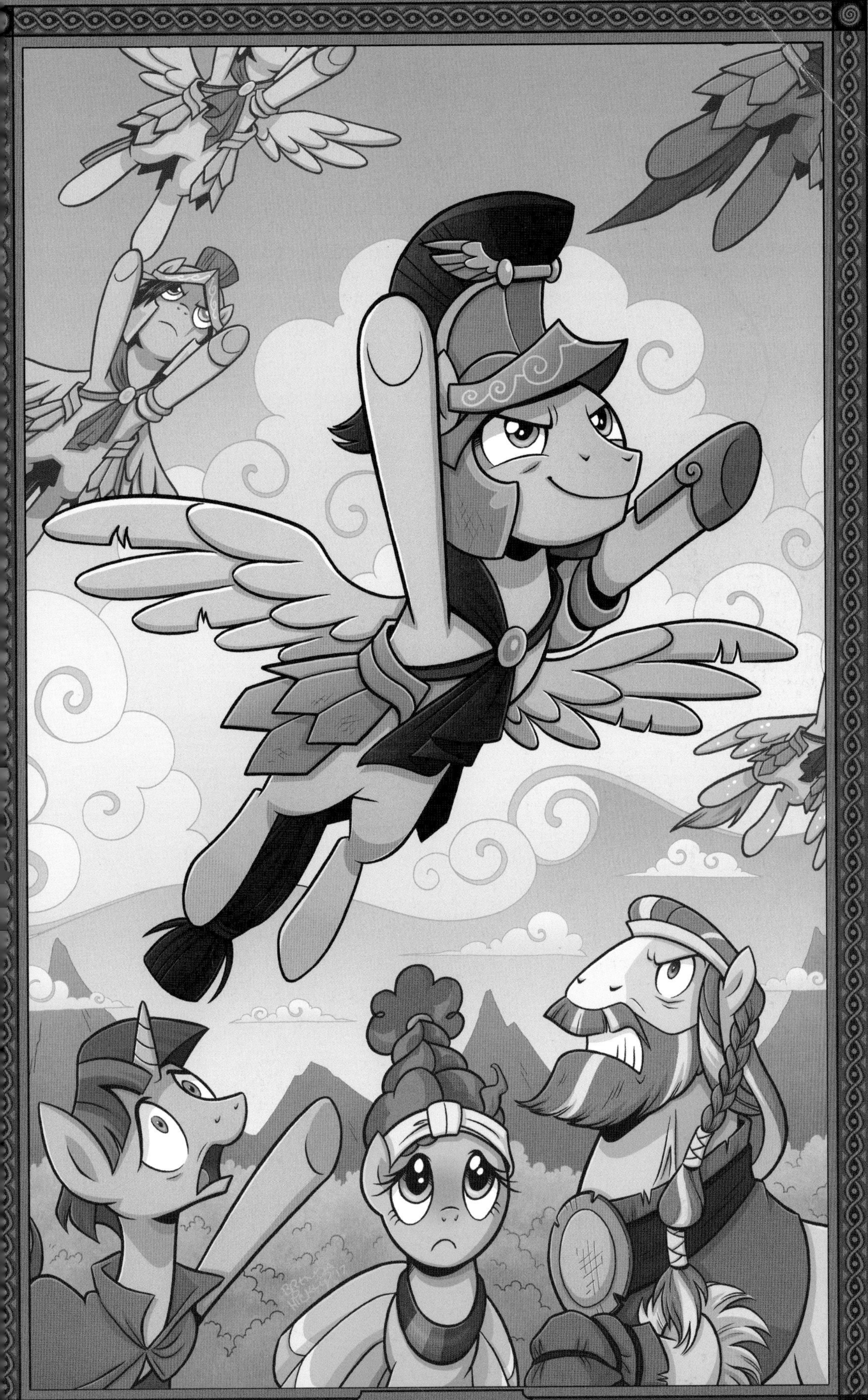
ART BY BRENDA HICKEY

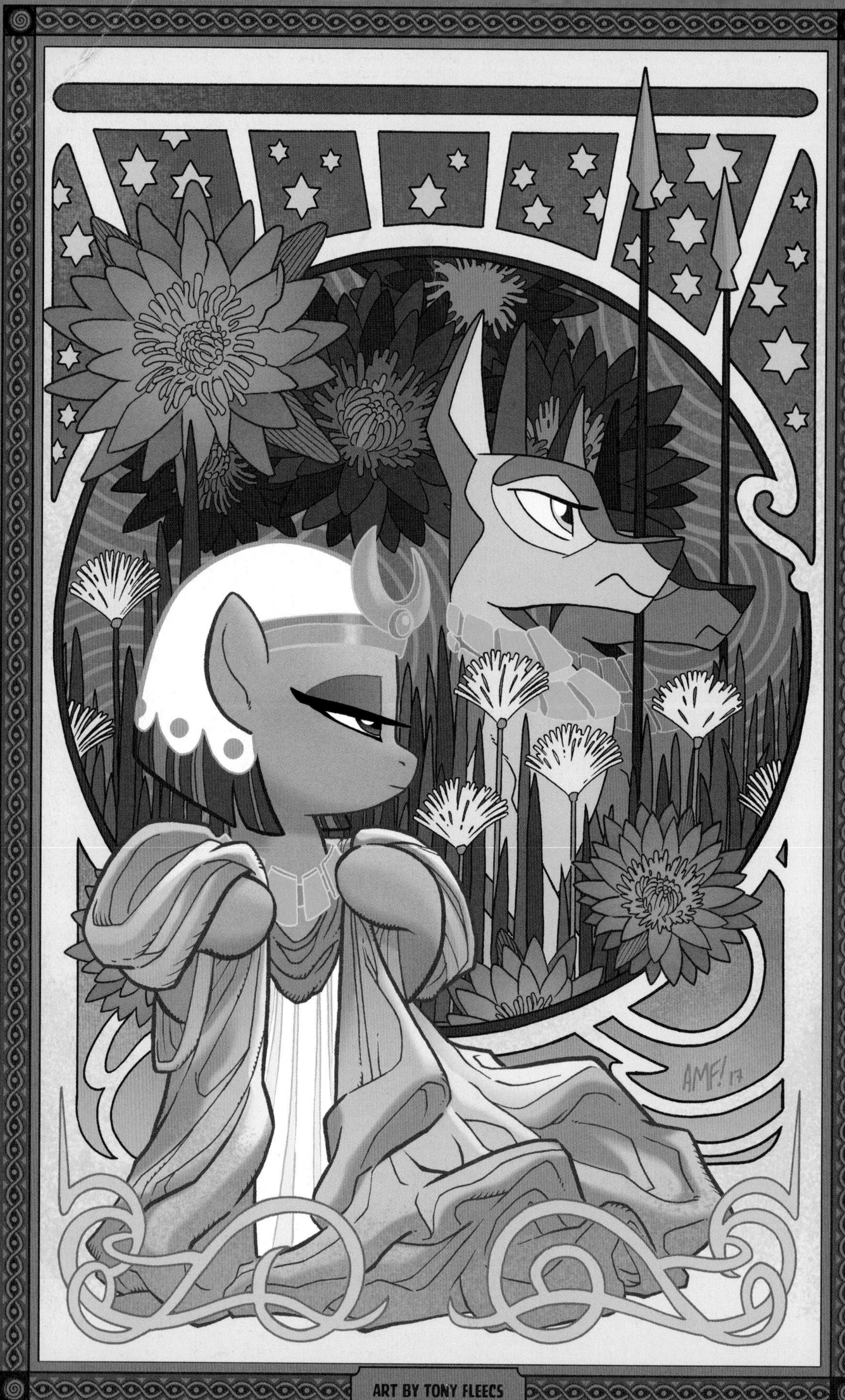
AMF! 17

ART BY TONY FLEECS

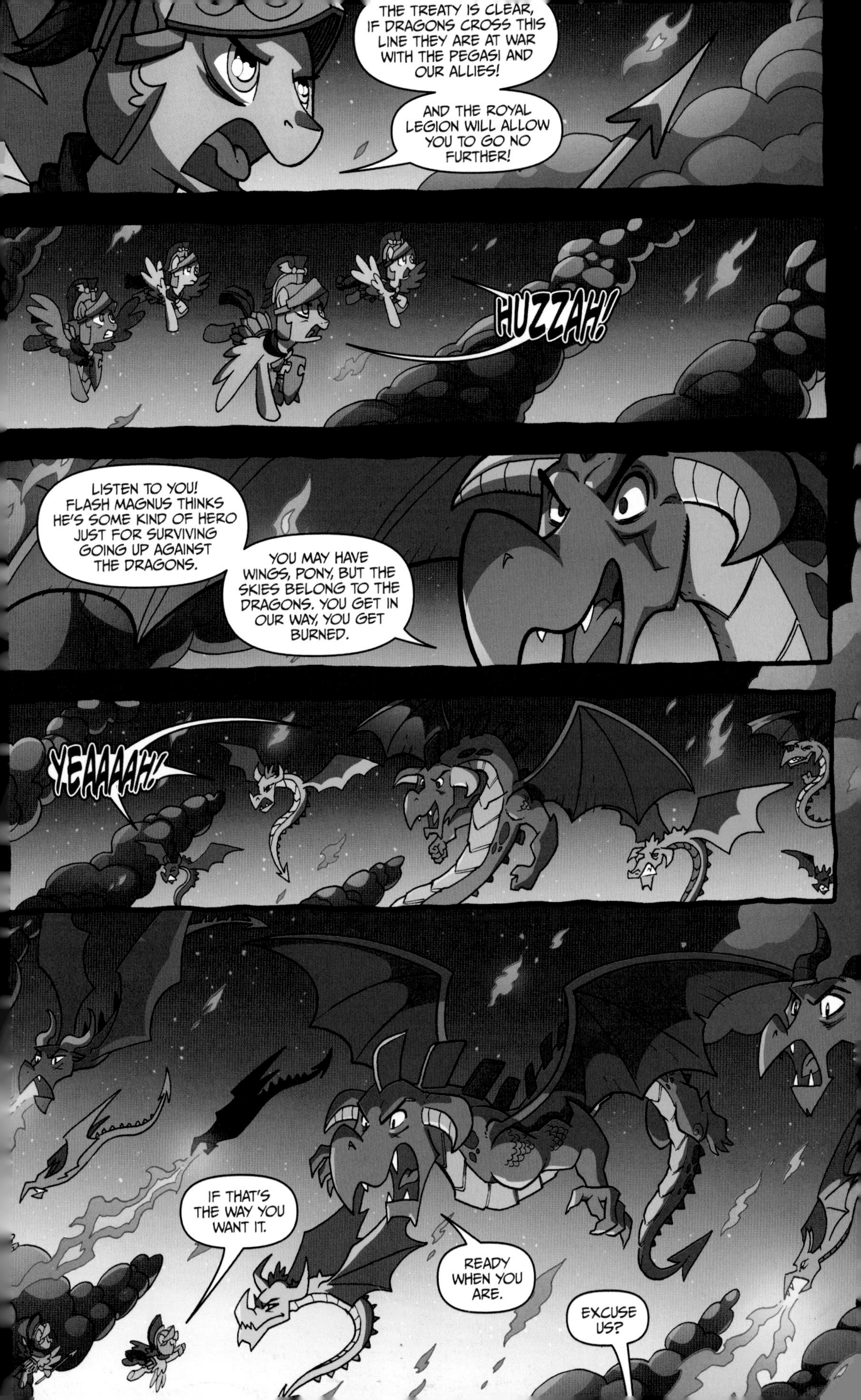
THE TREATY IS CLEAR, IF DRAGONS CROSS THIS LINE THEY ARE AT WAR WITH THE PEGASI AND OUR ALLIES!
AND THE ROYAL LEGION WILL ALLOW YOU TO GO NO FURTHER!
HUZZAH!
LISTEN TO YOU! FLASH MAGNUS THINKS HE'S SOME KIND OF HERO JUST FOR SURVIVING GOING UP AGAINST THE DRAGONS.
YOU MAY HAVE WINGS, PONY, BUT THE SKIES BELONG TO THE DRAGONS. YOU GET IN OUR WAY, YOU GET BURNED.
YEAAAAH!
IF THAT'S THE WAY YOU WANT IT.
READY WHEN YOU ARE.
EXCUSE US?

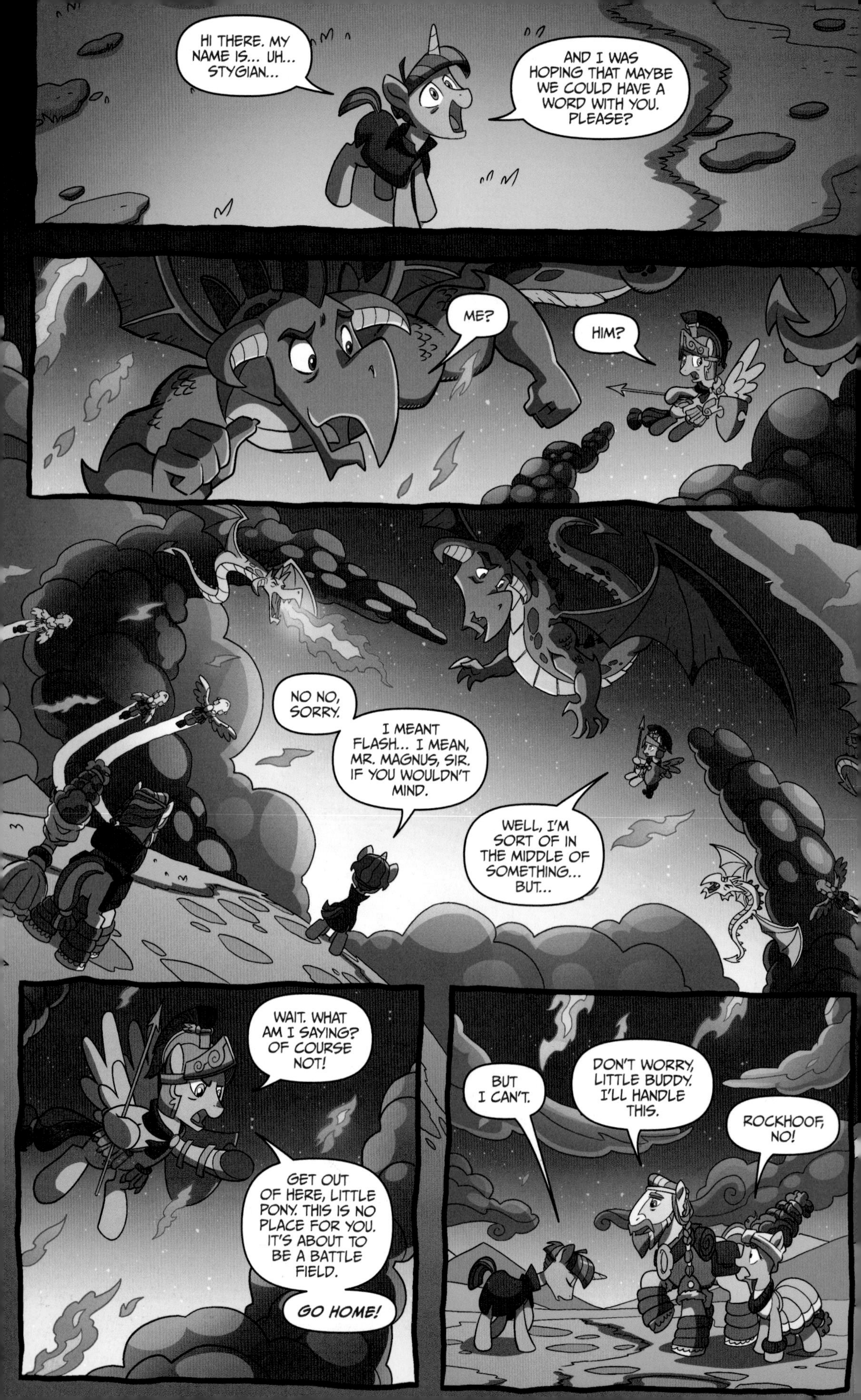
HI THERE. MY NAME IS... UH... STYGIAN...
AND I WAS HOPING THAT MAYBE WE COULD HAVE A WORD WITH YOU. PLEASE?
ME?
HIM?
NO NO, SORRY.
I MEANT FLASH... I MEAN, MR. MAGNUS, SIR. IF YOU WOULDN'T MIND.
WELL, I'M SORT OF IN THE MIDDLE OF SOMETHING... BUT...
WAIT. WHAT AM I SAYING? OF COURSE NOT!
GET OUT OF HERE, LITTLE PONY. THIS IS NO PLACE FOR YOU. IT'S ABOUT TO BE A BATTLE FIELD.
GO HOME!
BUT I CAN'T.
DON'T WORRY, LITTLE BUDDY. I'LL HANDLE THIS.
ROCKHOOF, NO!

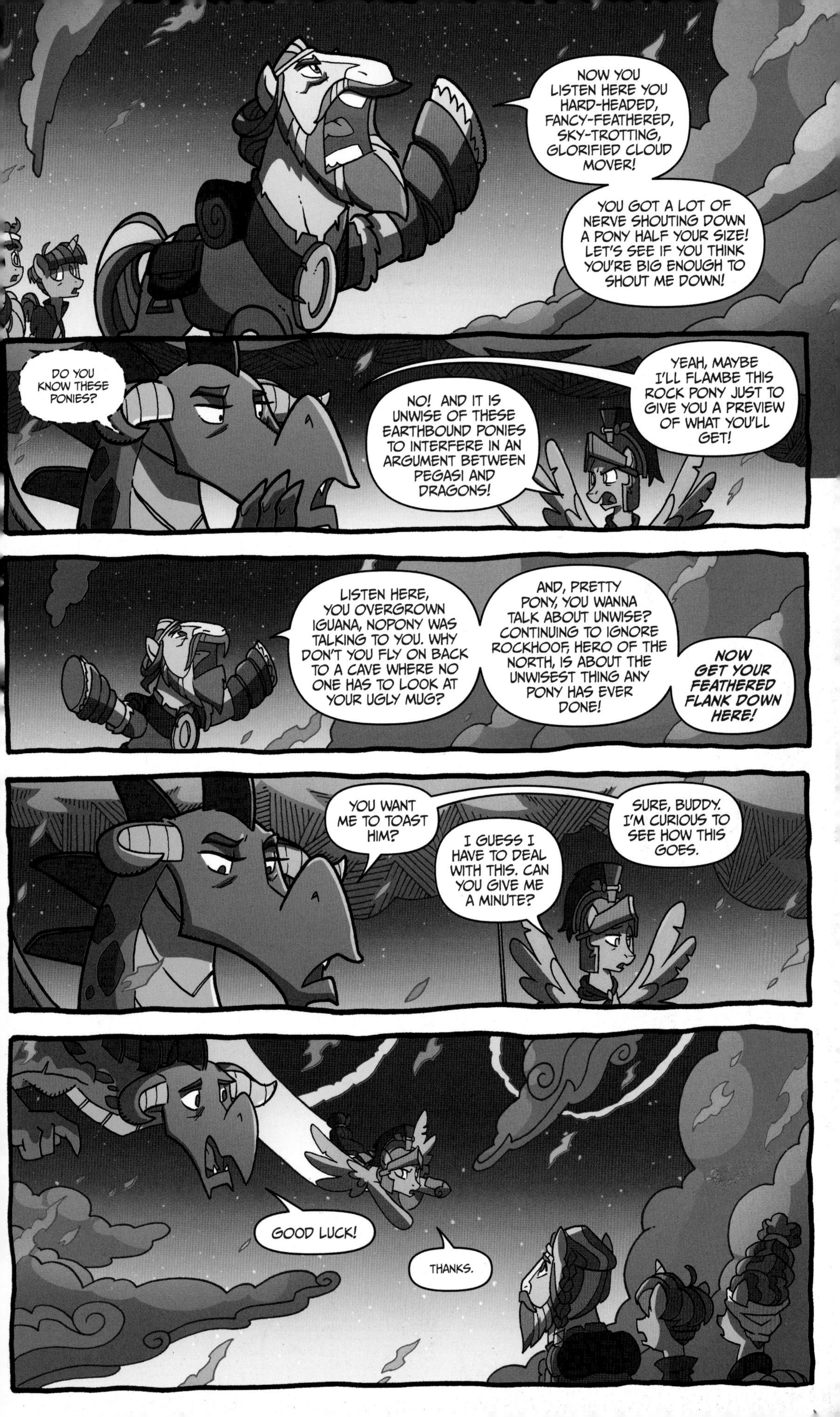
NOW YOU LISTEN HERE YOU HARD-HEADED, FANCY-FEATHERED, SKY-TROTTING, GLORIFIED CLOUD MOVER!
YOU GOT A LOT OF NERVE SHOUTING DOWN A PONY HALF YOUR SIZE! LET'S SEE IF YOU THINK YOU'RE BIG ENOUGH TO SHOUT ME DOWN!
DO YOU KNOW THESE PONIES?
NO! AND IT IS UNWISE OF THESE EARTHBOUND PONIES TO INTERFERE IN AN ARGUMENT BETWEEN PEGASI AND DRAGONS!
YEAH, MAYBE I'LL FLAMBE THIS ROCK PONY JUST TO GIVE YOU A PREVIEW OF WHAT YOU'LL GET!
LISTEN HERE, YOU OVERGROWN IGUANA, NOPONY WAS TALKING TO YOU. WHY DON'T YOU FLY ON BACK TO A CAVE WHERE NO ONE HAS TO LOOK AT YOUR UGLY MUG?
AND, PRETTY PONY, YOU WANNA TALK ABOUT UNWISE? CONTINUING TO IGNORE ROCKHOOF, HERO OF THE NORTH, IS ABOUT THE UNWISEST THING ANY PONY HAS EVER DONE!
NOW GET YOUR FEATHERED FLANK DOWN HERE!
YOU WANT ME TO TOAST HIM?
I GUESS I HAVE TO DEAL WITH THIS. CAN YOU GIVE ME A MINUTE?
SURE, BUDDY. I'M CURIOUS TO SEE HOW THIS GOES.
GOOD LUCK!
THANKS.

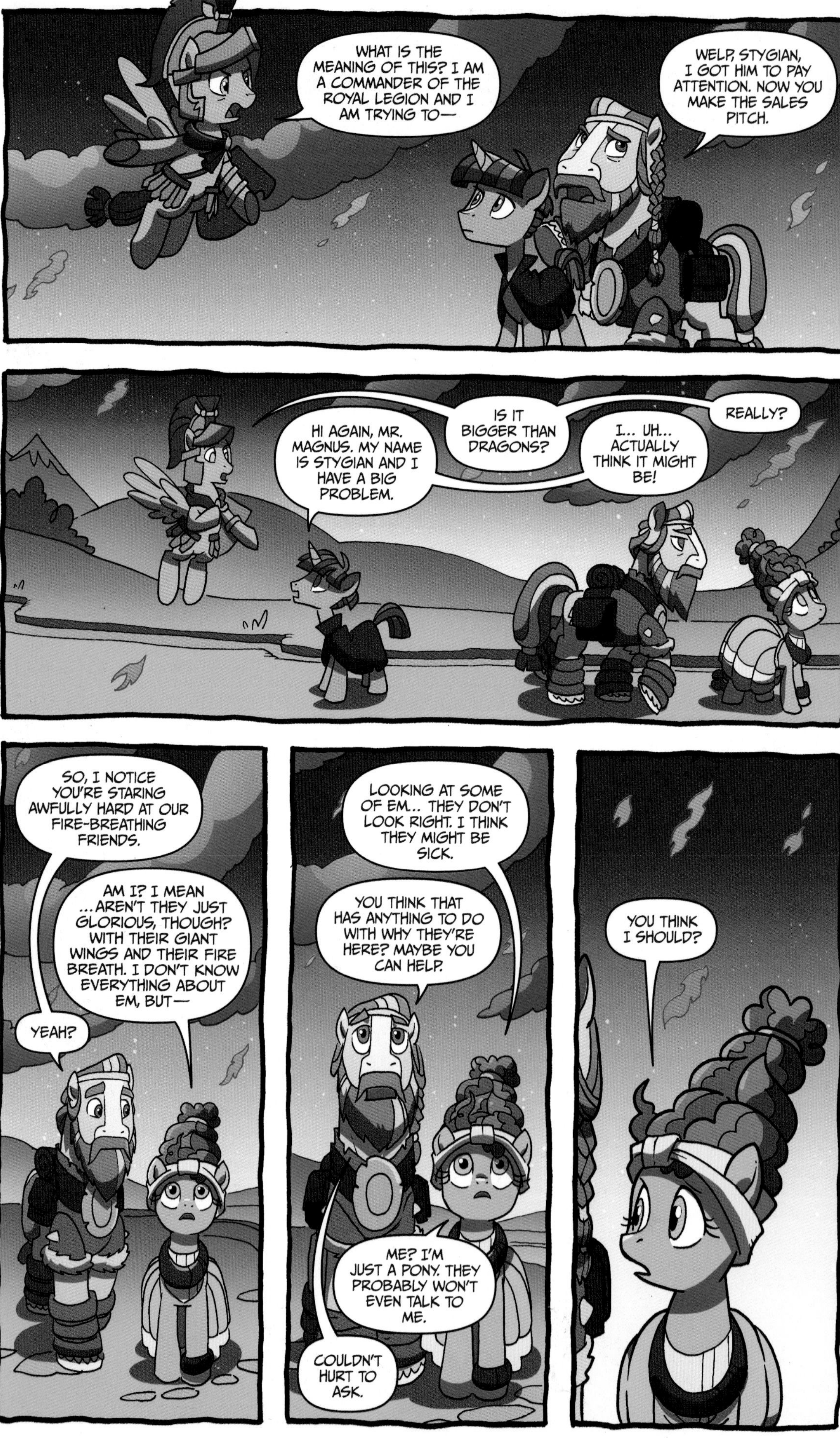
WHAT IS THE MEANING OF THIS? I AM A COMMANDER OF THE ROYAL LEGION AND I AM TRYING TO—
WELP, STYGIAN, I GOT HIM TO PAY ATTENTION. NOW YOU MAKE THE SALES PITCH.
HI AGAIN, MR. MAGNUS. MY NAME IS STYGIAN AND I HAVE A BIG PROBLEM.
IS IT BIGGER THAN DRAGONS?
I... UH... ACTUALLY THINK IT MIGHT BE!
REALLY?
SO, I NOTICE YOU'RE STARING AWFULLY HARD AT OUR FIRE-BREATHING FRIENDS.
AM I? I MEAN ...AREN'T THEY JUST GLORIOUS, THOUGH? WITH THEIR GIANT WINGS AND THEIR FIRE BREATH. I DON'T KNOW EVERYTHING ABOUT EM, BUT—
YEAH?
LOOKING AT SOME OF EM... THEY DON'T LOOK RIGHT. I THINK THEY MIGHT BE SICK.
YOU THINK THAT HAS ANYTHING TO DO WITH WHY THEY'RE HERE? MAYBE YOU CAN HELP.
ME? I'M JUST A PONY. THEY PROBABLY WON'T EVEN TALK TO ME.
COULDN'T HURT TO ASK.
YOU THINK I SHOULD?

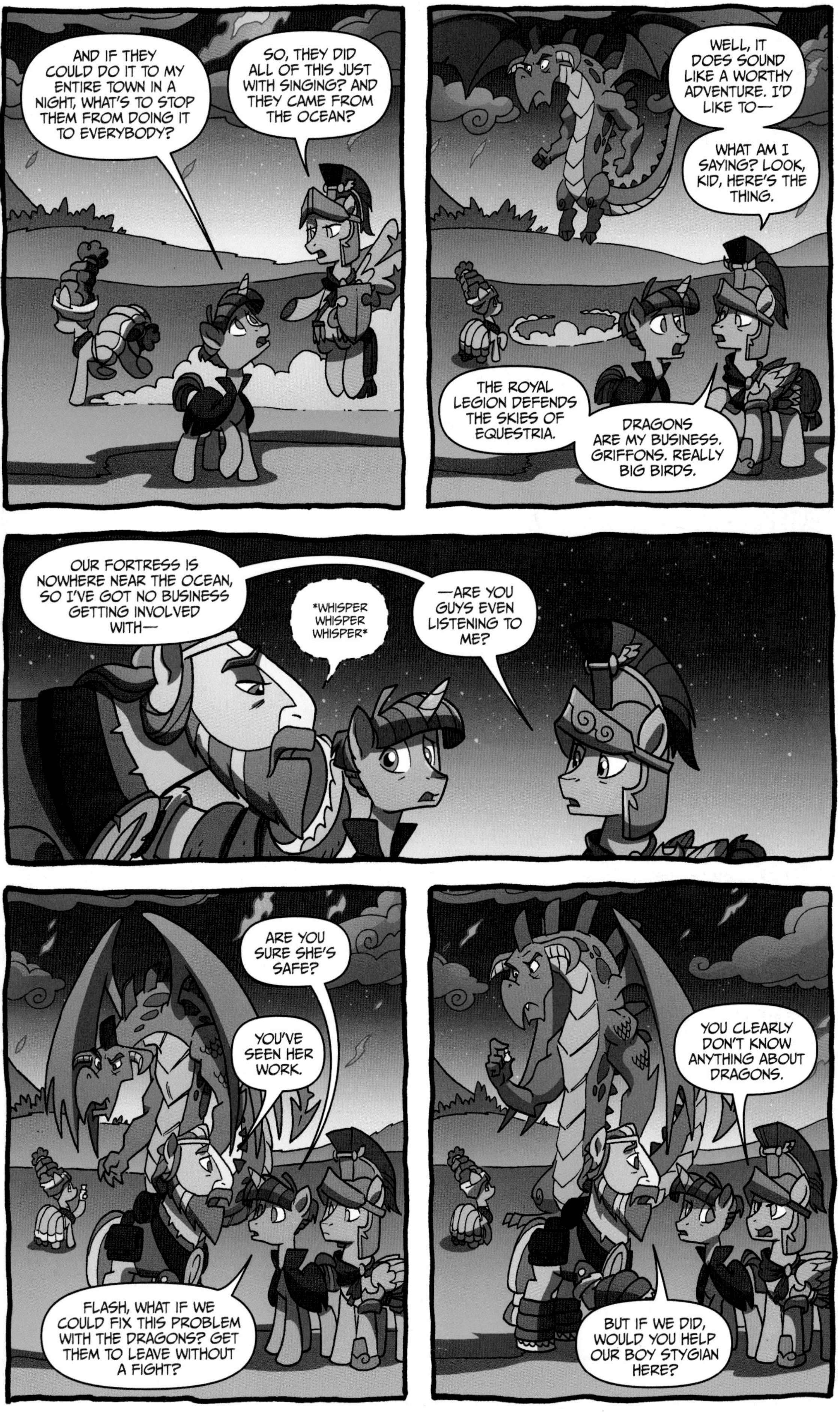
AND IF THEY COULD DO IT TO MY ENTIRE TOWN IN A NIGHT, WHAT'S TO STOP THEM FROM DOING IT TO EVERYBODY?
SO, THEY DID ALL OF THIS JUST WITH SINGING? AND THEY CAME FROM THE OCEAN?
WELL, IT DOES SOUND LIKE A WORTHY ADVENTURE. I'D LIKE TO—
WHAT AM I SAYING? LOOK, KID, HERE'S THE THING.
THE ROYAL LEGION DEFENDS THE SKIES OF EQUESTRIA.
DRAGONS ARE MY BUSINESS. GRIFFONS. REALLY BIG BIRDS.
OUR FORTRESS IS NOWHERE NEAR THE OCEAN, SO I'VE GOT NO BUSINESS GETTING INVOLVED WITH—
WHISPER WHISPER WHISPER
—ARE YOU GUYS EVEN LISTENING TO ME?
ARE YOU SURE SHE'S SAFE?
YOU'VE SEEN HER WORK.
FLASH, WHAT IF WE COULD FIX THIS PROBLEM WITH THE DRAGONS? GET THEM TO LEAVE WITHOUT A FIGHT?
YOU CLEARLY DON'T KNOW ANYTHING ABOUT DRAGONS.
BUT IF WE DID, WOULD YOU HELP OUR BOY STYGIAN HERE?

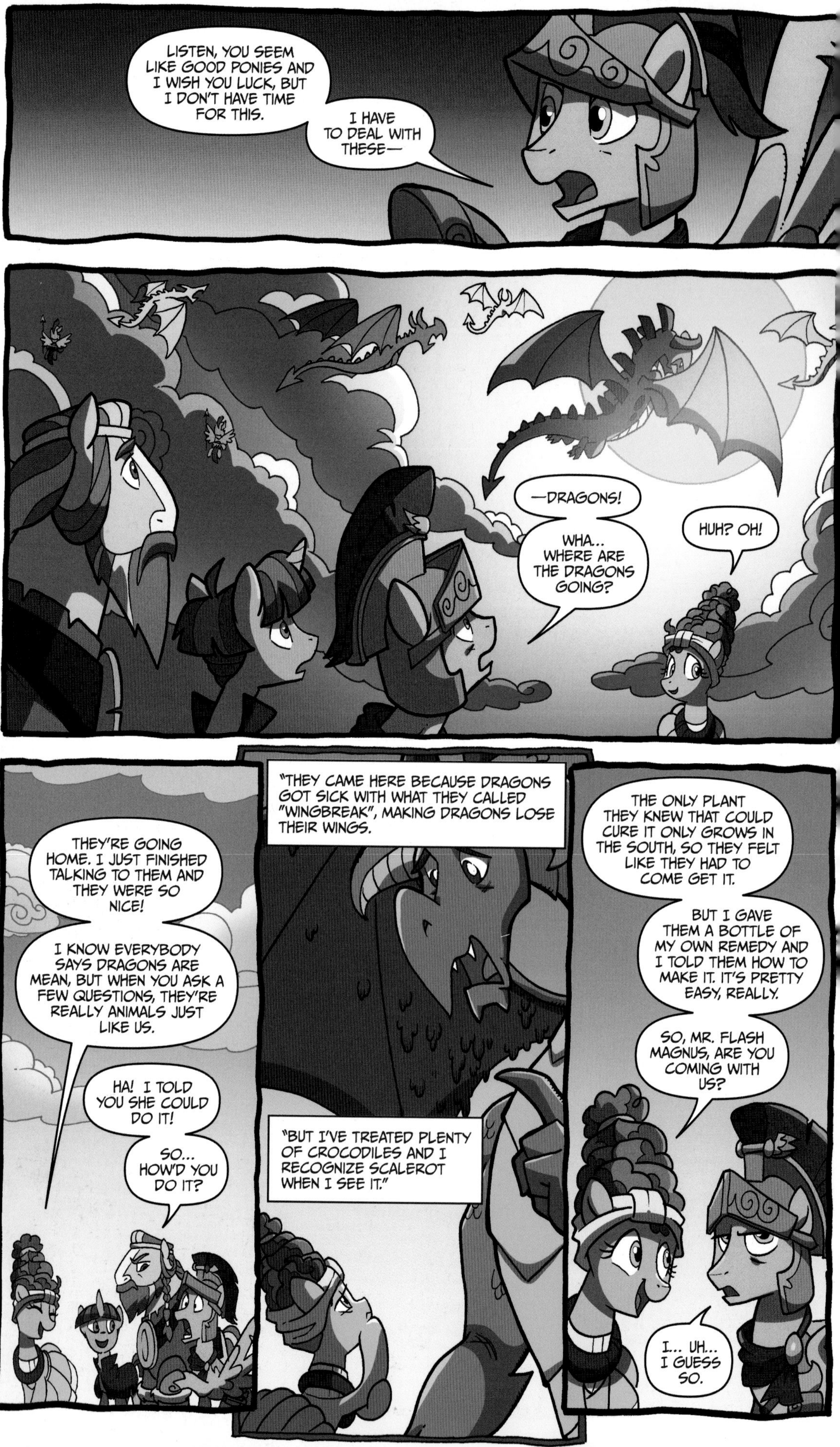
LISTEN, YOU SEEM LIKE GOOD PONIES AND I WISH YOU LUCK, BUT I DON'T HAVE TIME FOR THIS.
I HAVE TO DEAL WITH THESE—
—DRAGONS!
WHA... WHERE ARE THE DRAGONS GOING?
HUH? OH!
THEY'RE GOING HOME. I JUST FINISHED TALKING TO THEM AND THEY WERE SO NICE!
I KNOW EVERYBODY SAYS DRAGONS ARE MEAN, BUT WHEN YOU ASK A FEW QUESTIONS, THEY'RE REALLY ANIMALS JUST LIKE US.
HA! I TOLD YOU SHE COULD DO IT!
SO... HOW'D YOU DO IT?
"THEY CAME HERE BECAUSE DRAGONS GOT SICK WITH WHAT THEY CALLED "WINGBREAK", MAKING DRAGONS LOSE THEIR WINGS.
"BUT I'VE TREATED PLENTY OF CROCODILES AND I RECOGNIZE SCALEROT WHEN I SEE IT."
THE ONLY PLANT THEY KNEW THAT COULD CURE IT ONLY GROWS IN THE SOUTH, SO THEY FELT LIKE THEY HAD TO COME GET IT.
BUT I GAVE THEM A BOTTLE OF MY OWN REMEDY AND I TOLD THEM HOW TO MAKE IT. IT'S PRETTY EASY, REALLY.
SO, MR. FLASH MAGNUS, ARE YOU COMING WITH US?
I... UH... I GUESS SO.

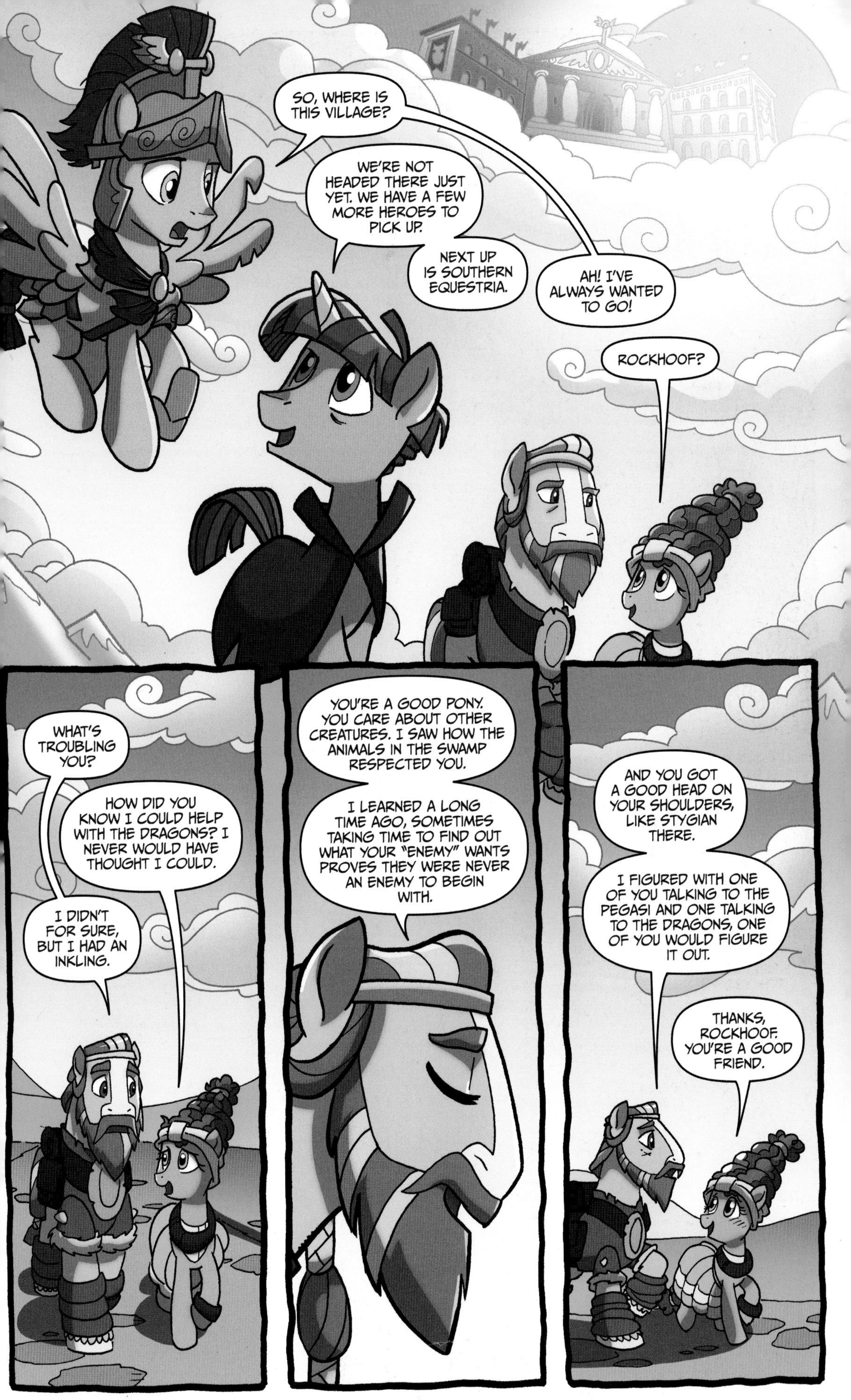
SO, WHERE IS THIS VILLAGE?
WE'RE NOT HEADED THERE JUST YET. WE HAVE A FEW MORE HEROES TO PICK UP.
NEXT UP IS SOUTHERN EQUESTRIA.
AH! I'VE ALWAYS WANTED TO GO!
ROCKHOOF?
WHAT'S TROUBLING YOU?
HOW DID YOU KNOW I COULD HELP WITH THE DRAGONS? I NEVER WOULD HAVE THOUGHT I COULD.
I DIDN'T FOR SURE, BUT I HAD AN INKLING.
YOU'RE A GOOD PONY. YOU CARE ABOUT OTHER CREATURES. I SAW HOW THE ANIMALS IN THE SWAMP RESPECTED YOU.
I LEARNED A LONG TIME AGO, SOMETIMES TAKING TIME TO FIND OUT WHAT YOUR "ENEMY" WANTS PROVES THEY WERE NEVER AN ENEMY TO BEGIN WITH.
AND YOU GOT A GOOD HEAD ON YOUR SHOULDERS, LIKE STYGIAN THERE.
I FIGURED WITH ONE OF YOU TALKING TO THE PEGASI AND ONE TALKING TO THE DRAGONS, ONE OF YOU WOULD FIGURE IT OUT.
THANKS, ROCKHOOF. YOU'RE A GOOD FRIEND.

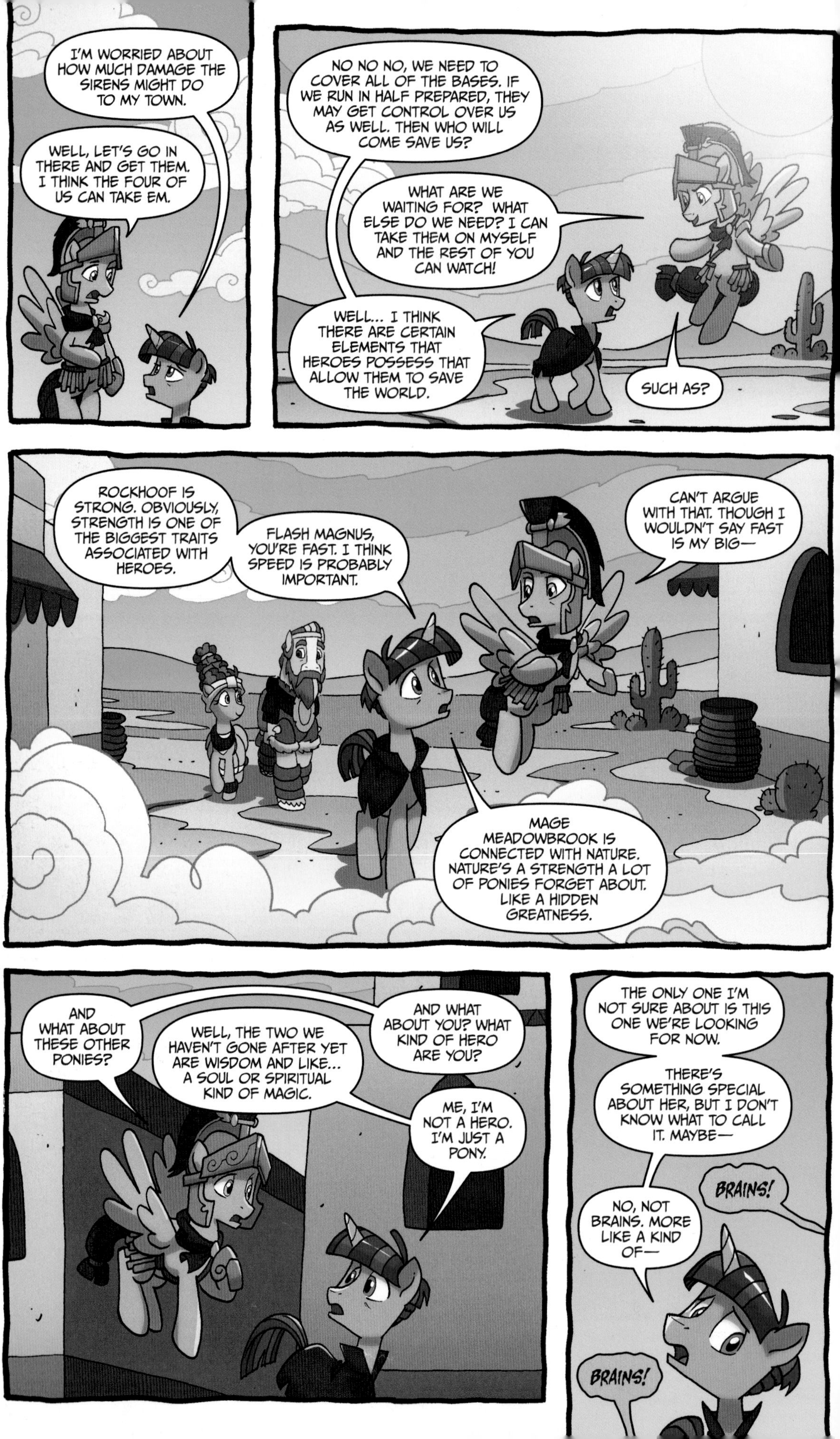

I'M WORRIED ABOUT HOW MUCH DAMAGE THE SIRENS MIGHT DO TO MY TOWN.
WELL, LET'S GO IN THERE AND GET THEM. I THINK THE FOUR OF US CAN TAKE EM.
NO NO NO, WE NEED TO COVER ALL OF THE BASES. IF WE RUN IN HALF PREPARED, THEY MAY GET CONTROL OVER US AS WELL. THEN WHO WILL COME SAVE US?
WHAT ARE WE WAITING FOR? WHAT ELSE DO WE NEED? I CAN TAKE THEM ON MYSELF AND THE REST OF YOU CAN WATCH!
WELL... I THINK THERE ARE CERTAIN ELEMENTS THAT HEROES POSSESS THAT ALLOW THEM TO SAVE THE WORLD.
SUCH AS?
ROCKHOOF IS STRONG. OBVIOUSLY, STRENGTH IS ONE OF THE BIGGEST TRAITS ASSOCIATED WITH HEROES.
FLASH MAGNUS, YOU'RE FAST. I THINK SPEED IS PROBABLY IMPORTANT.
CAN'T ARGUE WITH THAT. THOUGH I WOULDN'T SAY FAST IS MY BIG—
MAGE MEADOWBROOK IS CONNECTED WITH NATURE. NATURE'S A STRENGTH A LOT OF PONIES FORGET ABOUT. LIKE A HIDDEN GREATNESS.
AND WHAT ABOUT THESE OTHER PONIES?
WELL, THE TWO WE HAVEN'T GONE AFTER YET ARE WISDOM AND LIKE... A SOUL OR SPIRITUAL KIND OF MAGIC.
AND WHAT ABOUT YOU? WHAT KIND OF HERO ARE YOU?
ME, I'M NOT A HERO. I'M JUST A PONY.
THE ONLY ONE I'M NOT SURE ABOUT IS THIS ONE WE'RE LOOKING FOR NOW.
THERE'S SOMETHING SPECIAL ABOUT HER, BUT I DON'T KNOW WHAT TO CALL IT. MAYBE—
BRAINS!
NO, NOT BRAINS. MORE LIKE A KIND OF—
BRAINS!

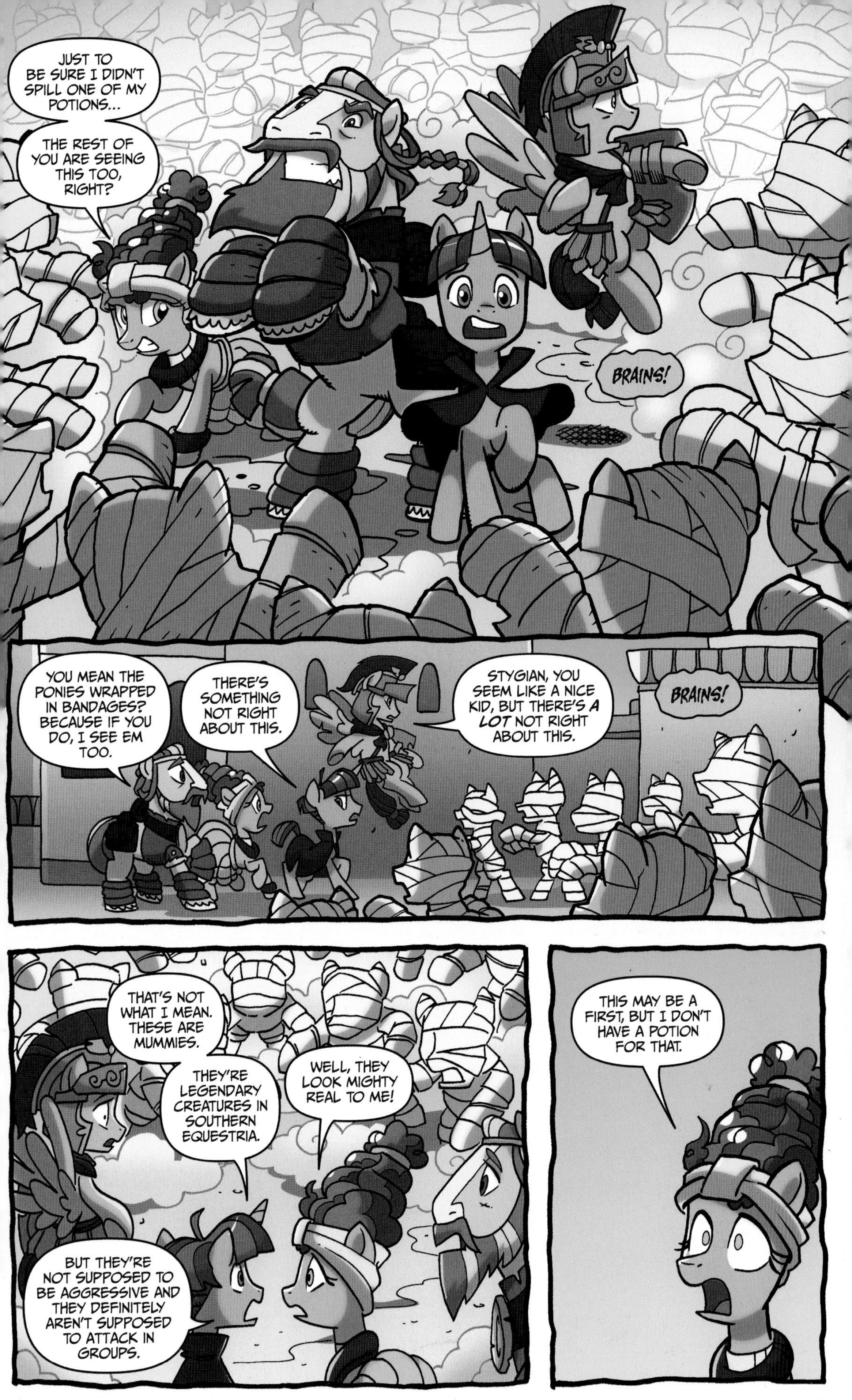
JUST TO BE SURE I DIDN'T SPILL ONE OF MY POTIONS...
THE REST OF YOU ARE SEEING THIS TOO, RIGHT?
BRAINS!
YOU MEAN THE PONIES WRAPPED IN BANDAGES? BECAUSE IF YOU DO, I SEE EM TOO.
THERE'S SOMETHING NOT RIGHT ABOUT THIS.
STYGIAN, YOU SEEM LIKE A NICE KID, BUT THERE'S A LOT NOT RIGHT ABOUT THIS.
BRAINS!
THAT'S NOT WHAT I MEAN. THESE ARE MUMMIES.
THEY'RE LEGENDARY CREATURES IN SOUTHERN EQUESTRIA.
WELL, THEY LOOK MIGHTY REAL TO ME!
BUT THEY'RE NOT SUPPOSED TO BE AGGRESSIVE AND THEY DEFINITELY AREN'T SUPPOSED TO ATTACK IN GROUPS.
THIS MAY BE A FIRST, BUT I DON'T HAVE A POTION FOR THAT.

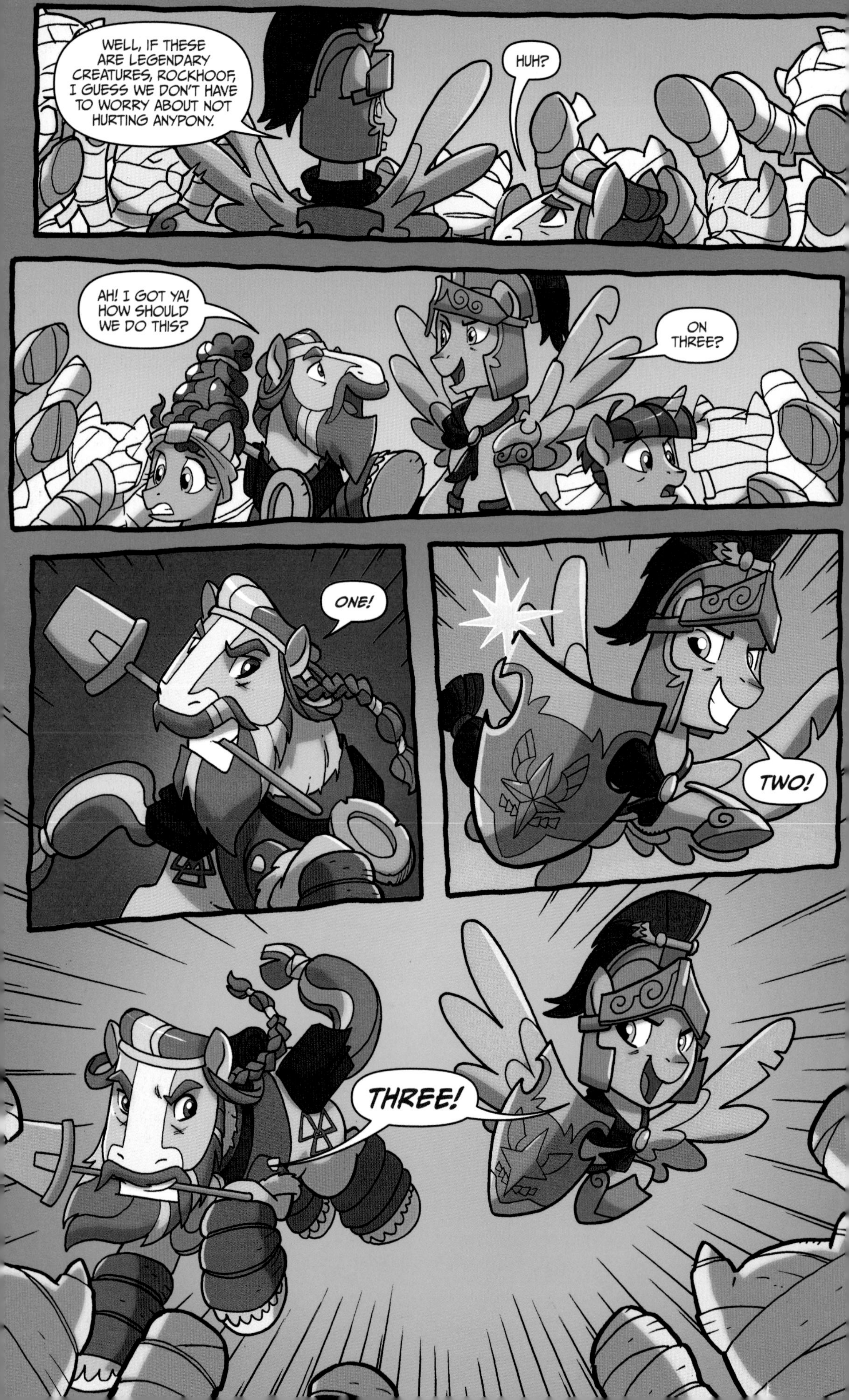
WELL, IF THESE ARE LEGENDARY CREATURES, ROCKHOOF, I GUESS WE DON'T HAVE TO WORRY ABOUT NOT HURTING ANYPONY.
HUH?
AH! I GOT YA! HOW SHOULD WE DO THIS?
ON THREE?
ONE!
TWO!
THREE!

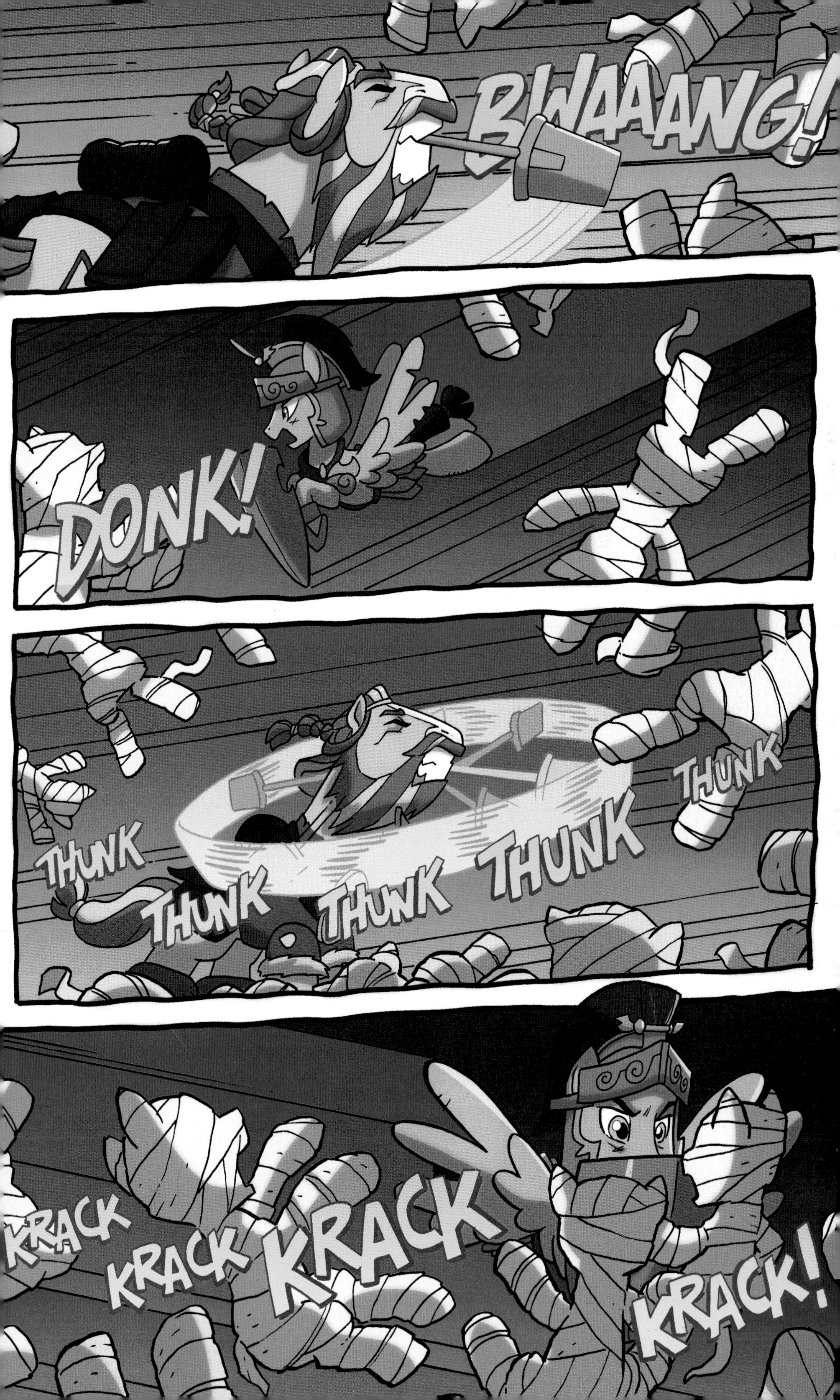
BWAAANG!
DONK!
THUNK
THUNK
THUNK
THUNK
THUNK
KRACK
KRACK
KRACK
KRACK!

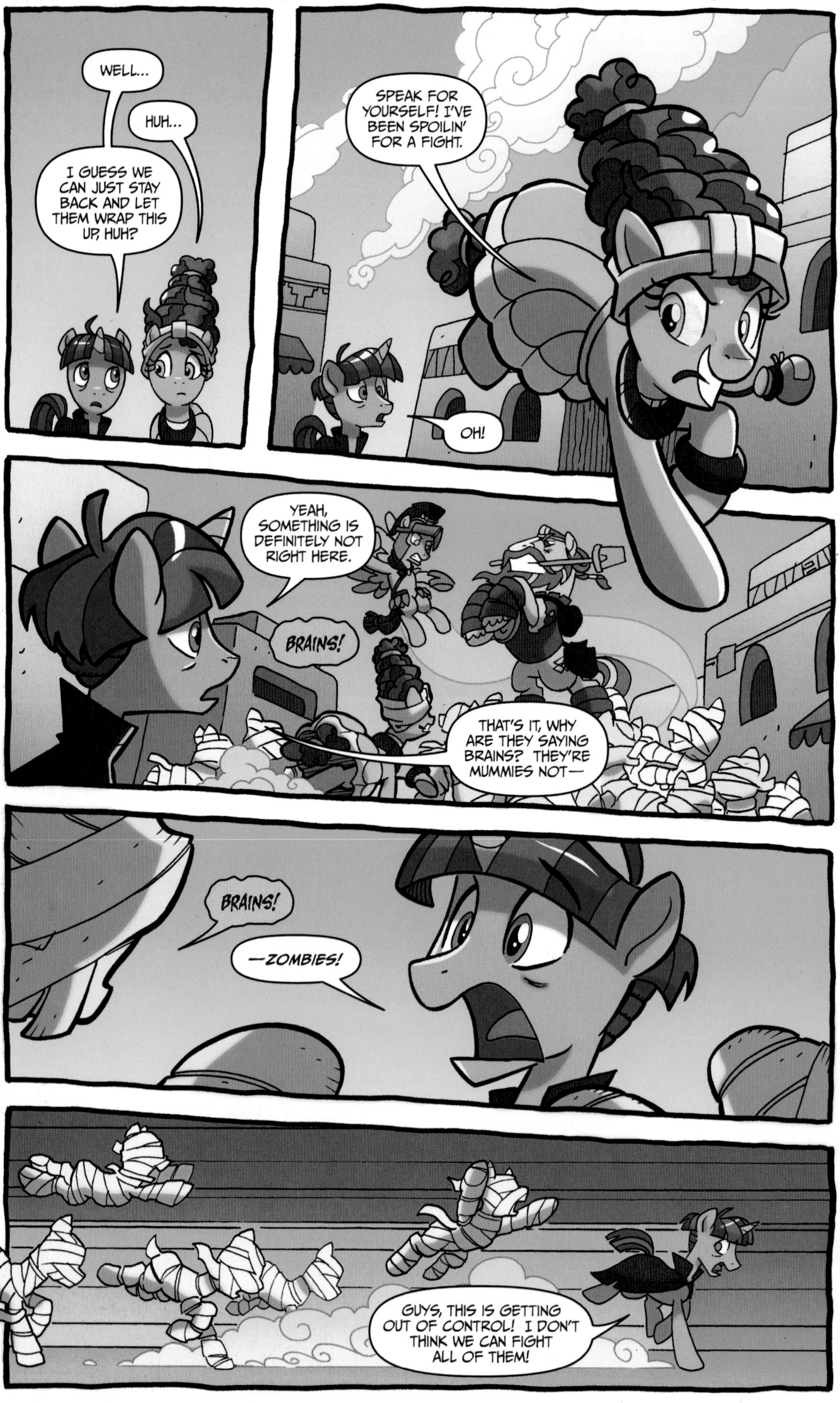
WELL...
HUH...
I GUESS WE CAN JUST STAY BACK AND LET THEM WRAP THIS UP, HUH?
SPEAK FOR YOURSELF! I'VE BEEN SPOILIN' FOR A FIGHT.
OH!
YEAH, SOMETHING IS DEFINITELY NOT RIGHT HERE.
BRAINS!
THAT'S IT, WHY ARE THEY SAYING BRAINS? THEY'RE MUMMIES NOT—
BRAINS!
—ZOMBIES!
GUYS, THIS IS GETTING OUT OF CONTROL! I DON'T THINK WE CAN FIGHT ALL OF THEM!

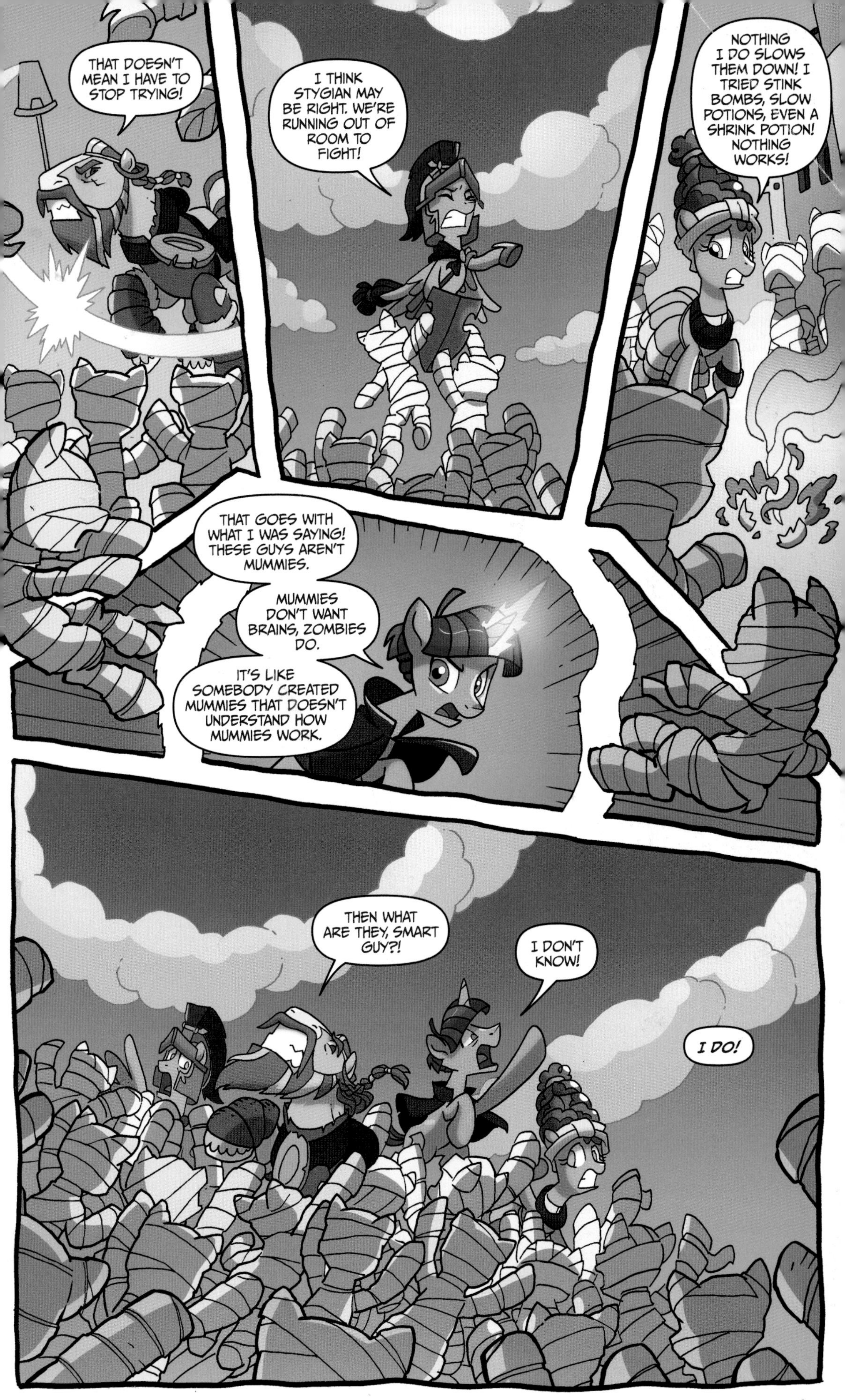
THAT DOESN'T MEAN I HAVE TO STOP TRYING!
I THINK STYGIAN MAY BE RIGHT. WE'RE RUNNING OUT OF ROOM TO FIGHT!
NOTHING I DO SLOWS THEM DOWN! I TRIED STINK BOMBS, SLOW POTIONS, EVEN A SHRINK POTION! NOTHING WORKS!
THAT GOES WITH WHAT I WAS SAYING! THESE GUYS AREN'T MUMMIES.
MUMMIES DON'T WANT BRAINS, ZOMBIES DO.
IT'S LIKE SOMEBODY CREATED MUMMIES THAT DOESN'T UNDERSTAND HOW MUMMIES WORK.
THEN WHAT ARE THEY, SMART GUY?!
I DON'T KNOW!
I DO!

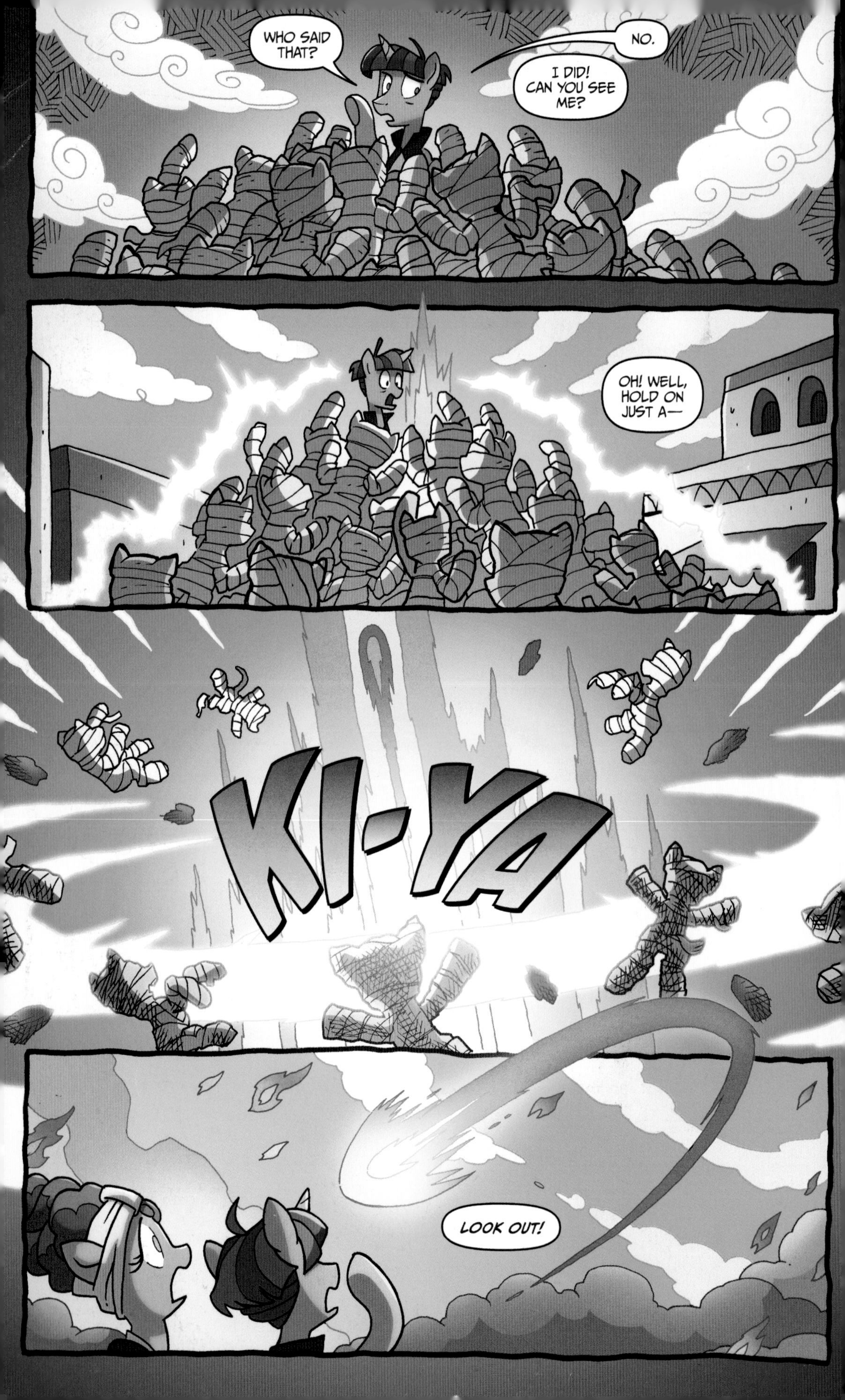
WHO SAID THAT?
NO.
I DID! CAN YOU SEE ME?
OH! WELL, HOLD ON JUST A—
KI-YA
LOOK OUT!

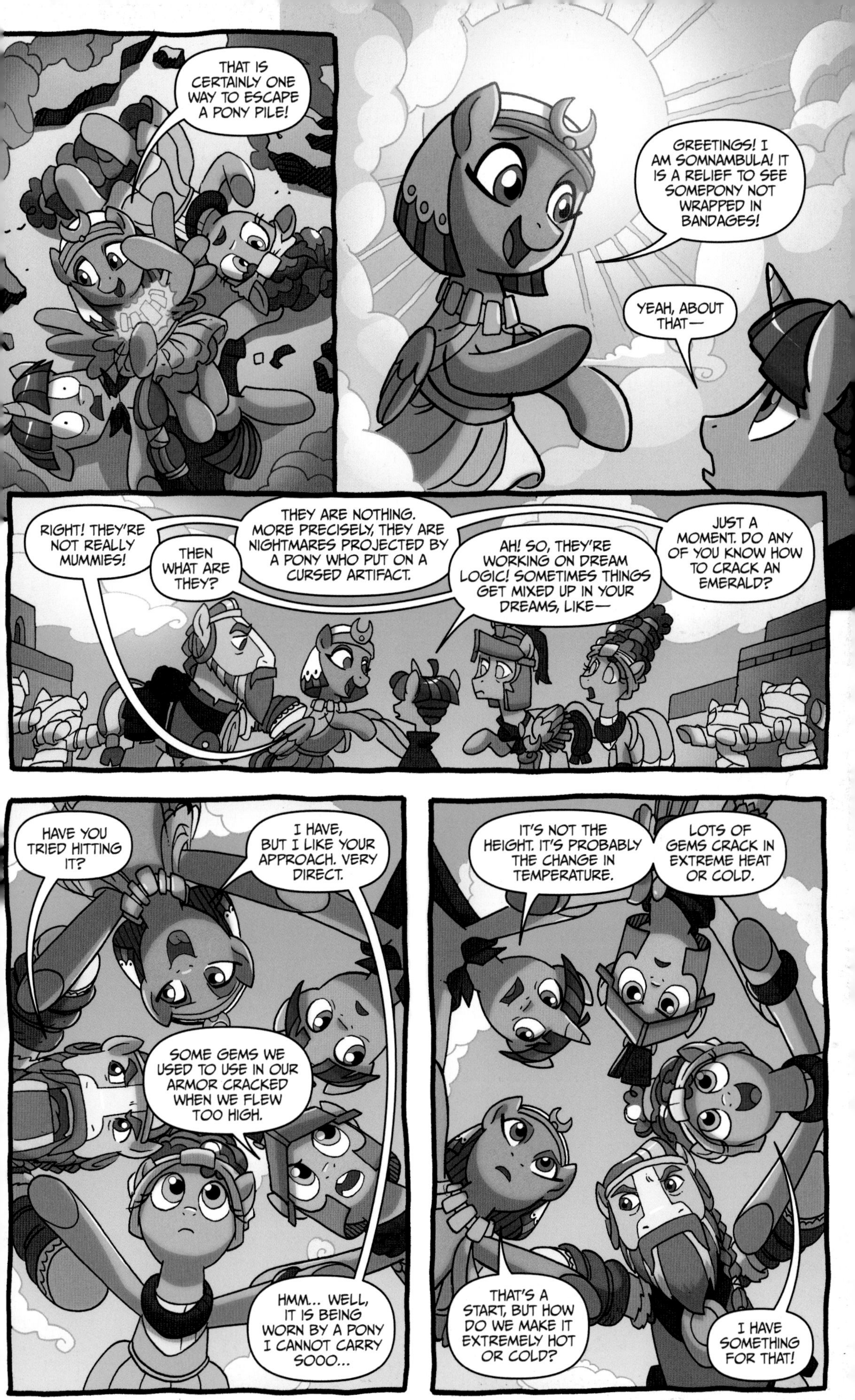
THAT IS CERTAINLY ONE WAY TO ESCAPE A PONY PILE!
GREETINGS! I AM SOMNAMBULA! IT IS A RELIEF TO SEE SOMEPONY NOT WRAPPED IN BANDAGES!
YEAH, ABOUT THAT—
RIGHT! THEY'RE NOT REALLY MUMMIES!
THEN WHAT ARE THEY?
THEY ARE NOTHING. MORE PRECISELY, THEY ARE NIGHTMARES PROJECTED BY A PONY WHO PUT ON A CURSED ARTIFACT.
AH! SO, THEY'RE WORKING ON DREAM LOGIC! SOMETIMES THINGS GET MIXED UP IN YOUR DREAMS, LIKE—
JUST A MOMENT. DO ANY OF YOU KNOW HOW TO CRACK AN EMERALD?
HAVE YOU TRIED HITTING IT?
I HAVE, BUT I LIKE YOUR APPROACH. VERY DIRECT.
SOME GEMS WE USED TO USE IN OUR ARMOR CRACKED WHEN WE FLEW TOO HIGH.
HMM... WELL, IT IS BEING WORN BY A PONY I CANNOT CARRY SOOO...
IT'S NOT THE HEIGHT. IT'S PROBABLY THE CHANGE IN TEMPERATURE.
LOTS OF GEMS CRACK IN EXTREME HEAT OR COLD.
THAT'S A START, BUT HOW DO WE MAKE IT EXTREMELY HOT OR COLD?
I HAVE SOMETHING FOR THAT!

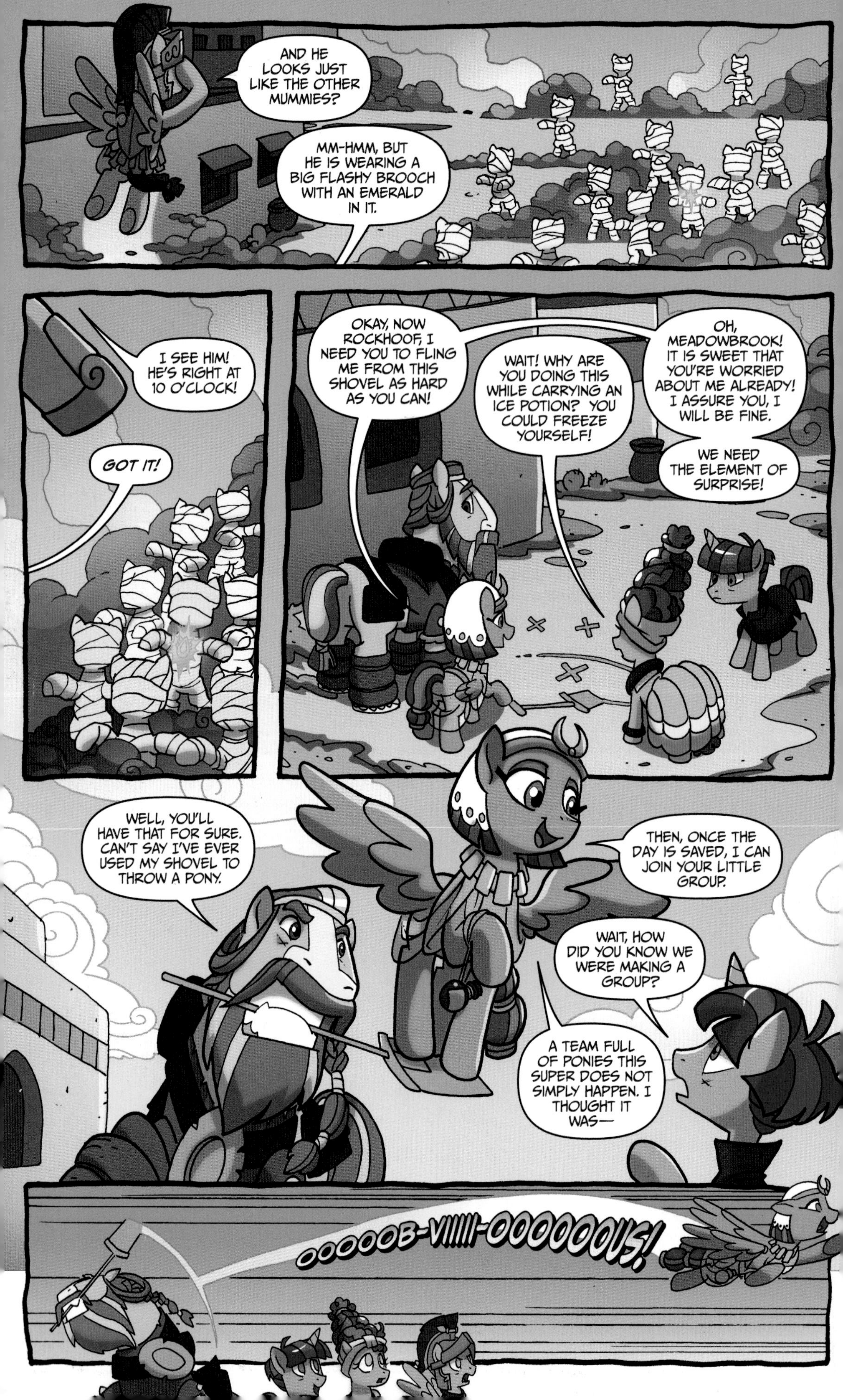
AND HE LOOKS JUST LIKE THE OTHER MUMMIES?
MM-HMM, BUT HE IS WEARING A BIG FLASHY BROOCH WITH AN EMERALD IN IT.
I SEE HIM! HE'S RIGHT AT 10 O'CLOCK!
GOT IT!
OKAY, NOW ROCKHOOF, I NEED YOU TO FLING ME FROM THIS SHOVEL AS HARD AS YOU CAN!
WAIT! WHY ARE YOU DOING THIS WHILE CARRYING AN ICE POTION? YOU COULD FREEZE YOURSELF!
OH, MEADOWBROOK! IT IS SWEET THAT YOU'RE WORRIED ABOUT ME ALREADY! I ASSURE YOU, I WILL BE FINE.
WE NEED THE ELEMENT OF SURPRISE!
WELL, YOU'LL HAVE THAT FOR SURE. CAN'T SAY I'VE EVER USED MY SHOVEL TO THROW A PONY.
THEN, ONCE THE DAY IS SAVED, I CAN JOIN YOUR LITTLE GROUP.
WAIT, HOW DID YOU KNOW WE WERE MAKING A GROUP?
A TEAM FULL OF PONIES THIS SUPER DOES NOT SIMPLY HAPPEN. I THOUGHT IT WAS—
OOOOOB-VIIIII-OOOOOOOUS!

ALMOST THERE!

STAY ON TARGET! STAY ON TARGET!

SMASH!

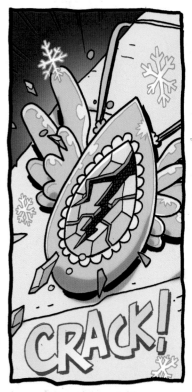

CRACK!

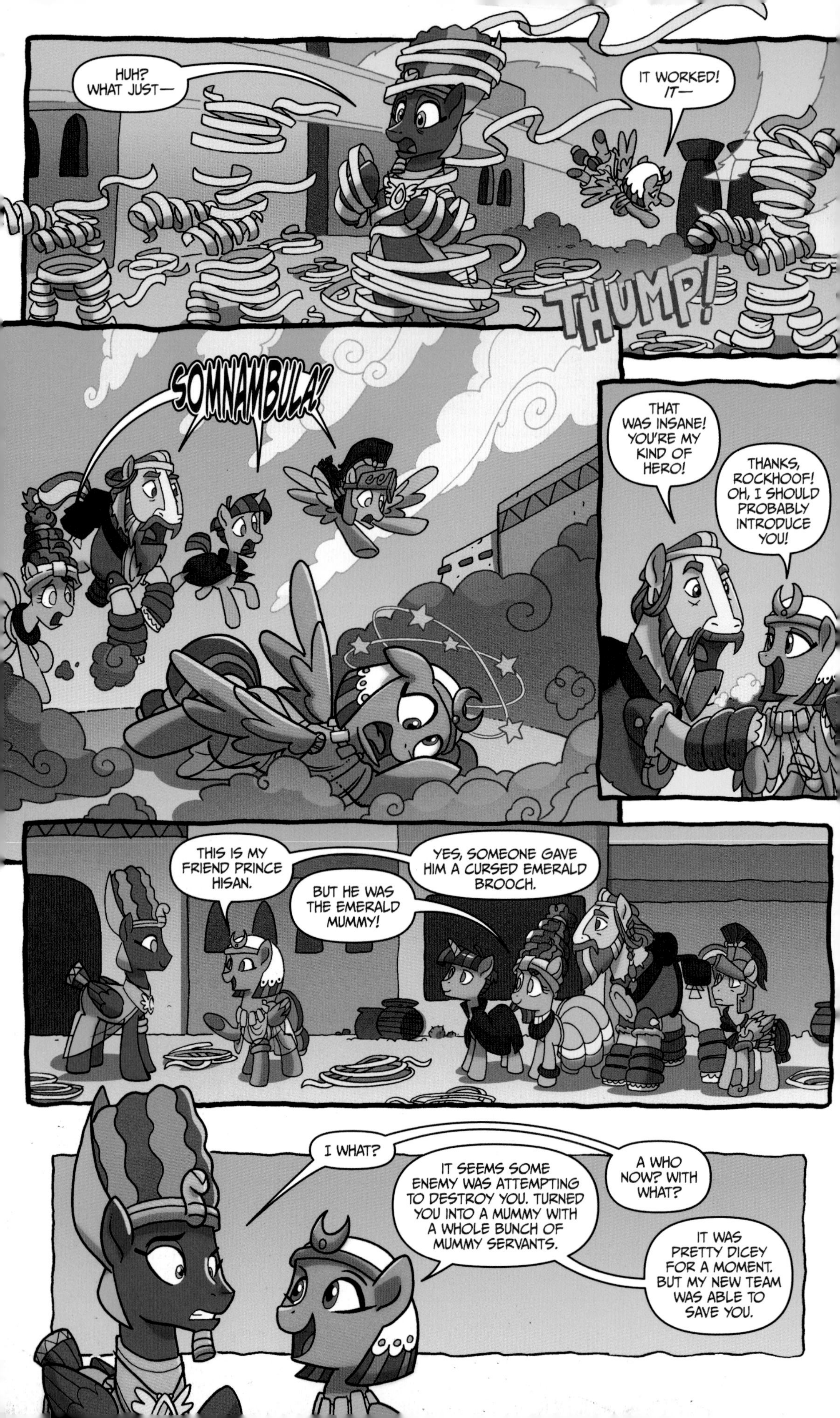
HUH? WHAT JUST—
IT WORKED! IT—
THUMP!
SOMNAMBULA!
THAT WAS INSANE! YOU'RE MY KIND OF HERO!
THANKS, ROCKHOOF! OH, I SHOULD PROBABLY INTRODUCE YOU!
THIS IS MY FRIEND PRINCE HISAN.
BUT HE WAS THE EMERALD MUMMY!
YES, SOMEONE GAVE HIM A CURSED EMERALD BROOCH.
I WHAT?
A WHO NOW? WITH WHAT?
IT SEEMS SOME ENEMY WAS ATTEMPTING TO DESTROY YOU. TURNED YOU INTO A MUMMY WITH A WHOLE BUNCH OF MUMMY SERVANTS.
IT WAS PRETTY DICEY FOR A MOMENT. BUT MY NEW TEAM WAS ABLE TO SAVE YOU.

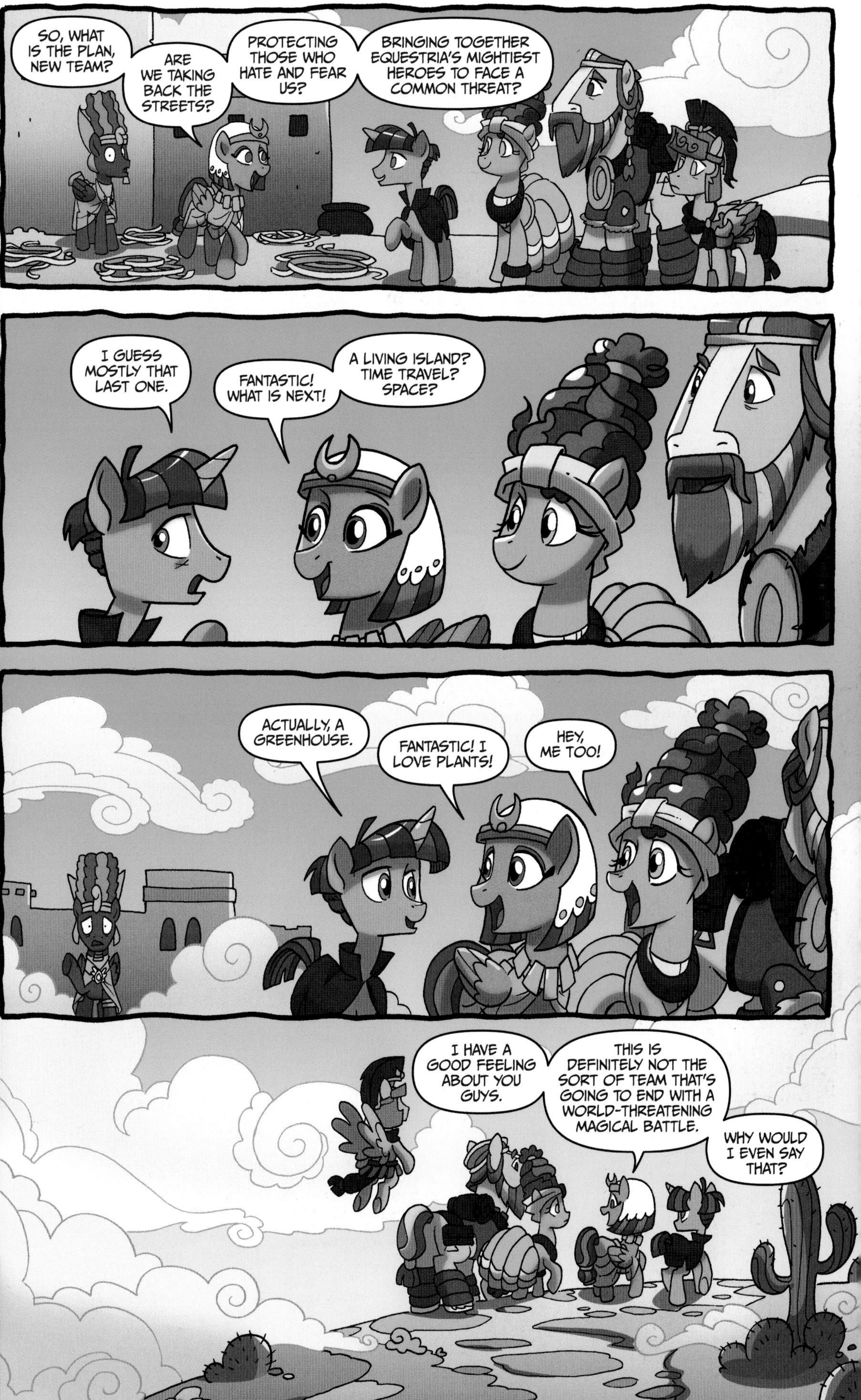
SO, WHAT IS THE PLAN, NEW TEAM?
ARE WE TAKING BACK THE STREETS?
PROTECTING THOSE WHO HATE AND FEAR US?
BRINGING TOGETHER EQUESTRIA'S MIGHTIEST HEROES TO FACE A COMMON THREAT?
I GUESS MOSTLY THAT LAST ONE.
FANTASTIC! WHAT IS NEXT!
A LIVING ISLAND? TIME TRAVEL? SPACE?
ACTUALLY, A GREENHOUSE.
FANTASTIC! I LOVE PLANTS!
HEY, ME TOO!
I HAVE A GOOD FEELING ABOUT YOU GUYS.
THIS IS DEFINITELY NOT THE SORT OF TEAM THAT'S GOING TO END WITH A WORLD-THREATENING MAGICAL BATTLE.
WHY WOULD I EVEN SAY THAT?

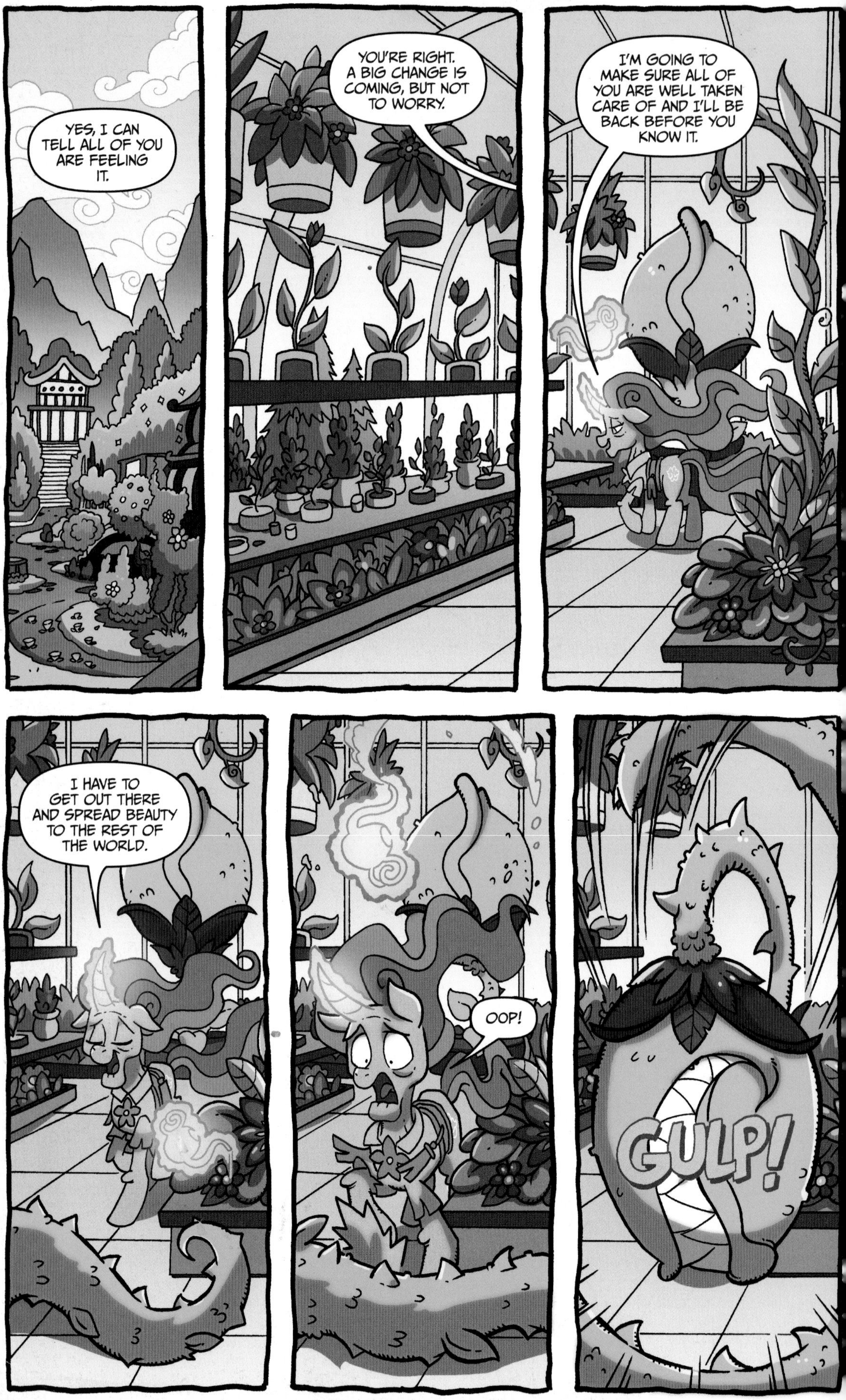
YES, I CAN TELL ALL OF YOU ARE FEELING IT.
YOU'RE RIGHT. A BIG CHANGE IS COMING, BUT NOT TO WORRY.
I'M GOING TO MAKE SURE ALL OF YOU ARE WELL TAKEN CARE OF AND I'LL BE BACK BEFORE YOU KNOW IT.
I HAVE TO GET OUT THERE AND SPREAD BEAUTY TO THE REST OF THE WORLD.
OOP!
GULP!

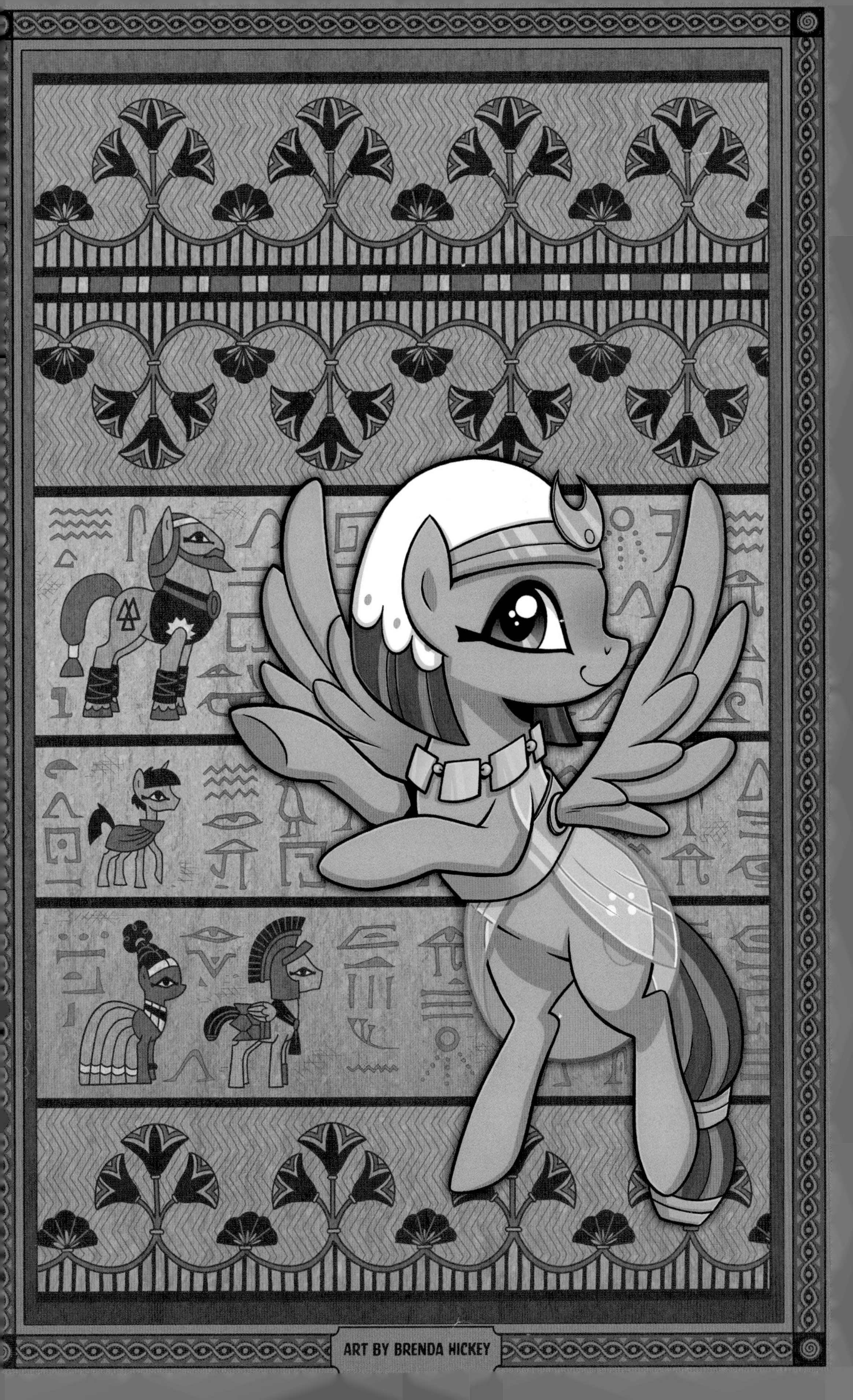
ART BY BRENDA HICKEY

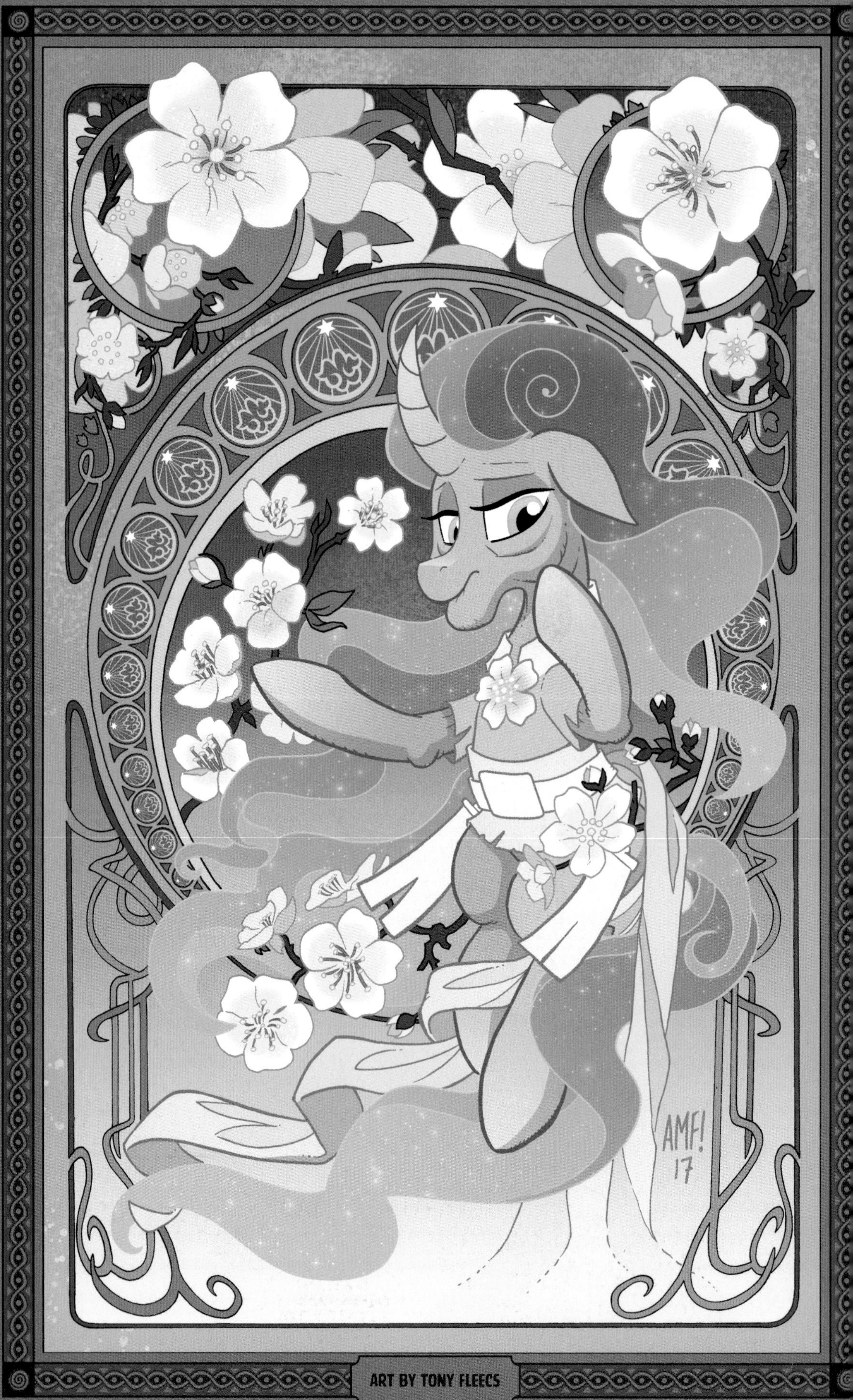
AMF!
17

ART BY TONY FLEECS

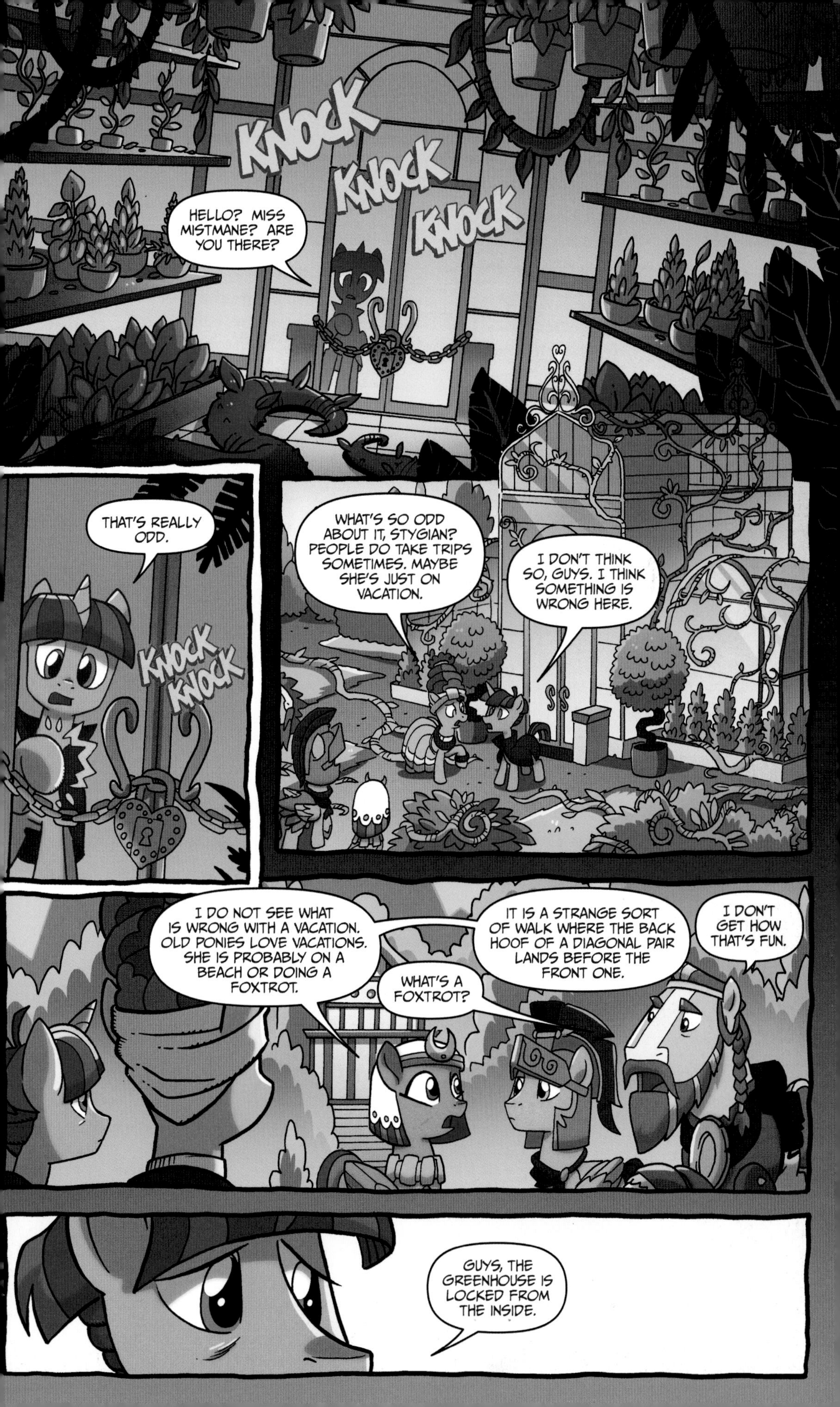
KNOCK
KNOCK
KNOCK
HELLO? MISS MISTMANE? ARE YOU THERE?
THAT'S REALLY ODD.
KNOCK KNOCK
WHAT'S SO ODD ABOUT IT, STYGIAN? PEOPLE DO TAKE TRIPS SOMETIMES. MAYBE SHE'S JUST ON VACATION.
I DON'T THINK SO, GUYS. I THINK SOMETHING IS WRONG HERE.
I DO NOT SEE WHAT IS WRONG WITH A VACATION. OLD PONIES LOVE VACATIONS. SHE IS PROBABLY ON A BEACH OR DOING A FOXTROT.
WHAT'S A FOXTROT?
IT IS A STRANGE SORT OF WALK WHERE THE BACK HOOF OF A DIAGONAL PAIR LANDS BEFORE THE FRONT ONE.
I DON'T GET HOW THAT'S FUN.
GUYS, THE GREENHOUSE IS LOCKED FROM THE INSIDE.

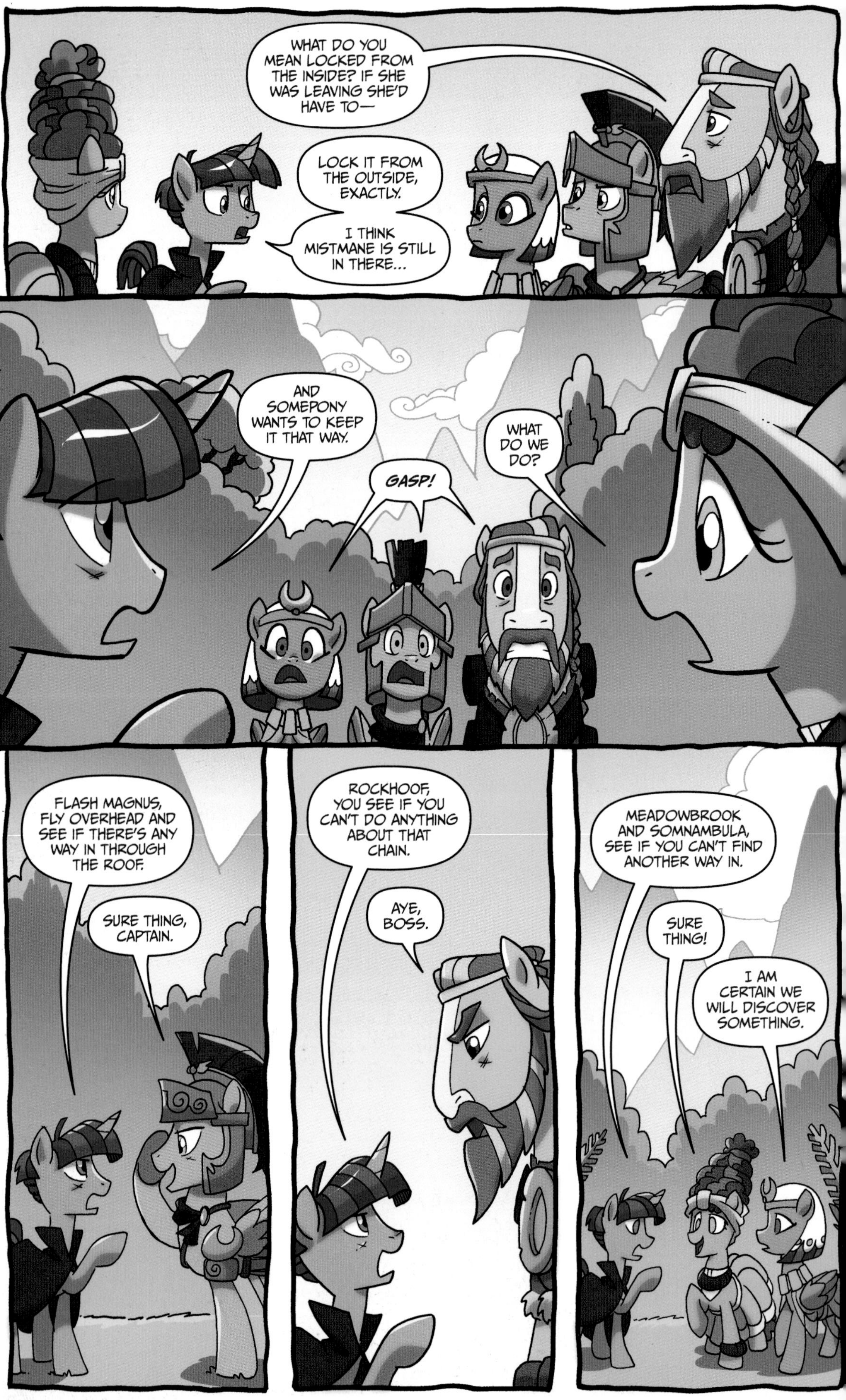
WHAT DO YOU MEAN LOCKED FROM THE INSIDE? IF SHE WAS LEAVING SHE'D HAVE TO—
LOCK IT FROM THE OUTSIDE, EXACTLY.
I THINK MISTMANE IS STILL IN THERE...
AND SOMEPONY WANTS TO KEEP IT THAT WAY.
GASP!
WHAT DO WE DO?
FLASH MAGNUS, FLY OVERHEAD AND SEE IF THERE'S ANY WAY IN THROUGH THE ROOF.
SURE THING, CAPTAIN.
ROCKHOOF, YOU SEE IF YOU CAN'T DO ANYTHING ABOUT THAT CHAIN.
AYE, BOSS.
MEADOWBROOK AND SOMNAMBULA, SEE IF YOU CAN'T FIND ANOTHER WAY IN.
SURE THING!
I AM CERTAIN WE WILL DISCOVER SOMETHING.

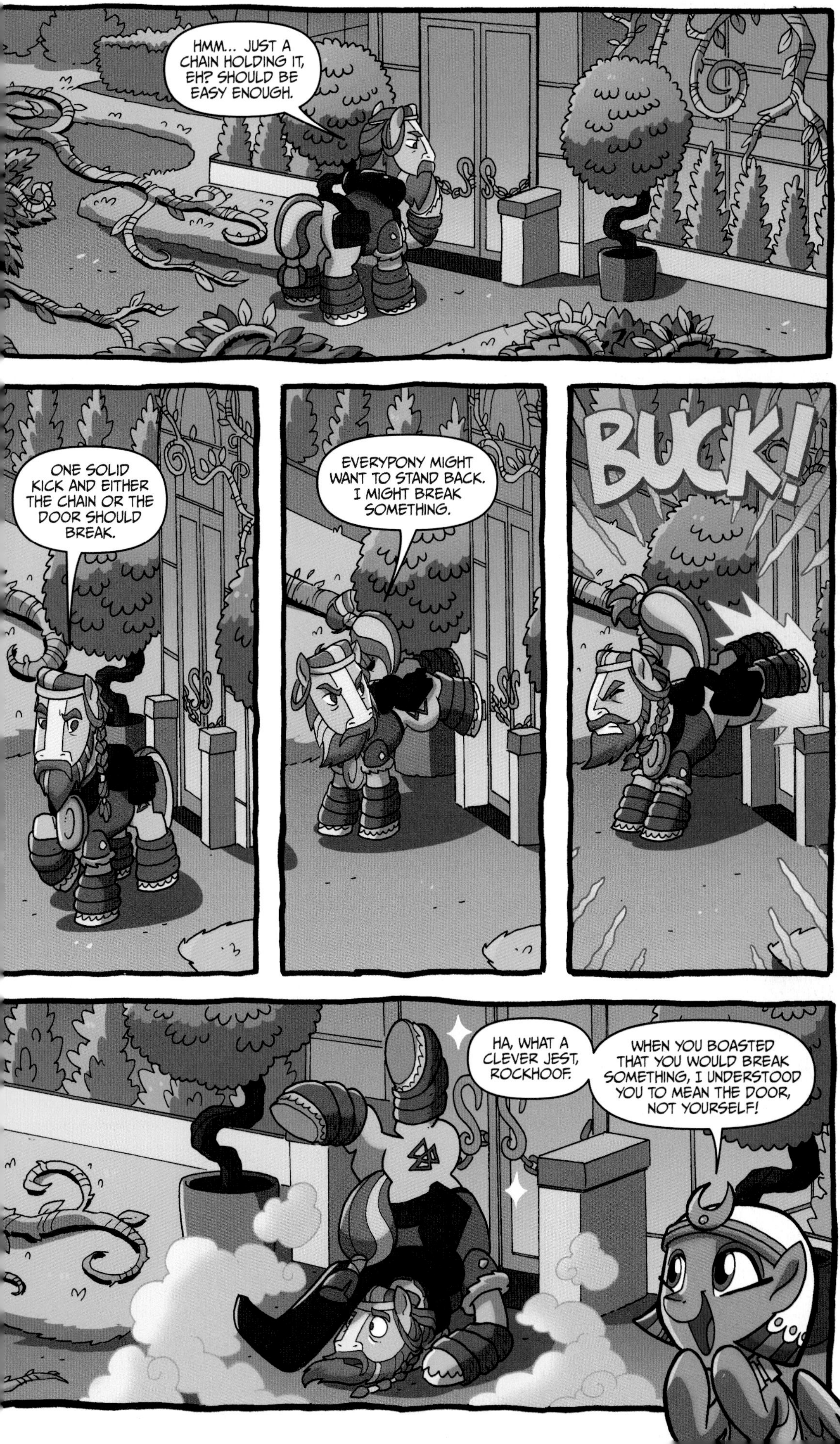

HMM... JUST A CHAIN HOLDING IT, EH? SHOULD BE EASY ENOUGH.
ONE SOLID KICK AND EITHER THE CHAIN OR THE DOOR SHOULD BREAK.
EVERYPONY MIGHT WANT TO STAND BACK. I MIGHT BREAK SOMETHING.
BUCK!
HA, WHAT A CLEVER JEST, ROCKHOOF.
WHEN YOU BOASTED THAT YOU WOULD BREAK SOMETHING, I UNDERSTOOD YOU TO MEAN THE DOOR, NOT YOURSELF!

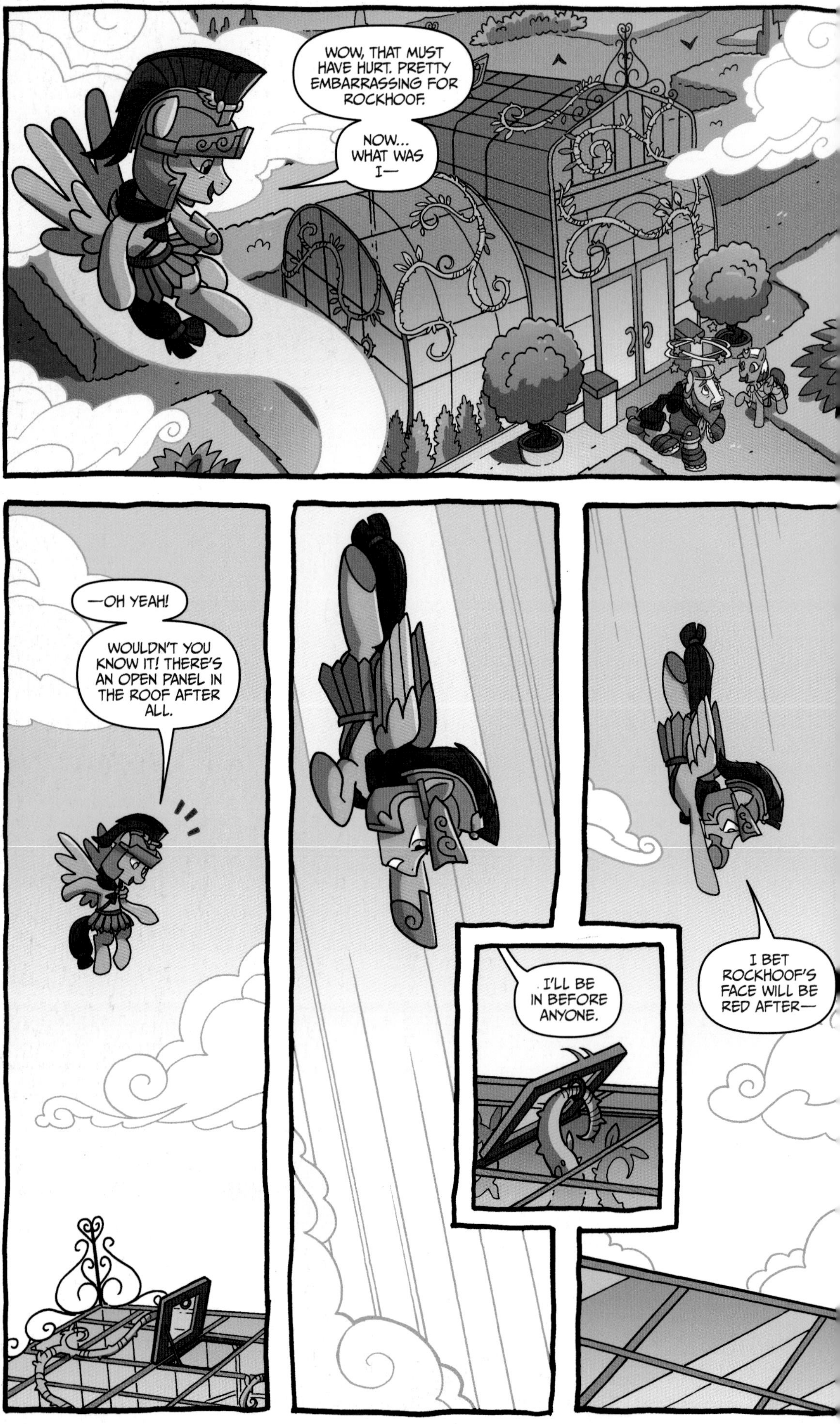
WOW, THAT MUST HAVE HURT. PRETTY EMBARRASSING FOR ROCKHOOF.
NOW... WHAT WAS I—
—OH YEAH!
WOULDN'T YOU KNOW IT! THERE'S AN OPEN PANEL IN THE ROOF AFTER ALL.
I'LL BE IN BEFORE ANYONE.
I BET ROCKHOOF'S FACE WILL BE RED AFTER—

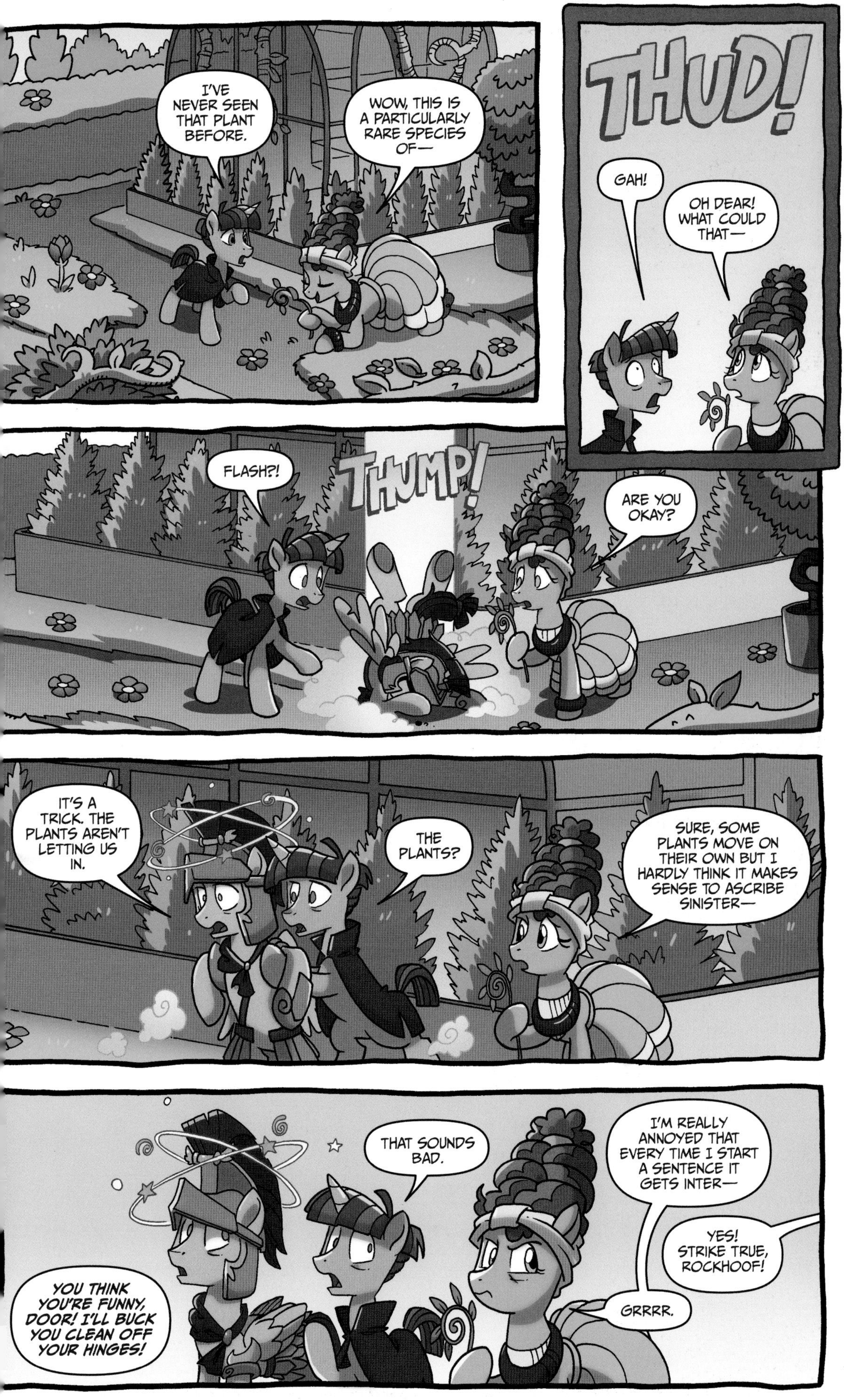

I'VE NEVER SEEN THAT PLANT BEFORE.
WOW, THIS IS A PARTICULARLY RARE SPECIES OF—
THUD!
GAH!
OH DEAR! WHAT COULD THAT—
FLASH?!
THUMP!
ARE YOU OKAY?
IT'S A TRICK. THE PLANTS AREN'T LETTING US IN.
THE PLANTS?
SURE, SOME PLANTS MOVE ON THEIR OWN BUT I HARDLY THINK IT MAKES SENSE TO ASCRIBE SINISTER—
THAT SOUNDS BAD.
I'M REALLY ANNOYED THAT EVERY TIME I START A SENTENCE IT GETS INTER—
YES! STRIKE TRUE, ROCKHOOF!
YOU THINK YOU'RE FUNNY, DOOR! I'LL BUCK YOU CLEAN OFF YOUR HINGES!
GRRRR.

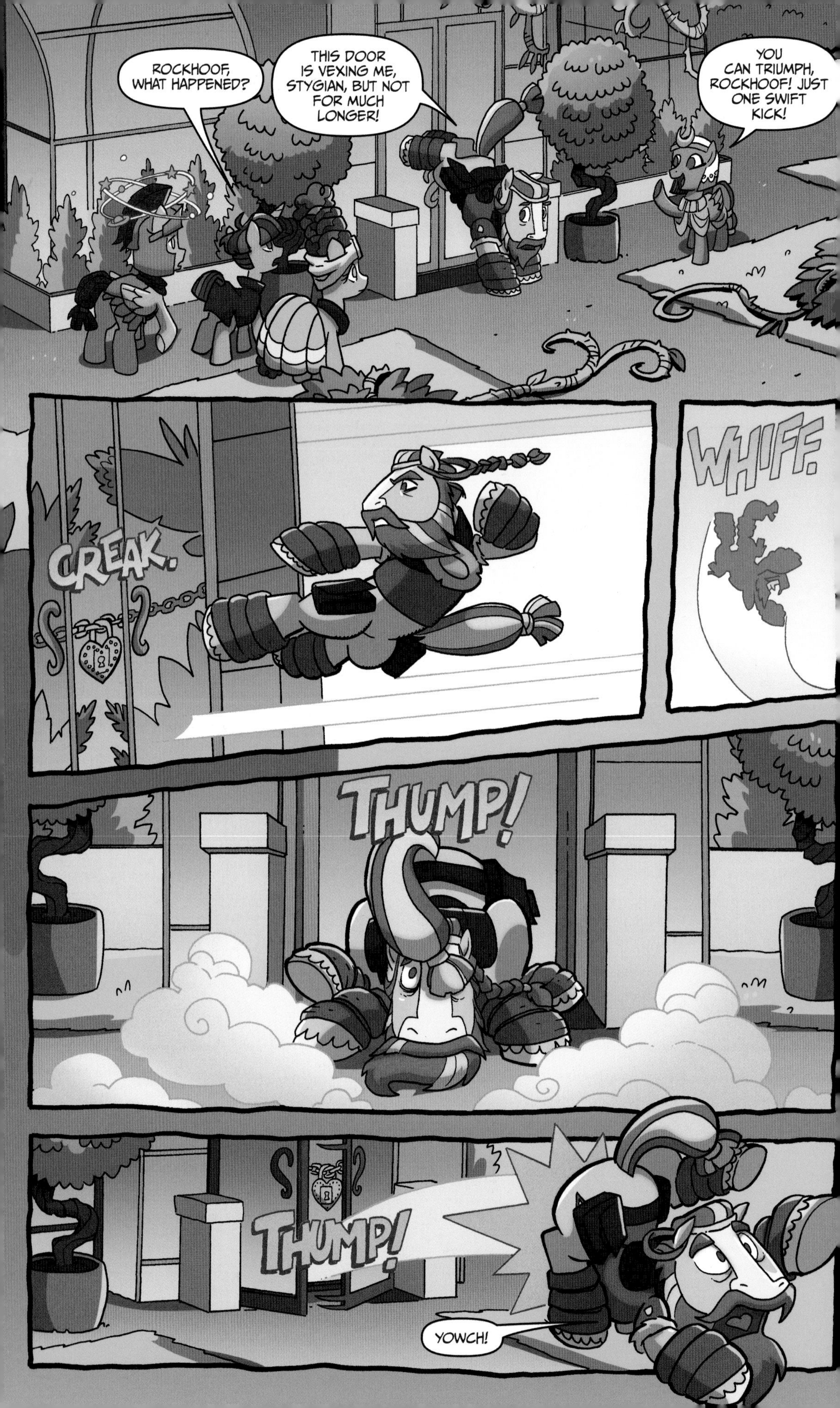
ROCKHOOF, WHAT HAPPENED?
THIS DOOR IS VEXING ME, STYGIAN, BUT NOT FOR MUCH LONGER!
YOU CAN TRIUMPH, ROCKHOOF! JUST ONE SWIFT KICK!
CREAK.
WHIFF.
THUMP!
THUMP!
YOWCH!

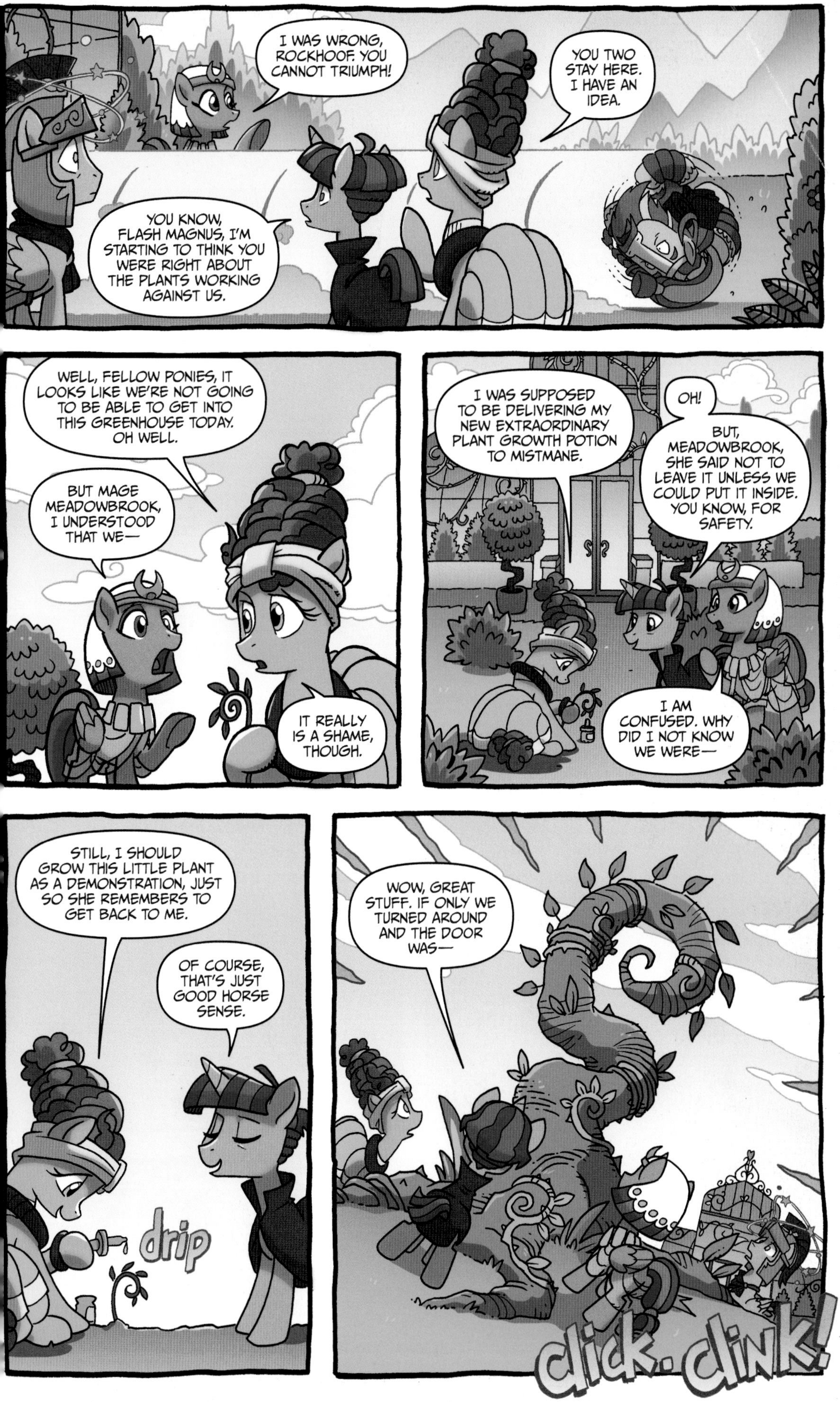
I WAS WRONG, ROCKHOOF. YOU CANNOT TRIUMPH!
YOU KNOW, FLASH MAGNUS, I'M STARTING TO THINK YOU WERE RIGHT ABOUT THE PLANTS WORKING AGAINST US.
YOU TWO STAY HERE. I HAVE AN IDEA.
WELL, FELLOW PONIES, IT LOOKS LIKE WE'RE NOT GOING TO BE ABLE TO GET INTO THIS GREENHOUSE TODAY. OH WELL.
BUT MAGE MEADOWBROOK, I UNDERSTOOD THAT WE—
IT REALLY IS A SHAME, THOUGH.
I WAS SUPPOSED TO BE DELIVERING MY NEW EXTRAORDINARY PLANT GROWTH POTION TO MISTMANE.
OH!
BUT, MEADOWBROOK, SHE SAID NOT TO LEAVE IT UNLESS WE COULD PUT IT INSIDE. YOU KNOW, FOR SAFETY.
I AM CONFUSED. WHY DID I NOT KNOW WE WERE—
STILL, I SHOULD GROW THIS LITTLE PLANT AS A DEMONSTRATION, JUST SO SHE REMEMBERS TO GET BACK TO ME.
OF COURSE, THAT'S JUST GOOD HORSE SENSE.
drip
WOW, GREAT STUFF. IF ONLY WE TURNED AROUND AND THE DOOR WAS—
click. clink!

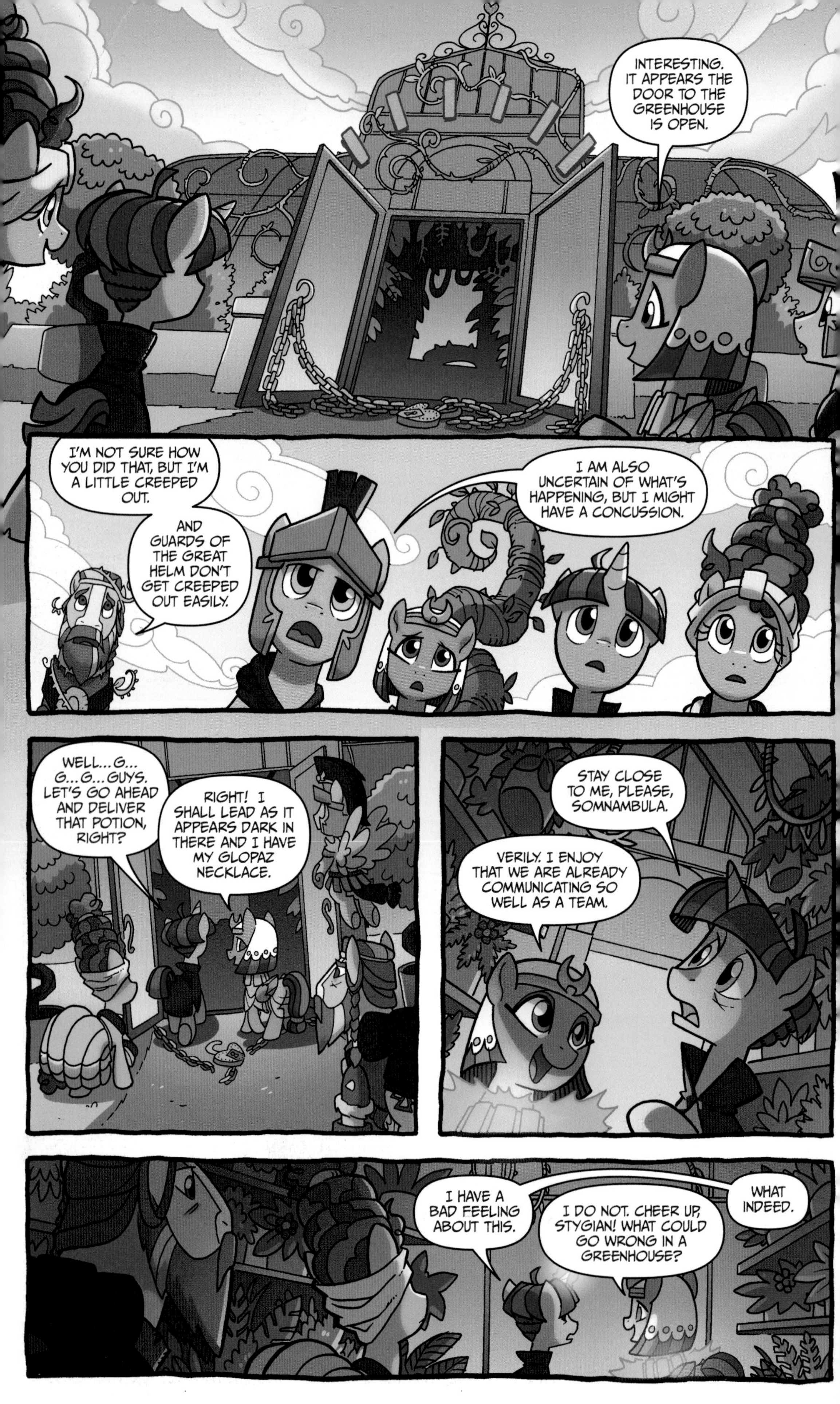
INTERESTING. IT APPEARS THE DOOR TO THE GREENHOUSE IS OPEN.
I'M NOT SURE HOW YOU DID THAT, BUT I'M A LITTLE CREEPED OUT.
AND GUARDS OF THE GREAT HELM DON'T GET CREEPED OUT EASILY.
I AM ALSO UNCERTAIN OF WHAT'S HAPPENING, BUT I MIGHT HAVE A CONCUSSION.
WELL... G... G... G... GUYS. LET'S GO AHEAD AND DELIVER THAT POTION, RIGHT?
RIGHT! I SHALL LEAD AS IT APPEARS DARK IN THERE AND I HAVE MY GLOPAZ NECKLACE.
STAY CLOSE TO ME, PLEASE, SOMNAMBULA.
VERILY. I ENJOY THAT WE ARE ALREADY COMMUNICATING SO WELL AS A TEAM.
I HAVE A BAD FEELING ABOUT THIS.
I DO NOT. CHEER UP, STYGIAN! WHAT COULD GO WRONG IN A GREENHOUSE?
WHAT INDEED.

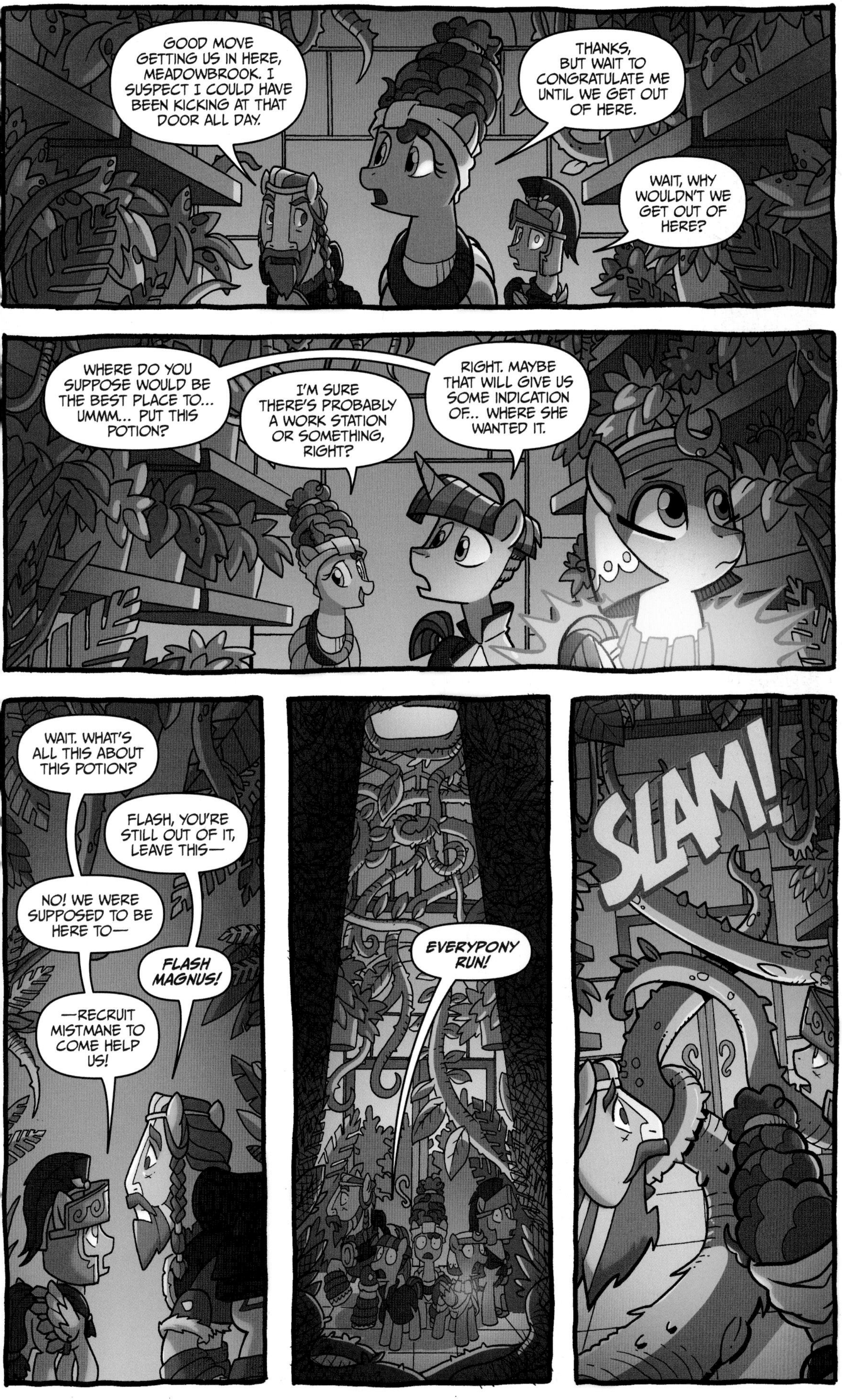
GOOD MOVE GETTING US IN HERE, MEADOWBROOK. I SUSPECT I COULD HAVE BEEN KICKING AT THAT DOOR ALL DAY.
THANKS, BUT WAIT TO CONGRATULATE ME UNTIL WE GET OUT OF HERE.
WAIT, WHY WOULDN'T WE GET OUT OF HERE?
WHERE DO YOU SUPPOSE WOULD BE THE BEST PLACE TO... UMMM... PUT THIS POTION?
I'M SURE THERE'S PROBABLY A WORK STATION OR SOMETHING, RIGHT?
RIGHT. MAYBE THAT WILL GIVE US SOME INDICATION OF... WHERE SHE WANTED IT.
WAIT. WHAT'S ALL THIS ABOUT THIS POTION?
FLASH, YOU'RE STILL OUT OF IT, LEAVE THIS—
NO! WE WERE SUPPOSED TO BE HERE TO—
FLASH MAGNUS!
—RECRUIT MISTMANE TO COME HELP US!
EVERYPONY RUN!
SLAM!

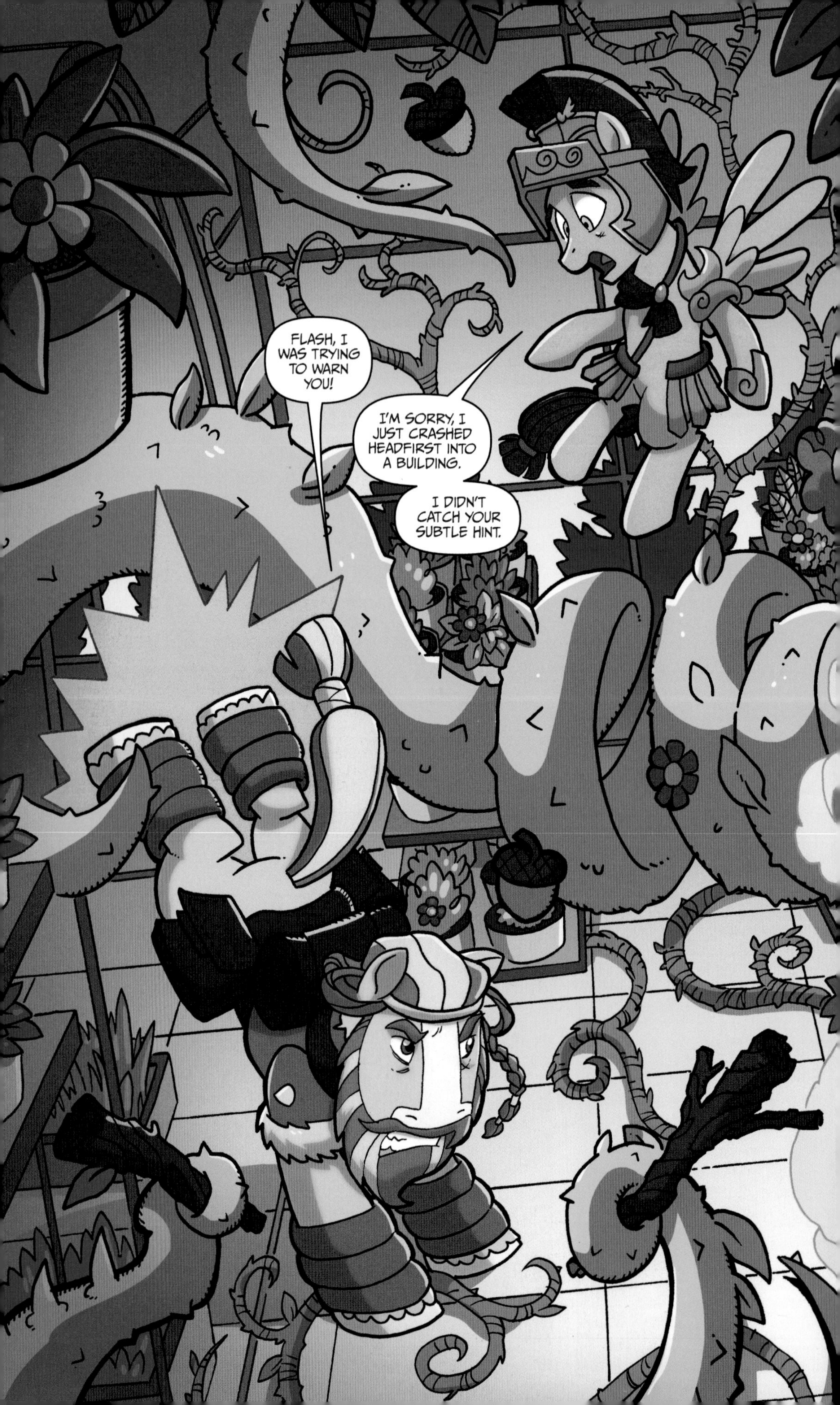
FLASH, I WAS TRYING TO WARN YOU!
I'M SORRY, I JUST CRASHED HEADFIRST INTO A BUILDING.
I DIDN'T CATCH YOUR SUBTLE HINT.

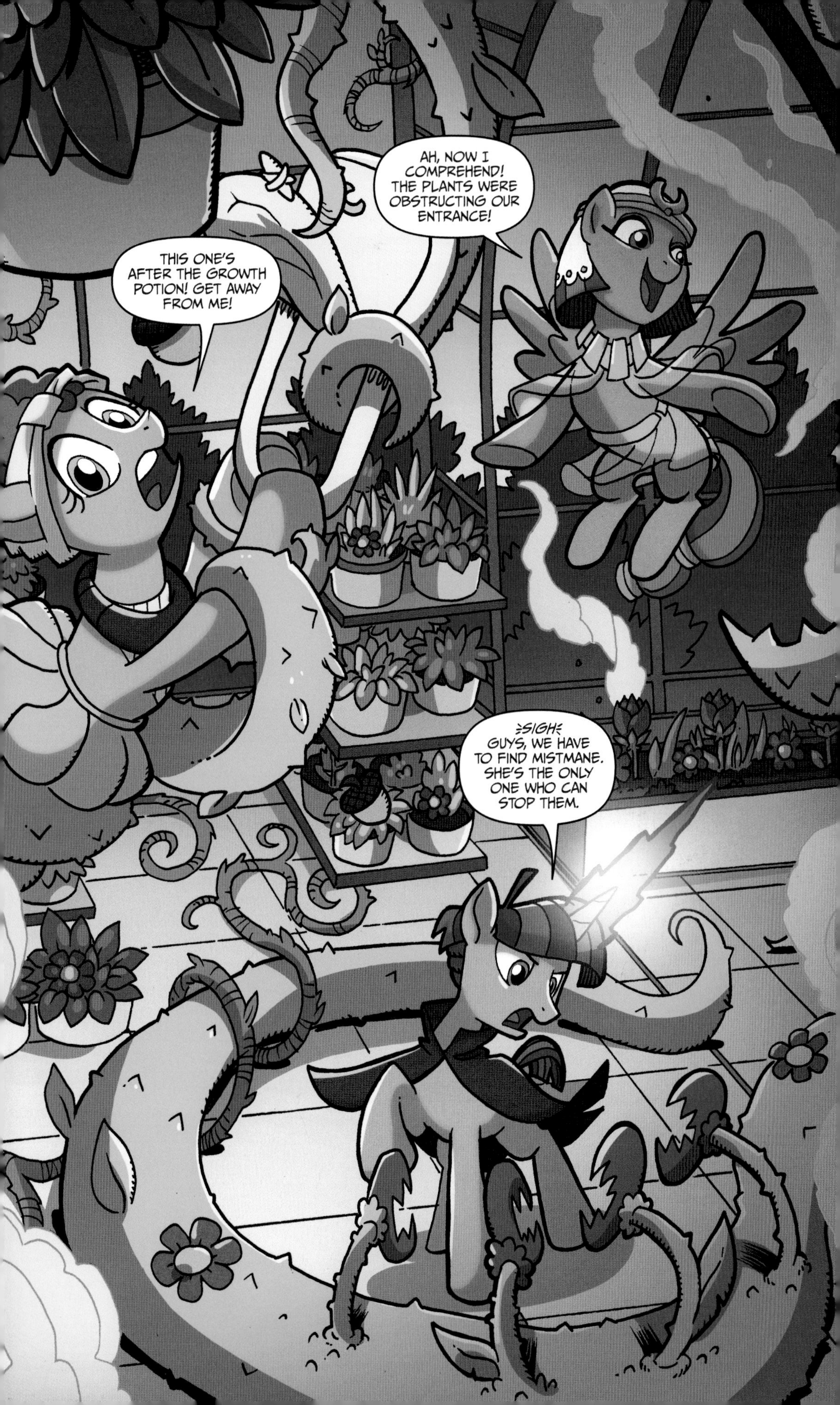
AH, NOW I COMPREHEND! THE PLANTS WERE OBSTRUCTING OUR ENTRANCE!
THIS ONE'S AFTER THE GROWTH POTION! GET AWAY FROM ME!
SIGH
GUYS, WE HAVE TO FIND MISTMANE. SHE'S THE ONLY ONE WHO CAN STOP THEM.

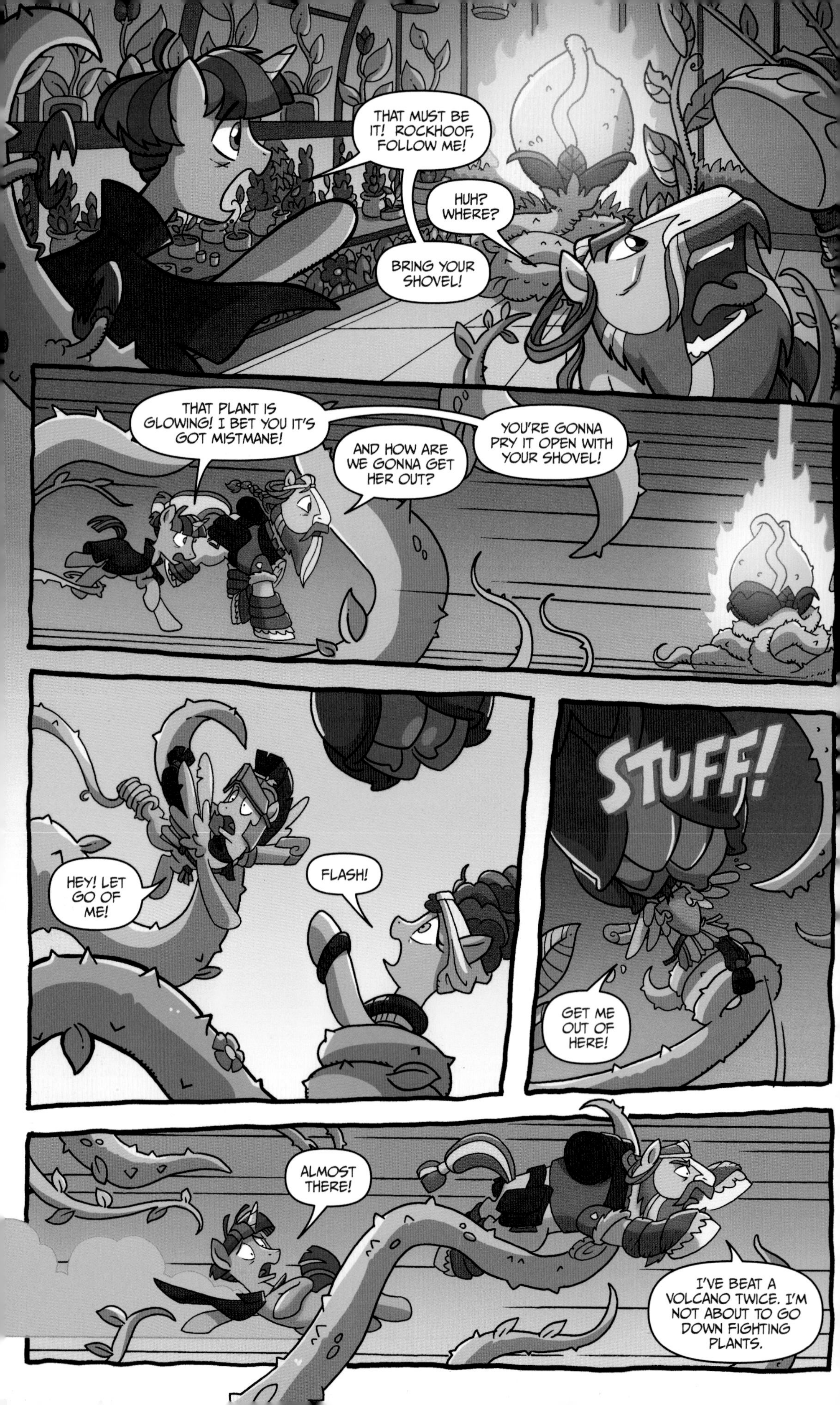

THAT MUST BE IT! ROCKHOOF, FOLLOW ME!
HUH? WHERE?
BRING YOUR SHOVEL!
THAT PLANT IS GLOWING! I BET YOU IT'S GOT MISTMANE!
AND HOW ARE WE GONNA GET HER OUT?
YOU'RE GONNA PRY IT OPEN WITH YOUR SHOVEL!
HEY! LET GO OF ME!
FLASH!
STUFF!
GET ME OUT OF HERE!
ALMOST THERE!
I'VE BEAT A VOLCANO TWICE. I'M NOT ABOUT TO GO DOWN FIGHTING PLANTS.

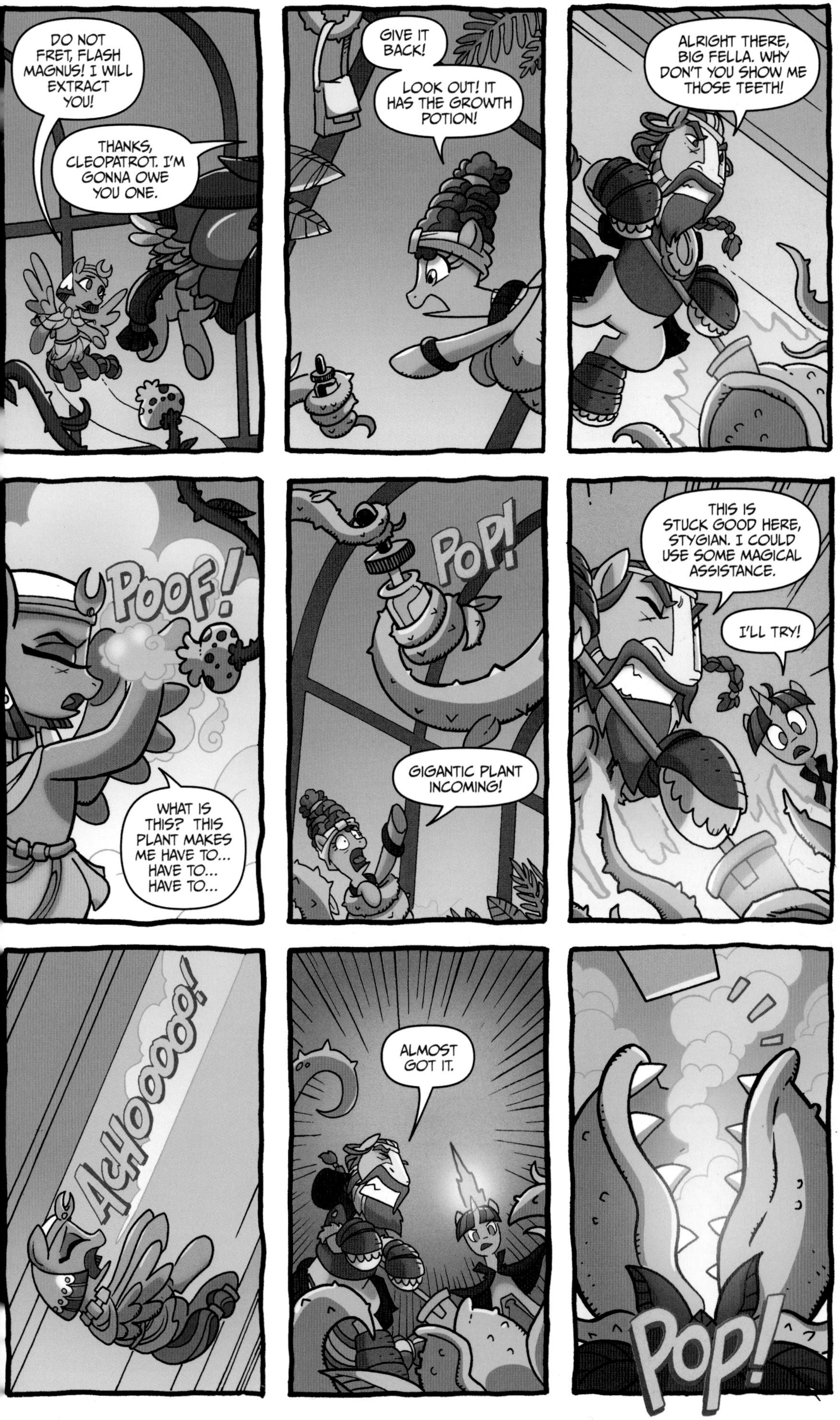
DO NOT FRET, FLASH MAGNUS! I WILL EXTRACT YOU!
THANKS, CLEOPATROT. I'M GONNA OWE YOU ONE.
GIVE IT BACK!
LOOK OUT! IT HAS THE GROWTH POTION!
ALRIGHT THERE, BIG FELLA. WHY DON'T YOU SHOW ME THOSE TEETH!
POOF!
WHAT IS THIS? THIS PLANT MAKES ME HAVE TO... HAVE TO... HAVE TO...
POP!
GIGANTIC PLANT INCOMING!
THIS IS STUCK GOOD HERE, STYGIAN. I COULD USE SOME MAGICAL ASSISTANCE.
I'LL TRY!
ACHOOOOO!
ALMOST GOT IT.
POP!

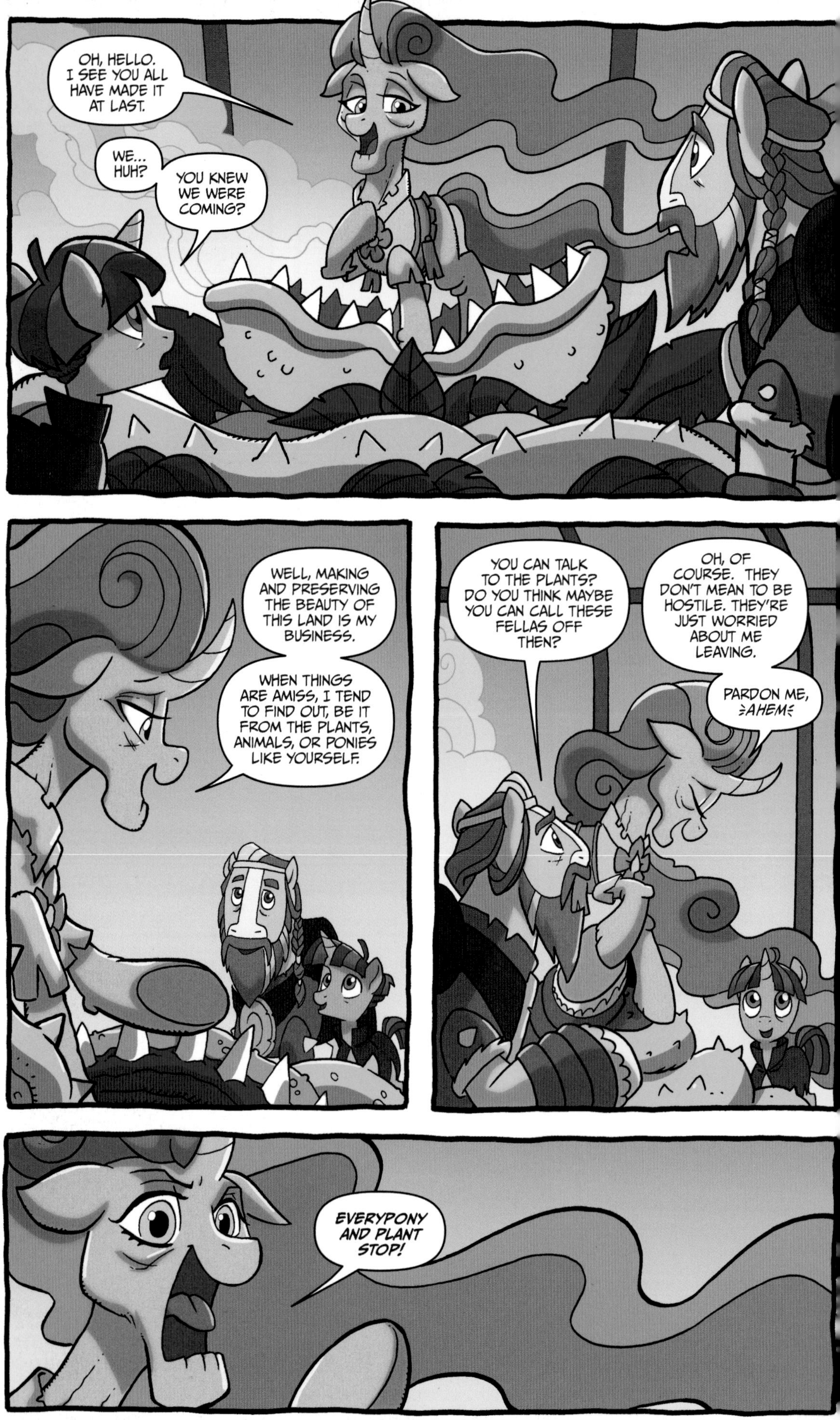
OH, HELLO. I SEE YOU ALL HAVE MADE IT AT LAST.
WE... HUH?
YOU KNEW WE WERE COMING?
WELL, MAKING AND PRESERVING THE BEAUTY OF THIS LAND IS MY BUSINESS.
WHEN THINGS ARE AMISS, I TEND TO FIND OUT, BE IT FROM THE PLANTS, ANIMALS, OR PONIES LIKE YOURSELF.
YOU CAN TALK TO THE PLANTS? DO YOU THINK MAYBE YOU CAN CALL THESE FELLAS OFF THEN?
OH, OF COURSE. THEY DON'T MEAN TO BE HOSTILE. THEY'RE JUST WORRIED ABOUT ME LEAVING.
PARDON ME, *AHEM*
EVERYPONY AND PLANT STOP!

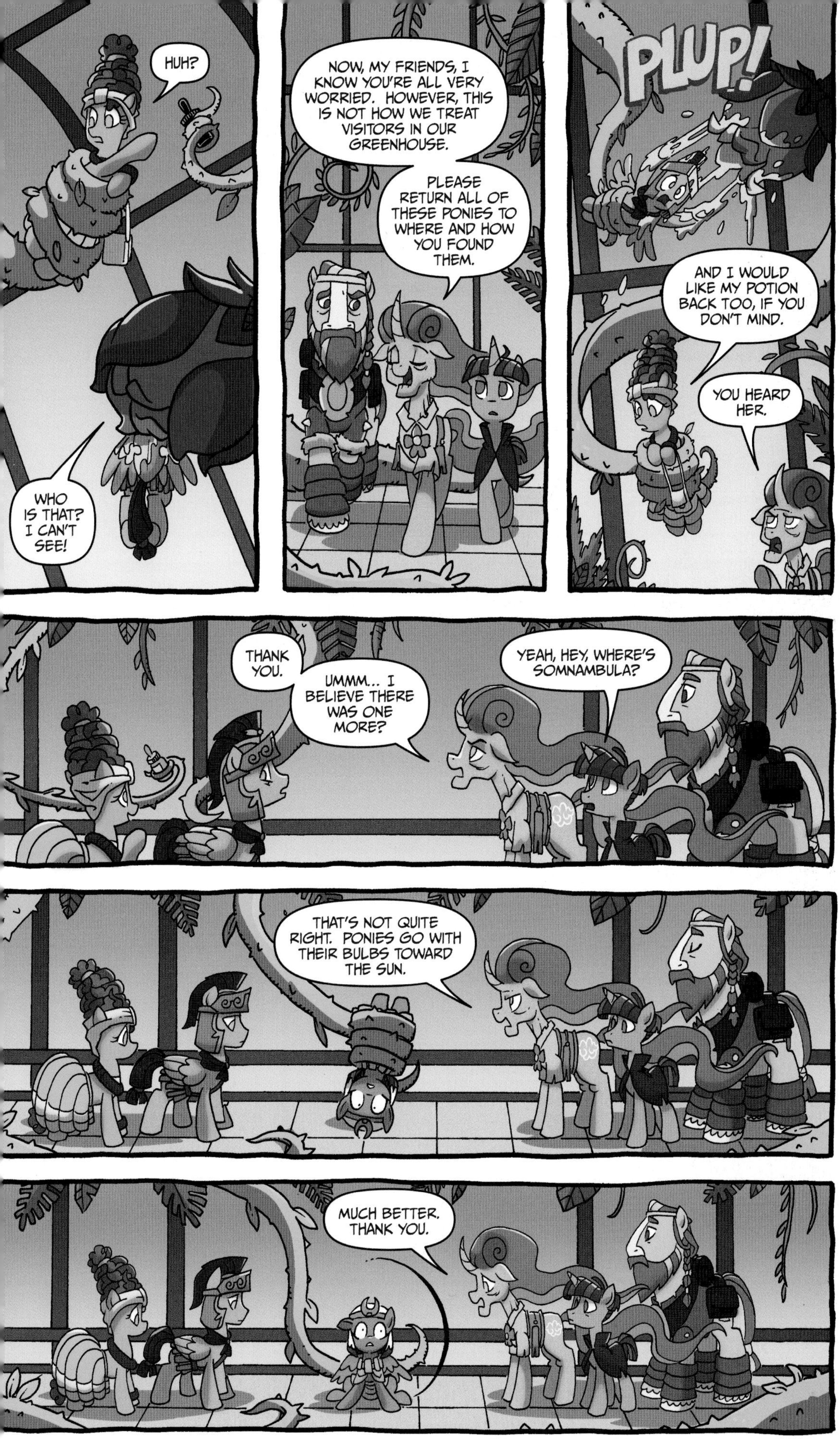
HUH?
WHO IS THAT? I CAN'T SEE!
NOW, MY FRIENDS, I KNOW YOU'RE ALL VERY WORRIED. HOWEVER, THIS IS NOT HOW WE TREAT VISITORS IN OUR GREENHOUSE.
PLEASE RETURN ALL OF THESE PONIES TO WHERE AND HOW YOU FOUND THEM.
PLUP!
AND I WOULD LIKE MY POTION BACK TOO, IF YOU DON'T MIND.
YOU HEARD HER.
THANK YOU.
UMMM... I BELIEVE THERE WAS ONE MORE?
YEAH, HEY, WHERE'S SOMNAMBULA?
THAT'S NOT QUITE RIGHT. PONIES GO WITH THEIR BULBS TOWARD THE SUN.
MUCH BETTER. THANK YOU.

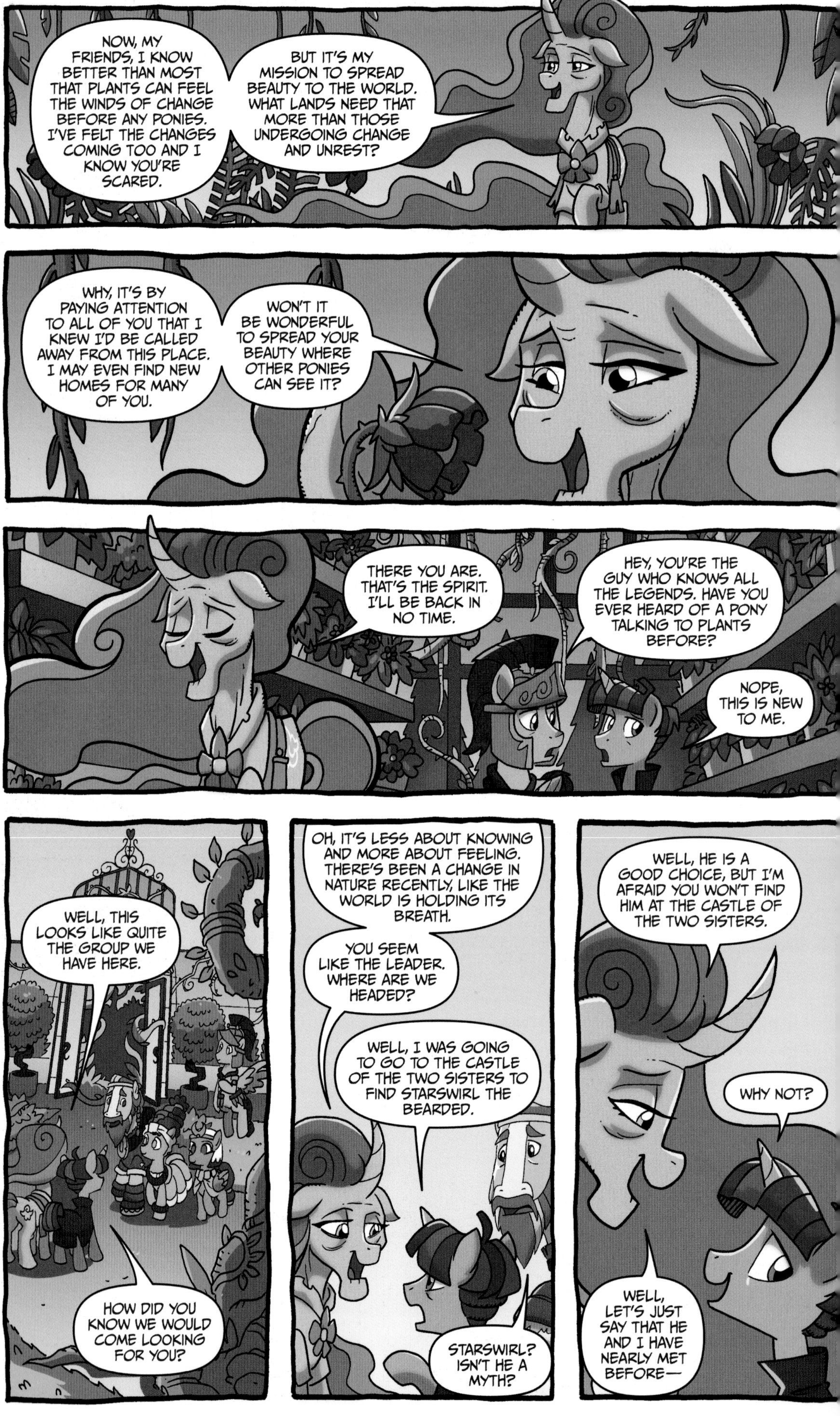
NOW, MY FRIENDS, I KNOW BETTER THAN MOST THAT PLANTS CAN FEEL THE WINDS OF CHANGE BEFORE ANY PONIES. I'VE FELT THE CHANGES COMING TOO AND I KNOW YOU'RE SCARED.
BUT IT'S MY MISSION TO SPREAD BEAUTY TO THE WORLD. WHAT LANDS NEED THAT MORE THAN THOSE UNDERGOING CHANGE AND UNREST?
WHY, IT'S BY PAYING ATTENTION TO ALL OF YOU THAT I KNEW I'D BE CALLED AWAY FROM THIS PLACE. I MAY EVEN FIND NEW HOMES FOR MANY OF YOU.
WON'T IT BE WONDERFUL TO SPREAD YOUR BEAUTY WHERE OTHER PONIES CAN SEE IT?
THERE YOU ARE. THAT'S THE SPIRIT. I'LL BE BACK IN NO TIME.
HEY, YOU'RE THE GUY WHO KNOWS ALL THE LEGENDS. HAVE YOU EVER HEARD OF A PONY TALKING TO PLANTS BEFORE?
NOPE, THIS IS NEW TO ME.
WELL, THIS LOOKS LIKE QUITE THE GROUP WE HAVE HERE.
HOW DID YOU KNOW WE WOULD COME LOOKING FOR YOU?
OH, IT'S LESS ABOUT KNOWING AND MORE ABOUT FEELING. THERE'S BEEN A CHANGE IN NATURE RECENTLY, LIKE THE WORLD IS HOLDING ITS BREATH.
YOU SEEM LIKE THE LEADER. WHERE ARE WE HEADED?
WELL, I WAS GOING TO GO TO THE CASTLE OF THE TWO SISTERS TO FIND STARSWIRL THE BEARDED.
STARSWIRL? ISN'T HE A MYTH?
WELL, HE IS A GOOD CHOICE, BUT I'M AFRAID YOU WON'T FIND HIM AT THE CASTLE OF THE TWO SISTERS.
WHY NOT?
WELL, LET'S JUST SAY THAT HE AND I HAVE NEARLY MET BEFORE—

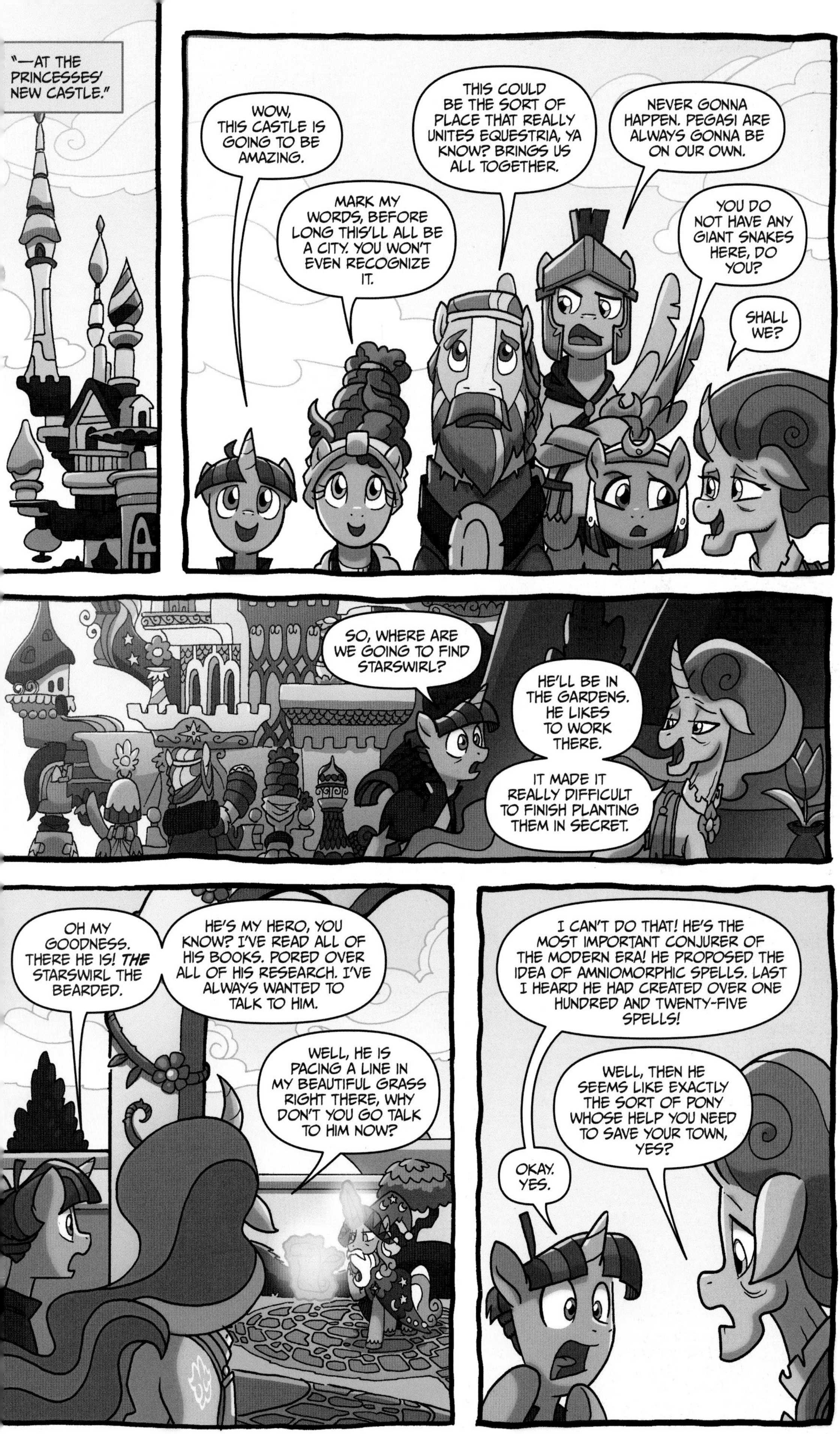
"—AT THE PRINCESSES' NEW CASTLE."
WOW, THIS CASTLE IS GOING TO BE AMAZING.
MARK MY WORDS, BEFORE LONG THIS'LL ALL BE A CITY. YOU WON'T EVEN RECOGNIZE IT.
THIS COULD BE THE SORT OF PLACE THAT REALLY UNITES EQUESTRIA, YA KNOW? BRINGS US ALL TOGETHER.
NEVER GONNA HAPPEN. PEGASI ARE ALWAYS GONNA BE ON OUR OWN.
YOU DO NOT HAVE ANY GIANT SNAKES HERE, DO YOU?
SHALL WE?
SO, WHERE ARE WE GOING TO FIND STARSWIRL?
HE'LL BE IN THE GARDENS. HE LIKES TO WORK THERE.
IT MADE IT REALLY DIFFICULT TO FINISH PLANTING THEM IN SECRET.
OH MY GOODNESS. THERE HE IS! *THE* STARSWIRL THE BEARDED.
HE'S MY HERO, YOU KNOW? I'VE READ ALL OF HIS BOOKS. PORED OVER ALL OF HIS RESEARCH. I'VE ALWAYS WANTED TO TALK TO HIM.
WELL, HE IS PACING A LINE IN MY BEAUTIFUL GRASS RIGHT THERE, WHY DON'T YOU GO TALK TO HIM NOW?
I CAN'T DO THAT! HE'S THE MOST IMPORTANT CONJURER OF THE MODERN ERA! HE PROPOSED THE IDEA OF AMNIOMORPHIC SPELLS. LAST I HEARD HE HAD CREATED OVER ONE HUNDRED AND TWENTY-FIVE SPELLS!
WELL, THEN HE SEEMS LIKE EXACTLY THE SORT OF PONY WHOSE HELP YOU NEED TO SAVE YOUR TOWN, YES?
OKAY. YES.

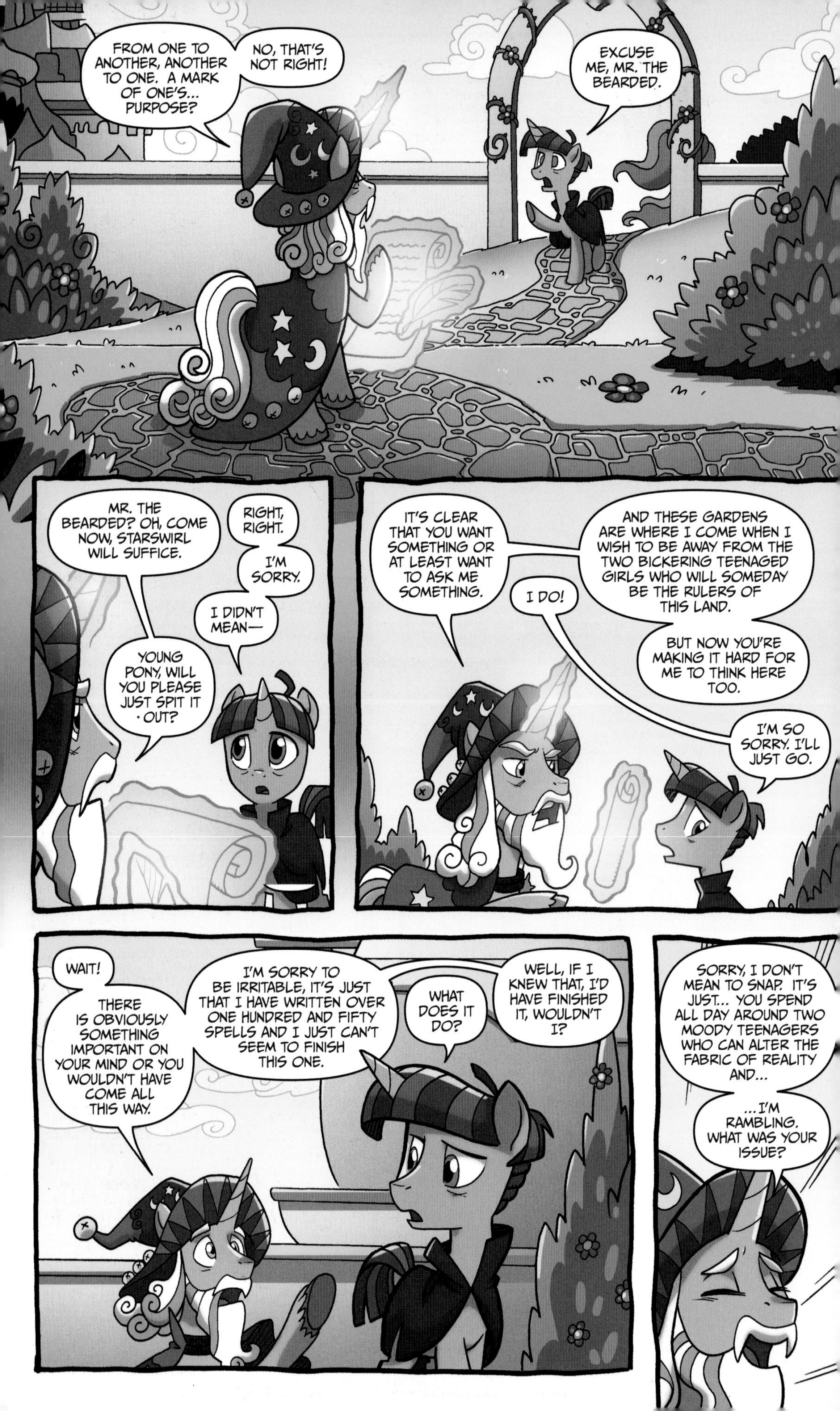
FROM ONE TO ANOTHER, ANOTHER TO ONE. A MARK OF ONE'S... PURPOSE?
NO, THAT'S NOT RIGHT!
EXCUSE ME, MR. THE BEARDED.
MR. THE BEARDED? OH, COME NOW, STARSWIRL WILL SUFFICE.
RIGHT, RIGHT.
I'M SORRY.
I DIDN'T MEAN—
YOUNG PONY, WILL YOU PLEASE JUST SPIT IT OUT?
IT'S CLEAR THAT YOU WANT SOMETHING OR AT LEAST WANT TO ASK ME SOMETHING.
AND THESE GARDENS ARE WHERE I COME WHEN I WISH TO BE AWAY FROM THE TWO BICKERING TEENAGED GIRLS WHO WILL SOMEDAY BE THE RULERS OF THIS LAND.
I DO!
BUT NOW YOU'RE MAKING IT HARD FOR ME TO THINK HERE TOO.
I'M SO SORRY. I'LL JUST GO.
WAIT!
THERE IS OBVIOUSLY SOMETHING IMPORTANT ON YOUR MIND OR YOU WOULDN'T HAVE COME ALL THIS WAY.
I'M SORRY TO BE IRRITABLE, IT'S JUST THAT I HAVE WRITTEN OVER ONE HUNDRED AND FIFTY SPELLS AND I JUST CAN'T SEEM TO FINISH THIS ONE.
WHAT DOES IT DO?
WELL, IF I KNEW THAT, I'D HAVE FINISHED IT, WOULDN'T I?
SORRY, I DON'T MEAN TO SNAP. IT'S JUST... YOU SPEND ALL DAY AROUND TWO MOODY TEENAGERS WHO CAN ALTER THE FABRIC OF REALITY AND...
...I'M RAMBLING. WHAT WAS YOUR ISSUE?

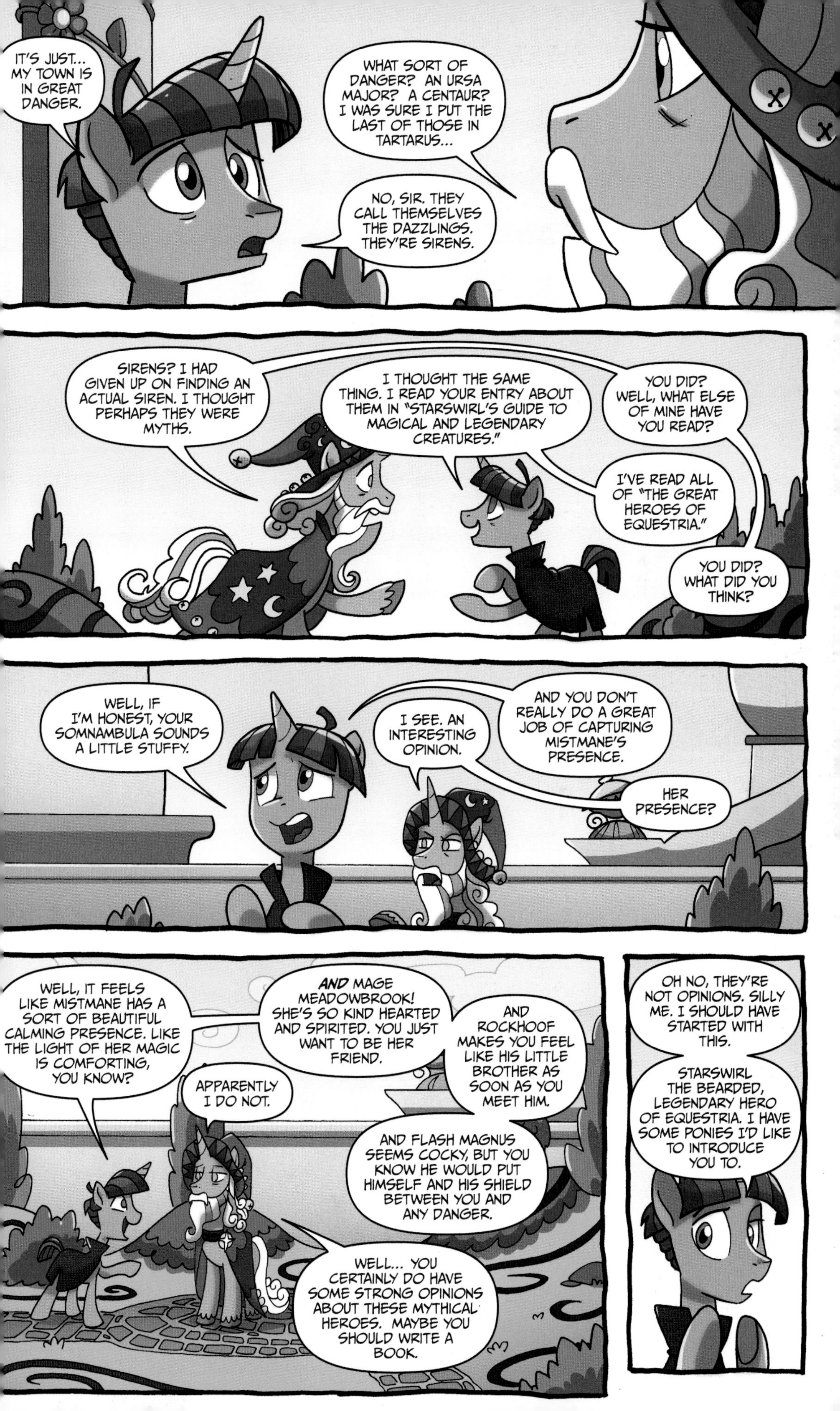

IT'S JUST... MY TOWN IS IN GREAT DANGER.
WHAT SORT OF DANGER? AN URSA MAJOR? A CENTAUR? I WAS SURE I PUT THE LAST OF THOSE IN TARTARUS...
NO, SIR. THEY CALL THEMSELVES THE DAZZLINGS. THEY'RE SIRENS.
SIRENS? I HAD GIVEN UP ON FINDING AN ACTUAL SIREN. I THOUGHT PERHAPS THEY WERE MYTHS.
I THOUGHT THE SAME THING. I READ YOUR ENTRY ABOUT THEM IN "STARSWIRL'S GUIDE TO MAGICAL AND LEGENDARY CREATURES."
YOU DID? WELL, WHAT ELSE OF MINE HAVE YOU READ?
I'VE READ ALL OF "THE GREAT HEROES OF EQUESTRIA."
YOU DID? WHAT DID YOU THINK?
WELL, IF I'M HONEST, YOUR SOMNAMBULA SOUNDS A LITTLE STUFFY.
I SEE. AN INTERESTING OPINION.
AND YOU DON'T REALLY DO A GREAT JOB OF CAPTURING MISTMANE'S PRESENCE.
HER PRESENCE?
WELL, IT FEELS LIKE MISTMANE HAS A SORT OF BEAUTIFUL CALMING PRESENCE. LIKE THE LIGHT OF HER MAGIC IS COMFORTING, YOU KNOW?
APPARENTLY I DO NOT.
AND MAGE MEADOWBROOK! SHE'S SO KIND HEARTED AND SPIRITED. YOU JUST WANT TO BE HER FRIEND.
AND ROCKHOOF MAKES YOU FEEL LIKE HIS LITTLE BROTHER AS SOON AS YOU MEET HIM.
AND FLASH MAGNUS SEEMS COCKY, BUT YOU KNOW HE WOULD PUT HIMSELF AND HIS SHIELD BETWEEN YOU AND ANY DANGER.
WELL... YOU CERTAINLY DO HAVE SOME STRONG OPINIONS ABOUT THESE MYTHICAL HEROES. MAYBE YOU SHOULD WRITE A BOOK.
OH NO, THEY'RE NOT OPINIONS. SILLY ME. I SHOULD HAVE STARTED WITH THIS.
STARSWIRL THE BEARDED, LEGENDARY HERO OF EQUESTRIA. I HAVE SOME PONIES I'D LIKE TO INTRODUCE YOU TO.

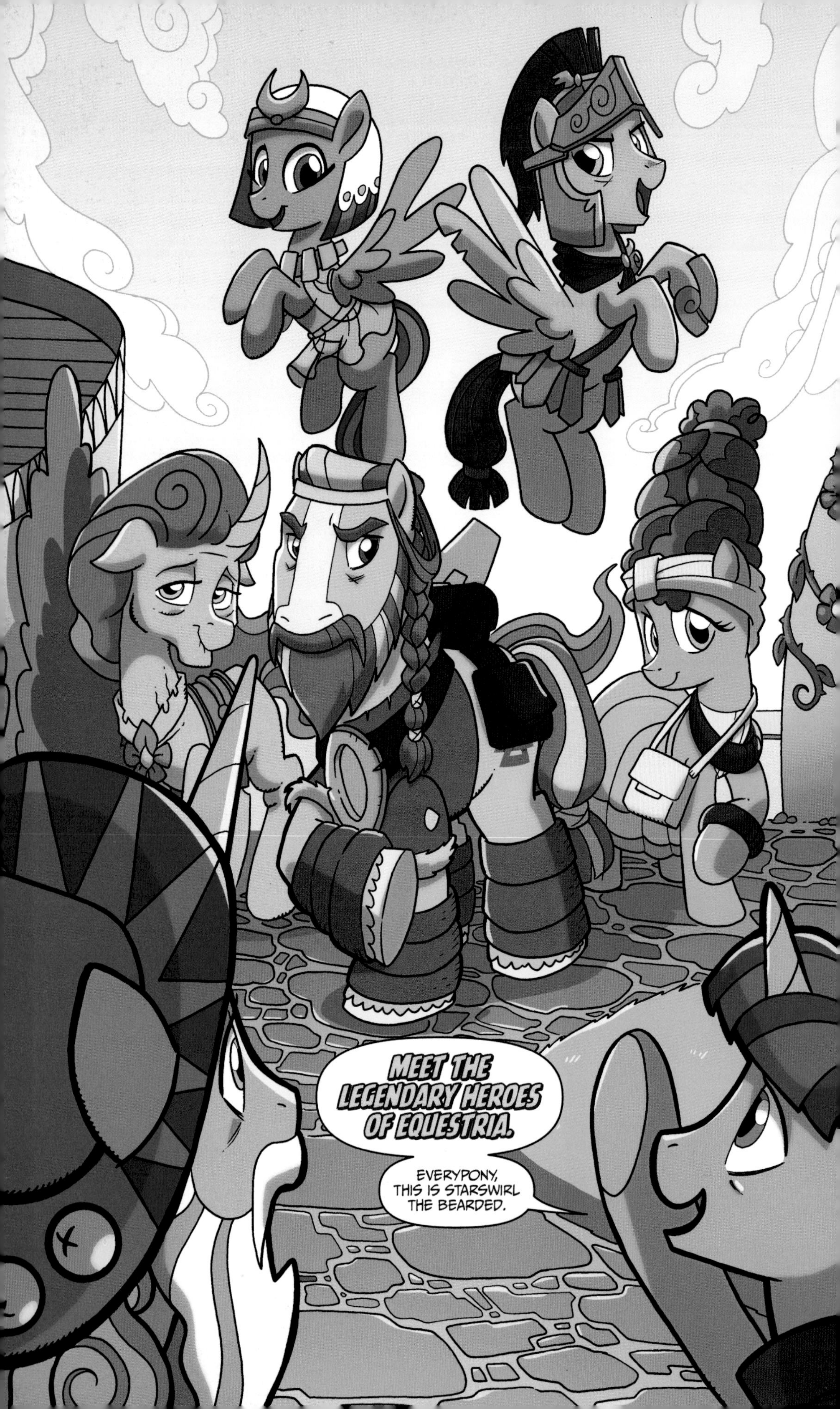
MEET THE LEGENDARY HEROES OF EQUESTRIA.
EVERYPONY, THIS IS STARSWIRL THE BEARDED.

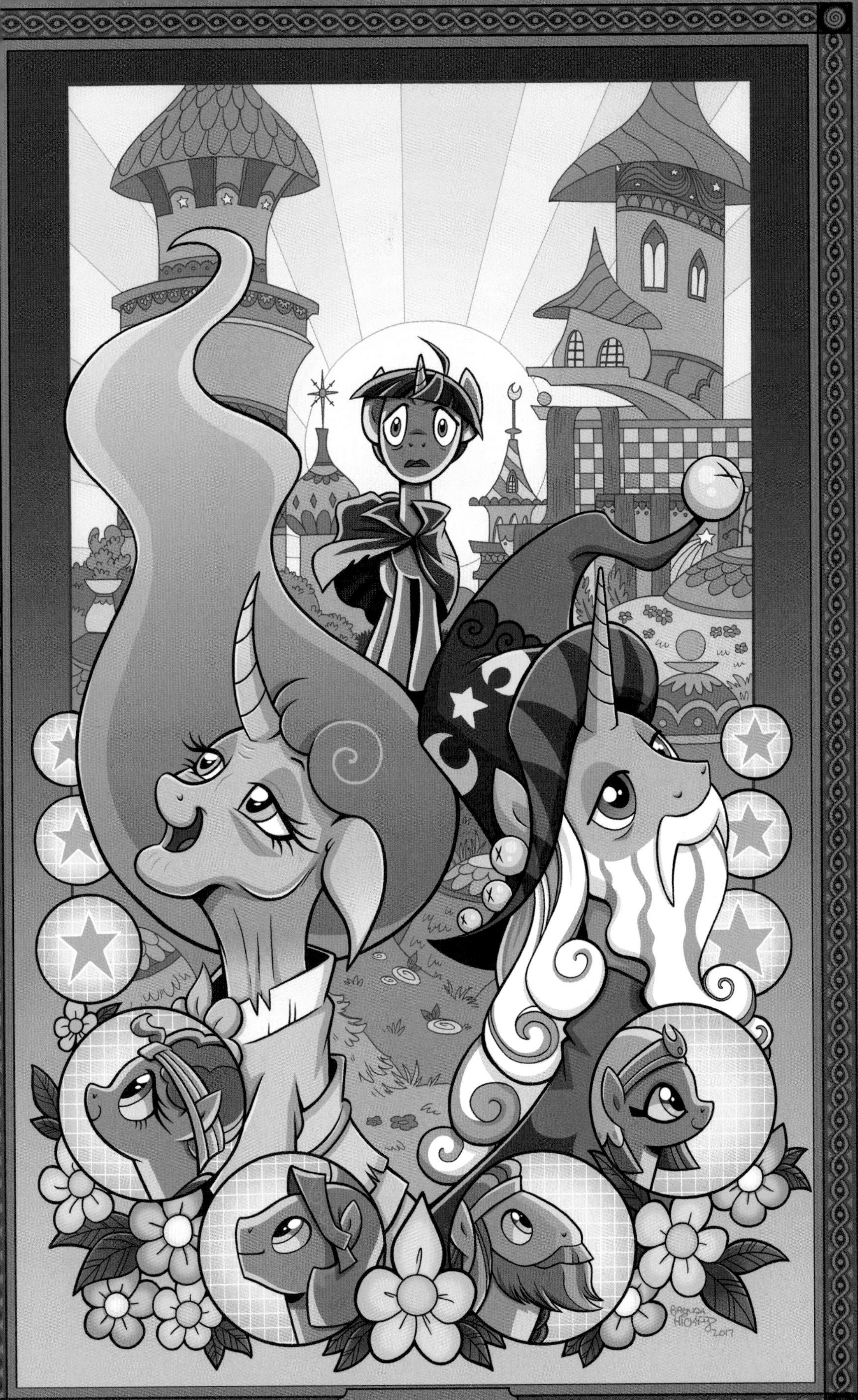

ART BY BRENDA HICKEY

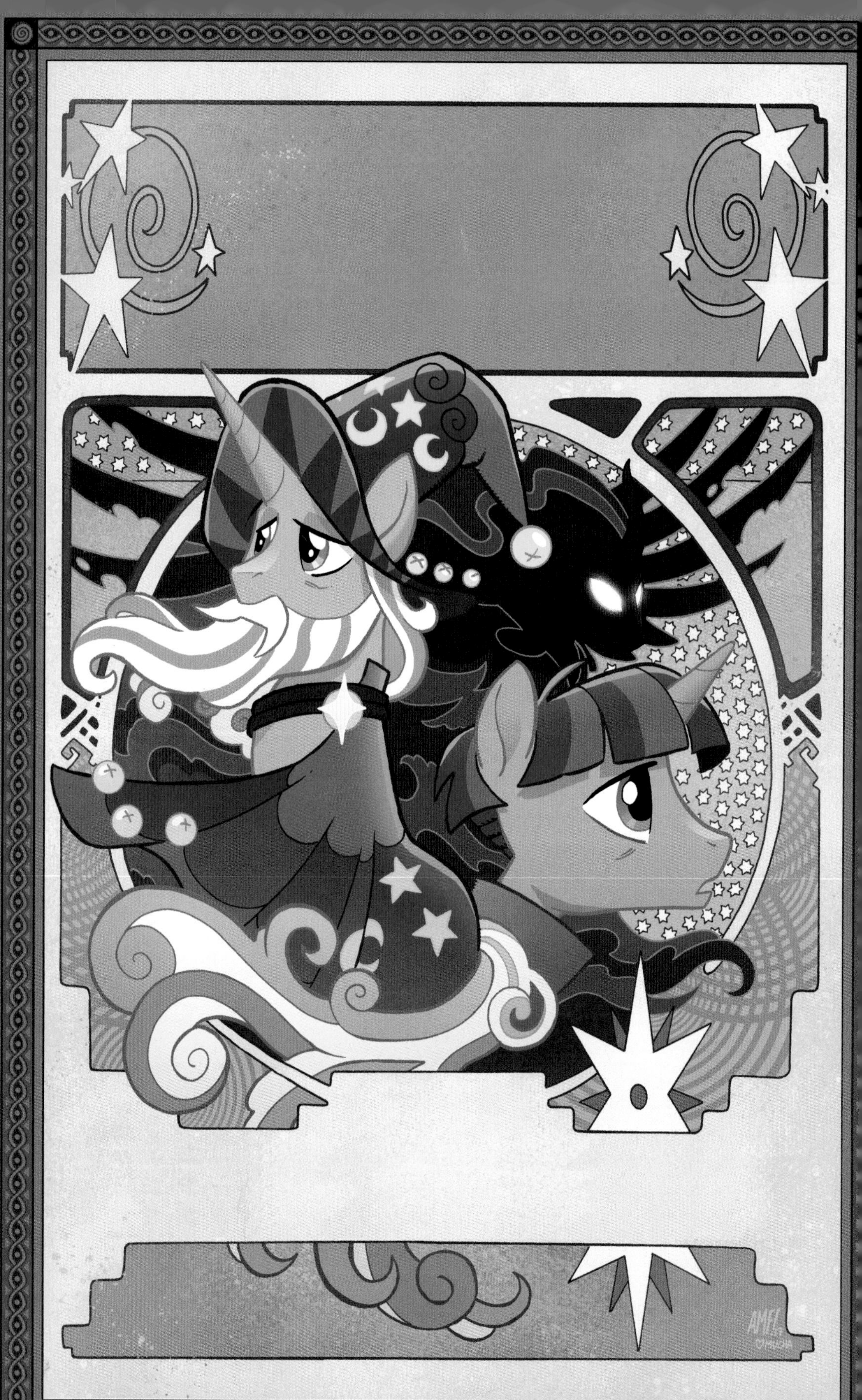
AMF! '17
♡MUCHA

ART BY TONY FLEECS

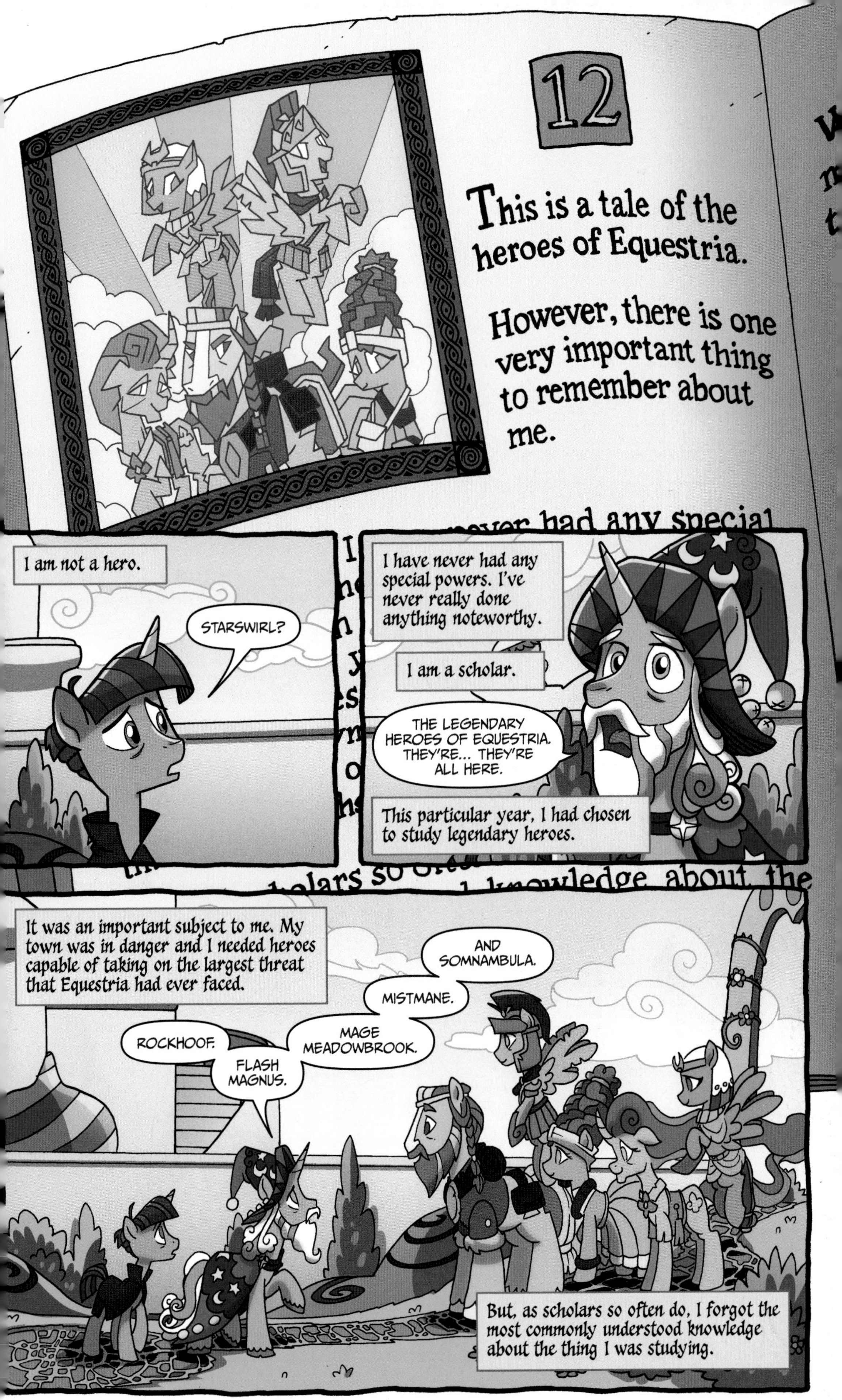
12
This is a tale of the heroes of Equestria.
However, there is one very important thing to remember about me.
I am not a hero.
STARSWIRL?
I have never had any special powers. I've never really done anything noteworthy.
I am a scholar.
THE LEGENDARY HEROES OF EQUESTRIA. THEY'RE... THEY'RE ALL HERE.
This particular year, I had chosen to study legendary heroes.
It was an important subject to me. My town was in danger and I needed heroes capable of taking on the largest threat that Equestria had ever faced.
ROCKHOOF.
FLASH MAGNUS.
MAGE MEADOWBROOK.
MISTMANE.
AND SOMNAMBULA.
But, as scholars so often do, I forgot the most commonly understood knowledge about the thing I was studying.

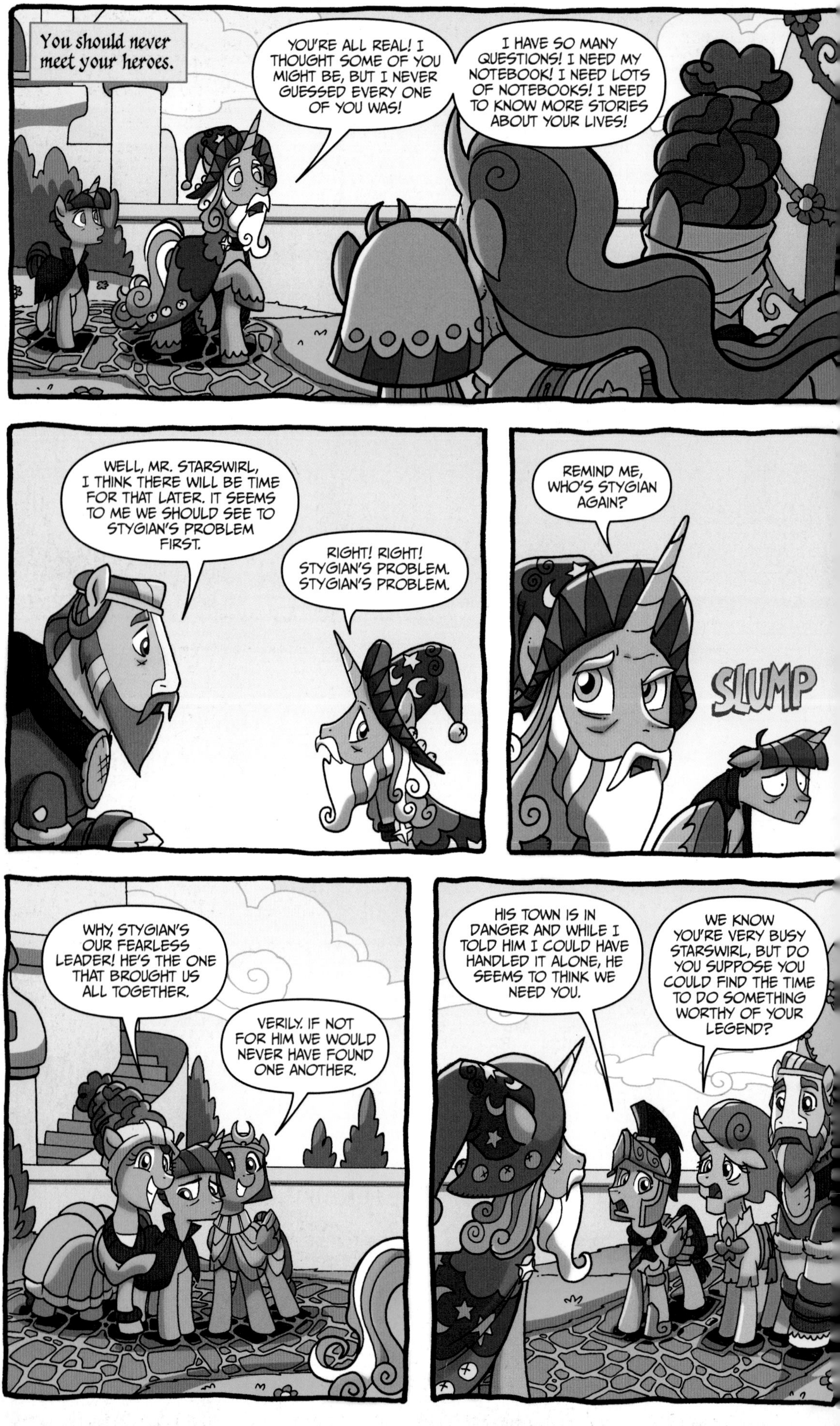
You should never meet your heroes.
YOU'RE ALL REAL! I THOUGHT SOME OF YOU MIGHT BE, BUT I NEVER GUESSED EVERY ONE OF YOU WAS!
I HAVE SO MANY QUESTIONS! I NEED MY NOTEBOOK! I NEED LOTS OF NOTEBOOKS! I NEED TO KNOW MORE STORIES ABOUT YOUR LIVES!
WELL, MR. STARSWIRL, I THINK THERE WILL BE TIME FOR THAT LATER. IT SEEMS TO ME WE SHOULD SEE TO STYGIAN'S PROBLEM FIRST.
RIGHT! RIGHT! STYGIAN'S PROBLEM. STYGIAN'S PROBLEM.
REMIND ME, WHO'S STYGIAN AGAIN?
SLUMP
WHY, STYGIAN'S OUR FEARLESS LEADER! HE'S THE ONE THAT BROUGHT US ALL TOGETHER.
VERILY. IF NOT FOR HIM WE WOULD NEVER HAVE FOUND ONE ANOTHER.
HIS TOWN IS IN DANGER AND WHILE I TOLD HIM I COULD HAVE HANDLED IT ALONE, HE SEEMS TO THINK WE NEED YOU.
WE KNOW YOU'RE VERY BUSY STARSWIRL, BUT DO YOU SUPPOSE YOU COULD FIND THE TIME TO DO SOMETHING WORTHY OF YOUR LEGEND?

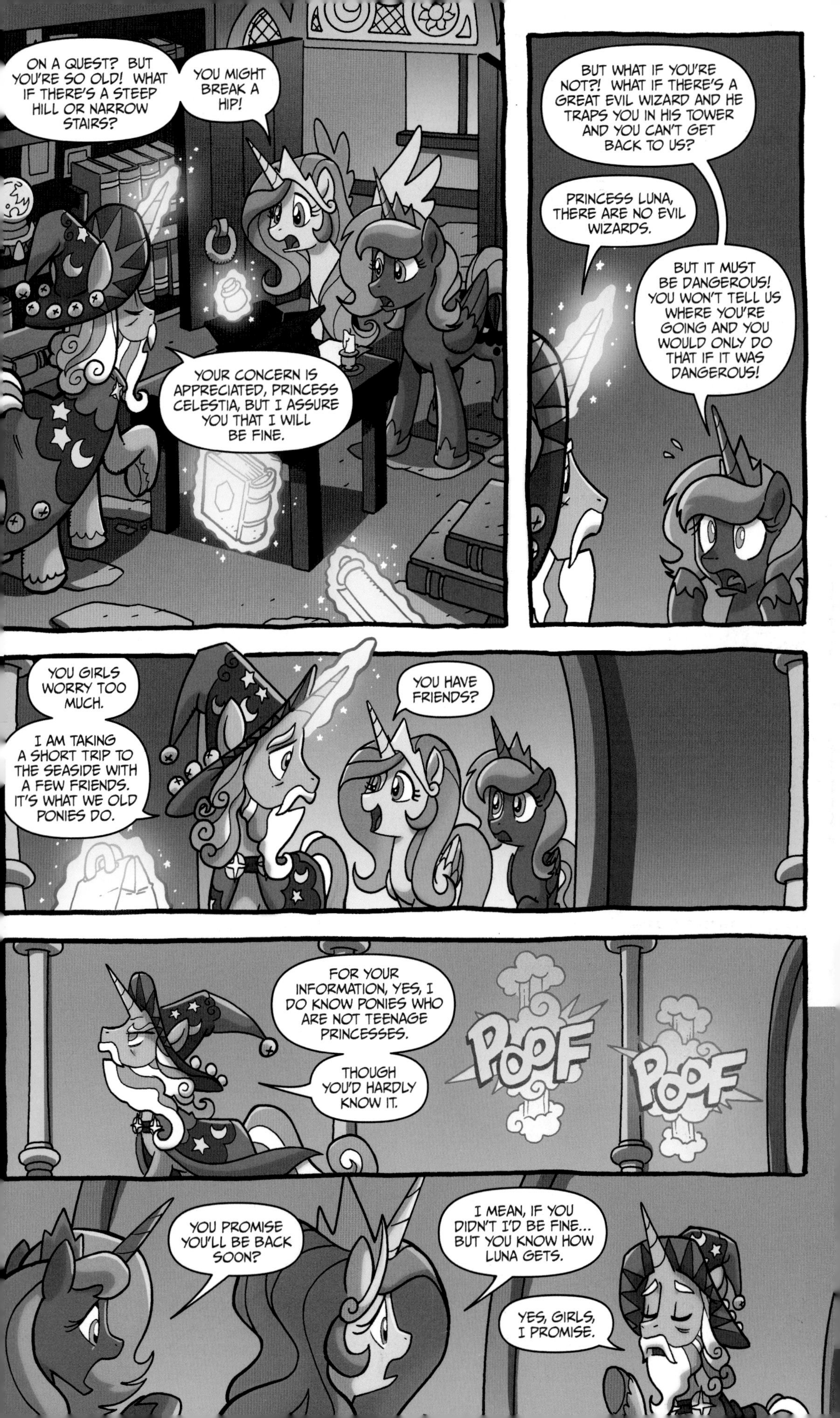

ON A QUEST? BUT YOU'RE SO OLD! WHAT IF THERE'S A STEEP HILL OR NARROW STAIRS?
YOU MIGHT BREAK A HIP!
YOUR CONCERN IS APPRECIATED, PRINCESS CELESTIA, BUT I ASSURE YOU THAT I WILL BE FINE.
BUT WHAT IF YOU'RE NOT?! WHAT IF THERE'S A GREAT EVIL WIZARD AND HE TRAPS YOU IN HIS TOWER AND YOU CAN'T GET BACK TO US?
PRINCESS LUNA, THERE ARE NO EVIL WIZARDS.
BUT IT MUST BE DANGEROUS! YOU WON'T TELL US WHERE YOU'RE GOING AND YOU WOULD ONLY DO THAT IF IT WAS DANGEROUS!
YOU GIRLS WORRY TOO MUCH.
I AM TAKING A SHORT TRIP TO THE SEASIDE WITH A FEW FRIENDS. IT'S WHAT WE OLD PONIES DO.
YOU HAVE FRIENDS?
FOR YOUR INFORMATION, YES, I DO KNOW PONIES WHO ARE NOT TEENAGE PRINCESSES.
THOUGH YOU'D HARDLY KNOW IT.
POOF
POOF
YOU PROMISE YOU'LL BE BACK SOON?
I MEAN, IF YOU DIDN'T I'D BE FINE... BUT YOU KNOW HOW LUNA GETS.
YES, GIRLS, I PROMISE.

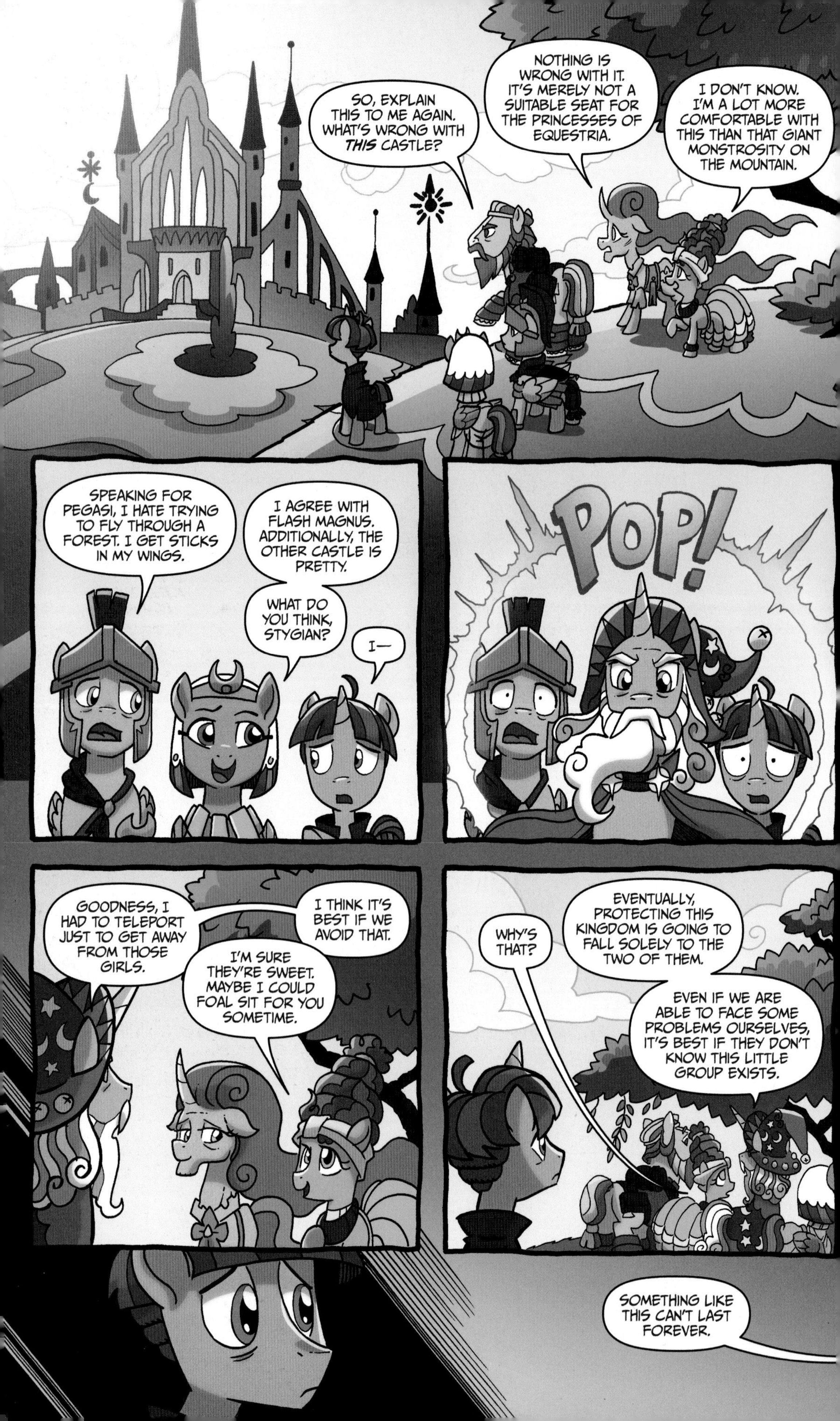
SO, EXPLAIN THIS TO ME AGAIN. WHAT'S WRONG WITH *THIS* CASTLE?
NOTHING IS WRONG WITH IT. IT'S MERELY NOT A SUITABLE SEAT FOR THE PRINCESSES OF EQUESTRIA.
I DON'T KNOW. I'M A LOT MORE COMFORTABLE WITH THIS THAN THAT GIANT MONSTROSITY ON THE MOUNTAIN.
SPEAKING FOR PEGASI, I HATE TRYING TO FLY THROUGH A FOREST. I GET STICKS IN MY WINGS.
I AGREE WITH FLASH MAGNUS. ADDITIONALLY, THE OTHER CASTLE IS PRETTY.
WHAT DO YOU THINK, STYGIAN?
I—
POP!
GOODNESS, I HAD TO TELEPORT JUST TO GET AWAY FROM THOSE GIRLS.
I THINK IT'S BEST IF WE AVOID THAT.
I'M SURE THEY'RE SWEET. MAYBE I COULD FOAL SIT FOR YOU SOMETIME.
WHY'S THAT?
EVENTUALLY, PROTECTING THIS KINGDOM IS GOING TO FALL SOLELY TO THE TWO OF THEM.
EVEN IF WE ARE ABLE TO FACE SOME PROBLEMS OURSELVES, IT'S BEST IF THEY DON'T KNOW THIS LITTLE GROUP EXISTS.
SOMETHING LIKE THIS CAN'T LAST FOREVER.

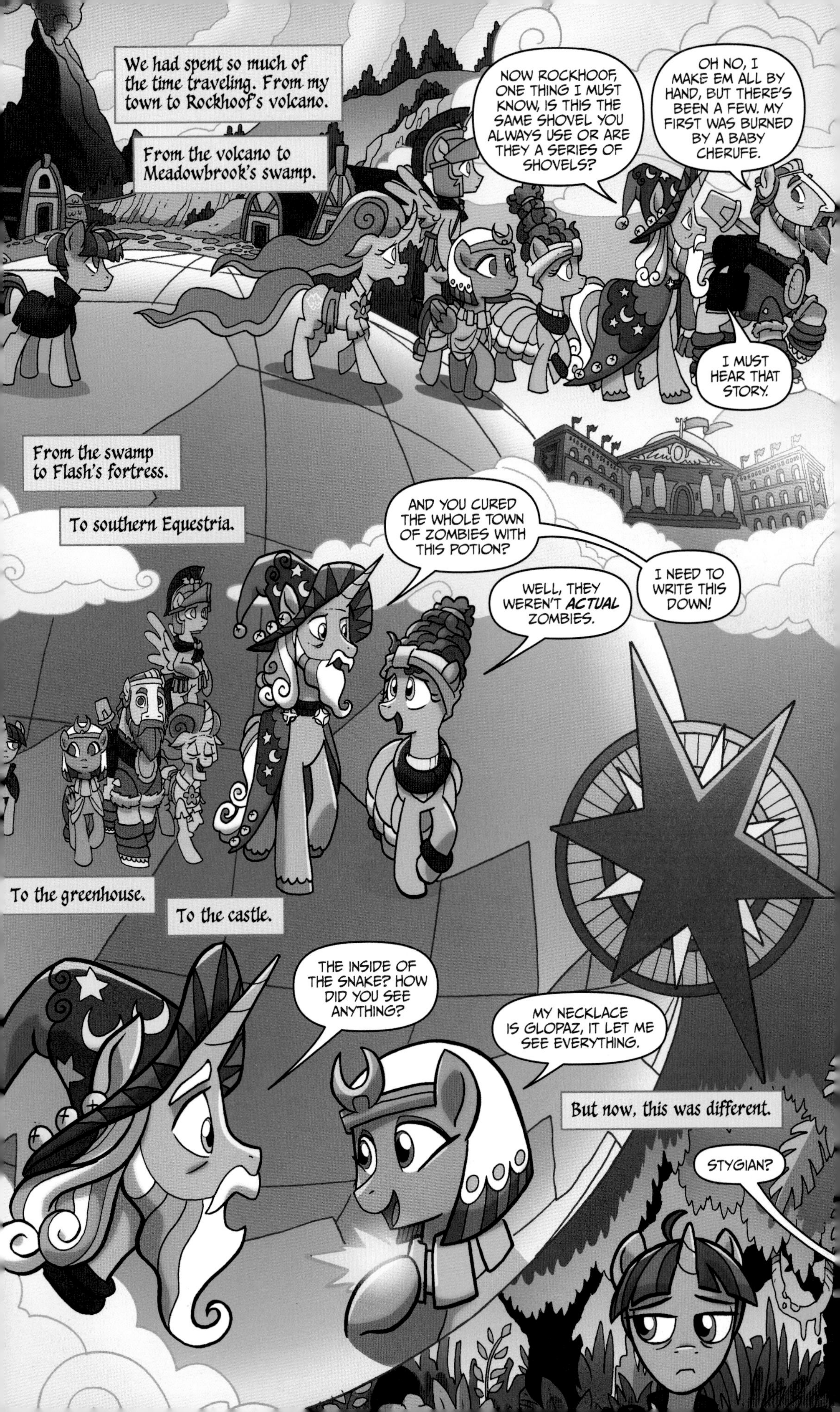
We had spent so much of the time traveling. From my town to Rockhoof's volcano.
From the volcano to Meadowbrook's swamp.
NOW ROCKHOOF, ONE THING I MUST KNOW, IS THIS THE SAME SHOVEL YOU ALWAYS USE OR ARE THEY A SERIES OF SHOVELS?
OH NO, I MAKE EM ALL BY HAND, BUT THERE'S BEEN A FEW. MY FIRST WAS BURNED BY A BABY CHERUFE.
I MUST HEAR THAT STORY.
From the swamp to Flash's fortress.
To southern Equestria.
AND YOU CURED THE WHOLE TOWN OF ZOMBIES WITH THIS POTION?
I NEED TO WRITE THIS DOWN!
WELL, THEY WEREN'T *ACTUAL* ZOMBIES.
To the greenhouse.
To the castle.
THE INSIDE OF THE SNAKE? HOW DID YOU SEE ANYTHING?
MY NECKLACE IS GLOPAZ, IT LET ME SEE EVERYTHING.
But now, this was different.
STYGIAN?

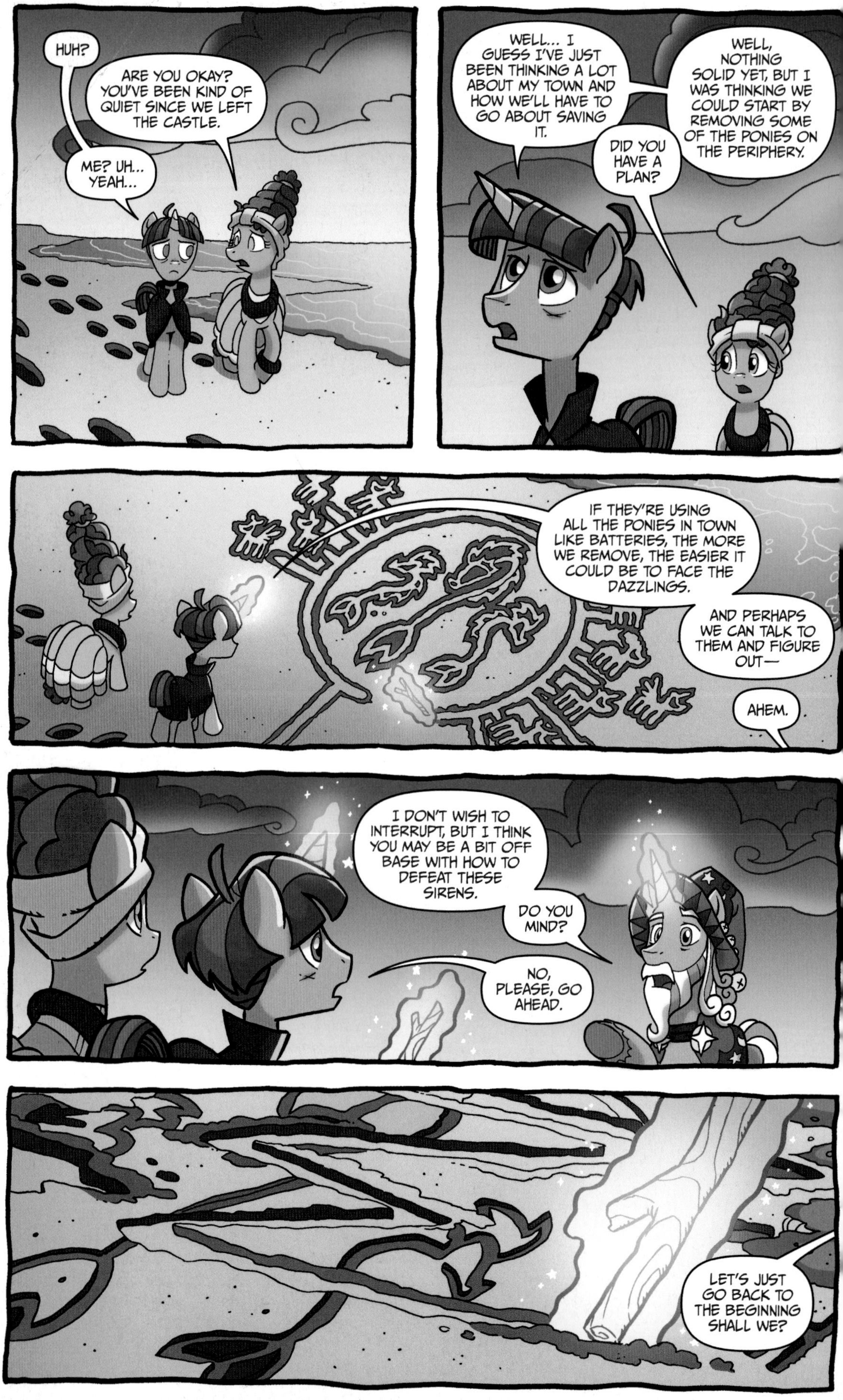
HUH?
ARE YOU OKAY? YOU'VE BEEN KIND OF QUIET SINCE WE LEFT THE CASTLE.
ME? UH... YEAH...
WELL... I GUESS I'VE JUST BEEN THINKING A LOT ABOUT MY TOWN AND HOW WE'LL HAVE TO GO ABOUT SAVING IT.
DID YOU HAVE A PLAN?
WELL, NOTHING SOLID YET, BUT I WAS THINKING WE COULD START BY REMOVING SOME OF THE PONIES ON THE PERIPHERY.
IF THEY'RE USING ALL THE PONIES IN TOWN LIKE BATTERIES, THE MORE WE REMOVE, THE EASIER IT COULD BE TO FACE THE DAZZLINGS.
AND PERHAPS WE CAN TALK TO THEM AND FIGURE OUT—
AHEM.
I DON'T WISH TO INTERRUPT, BUT I THINK YOU MAY BE A BIT OFF BASE WITH HOW TO DEFEAT THESE SIRENS.
DO YOU MIND?
NO, PLEASE, GO AHEAD.
LET'S JUST GO BACK TO THE BEGINNING SHALL WE?

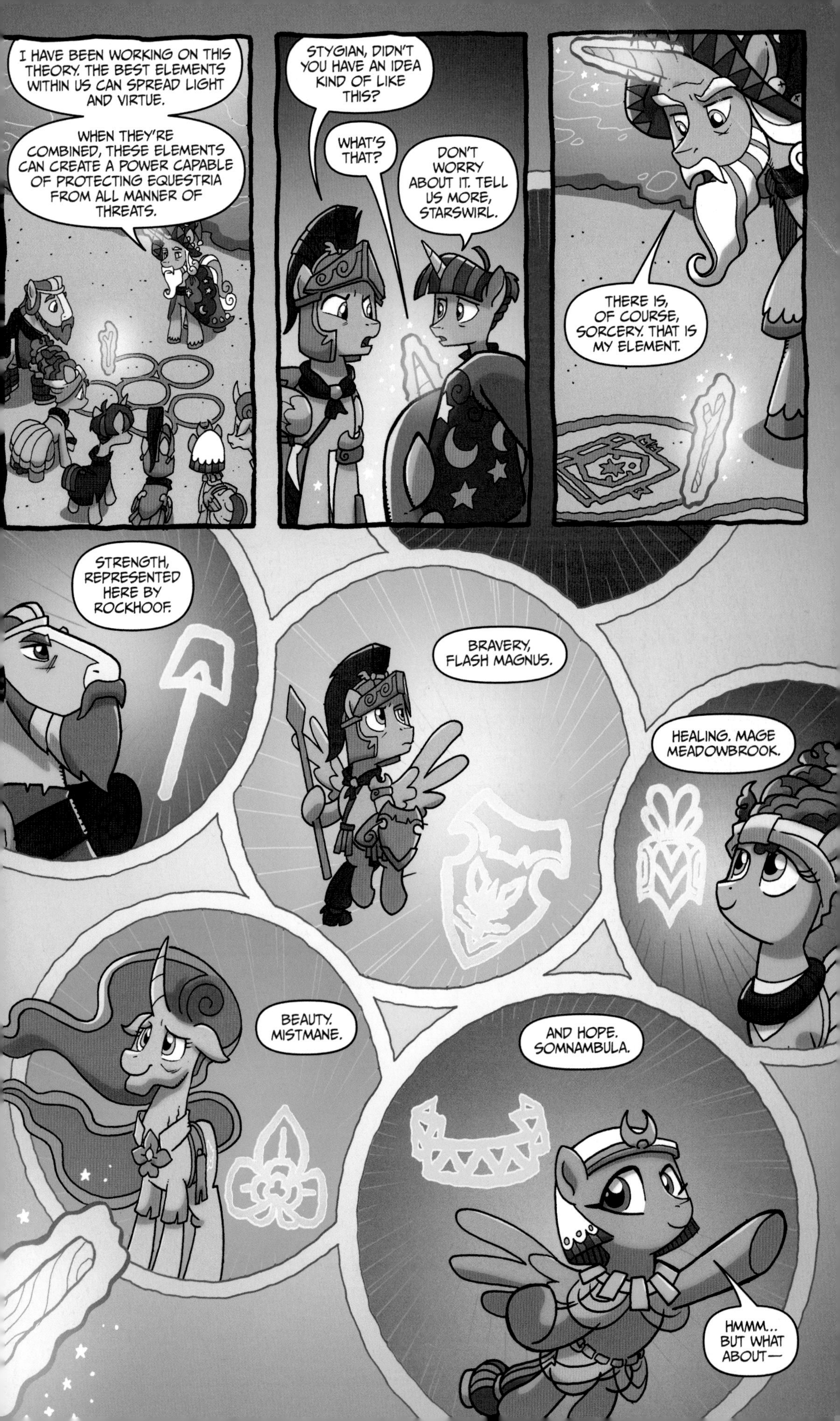
I HAVE BEEN WORKING ON THIS THEORY. THE BEST ELEMENTS WITHIN US CAN SPREAD LIGHT AND VIRTUE.
WHEN THEY'RE COMBINED, THESE ELEMENTS CAN CREATE A POWER CAPABLE OF PROTECTING EQUESTRIA FROM ALL MANNER OF THREATS.
STYGIAN, DIDN'T YOU HAVE AN IDEA KIND OF LIKE THIS?
WHAT'S THAT?
DON'T WORRY ABOUT IT. TELL US MORE, STARSWIRL.
THERE IS, OF COURSE, SORCERY. THAT IS MY ELEMENT.
STRENGTH, REPRESENTED HERE BY ROCKHOOF.
BRAVERY, FLASH MAGNUS.
HEALING. MAGE MEADOWBROOK.
BEAUTY. MISTMANE.
AND HOPE. SOMNAMBULA.
HMMM... BUT WHAT ABOUT—

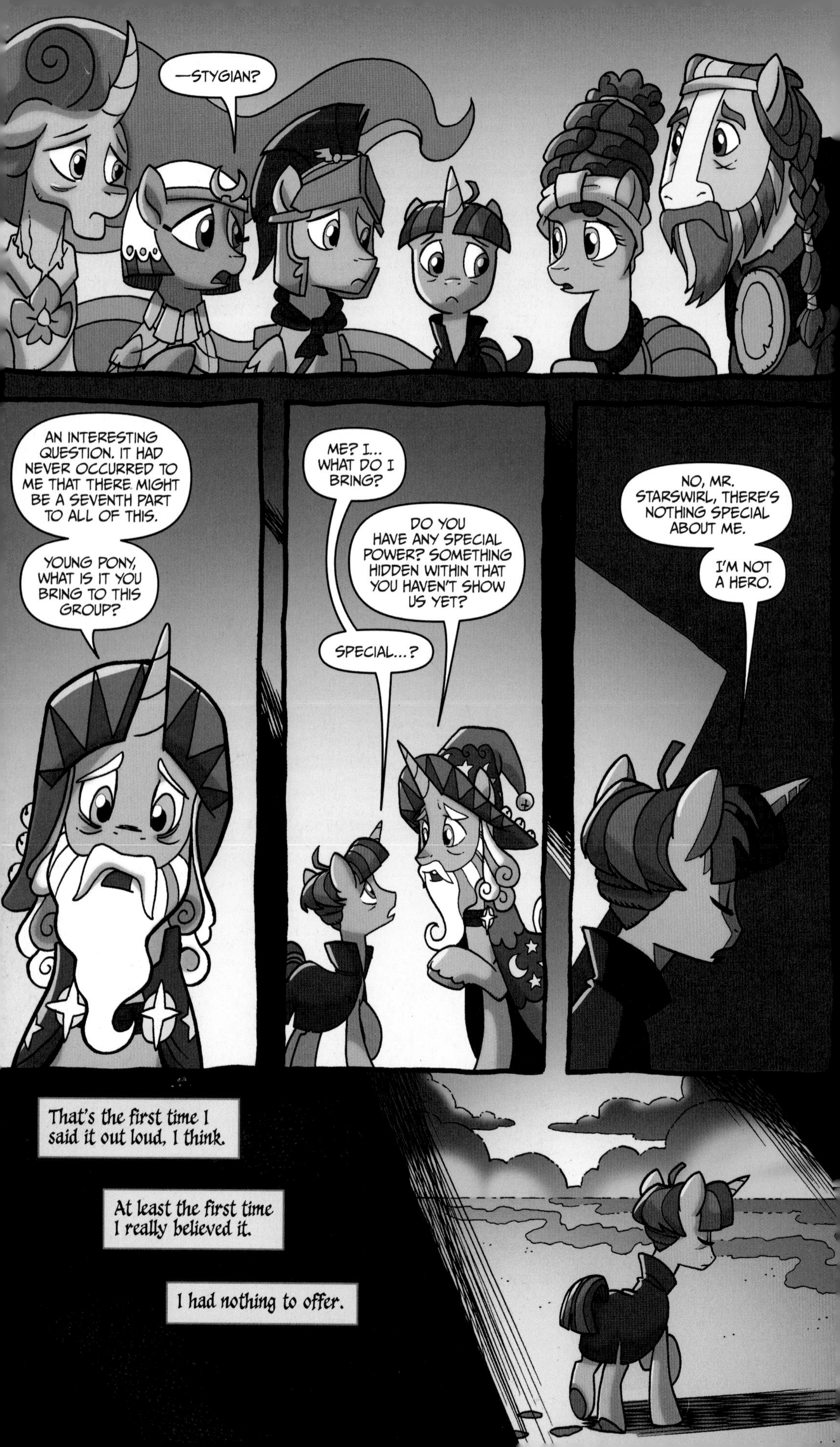
—STYGIAN?
AN INTERESTING QUESTION. IT HAD NEVER OCCURRED TO ME THAT THERE MIGHT BE A SEVENTH PART TO ALL OF THIS.
YOUNG PONY, WHAT IS IT YOU BRING TO THIS GROUP?
ME? I... WHAT DO I BRING?
DO YOU HAVE ANY SPECIAL POWER? SOMETHING HIDDEN WITHIN THAT YOU HAVEN'T SHOW US YET?
SPECIAL...?
NO, MR. STARSWIRL, THERE'S NOTHING SPECIAL ABOUT ME.
I'M NOT A HERO.
That's the first time I said it out loud, I think.
At least the first time I really believed it.
I had nothing to offer.

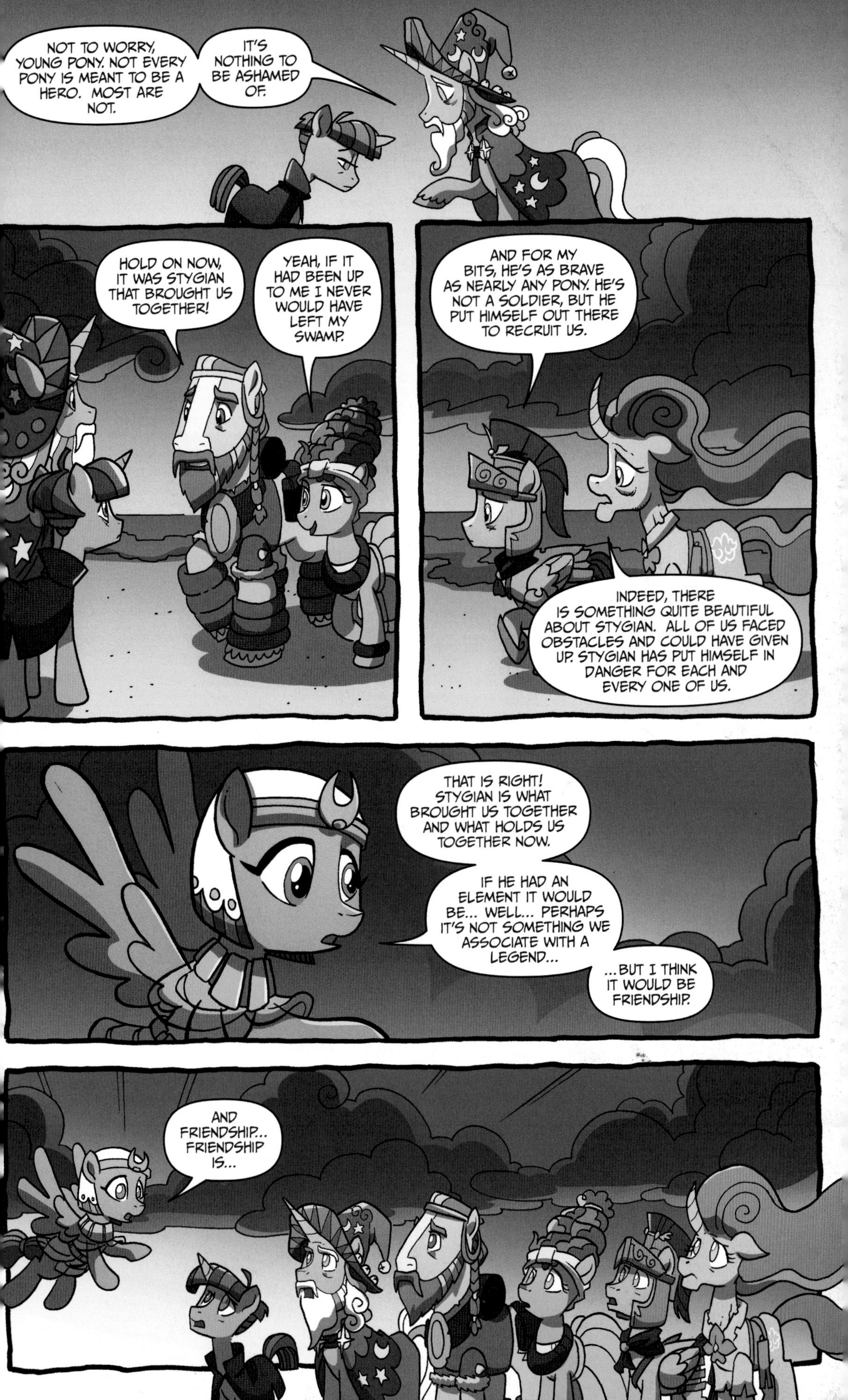
NOT TO WORRY, YOUNG PONY. NOT EVERY PONY IS MEANT TO BE A HERO. MOST ARE NOT.
IT'S NOTHING TO BE ASHAMED OF.
HOLD ON NOW, IT WAS STYGIAN THAT BROUGHT US TOGETHER!
YEAH, IF IT HAD BEEN UP TO ME I NEVER WOULD HAVE LEFT MY SWAMP.
AND FOR MY BITS, HE'S AS BRAVE AS NEARLY ANY PONY. HE'S NOT A SOLDIER, BUT HE PUT HIMSELF OUT THERE TO RECRUIT US.
INDEED, THERE IS SOMETHING QUITE BEAUTIFUL ABOUT STYGIAN. ALL OF US FACED OBSTACLES AND COULD HAVE GIVEN UP. STYGIAN HAS PUT HIMSELF IN DANGER FOR EACH AND EVERY ONE OF US.
THAT IS RIGHT! STYGIAN IS WHAT BROUGHT US TOGETHER AND WHAT HOLDS US TOGETHER NOW.
IF HE HAD AN ELEMENT IT WOULD BE... WELL... PERHAPS IT'S NOT SOMETHING WE ASSOCIATE WITH A LEGEND...
...BUT I THINK IT WOULD BE FRIENDSHIP.
AND FRIENDSHIP... FRIENDSHIP IS...

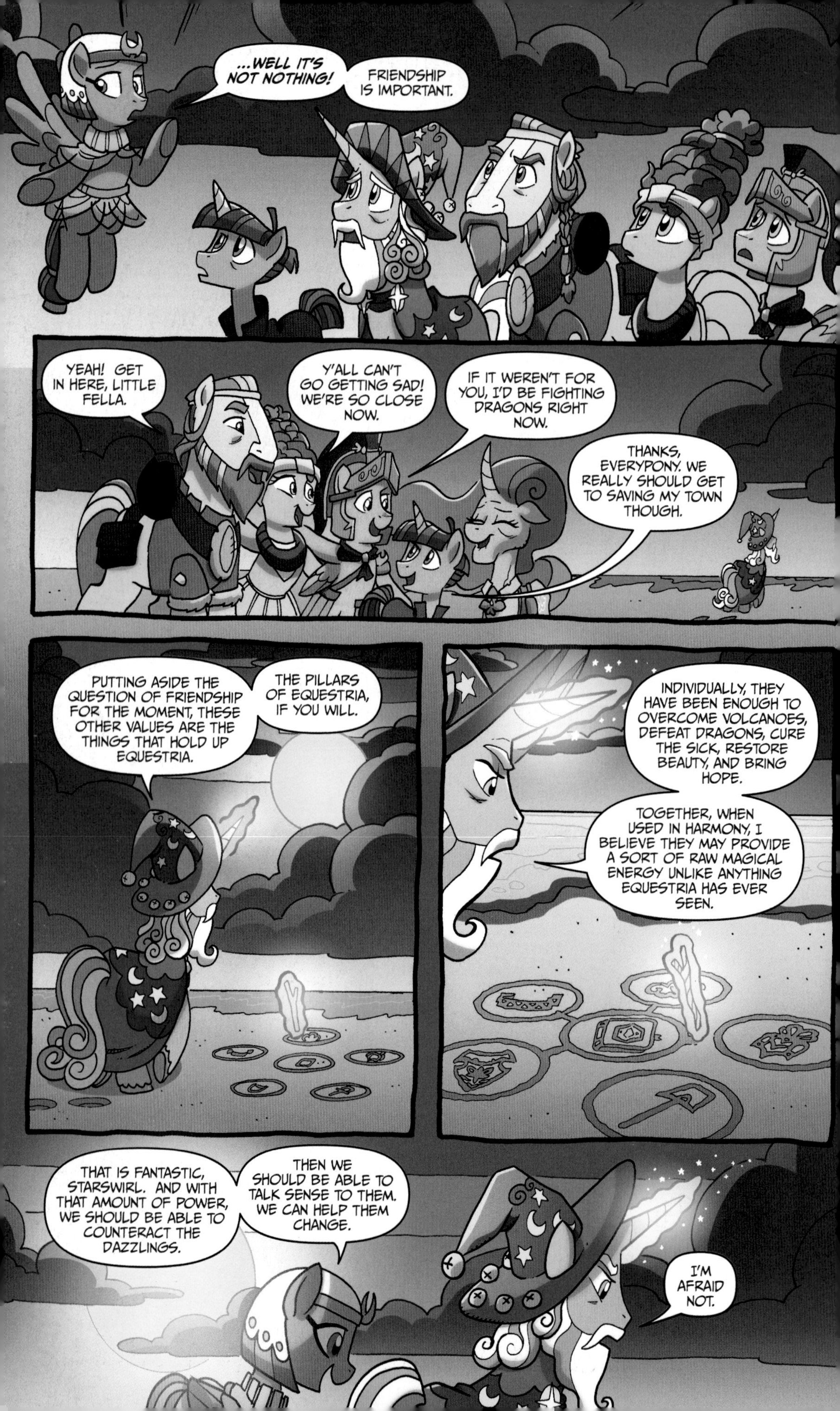
...WELL IT'S NOT NOTHING!
FRIENDSHIP IS IMPORTANT.
YEAH! GET IN HERE, LITTLE FELLA.
Y'ALL CAN'T GO GETTING SAD! WE'RE SO CLOSE NOW.
IF IT WEREN'T FOR YOU, I'D BE FIGHTING DRAGONS RIGHT NOW.
THANKS, EVERYPONY. WE REALLY SHOULD GET TO SAVING MY TOWN THOUGH.
PUTTING ASIDE THE QUESTION OF FRIENDSHIP FOR THE MOMENT, THESE OTHER VALUES ARE THE THINGS THAT HOLD UP EQUESTRIA.
THE PILLARS OF EQUESTRIA, IF YOU WILL.
INDIVIDUALLY, THEY HAVE BEEN ENOUGH TO OVERCOME VOLCANOES, DEFEAT DRAGONS, CURE THE SICK, RESTORE BEAUTY, AND BRING HOPE.
TOGETHER, WHEN USED IN HARMONY, I BELIEVE THEY MAY PROVIDE A SORT OF RAW MAGICAL ENERGY UNLIKE ANYTHING EQUESTRIA HAS EVER SEEN.
THAT IS FANTASTIC, STARSWIRL. AND WITH THAT AMOUNT OF POWER, WE SHOULD BE ABLE TO COUNTERACT THE DAZZLINGS.
THEN WE SHOULD BE ABLE TO TALK SENSE TO THEM. WE CAN HELP THEM CHANGE.
I'M AFRAID NOT.

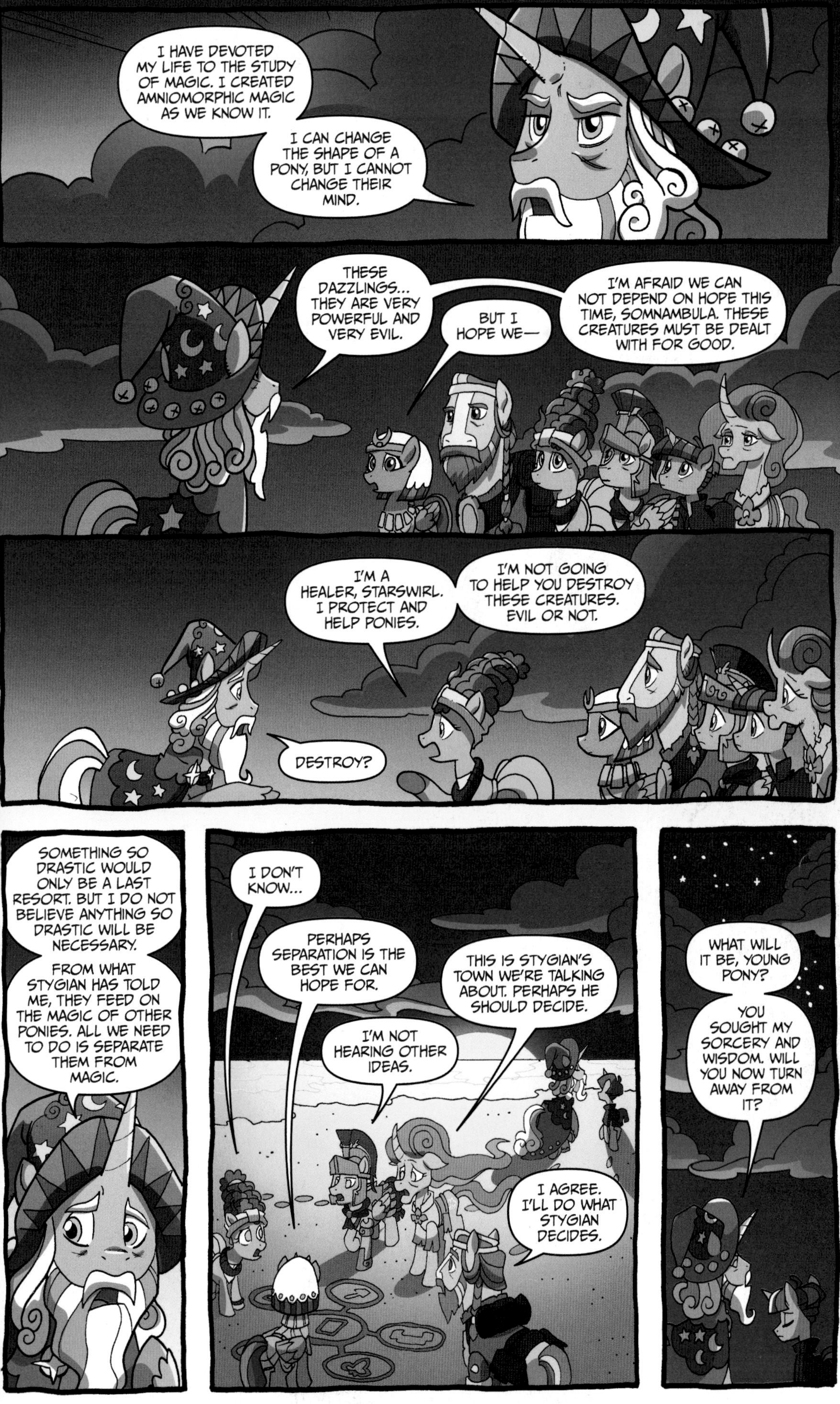

I HAVE DEVOTED MY LIFE TO THE STUDY OF MAGIC. I CREATED AMNIOMORPHIC MAGIC AS WE KNOW IT.
I CAN CHANGE THE SHAPE OF A PONY, BUT I CANNOT CHANGE THEIR MIND.
THESE DAZZLINGS... THEY ARE VERY POWERFUL AND VERY EVIL.
BUT I HOPE WE—
I'M AFRAID WE CAN NOT DEPEND ON HOPE THIS TIME, SOMNAMBULA. THESE CREATURES MUST BE DEALT WITH FOR GOOD.
DESTROY?
I'M A HEALER, STARSWIRL. I PROTECT AND HELP PONIES.
I'M NOT GOING TO HELP YOU DESTROY THESE CREATURES. EVIL OR NOT.
SOMETHING SO DRASTIC WOULD ONLY BE A LAST RESORT. BUT I DO NOT BELIEVE ANYTHING SO DRASTIC WILL BE NECESSARY.
FROM WHAT STYGIAN HAS TOLD ME, THEY FEED ON THE MAGIC OF OTHER PONIES. ALL WE NEED TO DO IS SEPARATE THEM FROM MAGIC.
I DON'T KNOW...
PERHAPS SEPARATION IS THE BEST WE CAN HOPE FOR.
I'M NOT HEARING OTHER IDEAS.
THIS IS STYGIAN'S TOWN WE'RE TALKING ABOUT. PERHAPS HE SHOULD DECIDE.
I AGREE. I'LL DO WHAT STYGIAN DECIDES.
WHAT WILL IT BE, YOUNG PONY?
YOU SOUGHT MY SORCERY AND WISDOM. WILL YOU NOW TURN AWAY FROM IT?

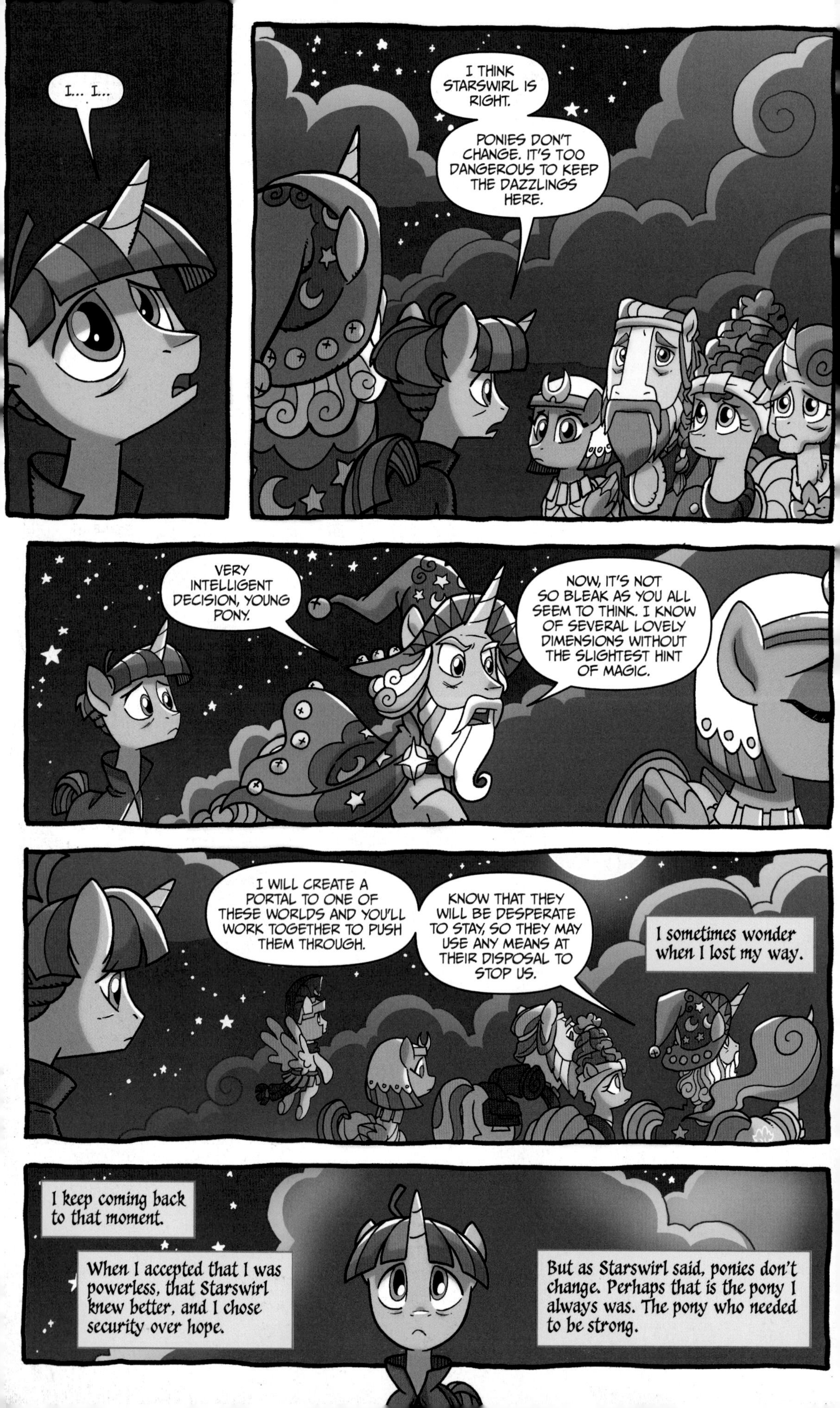
I... I...
I THINK STARSWIRL IS RIGHT.
PONIES DON'T CHANGE. IT'S TOO DANGEROUS TO KEEP THE DAZZLINGS HERE.
VERY INTELLIGENT DECISION, YOUNG PONY.
NOW, IT'S NOT SO BLEAK AS YOU ALL SEEM TO THINK. I KNOW OF SEVERAL LOVELY DIMENSIONS WITHOUT THE SLIGHTEST HINT OF MAGIC.
I WILL CREATE A PORTAL TO ONE OF THESE WORLDS AND YOU'LL WORK TOGETHER TO PUSH THEM THROUGH.
KNOW THAT THEY WILL BE DESPERATE TO STAY, SO THEY MAY USE ANY MEANS AT THEIR DISPOSAL TO STOP US.
I sometimes wonder when I lost my way.
I keep coming back to that moment.
When I accepted that I was powerless, that Starswirl knew better, and I chose security over hope.
But as Starswirl said, ponies don't change. Perhaps that is the pony I always was. The pony who needed to be strong.

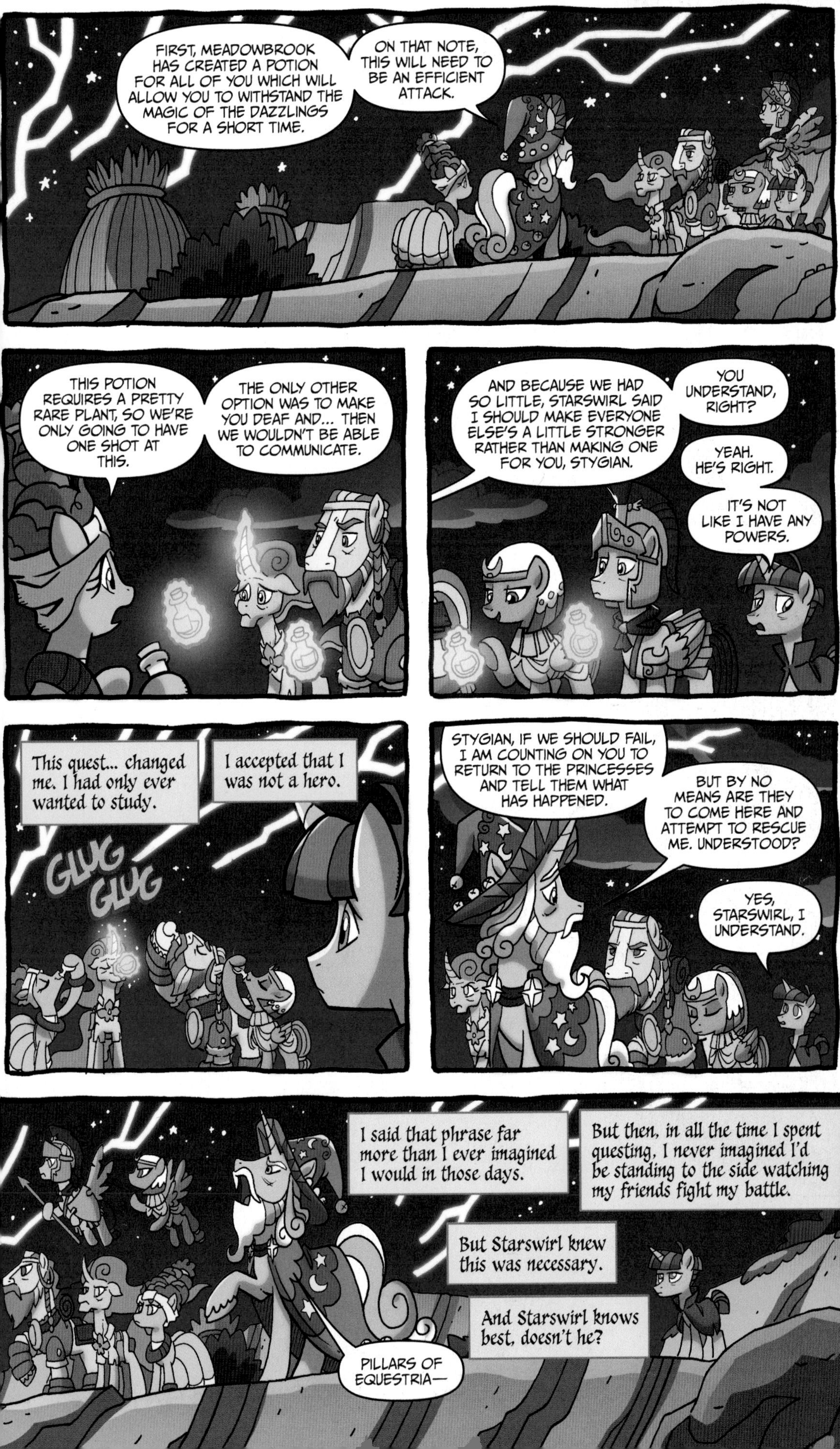
FIRST, MEADOWBROOK HAS CREATED A POTION FOR ALL OF YOU WHICH WILL ALLOW YOU TO WITHSTAND THE MAGIC OF THE DAZZLINGS FOR A SHORT TIME.
ON THAT NOTE, THIS WILL NEED TO BE AN EFFICIENT ATTACK.
THIS POTION REQUIRES A PRETTY RARE PLANT, SO WE'RE ONLY GOING TO HAVE ONE SHOT AT THIS.
THE ONLY OTHER OPTION WAS TO MAKE YOU DEAF AND... THEN WE WOULDN'T BE ABLE TO COMMUNICATE.
AND BECAUSE WE HAD SO LITTLE, STARSWIRL SAID I SHOULD MAKE EVERYONE ELSE'S A LITTLE STRONGER RATHER THAN MAKING ONE FOR YOU, STYGIAN.
YOU UNDERSTAND, RIGHT?
YEAH. HE'S RIGHT.
IT'S NOT LIKE I HAVE ANY POWERS.
This quest... changed me. I had only ever wanted to study.
I accepted that I was not a hero.
GLUG GLUG
STYGIAN, IF WE SHOULD FAIL, I AM COUNTING ON YOU TO RETURN TO THE PRINCESSES AND TELL THEM WHAT HAS HAPPENED.
BUT BY NO MEANS ARE THEY TO COME HERE AND ATTEMPT TO RESCUE ME. UNDERSTOOD?
YES, STARSWIRL, I UNDERSTAND.
I said that phrase far more than I ever imagined I would in those days.
But then, in all the time I spent questing, I never imagined I'd be standing to the side watching my friends fight my battle.
But Starswirl knew this was necessary.
And Starswirl knows best, doesn't he?
PILLARS OF EQUESTRIA—

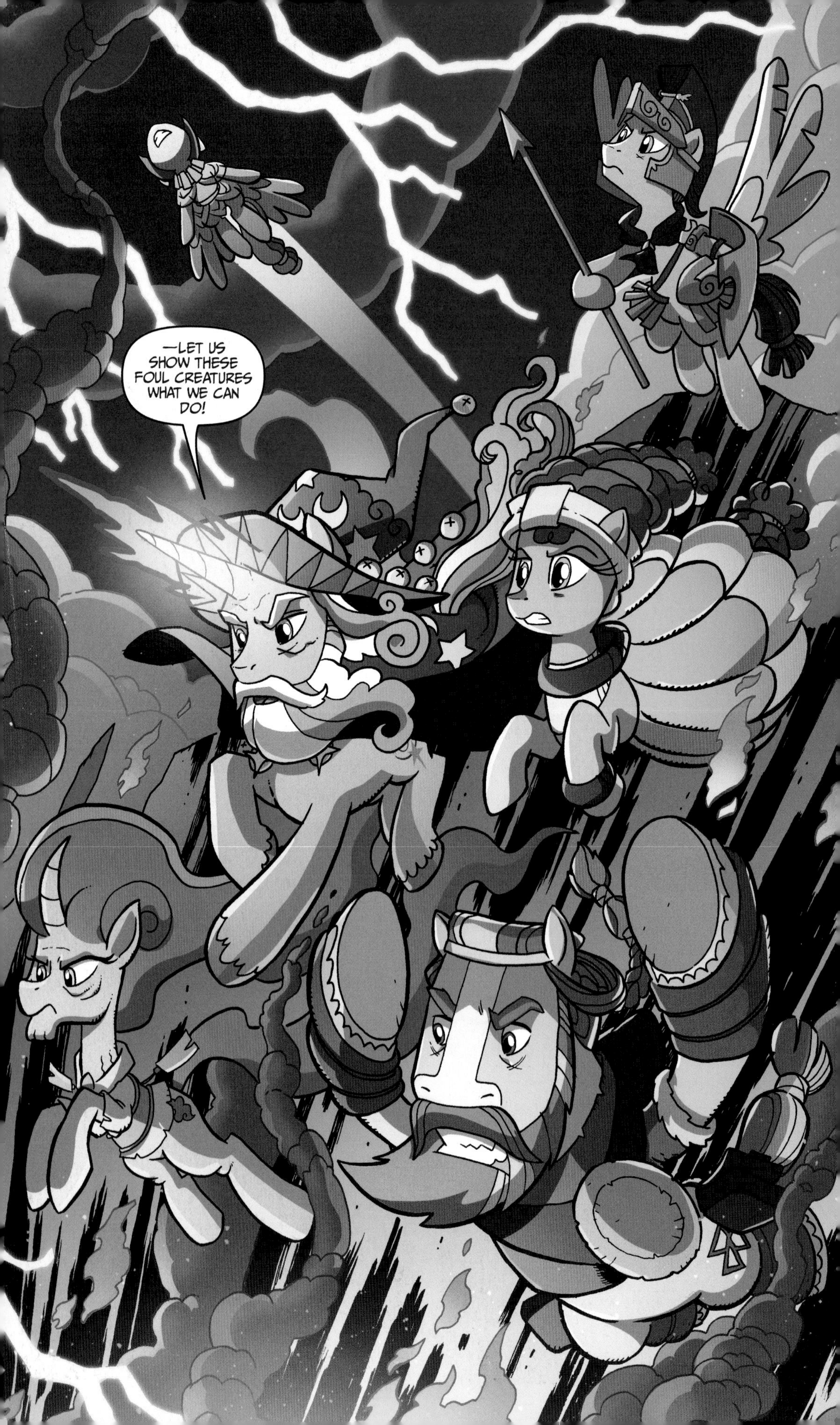
—LET US SHOW THESE FOUL CREATURES WHAT WE CAN DO!

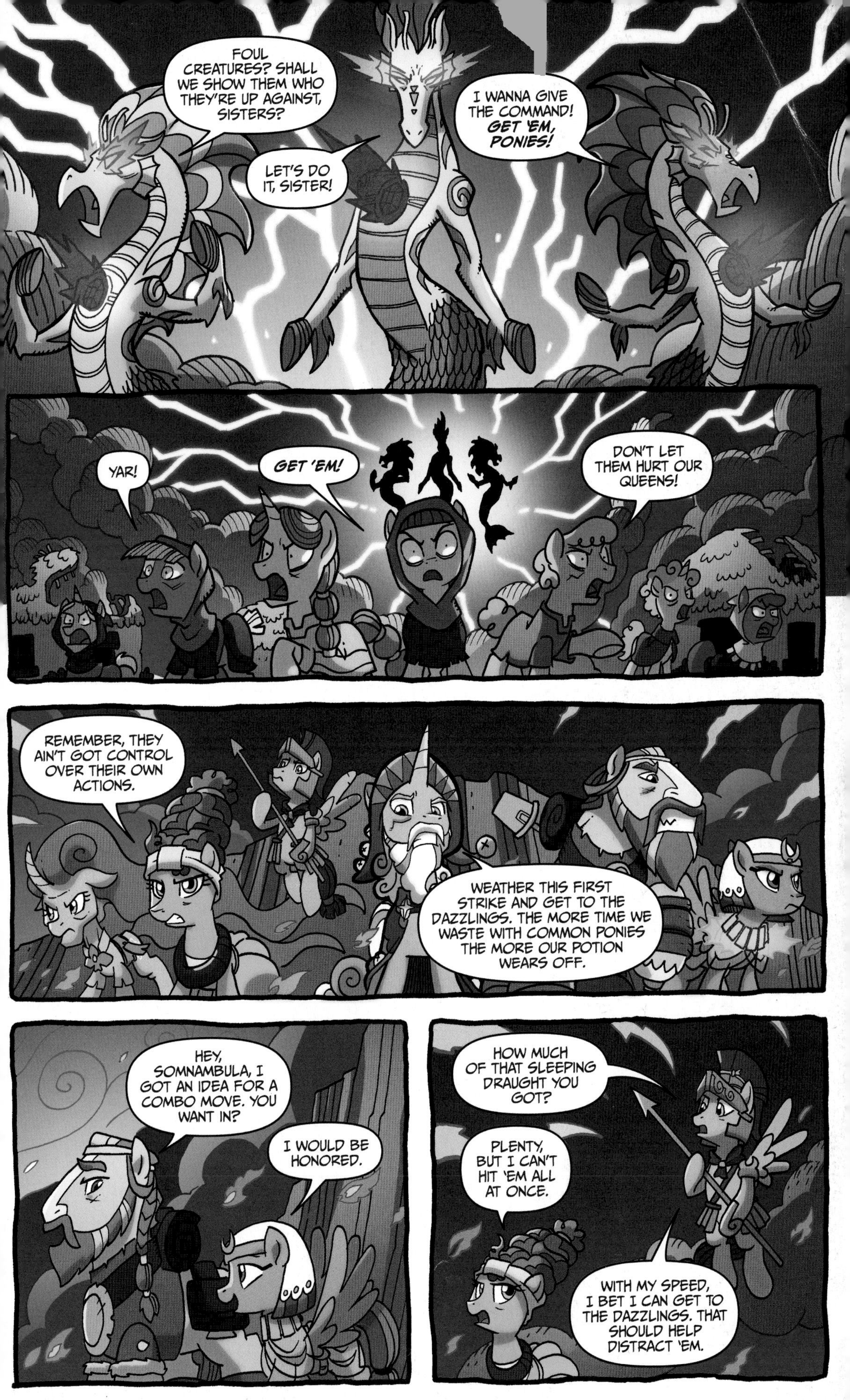
FOUL CREATURES? SHALL WE SHOW THEM WHO THEY'RE UP AGAINST, SISTERS?
LET'S DO IT, SISTER!
I WANNA GIVE THE COMMAND! GET 'EM, PONIES!
YAR!
GET 'EM!
DON'T LET THEM HURT OUR QUEENS!
REMEMBER, THEY AIN'T GOT CONTROL OVER THEIR OWN ACTIONS.
WEATHER THIS FIRST STRIKE AND GET TO THE DAZZLINGS. THE MORE TIME WE WASTE WITH COMMON PONIES THE MORE OUR POTION WEARS OFF.
HEY, SOMNAMBULA, I GOT AN IDEA FOR A COMBO MOVE. YOU WANT IN?
I WOULD BE HONORED.
HOW MUCH OF THAT SLEEPING DRAUGHT YOU GOT?
PLENTY, BUT I CAN'T HIT 'EM ALL AT ONCE.
WITH MY SPEED, I BET I CAN GET TO THE DAZZLINGS. THAT SHOULD HELP DISTRACT 'EM.

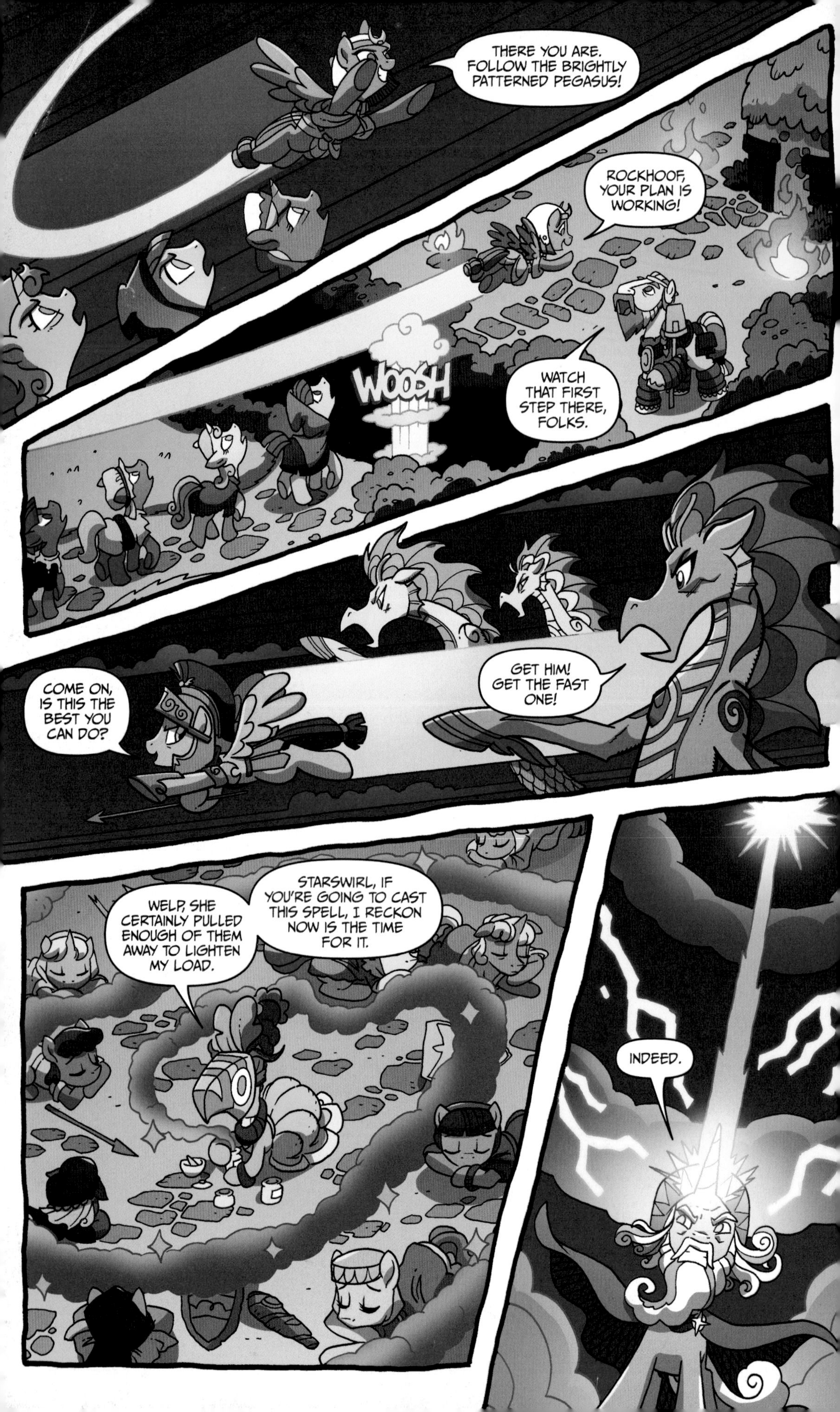
THERE YOU ARE. FOLLOW THE BRIGHTLY PATTERNED PEGASUS!
ROCKHOOF, YOUR PLAN IS WORKING!
WOOSH
WATCH THAT FIRST STEP THERE, FOLKS.
COME ON, IS THIS THE BEST YOU CAN DO?
GET HIM! GET THE FAST ONE!
WELP, SHE CERTAINLY PULLED ENOUGH OF THEM AWAY TO LIGHTEN MY LOAD.
STARSWIRL, IF YOU'RE GOING TO CAST THIS SPELL, I RECKON NOW IS THE TIME FOR IT.
INDEED.

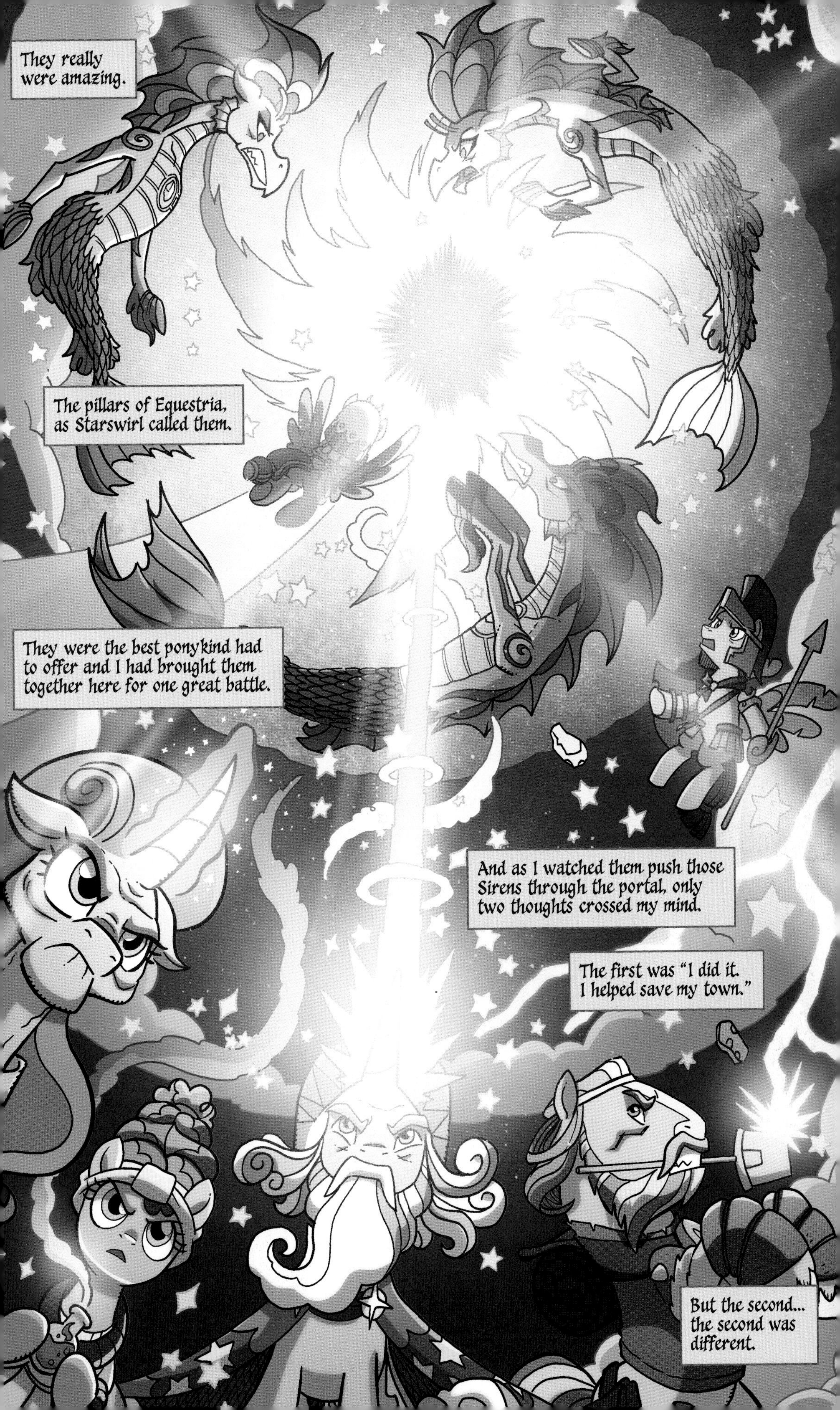
They really were amazing.
The pillars of Equestria, as Starswirl called them.
They were the best ponykind had to offer and I had brought them together here for one great battle.
And as I watched them push those Sirens through the portal, only two thoughts crossed my mind.
The first was "I did it. I helped save my town."
But the second... the second was different.

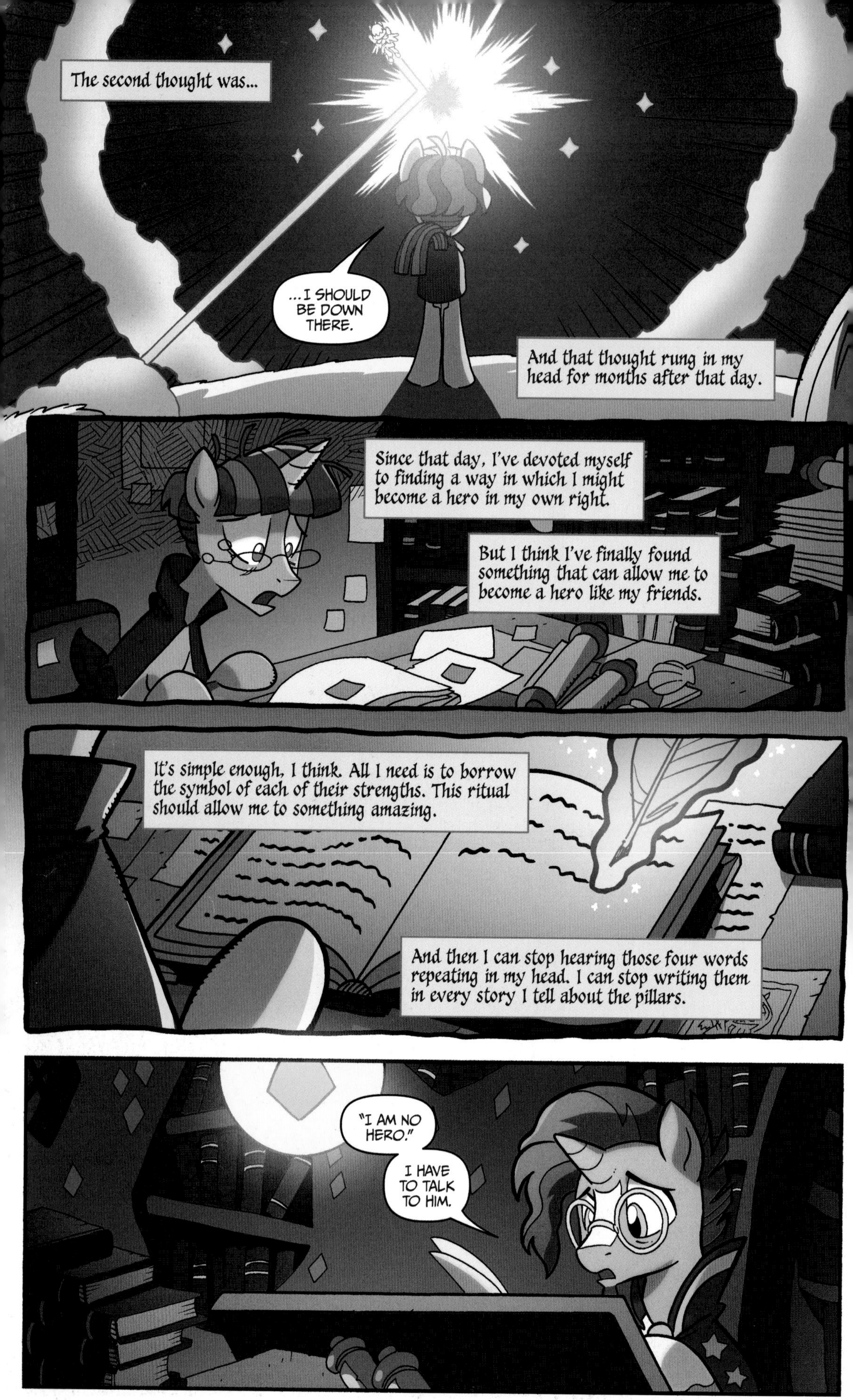
The second thought was...
...I SHOULD BE DOWN THERE.
And that thought rung in my head for months after that day.
Since that day, I've devoted myself to finding a way in which I might become a hero in my own right.
But I think I've finally found something that can allow me to become a hero like my friends.
It's simple enough, I think. All I need is to borrow the symbol of each of their strengths. This ritual should allow me to something amazing.
And then I can stop hearing those four words repeating in my head. I can stop writing them in every story I tell about the pillars.
"I AM NO HERO."
I HAVE TO TALK TO HIM.

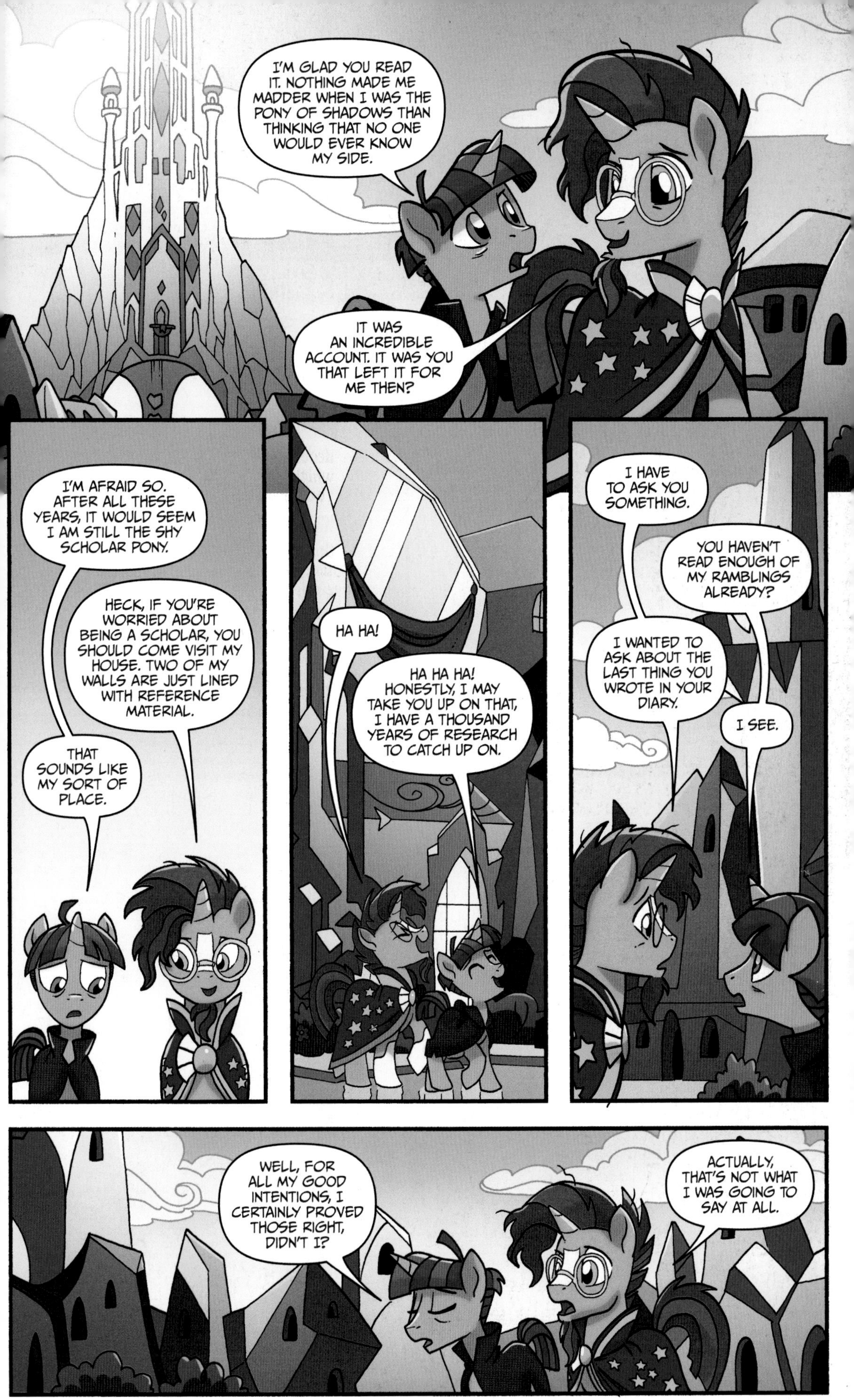

I'M GLAD YOU READ IT. NOTHING MADE ME MADDER WHEN I WAS THE PONY OF SHADOWS THAN THINKING THAT NO ONE WOULD EVER KNOW MY SIDE.
IT WAS AN INCREDIBLE ACCOUNT. IT WAS YOU THAT LEFT IT FOR ME THEN?
I'M AFRAID SO. AFTER ALL THESE YEARS, IT WOULD SEEM I AM STILL THE SHY SCHOLAR PONY.
HECK, IF YOU'RE WORRIED ABOUT BEING A SCHOLAR, YOU SHOULD COME VISIT MY HOUSE. TWO OF MY WALLS ARE JUST LINED WITH REFERENCE MATERIAL.
THAT SOUNDS LIKE MY SORT OF PLACE.
HA HA!
HA HA HA! HONESTLY, I MAY TAKE YOU UP ON THAT, I HAVE A THOUSAND YEARS OF RESEARCH TO CATCH UP ON.
I HAVE TO ASK YOU SOMETHING.
YOU HAVEN'T READ ENOUGH OF MY RAMBLINGS ALREADY?
I WANTED TO ASK ABOUT THE LAST THING YOU WROTE IN YOUR DIARY.
I SEE.
WELL, FOR ALL MY GOOD INTENTIONS, I CERTAINLY PROVED THOSE RIGHT, DIDN'T I?
ACTUALLY, THAT'S NOT WHAT I WAS GOING TO SAY AT ALL.

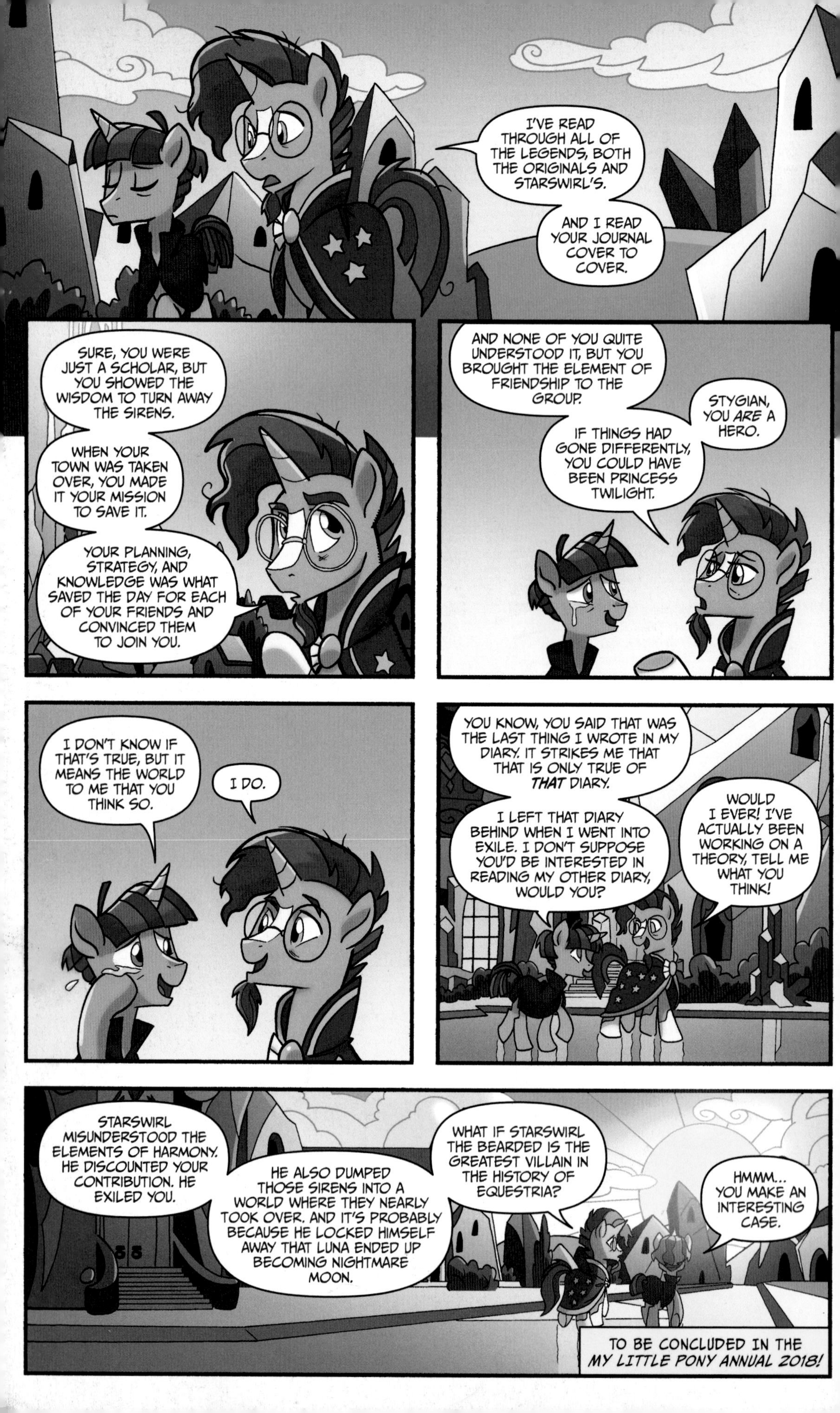
I'VE READ THROUGH ALL OF THE LEGENDS, BOTH THE ORIGINALS AND STARSWIRL'S.
AND I READ YOUR JOURNAL COVER TO COVER.
SURE, YOU WERE JUST A SCHOLAR, BUT YOU SHOWED THE WISDOM TO TURN AWAY THE SIRENS.
WHEN YOUR TOWN WAS TAKEN OVER, YOU MADE IT YOUR MISSION TO SAVE IT.
YOUR PLANNING, STRATEGY, AND KNOWLEDGE WAS WHAT SAVED THE DAY FOR EACH OF YOUR FRIENDS AND CONVINCED THEM TO JOIN YOU.
AND NONE OF YOU QUITE UNDERSTOOD IT, BUT YOU BROUGHT THE ELEMENT OF FRIENDSHIP TO THE GROUP.
IF THINGS HAD GONE DIFFERENTLY, YOU COULD HAVE BEEN PRINCESS TWILIGHT.
STYGIAN, YOU *ARE* A HERO.
I DON'T KNOW IF THAT'S TRUE, BUT IT MEANS THE WORLD TO ME THAT YOU THINK SO.
I DO.
YOU KNOW, YOU SAID THAT WAS THE LAST THING I WROTE IN MY DIARY. IT STRIKES ME THAT THAT IS ONLY TRUE OF *THAT* DIARY.
I LEFT THAT DIARY BEHIND WHEN I WENT INTO EXILE. I DON'T SUPPOSE YOU'D BE INTERESTED IN READING MY OTHER DIARY, WOULD YOU?
WOULD I EVER! I'VE ACTUALLY BEEN WORKING ON A THEORY, TELL ME WHAT YOU THINK!
STARSWIRL MISUNDERSTOOD THE ELEMENTS OF HARMONY. HE DISCOUNTED YOUR CONTRIBUTION. HE EXILED YOU.
HE ALSO DUMPED THOSE SIRENS INTO A WORLD WHERE THEY NEARLY TOOK OVER. AND IT'S PROBABLY BECAUSE HE LOCKED HIMSELF AWAY THAT LUNA ENDED UP BECOMING NIGHTMARE MOON.
WHAT IF STARSWIRL THE BEARDED IS THE GREATEST VILLAIN IN THE HISTORY OF EQUESTRIA?
HMMM... YOU MAKE AN INTERESTING CASE.
TO BE CONCLUDED IN THE *MY LITTLE PONY ANNUAL 2018!*

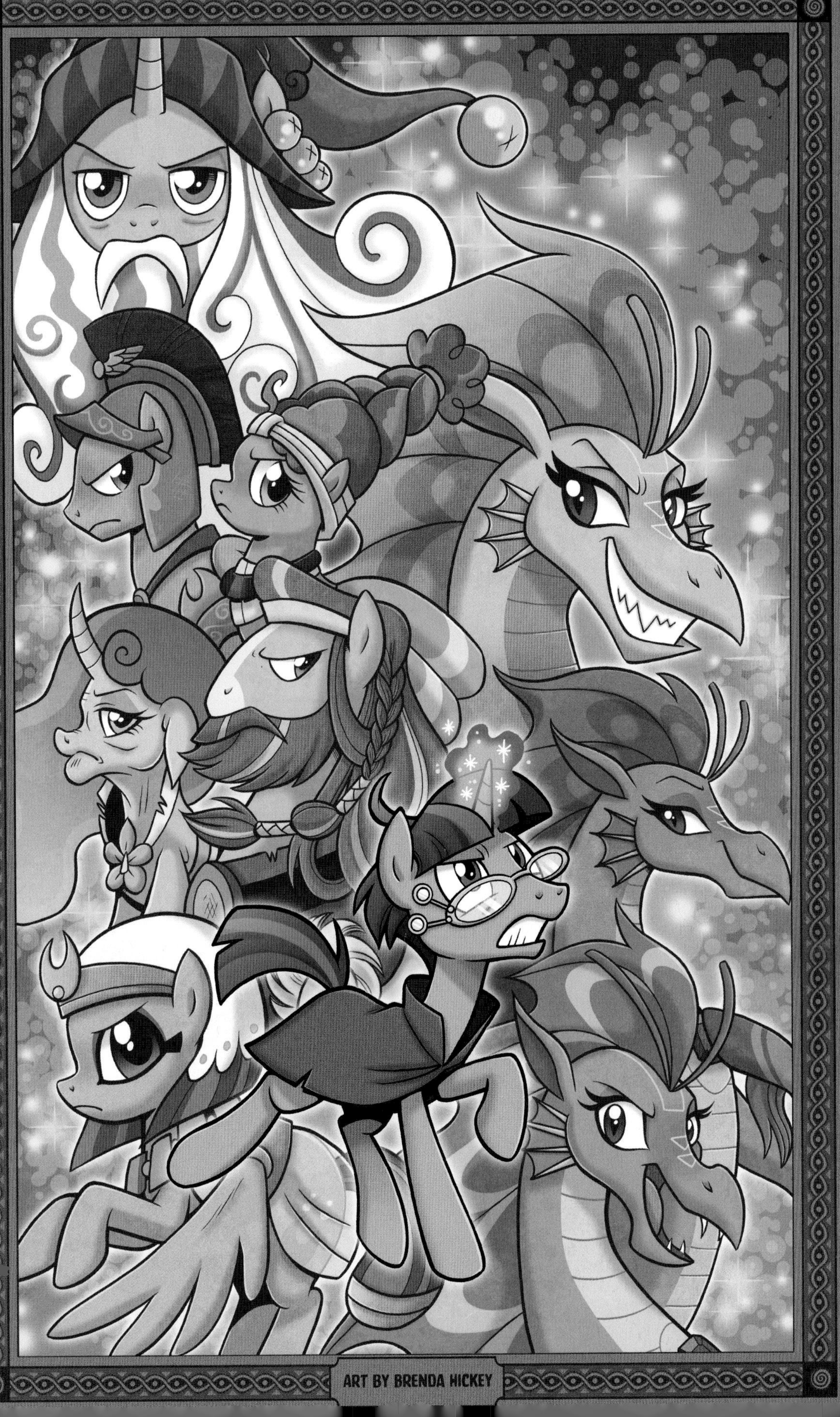
ART BY BRENDA HICKEY

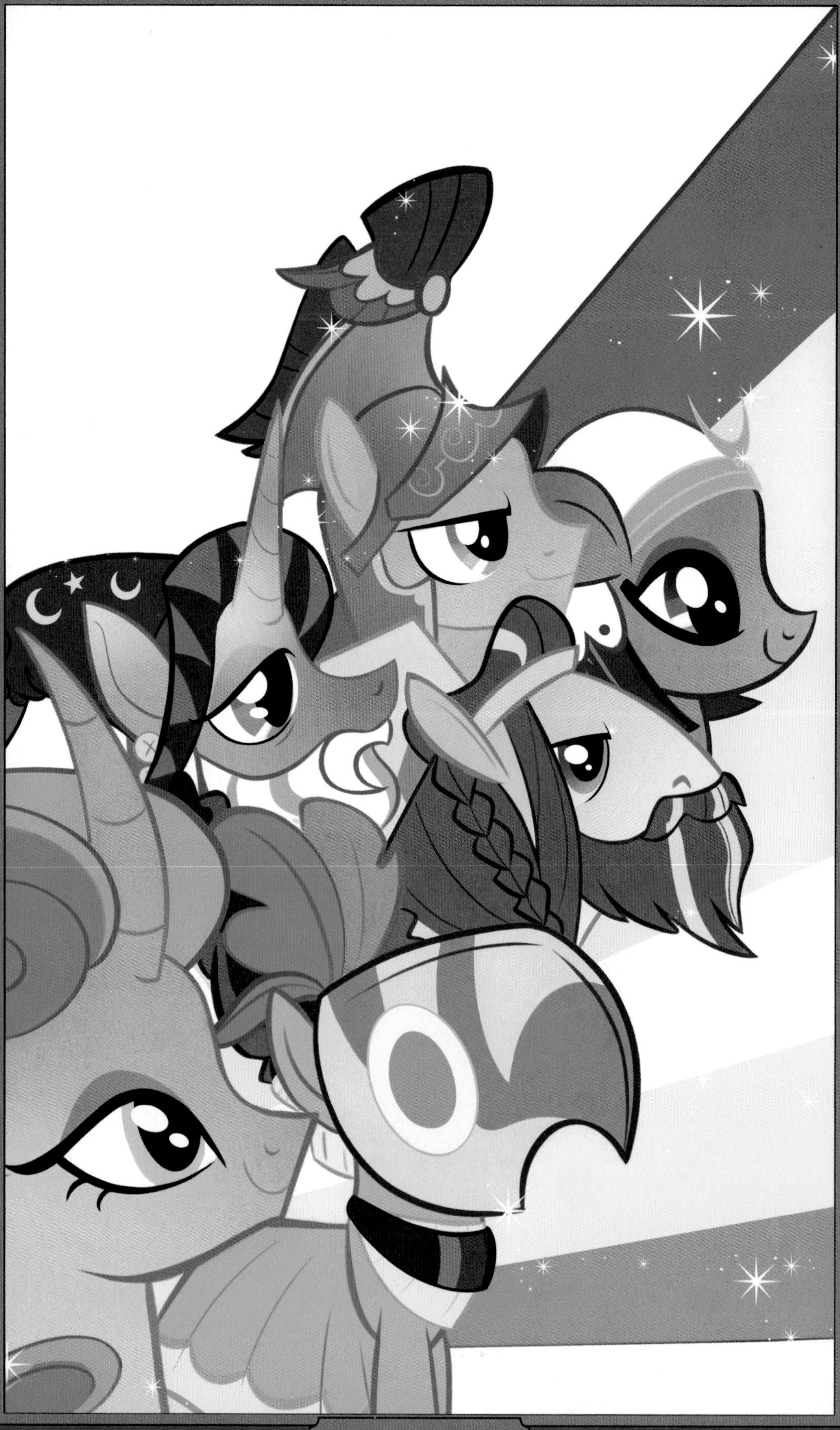

ART BY NICOLETTA BALDARI

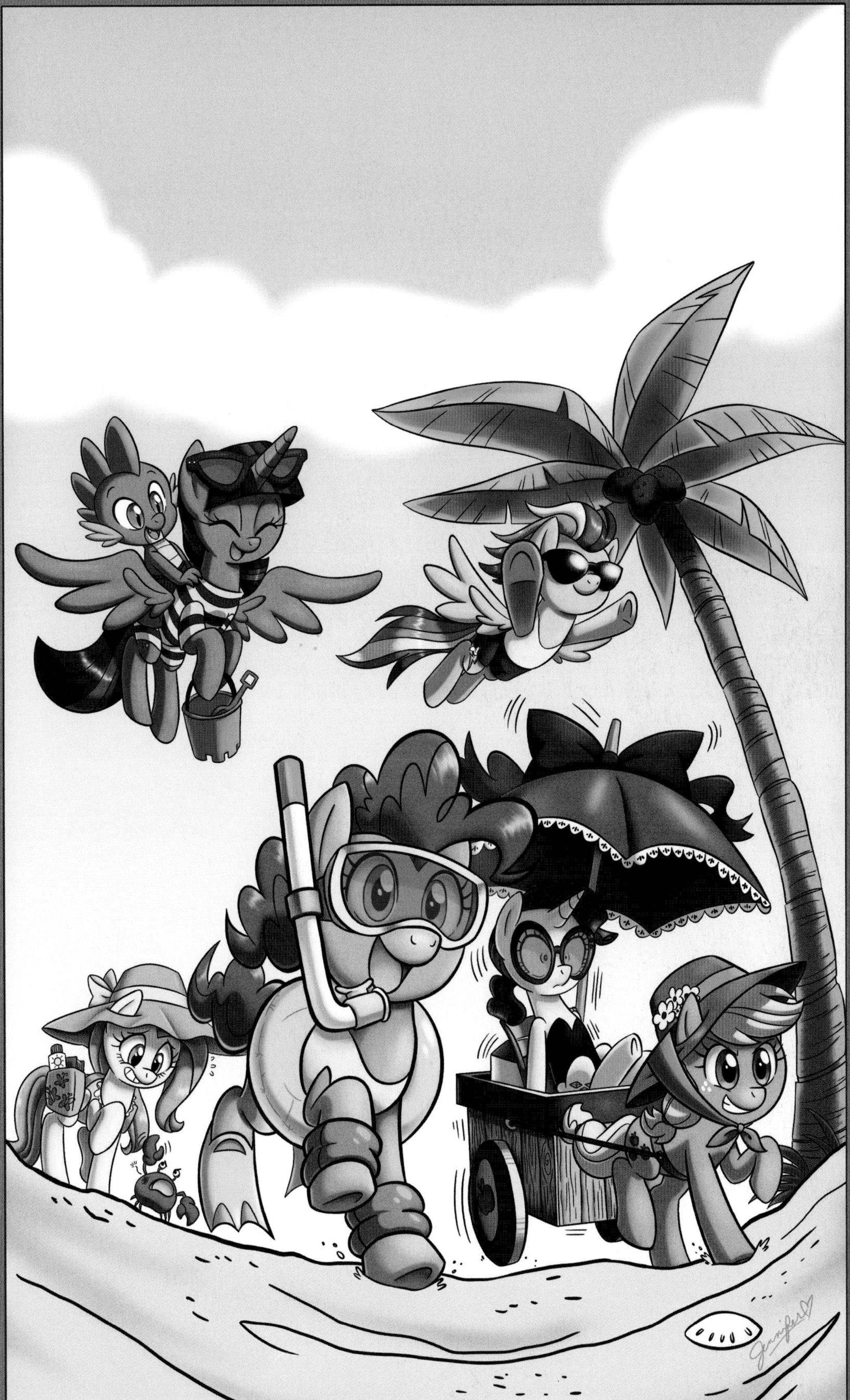

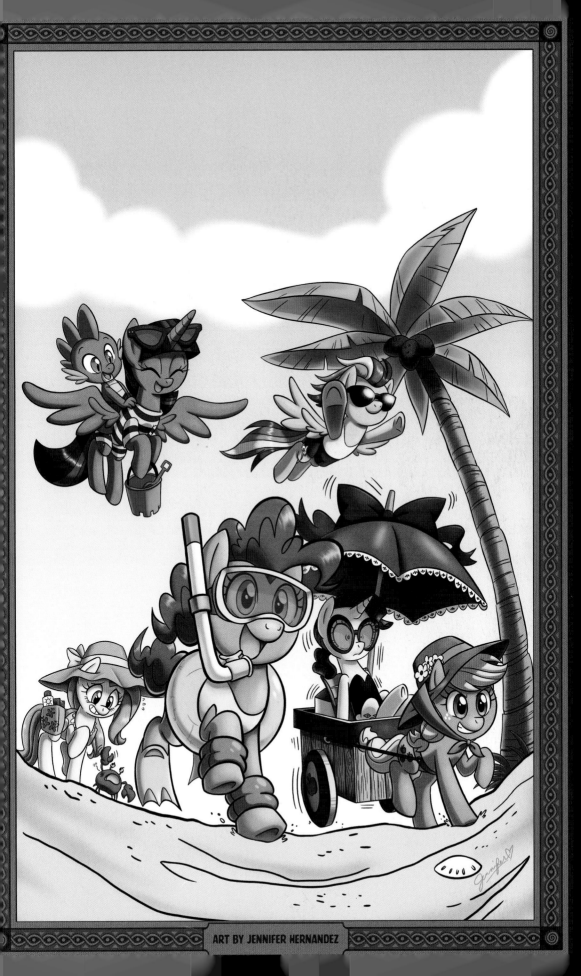

ART BY JENNIFER HERNANDEZ

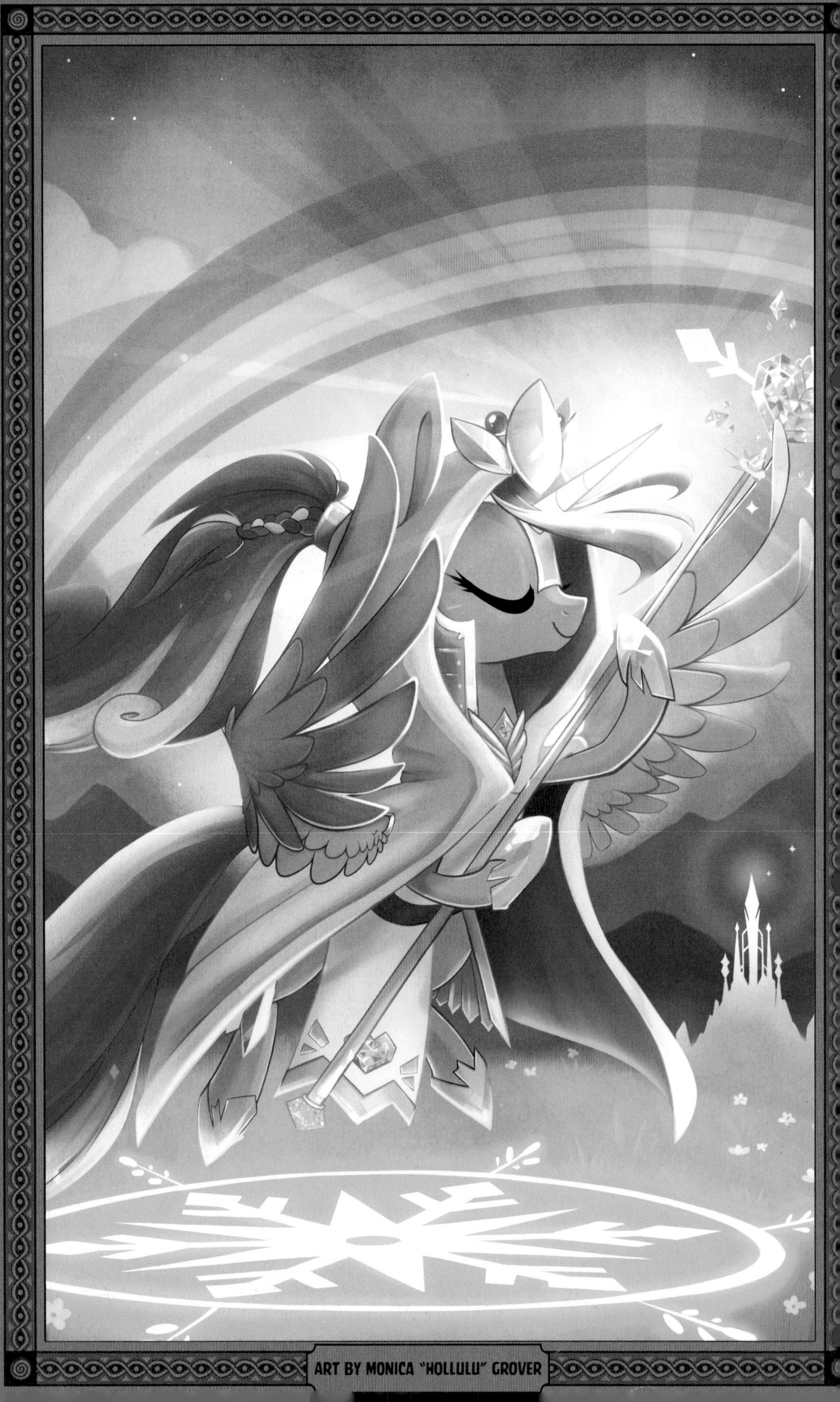
ART BY MONICA "HOLLULU" GROVER

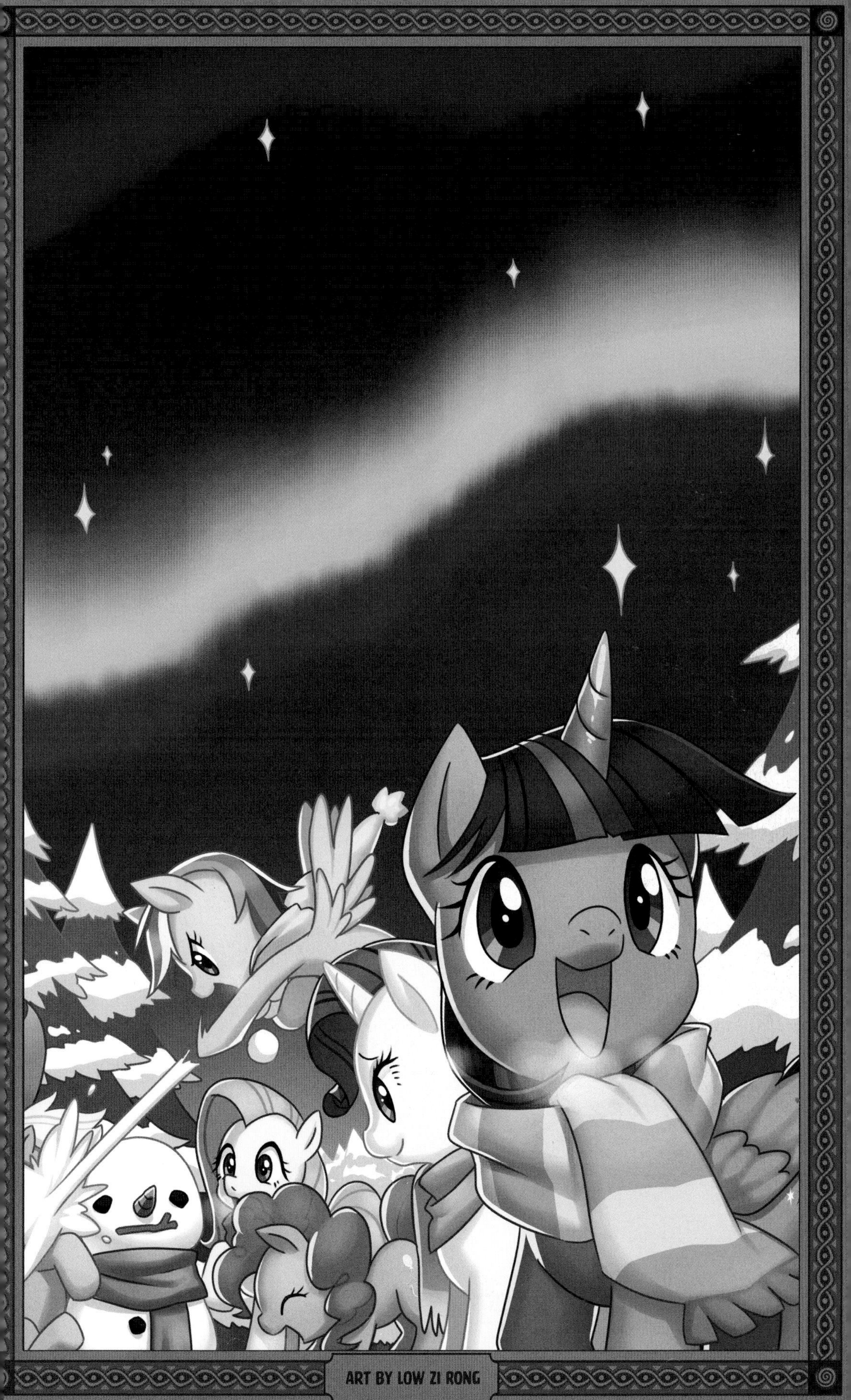
ART BY LOW ZI RONG

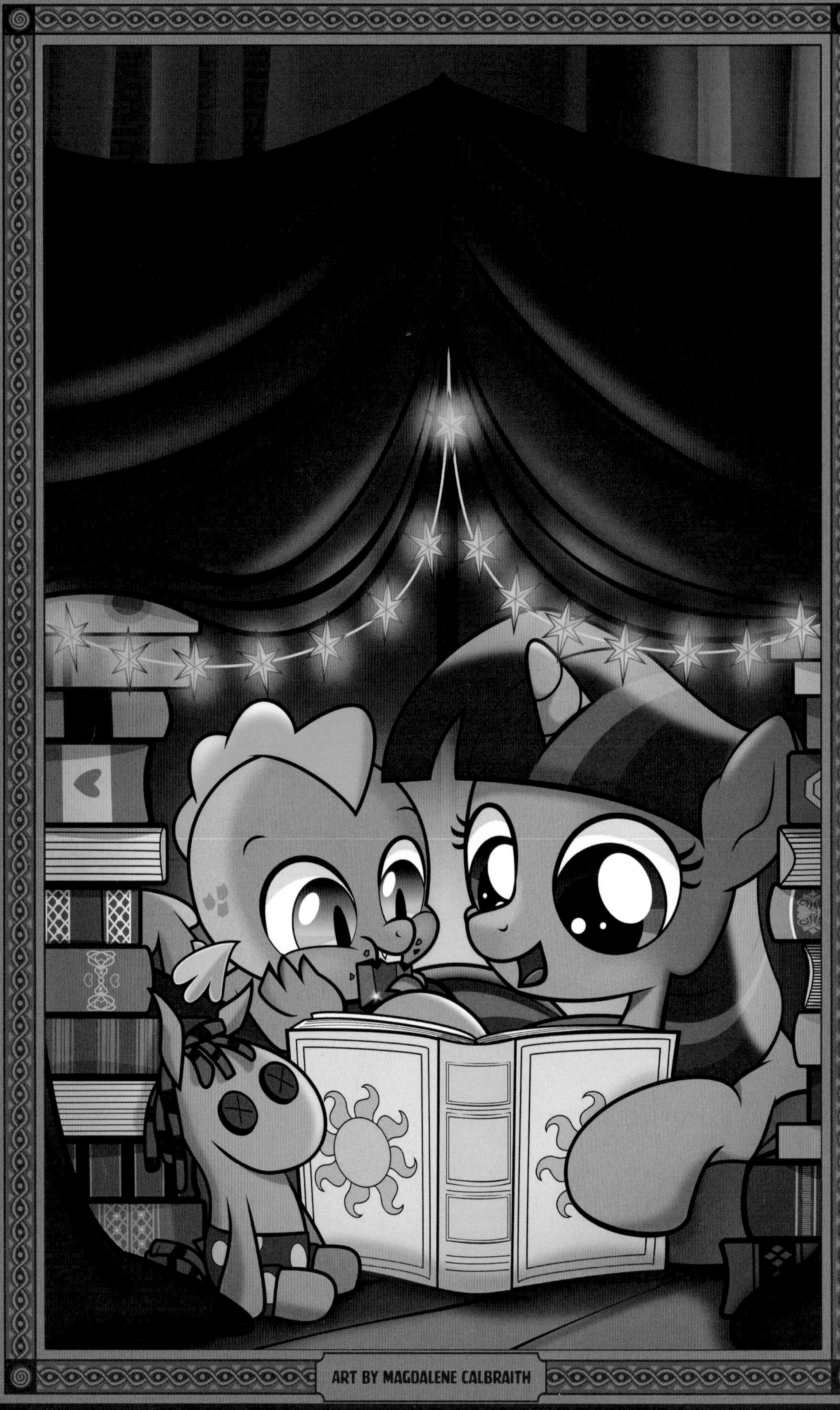

ART BY MAGDALENE CALBRAITH

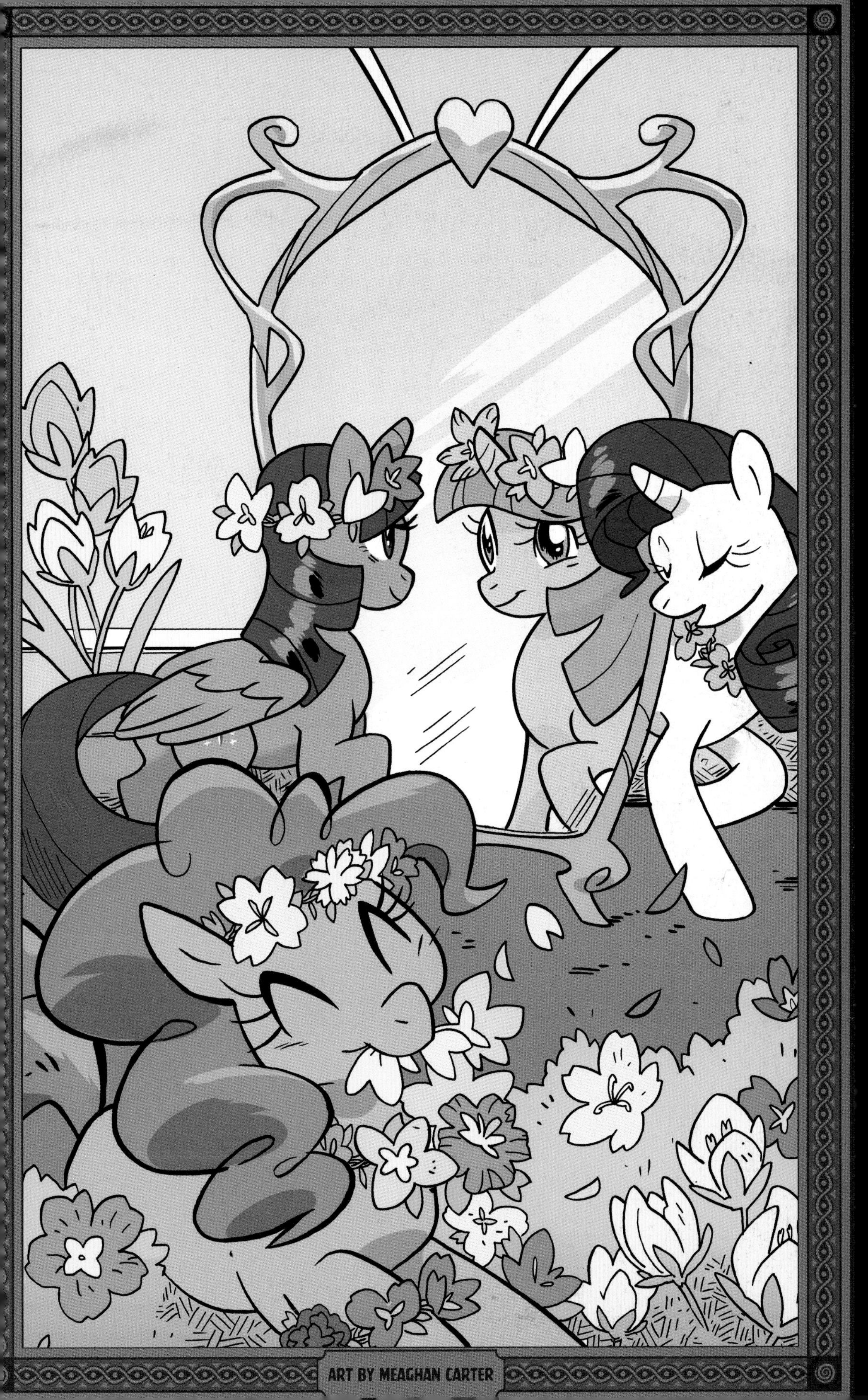

ART BY MEAGHAN CARTER

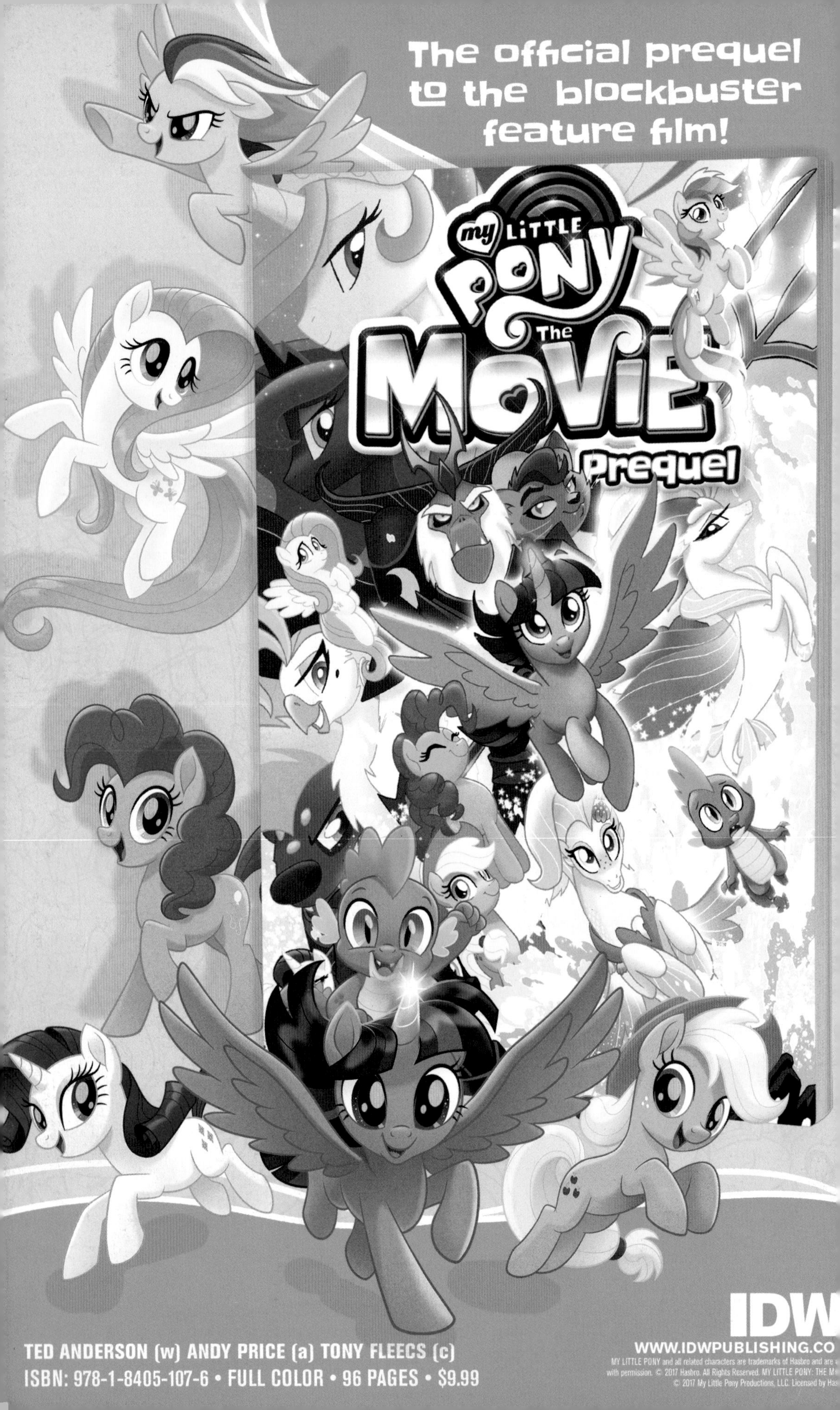

The official prequel to the blockbuster feature film!
My Little Pony The Movie Prequel
TED ANDERSON (w) ANDY PRICE (a) TONY FLEECS (c)
ISBN: 978-1-8405-107-6 • FULL COLOR • 96 PAGES • $9.99
IDW
WWW.IDWPUBLISHING.CO
MY LITTLE PONY and all related characters are trademarks of Hasbro and are
with permission. © 2017 Hasbro. All Rights Reserved. MY LITTLE PONY: THE M
© 2017 My Little Pony Productions, LLC. Licensed by Has

my LITTLE PONY
Legends of Magic

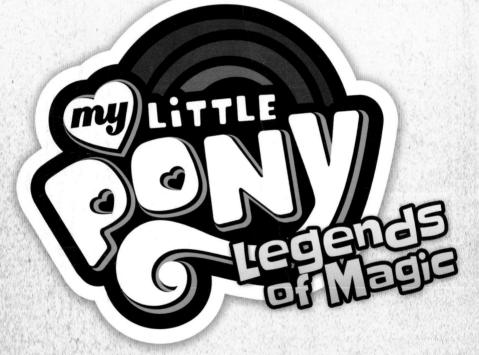